For the Good of All

Marc Stevens

To the men and women in uniform, past and present, who protect this great nation. My family and I are forever in your debt.

For the Good of All, is the sequel to the
Amazon First Contact Sci-Fi best seller,
First of my Kind.

Nathan Myers and the crew of the Legacy find themselves
at war with the predatory races and murderous corruption
so prevalent in the galaxy. The shadowy criminal figures
who stand to lose the most from Nathan's victories, have
placed a billion-credit bounty on his head. To make
matters worse, the Scrun and Murlaks have assassination
squads actively pursuing Nathan and his crew. In order to
survive Nathan must find allies willing to stand with them.
Finding an ally without ulterior motives is easier said than
done. No matter the odds Nathan and his crew will battle
their way through hell and back, For the Good of All.

Table of Contents

1

I open my eyes and, for some strange reason, am standing on an outcropping. I do not know why I am here or how I found my way to this place. It is bleak and unbearably hot. Everywhere I look, shimmering waves of heat distort the barren landscape. A stench permeates the stifling atmosphere and offends my senses. The familiarity makes me cringe. Death — this place smells of violent death. I edge forward and look into the abyss spread out before me and my breath catches in my throat. There are beings of every description below me. They infest the dreadful terrain and are fighting or struggling. It is hard to determine from my vantage point what could cause such turmoil. The moaning wail of their anger and despair is audible and its pitch sickening.

In the distance, I hear a low rumble that is gaining intensity. The anguish below me takes on a new tone and urgency. It is the sound of fear and terror. The rumble is competing with the din of uncontrollable panic. I look to the horizon and whatever is happening is closer now. Dark rolling clouds obscure the sky and I see flashes that look like lightning. The bizarre cyclone is increasing in volume, and it's now accompanied by concussive thumps I feel through my boots. Each brilliant flash of light stabs tiny spikes of pain into my corneas. The sounds of destruction coming from the hellish storm overcome all others.

Anxiety is gripping me; I try to turn away, but I am unable. I try closing my eyes to keep from comprehending what I am seeing, but I cannot. NO! PLEASE NO!

The storm is close. I see bodies being ripped asunder and thrown about like rag dolls. Huge swaths of aliens are turned into clouds of scarlet mist by bright flashing beams of energy. I can now make out a lone figure, and my legs want to buckle at the sight of the carnage it leaves in its wake. It is the Oolaran beast that resides in my brain and inhabits my body during combat. Two fiery red eyes peer out from the visor of the gore-covered armor. They bore into my soul, rending the bonds that protect and hold my Earthman moralities. I can feel the need to kill, to kill everything that stands against it, infecting me.

I bolt upright in my bed, covered in sweat. I heard the artificial intelligence of my ship, the Legacy, addressing me.

"Commander, I have awakened you because I sense your distress. The troubling manifestations of your human mind are the byproduct of the tremendous pressure you endured freeing Tria from her captors. In time, they will pass."

Throwing off my cover I sit on the edge of my bed, trying to erase the images from my brain. With the help of my crew, I would rein in the monster trying to possess me.

But the beast would now reward my efforts with its revenge. It would take over my dreams and use them to display its deadly prowess. It would demonstrate the proper use of my training. It would give new meaning to the phrase "Be all you can be."

"Justice, how is Tria doing?"

"Commander, her broken limbs are responding well to the nanites I have programmed to repair the fractures. When her bones mend, I shall begin the carbon fiber lamination process of the Oolaran weaponization program."

Shaking my head, I went to my shower. Standing under the hot water, I used my implants to reduce the temperature to the point it was brisk and cool. The Oolaran weaponization program was the source of my horrific nightmares. To help insure my survival, I had my ship's A.I. download the alien training and imprinting to my implants. The program was designed to make hardened soldiers out of the normally passive Oolaran citizens. At the time of development, our galaxy was facing conquest by a race of bio machines: in a feat of mindboggling achievement, the predatory race called the Prule made the intergalactic trip from Andromeda to the fringe of the Milky Way. The Prule's single-minded purpose was to conquer or destroy a galaxy and recover the resources necessary to expand their empire — they were indifferent to either outcome so long as it accomplished

11

their intended goals. Any species subjugated by the Prule would live out the rest of their short existence gathering resources and suppling biological materials for the enemy of all races.

Several of the most technologically advanced species in our galaxy formed an alliance and fought the Prule to a standstill. Recently discovered records speculate our galaxy banded together and kicked the Prule out of the Milky Way. Finding records or actual proof to verify this information is an ongoing quest of the few races who have access to the small amount of data available. Until we know for sure what happened, we can only contemplate the outcome. All of these events took place hundreds of years ago. What I know for sure was indoctrinating myself with alien technology, without spending a significant amount of time studying it for possible side effects, was not one of my better choices. Digressing was giving me a headache, so I concentrated on the future.

"Justice, what is our transition status?"

"Commander, I have detected no serious faults in the dark matter collection matrix. In eighty-two minutes, I will have sufficient energy to transition back to Alpha Base. I will alert you when all systems are optimal."

"Roger that, Justice. I am going to the galley to pick up breakfast for Tria and I. Keep me posted if something unexpected comes up."

I queried my implants and found everyone except Tria in their quarters sleeping. I don't know how I knew Tria was awake, but I did. After swinging by the galley, I went to the med bay. I steeled my emotions to contain the beast. It loves to rear its ugly head when I become angry. It's easy for me to get that way when I see Tria's beautiful face battered and bruised. Three of her four arms were broken and in stasis cast. When I enter the room, Tria's restoration pod was open, and she was trying her best to give me a smile. Her effort quashes the beast's attempts at feeding on my anger. It scurries to some hidden, dark corner of my mind like a vampire fleeing the sunrise. I smiled back, and the beast faded from my thoughts.

"I had a feeling you might be awake. And possibly hungry."

Her gorgeous emerald eyes sparkle at me when she speaks.

"Have you ever considered the possibility I might have summoned you, Nathan Myers?"

My smile broadens. "I didn't know Chaalt warriors had such powers. Are you revealing your people's secrets to a backward-thinking alien?"

Her laugh was like the musical notes of a favorite song. I would never grow tired of hearing it.

"I brought you a delicacy from Earth. Justice assured me it would not poison you."

She smiled because she had already tasted my adopted family's blueberry preserves. It was one of the few food items I had brought from Earth that Justice did not throw out the airlock — he found the bacteria count on everything else unsuitable for storage and not to his liking. He knew I would freak out, so the fruit preserves were the bone he threw me in compromise. I prepared two pieces of imitation wheat toast with the last of the jelly, leaving one whole and the other cut into small squares. I brought a cup of Justice's dishwater coffee and a glass of room temperature water with a straw in it. As I leaned forward to place the meal tray on the side table of the pod, Tria reached up and placed her one good hand on my cheek. It was an intimate Chaalt greeting usually done with two of her four hands. The touch was electrifying. I swallowed down the knot that was forming in my throat. Reaching out with both of my hands, I returned the gesture. She looked a little disappointed until I leaned in and planted an Earthman kiss on her lips. The warm smile and the sparkle in her eyes seemed to warm the whole med bay.

"My father says your Earth gesture of affection is unsanitary and will infect me with bacteriological contagions."

14

I already knew she was, like me, impervious to disease. Rolling my eyes at her, I open my mouth and let slip what was on my Earth boy mind.

"That's not the Earth gesture of affection he should worry about."

As soon as I said it, I bit down on my tongue. My face turned crimson with heat. *Myers, you idiot, keep your mind out of the gutter!* Her laughter was loud and from the heart. It took the sting from the way I was berating myself. She locked me with those beautiful green eyes, and I suddenly felt feverish. A tingling sensation overcame me. Goosebumps covered my body. My legs felt weak. What the hell was going on?

"Can you feel me, Nathan?"

Looking at the beautiful battered alien, I could not break eye contact with her. She had a look on her face I had never seen before. At first it was shocked surprise, but then it changed to something else. I tried to speak, but it came out disjointed.

"I...felt...I mean I feel...different...I..."

She pulled me close and whispered: "I embrace you with my aura. You are the first not of my species to experience Sha'leen and embrace its touch. To most, it is...toxic."

I would not admit it, but I was on the verge of falling to the floor because my legs felt like rubber.

"I have been aware of your aura emissions since the time you freed me from Drayen's prison. Females of my species sense those who radiate such energy. It is an extremely rare characteristic, and I am drawn to it. Your aura shines like star light, and it caresses my spirit."

Another wave hits me. I grip the edge of the med pod to keep from falling. Tria holds on to my arm and my eyes open wide. I feel like I took the deepest breath of my life and let it out.

"Can you feel me, Nathan?"

"YES."

Justice must have been going through sensory overload because he broke the spell that was gripping me.

"Commander?"

The sensations abruptly stopped.

"Commander?"

"Yes Justice, I hear you. Is there a problem?"

"No Commander, I need to consult with you."

Justice did not sound like his normal self, and I had a sneaking suspicion why.

"Justice, has charging the energy matrix caused a fault in your speech processing?"

"No Commander, systems will be optimized for transition in twenty minutes. I have calculated all planetary movement around the local star of Alpha base and plotted the target destination."

"Wonderful, Justice. Is there anything else you feel the need to tell me?"

"No Commander, I...yes. The lower rail cannon experienced a minor fluctuation in the number three guide rail during our last engagement. It might be an indication of a misalignment. Aiming errors of point one inch are possible if left unchecked. It will require visual inspection by Engineer Coonts to determine if I am correct."

The way Justice was responding might indicate that more than the rail cannon needed looking into. I knew, while aboard the Legacy, the A.I. could interact with my implants and get a good dose of what was going on in my head. He may have gotten a bigger bite of Sha'leen than he could chew. Tria sure rocked my socks with it.

"If that is all, Justice, call me at T-minus two minutes please."

"Yes, of course Commander, I will—"

"JUSTICE, T-MINUS TWO PLEASE!"

"Affirmative, Commander!"

Tria did not say a word, but her smile said all that was necessary. She reached out for one of the small pieces of jelly toast and I batted her hand away. She gave me a questioning look. I took the toast and held it in front of her swollen lips until she opened her mouth. I popped it in. She closed her eyes, chewing slowly, savoring the sweet, fruity taste. Holding the cup of water until the straw touched her lips, she drank. She put her arm around me and we finished our meal in silence.

2

Justice had regained his composure and alerted me we were T-Minus two minutes and counting. I checked the crew's status with my implants. They were all sleeping. There was no point in waking them. Our last mission was a real bitch, and we were all put through the wringer. I reached out and held Tria's hand. She looked up at me. I thought she was talking but I did not hear her words. Even the Legacy's usual sounds were muted. I could not hear a single sound. I tried calling to Tria but could hear nothing. Everything around me was shining an almost blinding white. I looked back at Tria and she vanished! Looking down at my feet, I faded away.

My eyes refocused and it was like nothing had happened. There was no discomfort of any kind. I was a little confused, thinking the transition had failed. My hearing returned and Tria was telling me that, if our molecules scatter, she was glad I was the last being she would ever see. Justice confirmed my uncertainty.

"Commander, our transition is complete and we are point one light year from Alpha base. I have contacted my subsystem and all is normal. The Grawl are doing well and are researching artifacts. Graf identified the containment vessel for what it was. The scientists discussed its examination but had concerns for what it might contain.

They left it untouched and are concentrating on the design characteristics of the nanites you recovered. We will make our approach and landing after I sweep the star system."

"Thank you, Justice! Please, carry on."

Knowing the Prule containment vessel had not been tampered with was a welcomed relief. I closed my eyes and thanked my maker. I now had a dedicated science and research team. It will be much easier to determine if discovered artifacts could be dangerous. I was considering adding a member of the science team to my crew roster. Having one onboard might prevent me from making a mistake that could have galactic repercussions. I already had a candidate in mind.

Tria looked up at me. "That was the most uneventful transition I have ever experienced."

Tria's comment was an understatement. She may have knowledge of such things, but I was amazed by what just happened. We had just traversed over three hundred thousand light years in the blink of an eye. Our previous excursions had taken days or weeks. This technology was a golden key capable of opening the door to the entire galaxy and possibly beyond. The potential was staggering. If we could somehow recover Justice's deleted star charts, we might have a map and the means to explore the rest of galaxy.

"That was the most incredible thing this Earthman has ever experienced."

Tria gave me another smile and said, "Go Nathan, and make sure that all is well. If I have needs, I will summon you."

I could not help but laugh on my way out of the med bay. I did not know if she was kidding me or not; everything about the Chaalt was a mystery. Little by little, Tria was filling me in on many things considered secret by her people.

I went to the forward lift tubes and made a fast ascent to the bridge. As the huge security doors parted, I came face to face with the Grawl engineer Coonts. He was the first alien species I had come in contact with. He was a little over four feet tall with a gray complexion and a large, bulbous head with large dark eyes. His race was responsible for the most reported sightings of aliens back on Earth. A lot of the facts I learned about his race were not flattering. His species was extremely intelligent, unscrupulous, and highly motivated to increase their technological expertise. The Grawl formula for success was designed to net them the power to do as they please, along with the considerable wealth that comes with that freedom. They did not care how they gained their tech, be it by begging, borrowing, or flat out stealing. The Grawl claimed to be civilized because they demilitarized hundreds of years in the past. In reality, it was a smokescreen to hide the fact they hire mercenaries by the scores to protect their ill-gotten gains. The Grawl's favorite motto was "We prefer to leave the dying to someone else." Coonts may have started down that road, but something about me drastically changed his insights. He was now the complete opposite of your standard Grawl template. He has proven to be smart, selfless and courageous. His goal to reform his race for the betterment of all made him a worthy addition to my crew.

"Commander, the Oolaran technology for hyperspace transition is remarkable. I woke to find my material form fading from reality to another dimension. When my awareness returned, I was amazed to find we were not traveling in interdimensional space. Our reality returning to normal spacetime in the star system of our base is an incredible accomplishment of engineering. The ability to manipulate spacetime in such a manner was most unexpected."

"Coonts, I am just a primitive backwards thinking alien, so what just happened is beyond my comprehension. The people of my world believe what we just experienced to be impossible and only the ramblings of fiction writers."

The smile on a Grawl's face is not a pretty sight, but I knew from experience what I was looking at and returned the gesture. We heard loud, thumping footsteps behind us, and the last member of my crew entered the bridge.

"You look rested, Commander. You must have slept as well as I did. Tell Justice to get the matrix charged so we can get back to base and spend a few rotations with our feet on solid ground."

Klutch Zuma is a Tibor Troop Master. He was a mercenary hired by nefarious criminals to protect them while they went about their illegal activities. He was a little over five feet tall and close to four feet wide. He had incredible body mass from being born on a world more than twice the size of Earth and four times the gravity. He easily weighed six or seven hundred pounds, none of it being fat. He tried to kill me once, and at the time, I was doing everything in my power to return the favor. If it were not for my crew, he may have completed the job. The battle was short and ugly. We killed four of his crew and I had managed to wound and disarm him. Rather than finish him, like he asked me to do, we talked about the criminals he worked for. The more he learned about them, the more he disliked what he had been suckered into doing. After a considerable amount of bullshitting, coercing and flat out bribing, I won the Tibor over to my side. Since that time, he has sworn his allegiance to me and has proven it beyond a shadow of a doubt more than once. The only reservation I had about the Tibor was his nonchalant use of his warrior's scent. When excited, a Tibor can produce an odor that could send a herd of disturbed skunks scurrying for fresh air. I opened my

23

mouth to tell him we had arrived at our base system, but Coonts beat me to it.

"Troop Master, if you were alert, you would have already noticed we have arrived in the star system of Alpha base."

Klutch gave the little Grawl a sideways look and I caught the faintest whiff of something really rotten. I backed up a couple of steps hoping for fresher air. Coonts was wishing he had phrased his words a little differently. The Tibor gave us a big toothy smile exposing a set of impressive gray choppers — it was a sight capable of making perfectly sound bladders defective. He reached out and shoved the little Grawl and let out a loud croaking laugh.

"HAH! Coonts, you are Throgg scatting me!"

When Coonts regained his footing, he chose his next words with more care.

"No Troop Master, we have made our transition and Justice is scanning the outer system for anomalous activity. We will be landing soon."

Klutch turned around and looked at the huge domed viewscreen that went from floor to ceiling, encompassing the entire bridge. The view was breathtaking because it appeared you were standing in outer space. He looked back at us in awe.

"I felt nothing. The sensation of transition has always awakened me in the past. This is indeed advanced technology. Is it possible to duplicate and install on our shuttles?"

I was thinking the same thing but knew the Grawl had been trying for over twenty years without success. Coonts once again answered before I could.

"Unfortunately, Troop Master, Grawl scientists and engineers tried for many solar rotations. We were unable to breach the Guardian-designed shield protecting the Oolaran DEHD core. We found that any brute force method we could devise would destroy the device. Rather than render it useless, we directed our research to other areas of the ship."

Coonts promptly turned and walked off the bridge. He was part of the research team that worked on the Legacy after it was discovered. His failures were not something he cared to revisit. Klutch looked at me as we both came to the same conclusion.

"Are you hungry Commander? I could eat two Dorta sea snakes."

Even though I had no idea what a Dorta sea snake looked like, my mind envisioned a picture of the Troop Master swallowing huge eel-like critters. My light breakfast started to boil. I quickly pushed the thought from my mind.

"No Klutch, I have already eaten with Tria."

"Is she doing well?"

"Yes, she is much better now and should be out of the med bay within this rotation."

"That is great news Commander! I look forward to seeing the Chaalt warrior back on duty. If you will excuse me, I will go to the galley."

My crew was aware that my relationship with Tria was changing into something other than a Commander-crewmate affiliation.

"Sure Klutch, I will catch up with you when we land."

Once, when the Tibor was really hungry, I had seen him eat twenty to thirty pounds of synthesized nutrients. His eating habits at times were memorable. I went to my command chair and sat down. It was a habit of mine when no one was around to spin the chair in a circle watching the stars go by. I knew it was childish, but it was so cool taking in an entire star system in one revolution. Justice decided I had been screwing around enough and broke up my revelry.

"Commander, if you are done practicing your primitive human pastime, I will give you my report."

"You sound kind of pissy today. Is there something you would like to talk about?"

"Yes Commander. I do not believe my observations of your interactions with Tria are in any way disruptive of your unique behavior while in her presence."

I knew this was coming. The A.I. had somehow altered its original programming to be more like a human. Justice was soaking up every emotion I exhibited and adding it to his human catalog of interaction. He had one in particular he was hoping to catalog, and the thought irritated the shit out of me. His introduction to Sha'leen had rattled the normally unflappable A.I., and to tell the truth, it had that same effect on me. His curiosity about the new human–Chaalt interaction was going to be unbearable.

"Justice, you spent more than a year on my planet. In that time, I am sure you properly interpreted the definition of privacy."

The A.I. was silent. It was his way of displaying impatience or annoyance at my lack of cooperation. Sometime in the future, I would pay for my responses by being subjected to the A.I.'s interpretation of human humor. It usually meant I would be on the receiving end of a childish prank.

"You said you had a report?"

27

"Yes Commander, the star system is secure and I am making our approach to Alpha Base. The Grawl scientists are aware of our return and have gathered in the hangar to greet you. They have been working non-stop since we departed and are very excited to show you the improvements they have made to Alpha Base."

"Thank you, Justice. That is great news. Can you give me an update on Tria's condition? I was wondering if her bone fractures were stable enough she could be released from the med bay?"

"Yes Commander, she has been insisting on her release since your visit early this morning. I have removed the rigid stasis casts and replaced them with less restraining protective devices. She has asked for a small delay in the next phase of the weaponization program."

"Oh really! Did she say why?"

"Yes Commander, she wishes to…spend time interacting with you."

I felt the temperature rise in my cheeks. The expectant tone in Justice's voice left nothing to my imagination.

3

Justice dropped us out of orbit and I watched our approach on the view dome. The moon our base was located on had just enough atmosphere to produce a fiery glow around the hull on our rapid descent. We were making a straight-in approach that appeared to be on a collision course with the side of a massive mountain range. Just when our demise seemed imminent, large entry doors rapidly opened in one of the mountains. The Legacy disappeared into the dark tunnel entrance and the camouflaged doors quickly closed, leaving no evidence the site was anything other than a mountain. As the Legacy passed through the atmospheric retention field, bright lights lit the way to the enormous spacecraft parking area.

I went to my cabin, put on a fresh, smart cloth uniform and walked out the door. Tria was walking down the corridor toward her quarters. She gave me a mischievous look.

"Tria, it's good to see you up and getting around..."

I suddenly became flushed and my legs weak. I stumbled against the wall. My eyes went wide when I looked back at her. I could hear her laughter but she never turned around; she just kept going. Gathering my wits, I steadied myself. I took another look back to where she had disappeared. She peeked out her doorway. I turned and ran on wobbly legs to the drop tube that would take me down to the personnel boarding hatch. As I exited the tube I gripped the side and shook my head. Coonts was standing with Klutch looking at what Justice was projecting on the bulkhead. It was an exterior view of the Legacy. I could see the Grawl scientists gathered outside, waiting for us to exit. Coonts looked up at me and saw I was a little disoriented.

"Are you well Commander? Do you need assistance?"

I tried my best to stand upright and act as if nothing happened.

"No, Coonts, I stumbled exiting the tube. I am fine."

"Are you sure Commander? You do not look your normal pallor."

I was glad when Tria's father stepped out of the drop tube behind me so I could change the subject. I put my hand on his right shoulder, giving him a customary Chaalt greeting. He looked puzzled. When he returned the greeting, his eyes momentarily widened. He quickly dropped his hand and his face returned to neutral. I could only think the reaction that flashed across his face had something to do with Tria smacking me around with her Sha'leen. I thought about it a little more and wondered if he could sense his daughter's aura on me.

"It is good to see you again, Scholar Burlor."

"Likewise, Nathan Myers. I am eager to inspect the containment vessel. We are fortunate it has not been tampered with."

"Of course, sir, this facility is at your disposal."

The Chaalt scholar nodded and stepped away to greet Coonts, then Klutch. *He must not approve of his daughter showing affection to a primitive alien.* I thought I wouldn't know until he told me and, so far, he had given no indication of doing so. Tria stepped out of the tube and I backed up a step. She had protective braces on three of her arms and was still badly bruised. The look of mischief returned to her face and she gave me a golden smile. The form-fitting smart cloth uniform accentuated her slim, graceful body. I swallowed and gave her a small shake of my head. She stepped forward and hooked her good arm in mine and we walked to the exit hatch. Coonts, Klutch and Tria's father were waiting for us. As a group, we walked off the Legacy to a roar of applause from the gathered scientists. Xul, Graf and Jaran were at the head of the greeting party. Xul turned to Graf and nodded. Graf held up his hands and the Grawl gathered around us ceased their applause. Xul turned back to us.

"Nathan Myers, Justice has related to us the great battles and suffering you and your crew endured. We are overjoyed you have returned."

31

I was about to address the crowd of scientists when Justice broadcast over the comms system.

"COMMANDER, six unknown vessels just transitioned into our star system at the exact coordinates the Legacy entered."

We were all shocked by the broadcast, and a feeling of dread gripped me. I couldn't help but think Eiger, the leader of the Murlak pirates, had somehow located our base. *He would only be here for one thing. Revenge.* I snapped out of it and started issuing orders.

"Tria, get your father aboard the Legacy now!"

I turned back to the Grawl gathering.

"Xul, I want the scientists to board the Legacy. I do not want panic. I want everyone aboard now! Coonts, Klutch, get geared up. I don't know what is happening but we cannot take the chance that Eiger has found us."

Tria appeared to be dragging her father up the boarding ramp. It sounded like they were arguing. Coonts and Klutch were standing on either side of the hatch barking orders and ushering the Grawl inside the Legacy as fast as they could. Looking back out into the hangar, I saw several Grawl stragglers attempting to get pieces of equipment or possibly personal items. I ran toward them, yelling out of frustration at their actions.

"LEAVE EVERYTHING AND GET ABOARD NOW!"

I grabbed those closest and forcefully turned them around and pushed them towards the loading ramp. The rest saw my actions and knew they wanted no part of disagreeing with me. They turned around and ran to the ship. The floor seemed to jump up at me and I fell to my knees. *What the hell was that? A moon quake?* Justice commed me and my blood turned to ice water.

"COMMANDER, THE UNKNOWN VESSELS JUMPED DIRECTLY INTO ORBIT ABOVE ALPHA BASE!"

Holy crap! Justice had once told me jumping a starship into a planet's gravity well was dangerous as hell and foolhardy to boot. Whoever was up there did not seem to give a damn where they jumped to. The quake must have been the moon's gravity rebounding from the blow it just received.

"JUSTICE, GET THE NEGATION SYSTEMS ONLINE AND OUR ENERGY CANNONS WARMED UP!"

"Commander, the emanations from our negation systems are undetectable. If I activate our weapons, the power sources have an energy signature that will give the unknown craft our exact position. The same will happen if I activate the shield dome."

Whoever it was knew we were here — otherwise they wouldn't be overhead. I was going to say screw it and have Justice activate the shields and get the weapons online. I was violently thrown into a stack of machine support spars by a compression wave of hot air, followed by a deafening thunder clap. I groaned as I rolled over, trying to figure out what just happened.

My eyes refocused, then grew to the size of quarters. Not thirty feet from me, I saw what looked like twenty columns of molten metal. My brain was still foggy from the blast, but my eyes were telling me I was looking at shiny pulsating pillars of mercury. They were in a circle with one at its center. The liquid metal appearance seemed to fall away, and in its place were armor-clad soldiers. I was shocked stupid. The soldiers all had four arms. They were Chaalt! The circle of troopers took a knee and each pointed two different wicked-looking combat rifles outward to every point on a compass. The soldiers were all clad in dark, cobalt blue armor with blacked out helmets. The armor looked heavy and was definitely exoskeleton-assisted. They wore side arms, fighting knives, and all had numerous devices adorning their armor that were either grenades or other death-dealing weapons.

The one standing in the middle, had blood-red armor trimmed in black and wore no helmet. She was definitely a Chaalt warrior. She may have been pretty at one time but not anymore. Her green eyes were similar to Tria's but darker and foreboding. Her hair was streaked with gray and pulled back into a short ponytail. The bands holding it were ringed with spikes. She had a scar running from her left ear along the jawbone that ended at her chin.

34

Cosmetic stuff like that was easy to fix and would have taken some of the *UGH* out of her ugly. She must have considered it a badge of honor. The armor she wore was not like the others; hers was form-fitting, and it was easy to see she was powerfully built. Her muscle structure was more like a man's than a woman's. She had pistols on her hips, but what caught my attention was the set of long handles protruding up from over both of her shoulders. They were ornate and looked like they were wrapped with gold braid. If I didn't know any better, I would have guessed they were *samurai* swords from Earth's past. I stared wondering why the Chaalt were here and how they found this place. The gaze the warrior was giving me had the beast inside me stirring. I could feel my anger rising at the uninvited intrusion. The thought of her ships parked over my base, showing any of my potential enemies where I might be, angered me further. The beast was egging me on.

"What are you doing here and why are you trespassing on my base?"

With utter contempt, the warrior spit out, "SILENCE! Primitive fool. I have no need for your mindless nonsense. If you interfere with my mission, you will die and I will destroy this place. DO YOU UNDERSTAND?"

The bitch could have said anything else in the world, but she had to make it a point to call me primitive. I had been called that so many times I swore the next alien

35

saying it without a really big smile on their face would get an ass-kicking. The beast was climbing out of the hole I thought I had buried him in. I reached down and picked up one of the support spars. It was a three-inch diameter metal tube with adjustable clamps on each end. It was also about the same size as a Louisville Slugger.

"You care to come over here and run that shit by me one more time?"

Looking like a ball player at home plate, I stood there slapping the spar into the palm of my hand. The Chaalt's eyes narrowed. *Wait...wait...just wait for it, it won't be long now.* In an unnatural burst of speed, the Chaalt leaped over the troops in front of her. I came back with the spar but before I could swing, she landed and unloaded a lightning bolt of a punch to my jaw.

I took two steps back reeling from the pain of the shot. *SON OF A BITCH! THAT HURT!* The Chaalt stood in front of me looking astonished. The beast loved it. My reflexes took control and I spun around with the spar swinging low. The surprised Chaalt tried jumping back but I caught her on the thigh with it. The spar had an unnatural curve to it now. She went down with a grunt. Two of her hands were going to the pistols. Tossing the spar, I dove on the Chaalt punching her in the side of the head. It was not my best effort but still a hell of a shot. She lost interest in the side arms but did however make it a point to return the favor using all four hands. Her

36

strength was incredible; she was definitely a brawler. She headbutted me and managed to split my lips open. I spit blood in her eye for the effort. She jerked me forward with two of her hands — I thought she was trying to wipe the spit on my uniform but was proven wrong when I received a very painful bite. That was dirty pool. I would go for an ear if she gave me an opportunity. The Oolaran soldier in me seemed to be enjoying the physical exercise. It was at this point I became aware of someone pulling me away and a stench that made me want to gag. Tria was yelling at us to stop.

Scholar Burlor was standing in front of the soldiers waving his arms and yelling, "HOLD YOUR FIRE!"

Klutch dragged me away from the Chaalt warrior. I noticed Coonts in his armor, his weapons pointed at the troops. Justice added his input as well.

"Commander, Scholar Burlor is saying the Chaalt invading our compound are the containment team sent to recover the Prule. It would be advisable to cease hostilities. The Chaalt are displaying very advanced technology and it would be prudent to at least listen to what they have to say."

Klutch released me and I wiped the blood from my mouth. Tria was helping the grizzled old bitch to her feet, but the hag pushed her away. That did not sit well with me. I reached down and picked up the warped spar.

"You push Tria again and I will break this off in your ass. If you need that translated, my A.I. can spell it out for you."

The old warrior looked like she could have chewed her way out of an airlock. In a blur of motion, she drew one of her weapons and pointed it in my face. Tria screamed and tried to step in front of me. I pulled her behind me. All of the portside rail cannon hatches popped open on the Legacy and the weapons swung around to point at the Chaalt containment team. Klutch pulled Tria out of the line of fire. The odor in the air was asphyxiating. No one seemed to notice.

I stood there staring down the barrel of the Chaalt's weapon. I reached up and casually placed my finger on one side of my nose and blew bloody snot between her feet. To my surprise, the corners of the warrior's mouth twitched upward, then the expression disappeared. She was still trying to stare a hole through me but holstered her weapon.

I looked back at her. "Are we going to talk now or do you want to go a couple more rounds?"

The expression on the warrior's face softened ever so slightly.

4

Scholar Burlor turned away from the troopers, walked over and stood between me and the Chaalt Commander. He looked at me.

"Please, let's be civilized and talk this out. There are no enemies here."

He turned and faced the Chaalt.

"As you can see, I am well and in control of the situation. Nathan Myers rescued my daughter and I from Eiger's forces. I will be able to lead this investigation without further assistance."

The surprised look on the Chaalt Commander's face was on full display. She did not break eye contact with me.

"Could you explain to me just how this simple-minded fool managed to survive an encounter with Eiger?"

Klutch had let go of Tria and she was now at my side. The Chaalt team leader gave her a sideways glance insinuating disapproval. Tria hooked her arms in mine. Her actions elicited a frown from the warrior. I leaned forward into the old Chaalt's face.

"I did what should have been done long ago by the gutless advanced races. Soldiers like you in particular. I...KICKED...THEIR...ASSES!"

Tria pulled me back. I smiled at the old Commander. Her face darkened with rage. Tria stepped in front of me.

"Do not incite her, Nathan. She is Kala Mor Dee."

"I don't give a crap what her name is. If she was the badass she makes herself out to be, she should have put an end to Drayen and Eiger a long time ago. Where I come from, that makes her all mouth and no ass."

I looked over Tria's shoulder. The old Commander's face was a steely-eyed mask of anger. "I hope you are picking up what I'm putting down."

Tria pulled me a couple of steps away. "Nathan! Kala Mor Dee is not her name, it is a title given to Operative Sael Nalen a great many years ago. It means "Deadliest of all."

That wiped the silly smirk off my face. I now grudgingly looked at the Operative with new found respect. I did not know how old Sael was, but my jaw still felt like she hit me with a hammer. "Tria, what the hell are they doing here and how did they find us?"

There was an expression of Tria's face I had seldom seen. It looked like hurt. She turned and looked at her

40

father. It was sinking in now. No one knew of this place until I brought Tria's father here. I gave him a withering stare and his eyes went wide.

Tria pulled me back around. "No Nathan, it is not as it seems! There are things that cannot be revealed. Please listen before you pass judgement."

The beast was a monkey on my back, and at the moment, it was biding its time by sticking me in the guts with a sharp stick. I know Tria would not betray my trust, but I needed some straight answers from someone, and I needed them now.

I looked at Operative Nalen. "How did you find this place?"

The old warrior's eyes narrowed. I could tell no one has ever been up in her grill before, and I was just getting started.

"I owe you no answers, human. That information is on a restricted need-to-know basis and until you make it on that list, your simple mind doesn't need to know."

Now the beast was kicking me in the balls. Man was I ever getting pissed! That would be the last time the gnarly old bat would call me simple-minded. Tria was pulling on my arm and shaking her head no. I could feel the venom coming and I needed to let it out before the beast did.

"You and your troops have ten minutes to get off my base and clear my orbitals. The clock is running. If you don't get your old wrinkled ass in gear, I will shoot them down!"

The Operative was dumbstruck at my outburst and her hands went to her pistols. I leaned into her face.

"Go ahead and draw your weapons! You think you have seen the worst of me? YOU HAVE NO IDEA WHAT I AM CAPABLE OF DOING!"

My hearing was zoning in and out. I could hear the beast that is my rage laughing out loud, then Tria yelling out, "NO NATHAN!"

The old warrior lost her look of anger. Her mouth opened in surprise and she took a step backwards. The beast was coming and she somehow knew it. I could hear Tria's father yelling. He was telling Sael Nalen that I went into Drayen's outpost and now there was only dust. I squeezed my eyes shut, trying to regain my self-control. I could see the aura Tria said I possessed. It was visible to me. It was no longer the bright, shining star light she told me about. It was turning a vile, inky black. It was fangs and claws with two hellish red eyes. It was the horror from my dreams and it was reaching out for Sael Nalen. The operative must have sensed the Oolaran demon inside of me. She drew her pistols and then her swords as she

42

continued to back up. I was trying to close the lid on Pandora's box, but my will to do so was ebbing.

The beast was yelling out. You may be called Kala Mor Dee, BUT I AM KALA MOR DEE!

I became aware I was being held in a tight embrace. My eyes came back to focus on my surroundings. Tria was holding me with fear in her eyes. The pained expression on her face beat down the will of the beast. I closed my arms around her and all thoughts of anger were gone. The Oolaran monster inside me was forced back into its prison. Looking around, I noticed everyone had given me a wide berth. I held Tria tight and kissed her lightly on the cheek. The beast was gone. She let go of me and turned away. She marched up to her father and in a not so kind voice, let him know how things were going to be.

"There will be no more secrets. You must be truthful so we can move forward for the good of all, or you can leave and never come back to this place."

Her father was speechless. I looked over to where Sael Nalen had retreated and her soldiers had formed a barricade. They again appeared to be shimmering columns of molten metal. The old warrior put her weapons away. Her troops became visible once again. They parted and the Operative approached us. She quickly regained her composure. I let the smallest of smiles cross my face when the old warrior stopped ten feet from me. *That was one of your smarter choices!*

"I cannot fathom why your maker would infect your aura with such a demon, but it is not a gift. Keep your hellish curse away from me, Human, or you will suffer the consequences."

Tria looked at me, hoping the Operative's threat would not incite the beast once more. I was forcing the Oolaran devil back into its cage, but its wretched mirth was grating. I closed my eyes and took a deep breath letting it out slowly, the beast fading with it. Sael Nalen was watching me carefully. She still had two of her hands on her pistols.

She looked at Tria's father. "Perhaps some things need to be addressed by the truth. Not all things, but some things. Scholar Burlor, your daughter is bound by an oath, but you are exempt from such things. Let the human know what is necessary. If I decide that it is not, I will let you know."

Tria's father had a look of relief on his face. Tria came back to my side and held onto my arm. I gave a sharp whistle that made everyone jump and stare at me. Looking at Klutch and Coonts, I held a finger up and twirled it over my head, then called out, "bring the scientists." That garnered me a frown from the Operative, but I didn't care.

I turned to her and said, "These are my people and what is said will go no further."

Sael Nalen nodded to Tria's father and he shook his head in agreement. The Grawl scientists made their way from the Legacy and gathered around me. One by one they all touched my hands and then stood quietly behind me. Tria's father looked impressed. Sael Nalen had a look of disbelief.

I looked at the Operative. "How did you find this place?"

She crossed both sets of arms and nodded in Scholar Burlor's direction. I again drew in a breath and let it out. Tria squeezed my arm a little tighter. Turning to her father, I gave him a questioning look.

"My people are familiar with DEHD core technology. We have a similar jump drive."

The Scholar was talking to me but was keeping eye contact with the Operative. He continued. "The Chaalt military has the ability to monitor certain exotic distortion waves."

The look on the Operative's face became stern. My patience was growing thin and I stepped in front of the Operative so the Scholar was forced to look at me. He hesitated. The Operative stepped from behind me looking angered. I ignored her.

45

"As you were saying Scholar Burlor?"

He continued. "There has not been a transition signature of an Oolaran designed jump drive for over two hundred years. The phenomenon was recorded and your entrance and exit locations plotted. It took little time to decipher the telemetry. Some of the information coincided with data I supplied to my superiors during my daughter's visit. Parallels were drawn and connected to the data. The containment teams were dispatched to investigate and assess the situation."

I chewed on the information for a few moments. "I take it all data on our discoveries was going to be disclosed to your superiors?"

The Scholar cleared his throat. "Yes."

"Was Sael Nalen ordered to seize the storage vessel if it contained a Prule?"

The Operative blurted, "Do not answer that question!"

I gave the old warrior an evil smile. "You just did, Sael Nalen."

The Operative grimaced at the silly mistake.

I turned my gaze back to the Scholar. "How did the containment team make their insertion?"

The Scholar started to answer. "You had no shie...

46

Sael Nalen yelled out, "SILENCE!"

I whirled to face the old Operative. Her stare was full of spite. Mine had turned noxious. I said out loud, "Justice!"

Justice broadcast for all to hear. "Shield dome active, Commander."

Sael turned her malice on Scholar Burlor. "You fool!"

Tria had all she could stomach. "This madness must stop! We are solving nothing. The fruitless display of authority is mindless stupidity. You will not find the answers you seek if you continue on this path. If you will not cooperate then leave! You sicken us with your arrogance. Your recklessness helps no one!"

The old warhorse had a look on her face that said the last meal she had eaten was spoiled. "The human's questions are self-serving and will settle nothing. We did not come here to reveal military secrets to a primate!"

The look on Tria's face said she was the one now running out of patience. "You will address him as Mister Myers or you will not address him at all! Do you understand what I say Sael Nalen or do we need to discuss it in private elsewhere?"

The look on the Operative's face was surprise, then anger. "You soil your ancestry by taking up with this…"

Tria was in the old Chaalt's face in the blink of an eye. "Go ahead Operative, say it! I dare you."

They stood eye to eye. There was an emanation coming from Tria I had only felt in combat. Her intentions were deadly. The Grawl standing behind us were moving back with looks of apprehension on their faces. They wondered if the conflict would start anew.

The Operative blinked then stepped back. Her next words were dripping with contempt. "Fine, but Mr. Myers will address me as Senior Operative!"

Tria's father came forward and made it a point to address me as Tria instructed. "Please Mr. Myers, let us examine the stasis vessel to determine the nature of what it might contain."

"I have conditions that will be met or there will be no cooperation."

Scholar Burlor looked at Sael Nalen, then back at me. "What do you require?"

"You will have your troops board your vessels and leave this star system. I have made countless enemies seeking revenge for their losses. Your ships located over my base of operations could lead to the detection of this facility."

Scholar Burlor tried to speak. "Mr. Myers, our military vessels have---"

48

The Senior Operative cut him off midsentence. "All but my flagship shall relocate to another star system. My ship will remain to patrol the outer regions of the system."

The look she was giving Tria's father translated to "hold your tongue." It was enough for me to surmise they had cloaking and negation capability on their warships. The Senior Operative extended her arm toward her troops palm up. Her troopers formed a small circle. She stared at me.

"Justice, disable the shield for twenty seconds."

"Affirmative, Commander, shield is now down. T-minus twenty seconds and counting."

The Operative curled her fingers upward. There was a flash and a thunderclap of air rushing in to fill the void they had once occupied. *I would love to get my hands on that tech.* The Grawl scientists started talking among themselves at the display of advanced tech. Every possible hypothesis was being discussed and the additional noise was distracting. Before the containment team made their sudden appearance, I was going to greet the Grawl. I was also going to ask them about the large structure that had been erected in the back of the hangar. There was now a building with an immense airlock on the side of it. The collection of artifacts that used to be stored in various places in the hangar area was nowhere to be seen. I had to assume they now occupied the new structure. A quick analysis with my implants estimated the square footage of the new building at over fifty thousand square feet. The Grawl had been very busy while the crew and I were gone. Turning my back to the Scholar and the Operative, I motioned to Xul and he separated from the scientists and stood before me.

"How can I be of service, Nathan Myers?"

I smiled at the little Grawl. He was one of the managing scientists I had rescued from the research station. Apparently, he was voted back into a leadership position by his peers.

"Xul, I need a quick debrief on the new building structure. I also want you and Graf to accompany Tria and I when we show the Chaalt our discoveries."

The Grawl scientist nodded then turned, holding up his hand with two fingers extended. *It reminded me of an old Earth sign of peace!* Graf came forward and they quietly conversed. Graf turned and held up three fingers, and Jaran joined him. The Grawl had established their chain of command in my absence. I wondered if their lack of implant use was because there was no central processing unit to channel the signals. At some point, we would address the issue. They spoke for a moment in low tones, then Jaran turned away and addressed the rest of the scientists. Xul and Graf stood at my side as Jaran and the rest of the Grawl moved to the personnel lifts that take you to the common areas.

5

I looked back at the Operative and it was obvious she was annoyed by the delay. The Scholar had a questioning look on his face. Taking Tria by the hand, I led her and the Grawl several steps away.

"Xul, we don't have time for a full debrief on all of your current research. I would, however, like to be up to speed on the new building."

"Yes of course! After much discussion, we determined it would be wise to construct a structure to protect us from the possibility of explosive decompression. This facility is hundreds of years old. The field in the entry tunnel retains the atmosphere in this area and, if the outer doors were open and the field failed, anyone not wearing a cloak suit would perish. We will address the redundancy issue with the retention field in the near future."

The expressions on my face alerted the Grawl scientist to the fact I needed a much shorter version of the briefing. Tria squeezed my arm to calm my impatience.

"My apologies Nathan Myers, the lower escape tunnel that leads to a remote hangar was filled with a huge supply of prefabricated building materials. We used a quantity of the materials with Justice's help to construct the building. We have built individual labs and storage areas for the artifacts. The compartmentalized storage areas will limit the possibility of accidental contamination of the entire base by foreign contagions or rogue nanites."

I had forgotten all about the escape tunnel. I never had a chance to investigate it because of the nonstop issues we had been encountering. Glancing over my shoulder at the angry looks, I turned back to the Grawl.

In a low voice, I said, "We are not going to give our...guests a guided tour. Take us directly to the containment vessel. Are there any artifacts not behind closed doors they can easily see?"

"Yes, the mineral blocks we have identified as having little value and the unknown spacecraft. They are just inside the large airlock doors. They can be moved to an enclosed storage, but it will take time to do so."

I didn't like giving the Operative a free look at anything we had recovered. I was still really pissed at the intrusion.

"No Xul, take us to the containment vessel and do not stop. I will usher them along if they hesitate."

The Grawl gave me a quick nod. "As you wish."

We walked back to the Scholar and the Operative. Tria's father looked relieved and the Operative agitated. Walking to the building, Xul approached a much smaller airlock on the opposite side. There was a security sensor next to the door that was biometrically coded to the Grawl scientists. He looked over his shoulder at me. I held up a finger and he paused.

"Justice, are the orbitals clear of spacecraft?"

"Yes Commander, the Senior Operative's flagship is currently at the outer edge of this system. The other vessels have transitioned to unknown destinations. I have taken note of their unique drive signatures and the similarities to our own transition distortion waves. I will now be able to track the Chaalt vessels."

I smiled at the Operative and her face darkened. I could tell she was on the verge of another tantrum. I nodded to Xul and he placed his hand on the security scanner. The outer door slid open and we went inside. We were swept with several sanitizing beams of light. The inner door opened to an area of about ten thousand square feet, according to my implants. It was brightly lit and sitting in front of the big atmosphere lock was the six spacecrafts. They were black cylindrical mirrors sitting on short stubby supports. They looked like missiles. Xul kept going, but Tria's father and the Operative were frozen in place. They had looks of astonishment on their faces. I almost collided with the Operative.

"Please follow Xul. You did not trespass on my base to study my artifact collection."

54

The comment netted me a small frown from the Senior Operative, but the amazement never left her face. Tria's father looked like he was stupefied.

The Scholar finally found his voice. "Mr. Myers, I have never heard of anyone possessing an intact Dagger. You have six."

Dagger! They had a name for them. It was a fitting moniker for the sharply pointed ships. It was not the reason the Operative was here, so I wanted to move on to settle the question of what was in the containment vessel once and for all.

"Please move along Scholar Burlor. I am well aware of the number of artifacts in my possession."

Tria's father tore his eyes away from the Daggers and followed Xul and Graf down the long corridor lined with oversized doorways. When we stopped at the end I was impressed with what was there. It was a large cubicle made of a dark gray material that resembled concrete. I wanted to ask where it came from but did not want to give away the fact I did not know in front of the Operative. The large door on the front was familiar; I had blown up a few just like it. It was a vault door similar to those found at the Grawl research facility I had destroyed. I was thoroughly impressed with the work the Grawl had done while I was away. I looked at Xul, giving him a small smile and a nod. He returned the gesture, making all turn to look at me. My face returned to neutral before they could catch the gesture. I waved the scientist on and he placed his hand on the security scanner on the side of the door. Xul stood aside and Graf placed his hand on the scanner, then called to Justice.

"Justice, please verify our identities."

There was a metallic clunk and the door started sliding open. *The Grawl did not know it yet but they all earned a million credits each.* The security measures were first class, as was the building design and construction. The more I thought about it, I decided their insight would net them two million credits each. It was a small fraction of my recent windfalls and the least I could do. Tria's father and the Operative entered the room. I stood back as they carefully inspected the containment chamber. The Scholar reached down to the back of one of the panels. He pulled a lever and the displays came alive. They had our attention now. This thing was hundreds of years old and still had an active power source.

The two Grawl scientists hastily pushed past me. They stood in awe as they watched the Chaalt Scholar at work. He was checking readouts running down a small display. His face was looking grimmer by the minute, and I did not know what to make of it. He touched a small round glowing ball on the side of the large tanks. It turned translucent and then clear. My eyes grew large. *Good God! What kind of horror were we seeing?* The large capsule-shaped body had six metallic legs, each ending with oversized serrated ice picks for feet. It had six long metal arms, two of which had six spiked fingers. The other four had machine devices that looked like mining and grappling tools. They might even be weapons for all I knew. The capsule itself looked heavily armored. It had several protrusions on the domed top and a couple of tubes extending from it on thick, flexible braided cables.

The Chaalt Scholar was rattled. "Mr. Myers, you have another first. You have a functioning Prule hunter in your possession. Your discoveries are incredible and may be the most important to this galaxy in more than a hundred solar rotations."

Justice commed me. "Commander, an unknown signal just emanated from your location. I was unable to block or jam it. I believe it was broadcast from a device on the Senior Operative."

"Justice, get the weapons on line and prepare for defensive action!"

The Senior Operative surprised the crap out of me. "That will not be necessary, Nathan Myers. I did send a signal but it was to inform my flagship that the Prule has been verified. I have no intention of seizing the containment vessel. Your security is good and it is about to become impenetrable. The more the vessel is handled, the more likely something catastrophic could happen. I will need to consult with my superiors for the best course of action."

I did not know if I should trust the Operative or not, so I turned to Tria. "Can I trust her word or do I tell them to leave?"

Tria looked the old warrior in the eyes. They stared at each other for almost thirty seconds. "Yes, we can trust her Nathan. She tells the truth." She looked at her father. "I expect the same from you."

The hurt on his face was obvious but he just nodded and remained silent. He turned around and started shutting down the containment vessels systems.

I looked at Sael Nalen. "What now?"

Once the containment vessel was completely shut down, she turned away from the container. "I am going to order this star system blockaded. My ships will return to increase security. A small fleet will join them shortly. All will cloak and take up strategic locations in and out of this system. When all are in place, your base and this star system will appear deserted once again. When I have made contact with my superiors, I will advise you of their intentions."

I thought about it for another moment. "If your superiors wish to stick to their original plan of seizing the containment vessel, then what?"

The Senior Operative stood silently looking at me. Her face betrayed nothing. She looked at Tria's father then turned back to me. "Nathan Myers, I now believe you are not the primitive fool I thought you were. I am sure you know the danger the Prule pose to this galaxy. Why would you want the responsibility of securing such a threat?"

It was a reasonable question and she was right. If something happened and the Prule hunter escaped, it would be on me. I needed to think carefully about what my response should be.

I looked at Tria and she quietly whispered to me. "You will know what to do. Perhaps we should discuss our options privately with the crew and the scientists."

I was beginning to believe I would not know what to do without this beautiful alien at my side. I gave her a small peck on the cheek and she gave me a smile that made my temperature go up a few degrees. She put both of her hands on my cheeks and planted a kiss square on my lips. Turning away, I caught the hint of a frown on the Operative's face that quickly disappeared. The old witch had to face the fact one of her own has taken up with a primitive alien from a backwards-thinking world.

Justice commed my implants. "Commander, the Senior Operative's starship has moved to our location. It is now one thousand feet about us. The five other Chaalt vessels have encircled this star system."

I approached Sael Nalen and Patriarch Burlor. "I must ask you to leave the artifact containment building until we have decided what we are going to do."

They did not like it, but they walked out of the cube. I nodded to Xul and he locked the vault door. We walked out of the building, and as we passed by the Daggers, our Chaalt guests could not keep their eyes off of them.

Graf locked the personnel hatch and I faced the Operative once more. "Regardless of the quality of your ships negation and cloaking systems, I do not want your flagship parked over my base. If you insist on remaining, you are to move to a large crevasse south of here. It is large enough for your ship and I won't be as pissy about you hanging around. As a convenience, I will drop my base's shield for an additional twenty seconds."

Justice broadcasted out loud. "Shield down Commander! T-minus twenty seconds and counting."

The Operative turned her back on me and stalked off. When she was about forty feet away, there was a flash and a gunshot-like report and she was gone. That was a freakin' awesome trick. One of these days, I would figure out a way to get my grubby Earth-boy mitts on the tech.

I called to Justice, "Justice, keep the shield up and the reactors hot on the weapons. I want them to ask nicely before they can come back."

"Affirmative, Commander."

Tria once again locked her arms in mine and I waved Xul and Graf over to join us. Coonts had shed his combat gear and joined Klutch at my side. Tria's father had a questioning look on his face that turned to resignation. He sat down on the long bench against the wall of the artifact building. We went down to the common areas and were met with another roar of applause. I could tell the scientists were worried about what might happen after my confrontation with the Chaalt Operative. I waved to the Grawl and they all followed Tria and I to the large, open cafeteria.

Holding up my hands, they quieted to a soft murmur. "Please sit. We have much to discuss. I need your input to help me determine my next steps."

Tria went to the counter and brought back a carafe of water and placed it at our table. I took a quick drink to clear my throat and addressed the crowd sitting around me.

"The Chaalt want the containment vessel because it holds a functioning Prule. I don't know if it would be wise for us to study the bio-machine or not. What I do know is we cannot let it break containment. If for some reason this should happen and it escapes, we will be responsible. I do not want to contemplate the consequences. I would like you to think about it and tell me what the best course of action is. Please take your time and discuss it. I must also tell you, when the Chaalt came here uninvited, it was their intention to seize the containment vessel. If you tell me we should keep the Prule, we may be forced to fight off a Chaalt assault. Please consider all options before you present them to Xul for my consideration. Thank you!"

The cafeteria erupted into a loud chatter. They were all talking at once. I was considering getting something to eat but the noise was annoying. I really wanted peace and quiet. I left Coonts, Klutch and the rest in at the table and decided I would eat aboard the Legacy. Making my way to the lifts, each Grawl I passed quieted and put their hand out so I would touch it. My family was growing. Glancing back, I saw Tria behind me, and she was getting the same treatment. I waited in front of the lift until she joined me. Her smile could melt butter at twenty feet. We stepped in the lift holding hands. When we came to the top, we stepped out together coming face to face with her father.

He started to say something and I cut him off. "Scholar Burlor, there is no need to explain yourself to me. You have your duty and I have mine. I can only hope what you and your superiors decide to do does not come into conflict with my immediate goals. I have committed what some might perceive as atrocities to protect your daughter, you and the Grawl you have met here. If Operative Nalen attempts to go against me and those I protect, I can assure you it will be a bloodbath of epic proportions."

The Scholar's eyes widened and his mouth opened. I turned my back on him and, without hesitation, Tria did the same. We were walking toward the Legacy when I caught a whiff of something very unpleasant. I looked over my shoulder and saw Tria's father in a running retreat. Coonts had a grimace on his face. The Tibor Troop Master had a huge toothy smile on his.

Justice addressed us. "Commander, the Chaalt flagship has taken cover in the crevasse. I have detected several microbursts of energy from that location. They are displaying very unique properties. They are leaving minute distortion waves similar to spacecraft transition waves. If I had not been directing the base's scanners at that exact location, I would have failed to detect them."

Just having the Chaalt close by was revealing a treasure trove of new intelligence on their military capabilities. My guess was they had a deep space communication system. It might even have the same properties as our jump drives. Instantaneous communication across millions of light years was priceless tech. I looked at Tria and I could tell she knew what I was thinking. She gave me an almost imperceptible nod. I turned away from her and cleared my throat, getting my crew mates' attention.

"Coonts, Klutch, any thoughts on the energy spikes?"

Klutch shrugged his wide shoulders. "Commander, I am a Troop Master, not a scientist. My job is to break scat and take titles. If I were to guess, I would say it was some form of comms traffic."

Coonts chimed in. "Many races, including mine, have been trying to get access to Chaalt tech or intelligence for a great many years. Even though Tria will not comment on the subject, her race is one of the most accomplished and advanced in the galaxy. To believe the recorded microbursts would be anything other than a very sophisticated communication device would be foolish. They obviously have real time comms capable of reaching their home worlds. It is very likely they are clarifying orders that will determine if they will attack our base or negotiate some sort of compromise."

The little Grawl rarely bullshitted. I was sure he had just laid out the most likely scenario. The look on the Grawl's face was grim, and it worried me. He clenched his hands behind his back and began pacing. When he finally stopped in front of me, the look was even grimmer.

"Commander, if the Chaalt bring the full weight of their military to bear, we will not survive the assault."

I turned to Tria and she looked me in the eyes. "If my people determine there is even the smallest probability we could release the Prule and let it escape, they will destroy this moon. Sael Nalen would only need her fleet to do so. There is the very real possibility we would receive no warning."

6

The stark reality of our predicament was starting to sink in. All my bluster and bullheadedness were now on the back burner. We would have to give up the containment vessel or face the consequences. It was a bitter pill to swallow, but the alternative was unthinkable.

Xul walked into the galley and he did not look happy. I waved him to our table and he sat down. "Nathan Myers, we have come to a consensus. All believe hostilities with the Chaalt will end with the loss of our lives. If that comes to pass, everything you have fought for and those brought to judgement for the good of all will have been for nothing. Your maker did not bring you here for this fruitless cause. There is still much to do and countless races that have no one to stand for them. If we perish now, evil will win and nothing will change."

Justice was listening. He decided that it was his turn and we needed to hear what he thought. "Commander, I have an idea."

I was jolted out of my morose state of mind. "I'm sorry, Justice, I failed to ask your opinion. It was an error on my part because you are in this situation as well. Please, let's hear what you have to say."

"Commander, the Chaalt obviously have some of the best tech currently available. Would it not make sense to discuss a trade, if not for the Prule containment vessel, perhaps one of the Daggers?"

Holy shit! Why didn't I come to that conclusion? The Earth-boy idiot was more worried about having to give rather than what I could gain.

"Justice, give me a short range comm channel I can reach Sael Nalen on!"

Everybody was all smiles now. "Comm channel open Commander."

"Senior Operative, I would like to talk with you and clarify our position."

The Operative came on immediately. "Mindless primate! It was you that was worried about your security. Now you broadcast on an unsecured comm channel."

I cut her off before she could get me really pissed again. "The shield will be down for three minutes, please come alone."

Justice killed the channel. He alerted me that the Chaalt flagship was fifteen seconds out. We went to the down tube and made our descent to the personnel hatch. We walked off the Legacy and heard the loud report of the compression wave. The Operative was doing the shiny liquid metal thing again. I was pretty sure it was a shield of some sort. It fell away and Sael had her hands on her weapons and was looking around cautiously. She came alone even though she thought it was a trick or a trap. I had to give it to the old warrior: she had a set of nads. She marched over to us with a look of rage on her face.

I shut her down with one sentence. "I would like to discuss turning the Prule over to you."

The angry Chaalt stopped like a set of new disc brakes. She suddenly squinted at me. "This had better not be some kind of human trick. I have little patience for any more of your scat!"

Justice was broadcasting to my implants so no one could hear him. "Commander I am picking up a continuous transmission signal coming from the Operative. I believe our discussions are being relayed to her ship and then on to her home world. It would be wise to choose your words carefully."

Justice was correct. I did not wish to present a less than stable and confident picture to the Operative's superiors. The outcome could be disastrous for us all. I need to make sure the Chaalt understand where I am coming from before they pass judgement on me.

"There will be no tricks Senior Operative. Your invasion of our base was unexpected and unwelcome. Your troops pointing their weapons at innocent people and your arrogant threats were the reason I responded in the manner I did. I protect all who live here. What would your people do if I were to go their homes and act the way you have? OH! I just remembered you have a Union blockade to prevent such Throgg scat!"

The Operative's attitude did a one eighty. She either realized I was playing it up for the microphone or she in fact was remorseful for the brute force entrance.

"Mr. Myers, I apologize for the intrusion. I was ordered to take every precaution because we had no intelligence on what we would find when we arrived. Our disagreement was...regrettable."

Now I was wondering if the old war horse was ordered to come back and play nice. Apparently the Chaalt know all about catching flies with honey.

"We are prepared to offer you a very generous finder's fee and an additional bonus for our intrusion."

Her offer confirmed my suspicions: she was ordered to play nice. I was relieved to know they did not want a conflict. I would still tread lightly because I could tell the Senior Operative was not on board with this tactic.

"My superiors have instructed me to award you twenty-five billion credits."

The Operative was stunned when we all stood stone faced giving her no recognition of the offer.

Turning my head to the side I talked over my shoulder. "Do we need any more credits?"

My crew and the Grawl scientist were shaking their heads negative.

"The numerous criminals we have brought to judgement offered up their ill-gotten gains in hopes I would spare their lives. They died destitute."

The reaction from the Operative was a look of newfound respect. The corners of her mouth curled slightly, and she gave me a nod of approval.

"We have no need for credits, but we do need new tech. While the advanced races turn their backs to the rampant crime and injustice going on before their very eyes, we do not! We need advanced technology to give us an edge over our enemies. The corruption we have uncovered involves a great many races. If we can stop even a small percentage, it will impact the lives of many. If your people were to join our cause we would make a much greater difference."

Sael Nalen's eye blinked then got wider. "I must discuss these matters with my superiors. I need to return to my ship. I will contact you before I return."

I wasn't sure what the strange looks meant, but I had the feeling she had been recalled. "Justice, deactivate the shield. I believe security is no longer an issue."

My comment netted me another minute smile. The Operative turned away. This time she walked a considerable distance before disappearing in a report that left no ringing in my ears. Justice again confirmed what was on my mind.

"Commander, the transmission signal halted several seconds before the Operative said she needed to discuss our request. I speculate she was recalled to determine if they will offer us technology."

"Those were my thoughts as well. Whether or not they will do so remains the question."

There was always the possibility they would offer more credits and then tell us to go buy what we need. I doubt we would be able to find a deep space comm system or a transporter. We would have to wait and see what happened. I was not alone in this, so I decided to call another meeting to decide what we would ask for if given a choice. We headed back to the common area and the Grawl scientists.

As I entered the room, I had everyone's attention. "I am sorry we have to continue playing games, but now there is the small possibility we may be offered new tech. I would like all of you to choose five items, and list them in priority of acquisition. List the items from 'most important' to 'would like to have.' Submit the list to Xul. If the opportunity arises, I will present it to the Chaalt."

The chatter and noise started all over again. I went to the lift waiting for Tria, Coonts and Klutch. When they joined me, we made our way back to the Legacy. Once aboard, we retired to our cabins. I had just taken a shower and climbed into bed when the door to my cabin opened and Tria came in. Justice took it upon himself to give Tria unfettered access to my personal space. She had a blanket wrapped around her. As she walked across my room she let it fall from her shoulders to the floor. She was only wearing braces on three of her four arms. My mouth went dry and my heart started racing. I cringed when an extruded appendage carefully set a carafe of water and two glasses on the small table next to my bed. "JUSTICE!" The appendage disappeared as if it had been cleaved off. Tria smiled at me. I suddenly felt feverish and covered in goose bumps. My breathing became shallow and fast.

"Can you feel me Nathan?"

"Yes"

She slid into bed with me and I was trembling. She embraced me with all of her arms. I kissed her.

"COMMANDER! Sael Nalen is in route to this location and will arrive in five minutes."

"ARE YOU FREAKIN' KIDDING ME?"

"No Commander. I can assure you I am as upset about this turn of events as you are."

"JUSTICE, NOT ONE MORE WORD!"

I heard Tria giggle. She got up and ran to my bathroom. I quickly dressed and told her I would see her later.

Again, I heard her laugh. Then she said, "Perhaps, Nathan Myers"

I rolled my eyes and started swearing in sentences. A cold shower might save me considerable embarrassment. I thought about who I was going to see and it quickly became unnecessary.

I didn't think I had been more than five minutes. I must have been mistaken, because the Operative stood with all of her arms crossed. She had a look of impatience written all over her less than attractive face. As I approached the Operative, the expression on her face changed from annoyance to shock, then surprise. Her expression finally settled to a frown. I suspected she sensed Tria's aura or Sha'leen or both on me. I was not here seeking her approval and really didn't give a shit what the Senior Operative thought about my relationship with Tria. My opinion of the Operative was that she needed to get laid and lighten up. If she was to get her battle scars fixed and ditch the guns and swords, she just might find someone crazy enough to try.

"I have no idea what Tria Burlor sees in you or your race. Her injuries must have affected her mind."

73

If the Operative was trying to get a rise out of me, it was working. I really did not wish to go down this road again. I closed my eyes and took a deep cleansing breath. I stepped right up into her personal space and looked her in the eyes.

"I know you are not delusional, Senior Operative. I also know you can sense what she sees in me and my race. Obviously, the truth does not sit well with you. I am sorry it is difficult for you to grasp the fact my race and I will eventually be the cure for the sickness spreading throughout the galaxy. With or without your help, what I have told you will come to pass."

The look on the Operative's face was once again full of anger and spite. The old bitch was so used to no one giving her shit she was on the verge of another meltdown. I started thinking if I could push her in that direction, maybe upper management might replace her with someone who had more tolerance and less bigotry.

"Look Senior Operative, I thought we had already established which of us has the bigger penis, so could you please just get on with it?"

At first, she looked puzzled. Then someone or something must have spoon fed her the translation. The look on her face turned deadly. I gave her my best Earth-boy smile and readied myself for what would surely come next. Her response shocked me.

Her homely face softened and she let out a barking laugh. "Your fearless overconfidence will one day get you eviscerated, you mindless primate!"

Easing my stance, I now felt like the pissing contests were finally over with.

"Old witch, I am glad you have finally come to your senses."

The briefest look of confusion crossed her face then vanished with another harsh laugh. "For reasons I cannot begin to understand, my people now consider it wise to bargain with you and your followers."

I gave her another Earth-boy smile. "You may now call me Nathan; all my friends do."

She looked at me for a moment and she smiled, the kind of smile one might see on a cat's face while it's looking at a mouse pinned under its claws. "You may call me Senior Operative because no one dares to do otherwise."

It was my turn to laugh and I let the comment go. "Your meeting was brief; can I take that as a sign your superiors have decided to share technology with us?"

Her look of neutrality gave me no hint as to what might be on her mind. It dawned on me she came to bargain and not just give tech away.

"We know the Prule hunter is of no use to you."

Before I could get mad and tell her to screw off, she quickly held up two of her hands and continued. "We do know there is a possibility that information gleaned from the bio-machine could unlock secrets to the galaxy of its origin. Do not misconstrue my statements. We place great value on these possibilities. However, it might not be the value you have determined it to be."

Looking over the Operative's shoulder, I saw Xul trying to catch my attention. Focusing back on the Operative, I excused myself and walked over to Xul. The words now coming from the Operative were not endearments. Xul handed me a small note and I examined it as he retreated to the down tube. I smiled because the first two items on the list were the same I wished for: the deep space comm system and the transporter. Next was all information the Chaalt might possess on the unknown spacecraft. That was indeed a noteworthy consideration. The one after that was another very good choice. Updated star charts. I might have bumped that one up to third, but the Grawl were much smarter than I was, so I had to agree. The last was interesting and another good choice: any Oolaran weapons that could be fitted to the Legacy. The Grawl were thinking of my safety as much as I thought about theirs. I turned back to the very annoyed Operative.

"As you were saying, Sael Nalen?"

I could tell she was ready to spit more venom for my use of her given name. Surprisingly, it was well watered down.

"Are all humans mindless fools such as you?"

"We have our fair share. Most are politicians and government officials. But hey, that means we might get lucky and find one who will take you for a mate."

The glare my comment garnered softened to a small smile.

"Human, in all my years as a soldier I have never met an alien such as you. All but my bitterest enemies grovel in my presence. Most willingly bend to my authority. I am actively questioning my sanity and find no reasonable explanation why I feel compelled to like an offensive beast such as you. I find your audacious levity and reckless insubordination refreshing. That being said, if you ever spout scat like that in front of my people I will cut your tongue out."

I smiled and blew her a kiss. "Old witch"

Her eyebrows went up and her eyes pinched shut. She shook her head and laughed. "Rancid beast!"

I was glad we finally understood each other and I would attempt to drop the theatrics. "Attempt" was the key word.

"Justice, please tell Xul, Graf and Tria's father to meet me in the artifact building."

"Affirmative Commander."

I was confident I would not be denied access to my own artifacts. I walked up and put my hand on the security scanner. The airlock opened and the Operative and I entered the decontamination chamber together. Once the process was complete, we entered the warehouse and the Operative made a beeline to the Daggers.

She looked at me. "Have you determined what these are?"

I decided to be honest with her. "We know they are spacecraft, probably fighters of some sort. We have had very little time to study them due to past events."

The careful scrutiny and the way she looked at the small starship told me she knew much more. I hinted to her that this was just the tip of the iceberg. "We have discovered several very interesting artifacts where we recovered the Daggers."

She nodded and turned to me, her curiosity aroused. "May I examine what you have recovered?"

I saw Xul, Graf and The Scholar approaching. Just coming out of the decontamination chamber behind them was Tria, Coonts and Klutch. I waved them over and we headed toward the hallway, giving us access to the stored artifacts.

7

I had Xul open the first large doorway we came to. The Scholar and the Operative entered while the rest of us stood just outside. The 699 and 2762 that filled the room was interesting, but not enough to get more than a cursory inspection. The thin sheets of material we had yet to identify were getting careful scrutiny from the Scholar. The Scholar turned back to me. The blank looks on our faces must have tipped him off we did not have a clue what it was.

"The material is artifact 481. You have enough to shield a small starship. It is a highly sought-after commodity because it is impervious to most forms of radiation. Due to its light weight and rugged durability, the more advanced races desire it for the fabrication of body armor."

I gave Xul a nod at the door across the hall. The strange look on his Grawl face radiated apprehension. He approached me and politely asked to speak with me in private.

Facing the Scholar and the Operative, I asked to be excused. "Could you please give us a moment? I will not be long and we will continue the tour."

Xul took my hand and walked me clear of our guest. When he thought we were out of earshot, he pulled me down so he could whisper to me. "Nathan Myers, we have not had time to discuss our current research. The room you wish to show the Chaalt is one of the new research labs. It has been set up and designed to study the nanites you discovered. The microscopic robots are of an amazing design. They are made from an unknown material that makes them exceptionally resilient. My point is: unless they have been programed to disassemble themselves, they will continue to do their programed tasks indefinitely. They are capable of an extraordinary range of uses."

"Okay, Xul, why are you concerned if the Operative or the Scholar sees them?"

"Commander, fifteen of the storage receptacles are full of nanites that have no designated programming. The other fifteen have been programmed as weapons. Our research has shown that it takes a trigger code to activate them. Once activated, they will devour whatever they are unleashed upon. They can disassemble a starship or a biological. They will not stop until a self-destruct command or a dormant command is given. They attack at the molecular level. Targets literally dissolve. I fear if the Chaalt should let this information pass on to the Galactic Union, we will be in direct conflict with their laws. Possession of weaponized nanites is considered illegal and leaves all of us subject to severe censure and possible internment."

"Thank you Xul. I see I should have spent my spare time getting a full debrief from you. Is there anything we can show them that will not endanger our security?"

"Yes, Nathan Myers, we have a large collection of encapsulated minerals or metals we have yet to identify."

I looked at the group in the hallway and all were getting fidgety, wondering what we were discussing. I jerked my head in their direction and we rejoined the group in the hallway.

"My crew and I have been away for an extended period of time. We have just returned and I have failed to ask for a full debrief on our recent discoveries. It has come to my attention that some of our artifacts will require a nondisclosure agreement before we can give you access. I cannot, at the present time, believe you can give me an absolute guarantee of secrecy. Please follow Xul and he will give you access to the balance of our discoveries we can show you without reservation."

The frowns I was getting told me the Scholar and Operative's curiosity was killing them. They now wondered what I was hiding from them. Xul walked down the hall to the second door on the left side. He touched the security scanner and it opened. The Scholar went in to investigate, but the Operative walked up to me. In a move that surprised me, she took me by the arm and walked me down the hall to the large open storage area. All eyes were on us; Tria in particular was watching intently. All of the things I could possibly think to say to the Operative right at the moment would piss her off. I was not a human known for keeping my mouth shut when prudence suggested I should. The stern looks on the Operative's face likewise implied I should refrain from blessing her with what might be considered intelligent conversation. For reasons unknown, I picked unintelligent conversation instead. When the Operative swung me around to face her, I startled her by putting my finger to her lips. Her eyebrows shot up and her eyes went wide.

"I know you can't help it, but you really need to control yourself. Tria is all the Chaalt female I am going to be able to handle at one time."

The punch was short and sharp. It was delivered perfectly to my solar plexus with her lower right hand. I don't think anyone behind me even saw it. I know I didn't. It instantly quieted the balance of my snide remarks. The strike was so unexpected it expertly evacuated the air from my lungs along with a small quantity of spit that landed on her cheek. She calmly leaned forward and cleaned it off with the collar of my uniform. She straightened my collar out and pressed it neatly back in place. I finally dragged enough air into my lungs to halt my wheezing gasps. The lukewarm smile on her face let me know she was enjoying my discomfort.

"You simple minded primate! It is difficult for me to understand why you find the need to make light of serious situations. You need to listen to what I have to say without further comment. If you want cutting edge tech from my people, you have to be more forthcoming with your discoveries. I have been given considerable leeway in what can be offered. Show me what you have hidden and I will decide whether or not I will disclose to my superiors the nature of the artifact."

My breathing had returned to normal and the Operative had my attention. I was thinking about the list in my pocket. "Justice, is the Operative still transmitting?"

"No, Commander. I find it interesting her transmissions ceased when you entered the artifact building."

She was startled we knew about the transmission signal. She was starting to understand just how unique of an A.I. Justice was.

I gave her a quizzical look. "Okay, but only you. I find the Scholar's divided loyalties unsettling. Where I come from, loyalty to family is everything."

"Your priorities are another reason I find myself liking you, human. It will not matter what the Scholar says about your discoveries. Now that he has verified the Prule hunter, he has demanded an immediate evacuation back to the home worlds. I find his lack of courage distasteful. He has formally requested me to reinstate Tria's service. If I were to do so, she would be sent home for retraining. He has shown little gratitude for you rescuing him and his daughter."

I looked back to where the Scholar now stood. My anger for his request was growing. Sael Nalen put her hand on my shoulder and I turned back to face her. She could see I was about to explode.

"Do not worry Nathan Myers. I have denied his request. He does not know it yet, but he will be permanently assigned to the science department on my flagship."

I found my respect for the Chaalt warrior was growing with each passing moment. What I thought was bias and bigotry may have been more along the lines of misunderstanding something not considered normal for her species. It was easy to like the Operative. She was direct and forthcoming. While she was not exactly a fountain of information, I could not blame her for holding her cards close.

I let my anger subside. "Is Tria aware of her father's intentions?"

"No Nathan Myers, I do not believe he has the spine to tell his daughter. I have no intention of doing so. It would solve nothing and only increase an already tense situation."

Letting the frown fall from my face, I looked the Operative in the eyes and truly felt I was seeing the real Chaalt hiding behind a warrior's façade. I liked what I saw and knew I was in the company of a kindred spirit. We were close enough together I leaned forward and gave her a peck on the cheek. The shock on her face quickly subsided into a warm smile I had never seen before.

"Do not attempt to work your guiles on me, human. I still cannot fathom what Tria sees in a mindless, backwards specimen such as you."

"Witch!"

"Primate."

We turned back to the waiting group. All stood in shocked silence. As we got closer I nodded to Xul and pointed to the nanite lab door. The alarmed expression on his face subsided and he quickly complied.

Tria came to my side and held my hand. "That was…interesting."

I leaned in and kissed her. She smiled. Looking up at the ceiling and shaking my head. I commented, "You have no idea."

Xul put his hand on the security scanner then stood back looking at me. "Nathan Myers, it will require multiple verifications."

Reaching down, I placed my hand on the device. Justice called out. "Identity verified."

The door slid open revealing an enclosed chamber, the first of three. It was cramped inside with the size of our group. We were swept with multiple beams of light. Xul lifted his arms above him and turned in a circle. All copied his actions. We stepped into the next chamber and then the following one, repeating the process in each. When the final vault-style door opened with a hiss of positive pressure, we entered a brightly lit laboratory. The walls, floor and ceiling were coated in a thick coat of a clear, plastic-like substance. It reminded me of the billet encapsulation containers. I realized the lab was air-and moisture-tight. The precautions the Grawl scientists had taken to ensure that no nanites could escape were remarkable. I made another adjustment to all of the scientist's bonuses. It would now total four million credits each.

Fifteen of the nanite vessels were against one wall and fifteen were against the other. In between was a large assortment of equipment and work stations. The number of analytical devices the Grawl took from their former research labs was impressive. I knew we had filled the cargo bay and all available spaces with crates and equipment, but I never knew the extent of our acquisitions. Apparently the Grawl had absconded with all the necessary devices and supplies for complete laboratories. Five million credits and counting.

Tria's father looked at several displays and devices. The look on his face was turning more incredulous by the minute. He turned to me. "You are in possession of weaponized nanites! This is a serious breach of Galactic Union laws. This is a criminal offense that must be reported!"

It did not take the Operative but a second to shut that crap down. "SILENCE!" This is now a Chaalt sanctioned research lab and you are bound by OUR laws of secrecy. Do you understand Scholar Burlor?"

The Scholar recoiled from the implications of her statement. He nodded to the Operative. Looking at her, I raised an eyebrow. At some point I would need a clarification on her designation. Her withering stare never left the Scholar.

"What was in the other storage room Scholar Burlor?"

The Scholar swiftly answered. "A large quantity of Containium, Cobalium and Trimellium."

It was the Operative's turn to raise her eyebrows. "Inform *our* scientists what those elements were once used for."

The Scholar swallowed and addressed us. "Our research has revealed they are the building blocks used to manufacture the shielding for Guardian and Sentinel exotic matter star drives. The material contains all emissions. Some theorize that, when cloaked, Guardian-designed military spacecraft are undetectable. It was further speculated it was the latest technology incorporated into their warships just before their mass disappearance. The elements are extremely rare and are considered priceless. No race we know of has knowledge of where these materials originated from."

This was amazing information. It also told me the Legacy must have been put in storage before the upgrades were installed on the Guardian fleet. The Legacy, even with our negation systems, was detectable by powerful close-range sensors of modern design. There was the possibility that could change in the near future.

It sounded like the Scholar was going to continue but was cut off by the Operative. "That will be all for now Scholar Burlor. Go wait outside for extraction."

A small smile crossed the Chaalt scholar's face. He hurried to the exit chambers. He had no idea he was about to get his morning meal watered down with a generous amount of piss. Tria looked puzzled, and I gave her good arm a little squeeze and a small shake of my head.

She looped her arms in mine and we looked to the Operative. "May I ask what you meant by stating this is now a Chaalt lab?"

"It means exactly that, Nathan Myers. You are now officially a sanctioned Chaalt covert research facility."

The frown on my face was getting darker by the minute. The warrior held up all of her hands to silence the protest forming on my lips.

"And as such, will be immune to any and all Galactic Union inquiries and interference. They will be informed a research lab exists in the general location of the fringe. It will fall under our military jurisdiction. We will surrender a small amount of dated tech and information connected to the supposed operations of this facility. You will be able to operate as you have, with no scrutiny from the Union."

Sael Nalen was one smooth operator. She managed to kill several big birds with one small stone — the biggest being the transfer of our base to the new designation of sovereign Chaalt territory. The transfer from mine to theirs had better come with a shit load of perks if they expect me to let them come and go as they please.

"We want your deep space communication capability."

The Operative eyed me. "It is a little early in the game to be demanding military secrets, Nathan Myers"

"I am not demanding anything. I am trading you one of the galaxy's greatest discoveries for tech I am sure you are working on upgrading or replacing. Look me in the eye and tell me you don't have the most current innovations in the works."

"Nathan Myers, what you ask for is the most current innovation. I told you I have leeway and will now exercise that option under certain conditions, the first being you are sworn to secrecy involving all aspects of the devices. You cannot talk about it or brag about it or even insinuate you have one. This means no one is allowed access to the interdimensional signal transmitters, or ISTs for short. As far as anyone else is concerned, there is no such thing as an IST. Since my race owns this tech, everything you broadcast will be monitored by us. I am warning you now: if there is something you do not want us to hear, do not use the device. For all of our benefits, do not place the device in your private cabin for any reason."

The Operative made it a point to give me the stink eye along with her last statement. I think she just might have exhibited a sense of humor. I rolled my eyes and shook my head. I wanted more because I was convinced the Chaalt had it to give.

"The ISTs are a good start, but we need an apple for apples trade."

The Operative gave me a perplexing look that turned incredulous.

"You want us to also supply you with fruit?"

I laughed at the confusion I had sown. The Operative did not think it was funny. "It is an old saying from the planet of my birth. It means we are going to need a little more than the ISTs."

The Operative did not think that was funny either. She balled up her lower right fist and smacked it into the opposite. "I have already warned you about making light of a serious situation, Nathan Myers."

"We want the transporter capability as well."

She was stunned at my request. It might have been a little much to ask for. I was going to throw in a Dagger but she cut me off.

"That will never come to pass, human! Transporter technology is our most closely guarded secret. None have ever lived to speak of it. It is only used on extremely dangerous insertions. There are never survivors from such an assault. You are most fortunate events turned out as they have or everyone here would have died."

I could tell she was serious. Her stare was boring right through me. I wasn't going to give up that easily. "All right, how about something not as valuable as your virginity?"

The Operative looked up at the ceiling shaking her head. Her face softened. "Mindless primate, if you continue your madness I will gladly beat the moronic chatter out of you."

"We would like to update our star charts."

She looked undecided then gave me a less than enthusiastic answer. "Perhaps with some modifications we could supply you with recent data to upgrade your existing logs. My generosity is at an end. There will be no more charitable donations."

I could tell my crew and the scientists had grown weary of our back and forth heated discussions. Xul was giving me a questioning look, and I already knew why. The secure storage room in the back of the lab had yet to be opened. It had to be where the Grawl stockpiled the eight hundred six-foot rods we decided were missiles. They were not with the other artifacts. It was not hard for me to surmise why the Grawl scientists housed them close by. They had to be the delivery system for the weaponized nanites.

I put my hands up getting everyone's attention. "You should all get something to eat and some rest. I will debrief you when the Operative and I have finalized our arrangements."

I put both of my hands on Tria's cheeks. With an annoyed look she batted them away and planted a wet one on me that made my knees knock. The Operative grimaced and stepped away.

"I will see you later and we will have a meal together."

She gave me an alarming smile. My legs felt a little rubbery and I got goose bumps. "TRIA!"

She disappeared with the crew and scientists into the Legacy. I turned back to try and complete my next request but was having difficulty gathering my thoughts. Sael Nalen was staring intently at me. She looked baffled. That's when I felt it. It was kind of numbing at first. Then it flared into a burning sensation. It was all I could do to keep from groaning out loud. The Operative was reaching out to me with her Sha'Leen. This was not a caress, it was a weapon. I was willing to bet she had never used it for anything else. The burning sensation was getting worse. I was not going to give her the pleasure of knowing it was getting to me. Forcing myself to stand up straight and put a cryptic look on my face, I walked to where she waited. She looked astonished. The pain and discomfort suddenly ceased. *Thank my maker!* I really did not think I could take much more.

"You don't look well Senior Operative; do you need to rest before we continue?"

She was studying me. "No, you fool, I am fine. As I said before, you have run out of free requests."

8

I stood, looking intently at the Operative. I was wondering if I should first offer the rare elements or go right to the Daggers. We already had good weapons on the Legacy. Tria telling me they were only fair compared to the originals made me want the real McCoy's. On the other hand, the other item on our list might possibly end up being a completely new weapon system if we could unlock its secrets. It was time to test the waters.

"Senior Operative, I am very interested in bringing the Legacy back to its full capabilities. I am willing to trade some of our other discoveries to acquire those assets."

The look on the Operative's face never changed. She obviously knew I would eventually start scratching at that door. I could tell she was trying to decide if she should open it or not.

"My people and I are not in the business of arming rebels and vigilantes."

The comment caught me off guard and, to tell you the truth, it kind of pissed me off. I had to think carefully about my response. Depending on whose eyes you were looking through, you could easily hang one if not both monikers around my neck.

I gave her a steely stare. "I find it hard to believe that is what you truly think we are. Common sense suggests if that was your true opinion, you would not be giving us IST systems."

The Operative smiled. "Once again you prove to me you are capable of intelligent thoughts. That, however, does not imply I no longer think you are three swings out of a tree."

I was finding it interesting she had not said a single word about the weaponized nanites. I was now wondering if the Chaalt had nanite weapons and were hiding them from the Galactic Union. Perhaps a test was in order to gauge her true feelings. I made my way to the storeroom and placed my hand on the scanner. Sael Nalen had followed me and now stood with both sets of arms crossed, not quite knowing what to expect next. With a clack, the door opened. Stacked floor to ceiling was the whole stash of missile tubes.

The Operative's looks went from curiosity to consternation. She stepped into the room and carefully inspected one of the tubes. She was astonished by our find.

"The odds of finding intact Daggers is miniscule. The odds of finding them with complete armament are astronomical. You may now possess enough leverage to acquire additional restricted military resources.

Transporter technology will definitely not be one of the items available."

Now we were getting somewhere. I held something the Chaalt wanted bad enough to admit it. Thinking back, I remembered my experiences dealing with the Zaens and the Ilor. It would be wise to think carefully about what I said or implied.

"I thought the whole idea of leverage was to pry heavy obstacles from one's path."

She smiled at my analogy. "Human, one can use leverage for any number of useful things. For instance, you could use leverage to remove your cranium from the orifice you so freely spread your endless supply of scat from."

Ouch, that burned. Touché, old witch. I could not help it — I now found myself really liking the grizzled old warrior. "Do you have Oolaran weapons we can install on the Legacy?"

I could tell she was also considering very carefully what she would disclose and what she shouldn't. "We have reverse-engineered the point defense beam weapons. We have those systems installed on our warships. It would be a simple matter to supply a limited number to arm your ship. The number ten comes to mind. What else is your small intellect fretting over?"

I had to admit the old war horse was shrewd. She was by no means naïve enough to think the first small gesture that came out of her mouth would suffice. "What about the anomaly weapon?"

The Operative narrowed her eyes at me. I could practically see the cogs turning. She was wondering if Tria had breached her oath of silence or if the A.I. revealed the nature of the weapons. I am sure the Operative was privy to any briefings involving intelligence gathered by Tria's father. With a vow of secrecy, I presumed he questioned Tria at length about the Legacy. She had no idea her father was turning over every scrap of intel to his superiors. Since he had very limited contact with Justice, she could only guess at how I knew about the weapons.

She lost the faraway look in her eyes. "We have salvaged one such weapon. It was a long time ago and we have had little luck getting it to function properly. We did not recover the weapon's original power source. Apparently due to the nature of its design, we were unable to duplicate its full capability. It also requires considerable input from an A.I. we have been unable to replicate as well."

Just because the Chaalt could not get it to work did not mean I no longer wanted it. "I know this might sound vaguely familiar, but I have to say it. I realize the weapon is of no use to you."

99

The Operative cracked a small smile that changed to a look of curiosity. "Scholar Burlor's information indicates you are not in possession of the original power source required to operate the weapon."

I smiled back like a cat that swallowed her favorite goldfish. "I am sure you have noticed by now, we are very lucky when it comes to finding things no one else seems able to."

She nodded in agreement. "Yes, I find it very interesting you are able to do so quite frequently. Is there any additional data I should know about?"

I loved the fact Tria's father had no knowledge of our Guardian transponder. I would let the Chaalt speculate all they wanted to. It was going to be one secret we were not telling anyone.

"Once you get to know me better, I think you will come to realize, humans are the luckiest species in the galaxy."

She made an unflattering noise with her mouth. "I will only agree that you are indeed lucky I have not killed you yet. I place considerable emphasis on the word, 'yet.'"

She was such a sweetheart. It was time to lay my cards on the table. "I am willing to give you a Dagger along with fifty missiles and the nanites to make them operational. In exchange, I want access to Oolaran weapons that can be fitted to my starship. I want all information you have on the Daggers, including equipment you have recovered to make them functional. I also want four armor suits like the one you are wearing. They are much lighter than our full combat rigs. Throw in some of those fancy rifles your troops enjoy pointing at me as well."

I could tell she was keeping a running tally. The changing expressions on her face said I was nearing the end of her patience and goodwill.

"Is there anything else, you thieving beggar?"

"I was only half way through my list. Believe me, you are getting the better end of the stick."

Her look of bewilderment told me to stop using Earth euphemisms. Her eyes suddenly rolled. "Stop your moronic rewordings."

She did not say we were done, so I carried on. "I want four of those assault shields you were using when you dropped into our base."

She held up two of her hands. "The weapons and shields are out of the question. The assault shields are as classified as our transporter technology. The weapons we manufacture would only function in Tria's hands. Tria still has her weapon ID chip. They are implanted in all military personnel. The DNA identifier encoded into the weapons micro A.I. will not allow use in the hands of another race. I was serious when I said the Chaalt people are not in the business of arming others. If the weapon was to fall into hostile hands, Chaalt military personnel have the ability to detonate their weapons power source. At maximum yield, the discharge could easily down an assault shuttle."

Oh well, the weapons we currently use have proven to be just as effective as the fancier beam rifles. The energy beam weapon on our combat suits and the recoded Tibor capacitive discharge pistols all had a detectable energy signature. The highly modified Earth-based weapons did not. Justice seemed to enjoy tinkering with the designs, and his knock-offs were much deadlier than the originals. Coonts had recently commented he could not locate the .44 pistol we had modified for him. The evil robot was no doubt fiddling with it. Until whatever he was doing was perfected, he would not unveil the fruit of his machinations.

The Operative must have thought I was thinking too hard. She interrupted my train of thought. "Nathan Myers, my people have been on a high state of alert since the Prule containment vessel was revealed. We are now standing down. The Union thought our preparations were a sign of war. My government has not revealed the nature of our mobilizations. My briefing has relieved anxieties and the Chaalt leadership has called for an immediate return to standard readiness. A statement was issued to all concerned parties. The Chaalt race just exercised our first of what might be many, large scale rapid response drills. That being said, we will not completely stand down until we are in control of the containment vessel."

I was wondering how many races were soiling their combat armor, trying to determine who was going to be the target of the Chaalt juggernaut. The Operative was now showing more than casual inferences she was getting annoyed.

I needed to make damn sure I was getting better than just a good trade. "I am not going to give away some of the greatest discoveries in the galaxy for a handful of trinkets from your second-hand store."

Sael Nalen again shook her head and slapped one of her hands over her eyes. She turned away from me and took a couple of steps away. She promptly turned and came back standing very close to me. "What makes you think my people want anything to do with weaponized nanites?"

"Sael Nalen, you may think of me as a primitive primate, which I might just be. But I am far from stupid. It occurred to me your race possesses such weapons. It is also not a leap of faith for me to determine they are not nearly as advanced as the Guardian artifacts."

The Operative gave me a Cheshire cat smile. She reached up and placed her hands on my cheeks. My eyes bugged out thinking she might be giving me an intimate Chaalt gesture of affection. That thought came to a screeching halt when she reddened my face with several less-than-gentle slaps.

"MY, my, you have excellent perception for a primate."

"You old witch!"

She laughed again. Were it not for the harsh edge, I would have found it pleasant. "Fine. I grow weary of this brinkmanship. You no longer have to bargain with me. I will take on the responsibility of properly reimbursing you for your discoveries."

She looped her arms in mine and we headed to the exit chambers. She did not say anything until we were finally outside of the artifacts building. The first thing we both noticed was my hangar queen shuttle being unloaded from the Legacy's hangar. My crew failed to heed my advice of R&R. It was quite apparent it had been partially disassembled.

The Operative looked at it and then cocked an eye at me. "Not one of your better discoveries." She saw the disdain on my face and laughed. "Or is it possibly one of your better investments?"

Extra smart-ass aliens had a way of getting under my skin. "Sael Nalen, I find your observations about as refreshing as the Fusra Pus virus."

She gave me a serious look then burst out in a deep belly laugh that made me do the same. "Yeah, that's what I got for trusting a Coram warlord to not screw me. I should have killed the Throgg but managed to still the beast inside of me before I did."

The Operative's smile instantly disappeared at the mention of my inner devil. She looked at me solemnly and gave me a small nod.

Justice broadcast for all to hear. "Commander, twelve Chaalt military vessels have arrived in our star system."

Sael Nalen turned to me. "My fleet has arrived and I wish to take control of the Prule containment vessel. Will you allow me to return it to my home worlds?"

"Senior Operative, I like you a hell of a lot better than I did several hours ago. But I do not love you enough to let you walk out of here with my artifacts. We need to make some kind of deal. I need assurances that would make me feel like I wasn't going to get screwed again."

"Nathan Myers, you shall receive poera for poera, and it will not involve fornication."

With that comment the Operative stepped close to me. It was a very awkward attempt to pucker up. She did it anyway and planted a loud smacking kiss on my cheek. She had the strangest look on her face when she stepped back. "I will need Tria to thoroughly explain why I felt the need to do that."

I did not get it either. A hand full of hours ago she was going to kill me and the feeling was mutual. "How do you want to load the containment vessel?"

The Operative looked like she was momentarily looking at some distant object. She had to be transmitting on a communication device of some kind. I would ask Justice what he thought later.

"I have dispatched three shuttles. They will need access."

Three shuttles? I was suddenly nervous. Why three when you only need one to haul the containment vessel. She was reading my expression.

"Have no fear Nathan Myers, nothing is amiss."

"I am going to need just a little bit of clarification before I open my base to your shuttles. On my world, trust is not given, it is earned."

She thought about the Earth saying and shook her head in agreement. "The first shuttle is for the team that will handle and remove the containment vessel. The other two are my tech and science teams. They are to install and set up several pieces of equipment you have acquired while running amok in the galaxy."

I was mystified by her comment. There was only one way to find out.

"Justice, open the outer doors for our guest."

"Affirmative, Commander. Entry tunnel doors opening."

I could see my crew turn and look down the tunnel. The entry lights flashed on after the first shuttle breached the atmospheric retention field. They were like mirrors. They were reflecting the bright lights off the surface of their hulls. The first one set down for a smooth landing. It was difficult to make out the ship's lines because it reflected its surroundings so perfectly. There was no noise save for the light clunk of the landing pads touching down. The mirrored surface faded to a gloss black. The shuttle was beautiful. It had smooth flowing lines and swept back wings for atmospheric flight. The star drives were integrated into the wings and tucked against the hull. There were no weapons evident, but I knew that was not the case. They were hidden somewhere within the hull and wings. Two of them were larger than the Tibor assault shuttle we once owned. The Tibor shuttle could be described as a truck; these were sports cars. The third was a lot bigger and boxy looking. It had to be a freight hauler of some kind. It spun around and landed with a large rear door facing us. The big door came down, making a ramp. A team of a dozen white-suited Chaalt exited the hauler. They had a fair-sized gravity sled moving between them. They came to a halt in from of us. I waved to my crew and got their attention. I held up a single finger and Xul separated from the group and hurried over to me.

"Xul, I am going to need a team to secure a quantity of nanites. We are going to give our new benefactors fifty missiles and the proper amount of nanites to arm them. Give them some from the weaponized batch. When you have completed that task, have the large atmosphere door opened on the artifact building. The Chaalt will be taking a Dagger with them."

Xul nodded and set off to assemble a team of scientists for the tasks at hand. The Operative was over by the freight hauler conversing with several of the white-clad Chaalt. She waved me over.

I might as well ham this up a little and eat crow in hopes it might net me something extra. "Yes, Senior Operative, how can I be of service?" I thought she was going to fall over she looked so surprised. I kept my face neutral and waited to hear what she had to say.

She cleared her throat and settled her emotions. "When your crew's duties permit, they will need to report to my Senior Tech specialist, Mork. He will run a few tests and also measure you and your crew for the recon armor fitting process."

"I am available now Senior Operative."

She rolled her eyes at me and told the tech to carry on. The tech's name seemed vaguely familiar, but I could not place from where. I let the thought pass. I followed the Chaalt inside the freight hauler. He led me to a pressure door, and when it opened, we entered into a lab. He had me stand against a grid on a wall and a beam of light swept me from all directions. Next, he sat me in a large chair and a dome lowered over my head. He started asking me questions.

"I am going to test you for exotic emission sensitivity. If you feel discomfort, inform me immediately."

I nodded and he started running his finger over a small data pad. A bright light flared inside the dome.

"I see you have implants. I cannot identify the design so if at any time you experience headaches let me know."

The brightness of the light was apparent even with my eyes closed. This guy was using it to look in my head. I reached down and covered my boys. I started hearing a noise like waves washing up on a beach. It gradually got louder then stopped. Next, I heard a ringing in my ears. It gradually increased until it was a shrill, ear-splitting whistle. I held my hands up and it ceased. I heard him comment to me.

"Excellent, you show no side effects or interference complications. Please remain calm and do not move. You will feel a small amount of discomfort when I install the Backscatter Data device."

It was always my experience when a doctor said those words, it was a code. When deciphered, it meant "where am I going to put this six-inch needle where it will hurt the most?"

9

I walked off the shuttle grimacing. I rubbed the spot behind my ear between my jaw bone and skull. Pulling my hand back, I was sure I would see blood. There was nothing. I was amazed the tech could drill a hole in the side of my head and not spill a drop of blood. Klutch came up to me.

"Commander, I was nearby and thought I heard you scream out. Is there a problem?"

I looked back at the tech. He had his arms crossed and was shaking his head. Klutch looked at him, then me. I scowled at the tech. "No Klutch, you need to get fitted for our new lightweight armor. Head up the ramp and Doctor Jekyll will fix you right up."

A baffling look crossed the Tibor's face. He walked up the ramp. Looking across the parking area I saw the big door on the artifact building open. The science team came out with the containment vessel strapped to the gravity sled. It was slowly moving across the parking area to the big boxy freight hauler. Tria and Coonts were walking in my direction and I met them half way. Taking Tria's hand, I smiled. I told them they needed to see the tech on the freighter. Tria gave me a peck on the cheek and released my hand. They wandered over and stood by the loading ramp of the freighter. The containment team secured the Prule storage tank and moved back to the artifact building for the Dagger.

There was a loud commotion and the crew of the freight hauler started jumping out of hatches. They were running in all directions. I saw Tech Mork on his hands and knees retching on the deck. Klutch came stomping down the ramp rubbing the side of his wide, bullet-shaped head. The look on his homely face said it all. I knew it was time to find something else to do far away from the Tibor Troop Master.

Giving the Tibor a wide berth, I made it a point to catch some fresh air and get close enough to Mork where he could hear me. "You will clean that up before you leave or the Troop Master will be paying you another visit."

I quickly moved off to find some atmosphere with a neutral bouquet. Spying the Operative, I moved in her direction. She was talking to Xul.

As I approached she frowned at me. "Your crew member's theatrics are NOT a welcome distraction and I will tolerate no further delays."

I looked around to ensure none of her people were within earshot. "Or what? You will attempt to put your potty mouth on my face again and drag me off to fornicate? I will file a formal protest with your superiors if that is your intentions."

112

I gave her my best Earth-boy smile. Her face darkened and she shouldered me aside. She stalked off to turn her ire on the crew balking at securing the Dagger.

"Rancid beast!"

I gave her a curt salute. "Old Witch."

Xul stood with his mouth gaping. I shrugged my shoulders. "Xul, have one of the other scientist finish up here. I want you, Graf and Jaran to report to the Chaalt freight hauler. You will be fitted with a new Chaalt data link. Let me know if there are any complications."

The little Grawl nodded and hurried to delegate the remainder of his tasks. Justice commed me. "Commander, the Chaalt technicians have delivered several IST units along with a dedicated power source. There are seven Backscatter transceiver units along with a central processor as well. I have reserved a storage area to install the equipment after I have thoroughly examined each device. I have written a new protocol program that will be capable of completely isolating individual pieces, or all of the equipment. In the unlikely event the new equipment interferes with shipboard operations, I can disable their capabilities."

"Thank you, Justice, your foresight is greatly appreciated. I can assume there were several more gifts left of us?"

113

"Yes Commander, there are four recon armor crates and a single Chaalt assault rifle. There is a huge assortment of Chaalt military supplies and munitions that will have to be cataloged. Because of the immense quantity, I recommend getting a number of Grawl scientists to start doing so as soon as possible. I have ten large crates containing point defense weapons. I have been informed they are reverse engineered replicas of Oolaran designs. I have two very large storage crates designated as the anomaly weapon that was originally installed as the Legacy's main battery. It lacks the necessary power source to make it functional."

Wow, Sael Nalen was not bullshitting me when she said I would receive a fair trade. There was an immense machine of some sort being off loaded out of a side door on the freight hauler. Sael Nalen was supervising the work and pointed in my direction.

A tech came running over and stopped in front of me. "Mr. Myers, where would you like your replicator placed?"

My mouth dropped open. I was not up on the latest alien tech but knew a replicator could manufacture most anything. With the right programming and the necessary materials, it had an almost unlimited capability. I pointed to the far wall, away from the tunnel entrance. He nodded and went back to work. I told Justice to fill me in later after he had a chance to survey everything. I saw Tria coming down the back ramp of the hauler. She had a frown on her pretty face and was rubbing the side of her head. I no longer felt the discomfort of the device insertion. It did not take me but a second to think of a way to make Tria forget about the irritation.

I walked up to her and, without saying a word, planted an Earthman kiss on her lips. She smiled and whispered, "Please, I would like another." I obliged her.

I heard the Operative yell out. "What are you fools staring at? Get back to work!"

I glanced about, noticing my display of unknown mannerisms had brought a screeching halt to the loading and unloading operations. Now everyone seemed to double their efforts. Tria looped her arms in mine. We were going to take a look at the munition crates. They were stacked twelve high and twenty deep and twenty across.

The Operative intercepted us. "Must you act like a primate in front of my subordinates? It is disruptive behavior and will cause further delays in our—"

I stepped up to her and kissed her on the cheek. Her eyes shot open and she was speechless. Tria put her hand over her mouth and turned away to keep from laughing out loud.

The Operative stalked off screaming, "I THOUGHT I TOLD YOU TO GET BACK TO WORK!"

Tria turned back to me. "Nathan, you must stop inciting her — she has been generous beyond belief. I wonder how much of this exchange was actually sanctioned by her superiors."

I laughed and said, "I don't think the description of what it does to her can be defined as inciting."

Tria gave me a puzzling look. She leaned in close and whispered to me. "You will have no need for another." My legs became rubber and my breath caught in my throat. I had goose bumps head to toe. She was holding me upright. The feeling left as quickly as it came. Tria smiled at me and walked in the direction of the Legacy. Looking around, I turned and followed her. My crewmates and the Grawl scientists were just leaving the artifacts building and Xul was closing the doors. Looking to the freight hauler, I saw the gravity sled with its load of missiles and containers of nanites disappear inside. Looking back at Tria, she gave me another smile that sent my temperature soaring. I could not help but think all was right. Then it was not.

It started with the shuttle crew's running back to the ships. I looked at the Operative and she was rapidly moving to where I stood. She stopped and yelled at the crews heading for the far shuttle. "Get aboard the freight hauler. We are leaving number two, it is defective!" The crews stopped and looked back at her in confusion. With a wave of her arm they turned and ran to the hauler. She ran up to me.

"We have a problem Nathan Myers. A Quill scavenger fleet has exited hyperspace in an adjoining star system. We still do not have complete numbers, but it appears to be a large number of vessels. There could be great danger if they find their way to this system."

I was shocked by the Operative's urgency. 'Who or what are Quill?"

"The Quill are an advanced predatory race that ravages the fringe. They infest all worlds they find and strip them of all resources. They are very formidable and have excellent weapons and good defensive systems. They are a race of Crits, or in your language, insects. They have a carapace that serves as their armor and also protects them from the void. Unless you know their weaknesses, you would not want to face them in battle. It is their custom to swarm when engaged in combat and overwhelm any foe not capable of repelling them. If they do not incur heavy enough losses to deter them, they will fight until they win. All who fall are stored for consumption. All recovered tech is developed for their own use."

The Operative was issuing orders to no one. I realized she was verbally using her data link. I was trying to digest everything she had just told me. What the crap! This was my bastion, my safety harbor, my fortress of solitude. Now an unknown was knocking at my door. I felt the beast stir.

I yelled at Sael Nalen as she headed for the remaining shuttle. "Can we help repair your shuttle?"

She yelled back as she hit the boarding ramp. "You mindless beast, there is nothing wrong with the shuttle. It is your final payment for services rendered. The two you see are prototypes and the production model is much larger and a different profile. Take care of it and it will take care of you."

With that she boarded the shuttle. I watched the door rapidly close and I called to Justice. "Justice, open the tunnel doors."

"Already open Commander. I overheard your discussion. My subsystem is in the process of terminating all unnecessary power feeds and shutting down non-essential equipment."

"Is the Legacy combat capable?"

"Yes Commander, ninety one percent of capability. Replacing our diminished supply of rail cannon munitions would bring us back to one hundred percent. We are currently at sixty-six percent of maximum loadout."

"Roger that, Justice. Square everything away and prepare for defensive actions. Recall the crew and let the scientists know that if hostilities break out in this system, they are to take refuge in the A.I. spaces. If the worst comes to pass, you know what must be done, correct?"

"Yes, Commander. If escape for personnel is not possible, I am to terminate this facility."

"Yes, let's hope that will not come to pass. Are you working on the IST and Backscatter transceivers?"

"Yes Commander, I hope to test the equipment in approximately forty minutes."

"Is my battle armor back to proper working order?"

"Affirmative, Commander. The departed Chaalt spacecraft have rejoined the mothership and three of the Operative's warships have encircled it. They are rapidly moving across this star system. I speculate they will make a transition once they are on the far side of our most distant gas giant. Sael Nalen's flagship and the remaining warship have jumped out of this system. It will take time for me to analyze the minute distortion waves left in the dark energy wake of their transitions. I do not think it will be necessary to track the Operative. When she disclosed the location of hostile forces as being in an adjoining star system, I used this base's sensor arrays to locate the distortion waves of the Quill spacecraft as they transitioned into the star system. The craft exhibit a very unique star drive signature. They are using an unknown pulse drive. I sense them as vibrations. The count is currently eighty-six separate signatures."

Sael Nalen had fourteen ships at her disposal and the opposition eighty-six. She was going to be in deep shit if she did not get back up. I remembered her saying they were going to stand down all forces that had been at a high state of readiness for an extended period of time. She also stated the Quill had good weaponry. Regardless of how superior the Chaalt warships might be, they could still get their shields overloaded by the sheer number of hostile ships firing on them.

"Justice, prepare to get underway. I want you to plot a jump that will put us just outside the star system. We will go full stealth and find a spot to observe the Quill ships."

"Affirmative Commander, the crew is aboard and the Legacy is ready for departure."

I saw Xul come around the side of the artifact building and he looked worried. I ran up to him and told him he was in charge till I got back. He nodded and said they would shut down all unnecessary emissions in case the hostiles jump to our star system.

He touched my hand and said: "Come back to us, Nathan Myers. We still have much to accomplish, and we cannot do it without you."

I leaned down and gave the Grawl my best smile and a quick embrace. "I will, Xul, because I cannot accomplish my goals without your help."

A Grawl smile was not a pretty thing. I had grown to accept the look and to me it was just fine. I turned and ran to the Legacy. Tria was standing on the ramp waiting for me. Just inside the hatch, I could see Coonts and Klutch. As soon as I hit the ramp Tria grabbed my hand and we ran through the hatch.

I greeted my crewmates then yelled to Justice. "Let's roll."

We went to the ready room, walking past our new recon armor. I was not about to take unknown equipment into battle. Going to my Zaen battle armor crate, I entered the access code and it opened. The diagnostics screen on the door of the crate was all green go codes. I went to the weapons rack and did a quick inspection of my highly modified shotgun. Our weapons were spotless and ready to go. The magazine pouches in the bins under the weapons were all full. I don't know why I bothered to look. I should know by now not to expect anything less. I went out the door with my crew following. We went up tube and then to the bridge. We took our seats and everyone's attitude changed to all business. Justice took us out of the tunnel at an insane velocity. One second, we were in the parking area; the next we were in space. I looked up at the full three-hundred-and-sixty-degree dome-shaped view screen.

"Tria, is there any additional data on the Quill you can share with us?"

"No, Commander. I have never encountered the species on any of my tours of duty."

"Coonts, Klutch, anything you can add?"

They both gave me blank stares. Coonts finally said: "Commander, due to the nature of the facilities we were sequestered on, we would have little knowledge of current events. At no time was I briefed on predatory race incursions."

Klutch just nodded his agreement and turned back to his hangar bay checklist. My Earth-boy curiosity was insatiable. I wondered what could make a hard ass like Sael Nalan get her panties in such a wad.

"Justice, do you have the target system's coordinates plotted?"

"Yes, Commander. I am ready to jump on your order. Standard transition time will be seven minutes twenty-two seconds. I will begin matrix charging when we arrive at our destination. DEHD core options will be available in approximately sixty minutes. All weapons are ready in all aspects."

"Roger that, Justice. Jump us to the target area."

The domed view screen turned to a single white spot then coalesced to the dark shimmering waves of interdimensional space. I was feeling the small shots of adrenaline that came with the thoughts of possible combat. The beast inside me stirred. He drank in the stimulant and I could feel his need for more. Tria must have sensed the change to my aura. She got up and stood by my side, placing her hand on my shoulder. The beast slithered back into the shadows of its cage. I noticed she no longer wore her support braces. I gave her a small smile when my mind wandered to more pleasant thoughts. She returned the gesture then returned to her chair at the comms station. The beast and its prison were nowhere to be found.

Justice gave me a sitrep on the equipment Sael gave us. "Commander, after careful study and analysis I have connected the IST unit and the Backscatter transceiver to their power sources. When power was established to the IST device, I became aware of two additional active transmitters. One could only be aboard the shuttle Sael Nalen left behind at Alpha base since the balance of the units given to us is aboard this ship. The other is in the distant star system we are now approaching. I speculate it is aboard the Operative's flagship. I also surmise she is now aware we are on our way. I have designed and installed failsafe power disrupter switches to the new devices. I have taken the liberty of temporarily disabling them. However, I will re-establish their power supplies on your order."

"Go ahead and turn them back on. There is no point in hiding if the Operative knows we are coming. If her IST is active she obviously does not think it can be detected by the Quill. Why she would think that, I have no idea. We were able to detect the signal, she should not assume others cannot. What is the nature of the Backscatter devices she had buried in our heads?"

"The device transmits a signal that closely matches the background noise emanated by the universe. It is almost impossible to sort out the data-laden signal from the countless emissions that make up the cacophony surrounding it."

Coonts must have seen me roll my eyes at the explanation Justice just gave me. "Commander, I think what Justice is stating is we now have a form of relatively secure comms between our implanted devices. I suspect they have a much shorter range than the IST device. It remains to be seen what the actual range of both devices will be and what shielding may disrupt them."

"Coonts' clarification is an accurate depiction, Commander. Now that you are aboard the Legacy, I have been able to scan the device. It appears to have grown microscopic leaders that have made their way into your tympanic membrane and several locations along your cerebral cortex. They have also established a connection with your existing implant array. I assume you will have individual data channels for each crew member and a group link for joint communication as well. It would be careless to dismiss the possibility you now have the capability of linking with the Senior Operative. If that is indeed the case, it leads to further speculation the Operative can monitor your comms while using the device."

I had mixed feelings about the possibility of big mother listening to our transmissions. It seemed harmless enough at the moment, but one never knows. A big smile crossed my face. The Operative just got a new code name.

"Justice, are you sure you can shut it down if we need to?"

"Yes, Commander. Unless the device is capable of remote activation, we can close down the signals by disrupting its power source. Exit transition in thirty seconds."

10

Our return to normal space time revealed a star system with two small, Mercury-sized rocky planets. They were orbiting well out in the system, away from the massive red giant that was the central star. In between the planets and the red giant was a huge asteroid field encircling the waning star. There were several dust-filled bands closer to the star that would one day be absorbed or obliterated when the red giant finally collapsed. The outer reaches of the asteroid field stretched until it was fairly close to the small rocky planets.

Forty-three red boxes appeared around one of the planets then the other. Justice magnified the observation screen as much as possible. The ships were big but not huge like the half-mile long Chaalt warships. The Quill ships reminded me of oblong pine cones. Each segment had a forward swept barb pointing to the narrow end. We could not count from this distance, but it looked like there were at least a hundred segments. The ships were equidistant around the planet and at a low altitude above the surface. Whatever they were doing on the surface was creating a plume of debris that obscured the narrow end of the alien ships. If I was to guess, I would say they were mining something they thought was valuable.

Justice had chosen his entry coordinates so we would be a safe distance from the asteroids and as close to the local star as possible. There was a very low probability the Quill had their sensors pointed directly at the star. We dove headlong into the rocky debris field and were weaving our way closer to the hostile ships. The fourteen Chaalt warships were nowhere to be found.

"Justice, have you located the wake disruptions from the Chaalt ships?"

"Negative, Commander. It would be sound military doctrine to covertly observe from within the asteroid field as we are doing. There is a great deal of movement within the bands of the field. It effectively erases all detectable traces of their travel."

Justice continued working his way through the asteroid field using all available clearings. We were getting closer but still a considerable distance from the Quill ships. My curiosity was getting the better of me. I was wondering about the star chart upgrades the Operative said she might give us.

"Justice, did you receive updated astrogation data?"

"Commander, the updated information came in the form of a data cube. The cube is of an unknown design and is capable of uploading vast quantities of data in micro seconds. For security reasons, I did not allow it access to my central data cores. When the Overseer

127

became aware of my concerns, it volunteered to be downloaded into the data cube. I first downloaded its awareness to a data transfer device of my design. I created several robust firewalls within the transfer module. The Overseer helped me establish the validity of the data chokes. Several tests were made to verify my apparatus was capable of containing any rogue programs or codes. Only then did I allow the Overseer to be transferred into the Chaalt data device. It is elated knowing that it is able to help us. The task could take an extended period of time to complete. The Overseer is going through each individual line of code and all encrypted data. If the Overseer finds questionable processes, it will alert me immediately. The Overseer also informed me it has found several files included in the cube that pertain to the Daggers. I will be monitoring my transfer module for any determinations and will alert you when I can transfer the updated information."

Justice was a thousand steps ahead of me. I never would have thought about the possibility of intrusive programs collecting sensitive information. I did not think the Chaalt would do harm to the Legacy or directly endanger my crew. However, I was pretty sure they would take any and all information they could get their tech hungry hands on. Justice broke my train of thought.

"Commander, the Backscatter link has increased energy consumption. I believe inbound message traffic is a certainty." Justice had hardly completed his statement when Sael Nalen started talking inside my head.

"Nathan Myers, why are you in my zone of operations? You are needlessly exposing your crew to what might prove to be a very dangerous situation."

"Last time I checked, it was determined you are not my boss or my commander. Besides Mother, I did not wish to see anything happen to you after all of the nice gifts you gave me."

A less than pleasant noise came over the link. It was followed by more than a few awkward moments of silence. I had the feeling the Operative might have relocated to a place she could freely say what was on her mind.

"You Throgg, I have never taken a mate. If I did choose to make such an unfortunate mistake and produce offspring, I would self-terminate before I would let the likes of you escape my loins."

I had to give it to her; she was now the queen of comebacks. "Now Mother, is that any way to talk to your only alien child?"

"Nathan, cease your mindless chatter! We are preparing to strike the Quill now that all have engaged their umbilical tubes. Do not move from your current position. I do not want you in our battlespace. We make numerous preprogramed transitions and a collision is possible."

There was nothing else to say. "Acknowledged Mother. We will be standing by."

When she said nothing more, I assumed the transmission was over. I looked over at Tria and she was smiling. Coonts and Klutch seemed oblivious to the conversation. They were hiding it well or considered it private. Either way, I had no further comments pertaining to the exchange. I ceded to her authority and that was that.

"Justice, hold position but continue passive scan."

"Acknowledged, Commander."

I would have liked a better seat to the upcoming battle. There were more than just a few asteroids in our direct line of sight. Justice would only move the Legacy when it became evident a piece of debris would cross our exact location.

"Commander, I detected fourteen separate transitions originating from the edge of the asteroid field. I am now detecting exit distortion waves very close to the hostile targets."

"Justice, move us as close to the edge of the asteroid field as you can without leaving it. I am really interested in seeing how the Operative takes care of business."

"Commander, asteroid movement in the outer band of the field is significant. To move farther would require continuous maneuvering to avoid collisions. I will illustrate sensor feed information to generate an interpretation of actual events."

The bridge view dome temporarily blacked out and then we saw outlines of the planets along with the hostile targets in red boxes. The blue oblong boxes of the Chaalt warships had non-stop green lines blinking between them and the Quill target boxes. I noticed all the Quill target boxes blinking, insinuating strikes. The Chaalt could only engage so many targets at one time. It had to be missile strikes. I pondered the reality of what I was seeing. Justice took the guess work out of the equation.

"Commander, data suggests the Chaalt launched a time-on-target assault. The attack coincided with stealth missile strikes. I detected no missile launches. I now surmise the length of time it took for the Chaalt to engage the Quill was in fact a predetermined delay to allow the cloaked missiles to reach their targets. Without knowing when or how the missiles were launched, I can only speculate as to whether or not they traversed the entire distance. There is a possibility they have an interdimensional capability and I failed to detect the diminutive transitions. Regardless of my hypothesis, sixty-one of the Quill ships have been destroyed outright or have crashed to the surface of the planets. Seven are still under power and have severed the large tubes extending to the planet's surface. The remaining eighteen targets are heavily damaged and have no active emissions from their star drives. They are, however, launching hundreds of missiles. I have detected strikes on the shields of Chaalt ships. The strikes indicate the Quill missiles are two hundred megaton fusion weapons. They rapidly deplete the Chaalt shields and force them to jump to another location to renew their attacks."

As I watched eleven more hostile ships disappeared from the screen. The Operative was kicking the shit out of the Quill. I figured she must have had a damn good reason for doing so. It did not look like there would be any survivors.

"Commander, I am detecting transition wave distortions I cannot identify. The distortions have increased in intensity. I now have an unknown number of Quill ships entering the star system. I am now detecting a separate exit transition that matches the profile of the Quill previously detected. The first transition propagation has ceased. I have sixteen Quill spacecrafts closing with Chaalt warships. They are exchanging heavy fire. The second exit is complete and another sixteen Quill ships are attacking the Chaalt from a second vector."

I was on the edge of my command chair, gripping the arms till my fingers hurt. A Chaalt warship came out of hyperspace directly in front of the second assault wave. It

132

came under withering fire and then we saw the star bright flashes of nuclear hellfire envelope the ship. It disappeared from the screen. *OH SHIT!* I did not know if this was a Quill response, tactic or a coincidence. It no longer mattered.

"JUSTICE, ATTACK THE SECOND WAVE NOW!"

The dome became a dizzying blur of movement as Justice rapidly extracted us from the asteroid field. We made a very short jump that suddenly filled the view dome with the bizarre pulsing star drives of the Quill ships. Now that we were close, I could see a faint violet glow around the spiked organic looking vessels. Justice poured fire from our main weapons directly into the drive nozzles of the first ship we encountered. He was pumping out full yield anti-matter missiles two at a time, every fifteen seconds. The first target's shields failed and it blew apart, sending huge pieces of its thorny hull into the other ships in the tight formation. The shields on three failed from the collisions. Our missiles flew into the unprotected star drives unimpeded. The rear ends of the ships blew outward in massive clouds of tinsel like debris. One detonated, momentarily blacking out the view screen. The other two were spinning end over end, spewing their contents as they started their endless journey into the void.

The shields on the front of the Legacy were glowing almost as much as the red giant behind us. We turned away and made a jump to keep our shields from failing.

"Commander, our shields are at twenty eight percent and regenerating. We are fortunate the Quill formation could not target us with their nuclear arsenal. The Quill ships have separated and no longer face such constraints. For reasons unknown, the Quill have made no intersystem transitions. They prefer instead to make swarm attacks on individual targets. I have detected the loss of another Chaalt warship. The Chaalt tactics now comprise of jumping in and out of interdimensional space. They are making hit and run attacks, then jumping away to avoid the nuclear missiles. We shall copy their tactics."

Not knowing if Sael Nalen's flagship was one of the ships destroyed was eating at me. I mourned the thousands of Chaalt lives that were lost. I said a prayer to my maker in hopes he might shelter their spirits. There was now a total of twelve Chaalt warships still fighting, thirteen counting the Legacy. I was not a huge fan of that particular number. The Chaalt had thinned the Quill numbers considerably and we now faced twenty-one remaining Quill ships. The hostiles gathered in loose formations of seven ships each. They were attempting to chase down the Chaalt warships when they came out of hyperspace. The Chaalt would quickly jump away and re-engage from another trajectory.

Justice was making it a point to introduce our weapons fire into the star drive nozzles of any Quill ship formation, turning away in pursuit of a Chaalt warship. The discharge from their star drives had no shielding. Shooting the ships right in the ass quickly turned to the target of choice. It was the Quill's Achilles heel. The crazed maneuvers of the hostile ships had our missiles chasing them around the already cluttered battle zone. We were wasting more and more of our finite supply of the Ilor-designed armaments. One out of five was destroyed due to collisions with debris. We came out of hyperspace and blundered into the detonation of a mega nuke. Our shields dropped to a dangerously low seventeen percent. The Legacy shook violently as the shock wave and hard radiation washed over our hull. Justice once again snap jumped us out toward the asteroid field.

I wanted to call out on my Backscatter link but knew if the Operative was still alive, she would not appreciate the distraction. Two more Quill ships disappeared from our screen. Justice turned us back to the fray and a Chaalt warship exited hyperspace in close proximity to us. Justice made a crazy sharp turn away from them. As we moved away Justice momentarily froze the view screen. I looked on in horror at the devastation we saw. Several decks were open to space and there was a hellish glow coming from just forward of the engineering spaces. The ship was mortally wounded and trailing atmosphere and debris, some of which were bodies of the

Chaalt crew. I looked over to Tria, her eyes were closed and she was slowly shaking her head.

A surviving three-ship formation of Quill was turning back in our direction. They were going after the badly damaged Chaalt ship. One of the Quill ships was streaming a thick, smoke-like trail behind it. The two ships on either side of it were using their shields to try and protect it. Looking at my crew, I saw grim faces.

"Justice, we can't let them re-engage the damaged Chaalt ship. We have to stop them. Ram the Quill ships if you have to, but don't let them destroy that ship. The crew was staring at me wide eyed then all three nodded in agreement. Justice turned the Legacy. We were now driving right at the oncoming Quill ships. He accelerated to maximum and poured all of our rail cannons and energy beams into the oncoming hostiles. The intense fire was a wedge forcing the two lead ships apart.

Justice called out, "BRACE FOR IMPACT!"

The view dome was obscured by our shield flare. The point defense weapons of the lead Quill ships had us lit up like a Christmas tree. I could have sworn I saw a huge explosion in front of us just before I was ripped from my seat. I came to lying on the deck. Tria was staring down at me. My head was throbbing. Klutch was helping Coonts to his feet. My crew was able to brace against their control boards. I did not have one, so I was thrown into the consoles between Coonts and Klutch. I could taste blood in my mouth.

Tria smiled at me and the pain from the prominent knot on my head instantly went away. "Nathan, it would have been wise to secure your combat harness before you ordered Justice to ram the Quill."

I could see a thin layer of smoke in the air. Tria helped me to my feet. "What the hell happened?"

Klutch looked around at me and gave me a toothy smile. "Justice put enough fire into the Crits that the trailing ship exploded. It caused enough damage to the lead ships that their shields faltered. He then detonated an anti-matter missile between them. We collided with the debris field. Justice is working on the damage now.

"Justice, how bad is the damage?"

"The starboard side of the ship suffered a hull breach on deck two. I have sealed those spaces. The cargo bay door is partially sprung and leaking atmosphere. We lost both starboard rail cannons. I managed to reset the shield emitters and have partial coverage of the damaged areas. The view dome is resetting as well. The battle is still ongoing and the Chaalt have lost an additional warship. The ship we were protecting is now maneuvering under power and has taken refuge in the asteroid field. The three-ship formation we attacked has left two ships intact and they are both drifting. Our main weapons are now back online. I recommend we do not give the Quill time to repair their battle damage."

I gave Tria a quick hug and she returned to her station. Coonts and Klutch both gave me an Earthman thumbs up. The view dome flickered and came back online. I could see the Chaalt were still mixing it up with the two remaining Quill formations. The number of red hostile indicators was twelve. The enemy formation gathered then split up into equal groups of four. Whoever was commanding the Quill still thought they could win this. If they had additional ships on the way, there was a good chance they would. I could only see eight blue boxes maneuvering wildly and jumping in and out of hyper space. Several ships on both sides had sustained damage and were leaking contaminants into the void. Justice got us moving again. We made a hard turn that lined us up on the first Quill ship drifting closest to us.

"Don't wait for me Justice, give them a shot of everything."

The Quill ship blew apart in a spectacular flash of debris. The other ship managed enough power to get their aft point defense weapons working. Justice turned hard to port, using our best shields to bear the brunt of the attack. He thanked them with a non-stop stream of rail cannon fire. The fire hose line of munitions blew a row of the spiny segments off the ship and into space. The enemy ship's short-range weapons promptly failed. We stared wide eyed at the alien ship when Justice magnified the view screen. The exterior of the ship was crawling with Quill. They were swarming like ants in their attempts to repair the ship. We got our first good look at the Crits. They resembled praying mantises with thick black bodies. It was the only glimpse we would get. Justice sent them all to hell with a barrage from our main weapons. The Quill bodies registered as small sparks on our forward shields as we plowed through the debris field searching for more targets.

11

I heard a small beep I had never noticed before. My link came alive. "Your suicidal tactics have me questioning your sanity. You have done well, Nathan Myers. You saved many lives, but the battle goes poorly. My people have recalled our warship crews and a strike force should be here within the hour. You should jump clear before you sustain further damage."

"Now Mother, you must remember the fruit does not fall far from its tree. Besides, we only came here to dump some obsolete ordnance. We have yet to complete the task."

I heard a bark of a laugh and a small beep, and then the link went dead. I personally did not think the battle was going that poorly. It was, at one time, one hundred and eighteen against fourteen. Two more bright flashes brought the enemy ship count down even farther. It was now ten hostiles against eight friendlies. Nine when you counted the Legacy. Justice called to us.

"Commander, after your last Backscatter communication, I was able to pinpoint its source. I have placed an identifier on the Senior Operatives flagship. Our supply of expendable munitions is down to minimum capacities. We have twenty-two anti-matter missiles and three hundred and eleven projectiles for the rail cannons. I have fault warnings on one of our Galactic Union beam weapons and will only use it as a last resort."

"Roger that, Justice. I don't see any point in saving anything for later. Take us back around and let's stomp some more bugs."

Justice zeroed in on a Quill straggler like a shark following a blood trail and jumped us in close. The Quill ship made an attempt to turn into us. The ship's point defense had our shields flaring bright with fire. We had a close-up view of the wounded vessel. There were hundreds if not thousands of Quill clinging to the outside of the ship. Most were firing some type of handheld weapons at the Legacy. Justice was giving some of the denser concentrations of bug troops precise, single-round shots from our remaining rail cannons. It looked like the Quill crews were amassing around the star drives, trying to protect them. I guess Justice must have thought we were too close to show them why it did not matter. He was making a turn to put some distance between us when a blinding flash whited out the view screen. The Legacy was violently thrown aside by a massive detonation. I was glad we had belted ourselves into our seats. The view screen flickered and came back to life. The universe was doing crazy corkscrew rotations that Justice quickly corrected.

"Justice, what the hell was that?"

"Commander, I postulate it was a trap. The debris field behind the damaged ship had a Quill nuclear missile hidden in the detritus. When I turned away they detonated the warhead, trying to destroy us before we could escape the blast zone. It will no longer be necessary to expend munitions on the target. The view dome zoomed in on the Quill ship. The star drive nozzles the Quill crew was trying to protect were no longer visible. The rear of the ship was bent to one side. The whole mess was spinning like a boomerang on a course that looked like it would end in the massive red central star. Out of the corner of my eye, I saw a Chaalt warship with a flag above the blue box surrounding it. It had just appeared at the edge of the asteroid field. It blinked once and disappeared again. To my horror it reappeared directly in the path of a Quill three ship formation. It collided with at least two of the three ships and all were now drifting without active shields registering on my view screen. The third Quill ship turned back around and was moving directly at Sael Nalen's flagship.

"JUSTICE, JUMP US IN THERE NOW!"

The jump only registered as a blink of an eye. As we exited hyperspace, one of the drifting Quill ships was in very close proximity to us. Justice did not hesitate to give them a double tap with our main weapons. The unshielded ship broke in half, vomiting its crew and equipment out into the void. We were making another hard turn to try and line up with the ship closing on the Operative's flagship. My eyes went wide when the Quill vessel rapidly closed the distance with the drifting Chaalt ship. If they attacked with nuclear missiles, the flagship would be destroyed. I was mystified when the Quill ship failed to open fire. I was stunned to disbelief when the Quill ship's central spine shot out like a harpoon and buried itself into the side of Sael Nalen's flagship. There was a long tube connected to the spine. The bugs were using it to reel their ship down to the damaged Chaalt warship. I could not believe what I had just witnessed.

OH SHIT! "Justice, we need to do something and we need to do it now!"

"Commander, the flag ship might be destroyed if I engage with our main weapon systems!"

I looked up wild eyed at where the rest of the Chaalt warships were. The five remaining friendlies were fully engaged with the last six Quill ships. It was a knife fight to the death. Justice took us through withering defensive fire that was rapidly degrading our shields. He all but parked on the rear of the Quill ship. He put at least a hundred of our remaining rail cannon rounds right between the drive nozzles of the enemy ship. The rear of the ship blew outward sending several large pieces of hull through our badly depleted shields. The impacts shook us violently. The control boards in front of my crewmates were covered in red warning lights. The point defense weapons were no longer pounding away at us. The Quill ship was starting to drift, but the umbilical tube was holding it secure. A bright flash shook the Legacy violently. We were being targeted and Justice started zig-zagging to shake any missiles that might be pursuing us. We made another sweeping loop and headed back to the Operative's stricken warship. Justice took us into point-blank range and gave the tube a burst with the rail cannon. It blew apart, spewing Quill troops. The Quill had been boarding the Chaalt ship.

I threw my combat harness off and yelled to my teammates, "ARMOR UP, we are going in heavy!"

Without hesitation, my crew headed for the ready room. As we came out of the down tube, I could see a glaring red light. It was on the access control panel that controlled the large hatch allowing entry into the hangar. Normally the door was always open, and the atmosphere retention field was operating around the clock. The light indicated the field was not functioning and the hangar doors were not sealed. The void was now waiting for us on the other side of the hatch.

We made a left into the ready room. Justice had our Zaen battle armor crates open and waiting for us. We stripped down and quickly put on our suit liners. I stepped up into my armor and it closed tightly around me. Looking at my HUD, I verified that my munitions backpack was at maximum capacity. Justice had selected one hundred and fifty rounds of high explosive and another hundred and fifty of anti-personnel ammunitions. He was not going to give me any chance at killing myself or my crewmates. The loadout did not include a single round of anti-matter munitions. I went to my weapons locker and started arming myself with the tools of my newfound profession. Reaching out, I pulled my double-barreled assault shotgun from its rack. I picked up a twelve-round magazine of explosive buckshot, slapping it in place on one side of the weapon. Reaching into another bin, I grabbed a mag of explosive penetrator slugs for the other side. On a shelf were several loose rounds. I loaded each barrel to bring the weapon to full capacity. I swung the weapon over my shoulder, clipping it to the mag lock on my munitions backpack. Pulling the handle grip of my Tibor fighting knife, I made sure it was secure in my lower leg scabbard.

I could feel the beast stirring. He was invading my subconscious thoughts. It yearned for combat and was willing me to do the same. My crewmates had been quiet and calm throughout the chaos of the last several hours. Now there was tension in the air and I already knew why. The last time I was in armed conflict, I had given myself over to the Oolaran soldier lurking inside me. The remorseless monster cared only for battle and the deaths of all who stood against it. It was indifferent to survival and oblivious to civilized rules of engagement. With the help of my crewmates, I would use all of my willpower to leash the beast and bend it to my will. Although I abhorred the manifestation's bloodthirsty ambitions, it was still a weapon that had served me well.

My crew was checking their loadouts and making sure all mag pouches and weapons were secure. They in turn did the same to each other. Tria walked up to me and smiled. The beast scurried to a dark place in the corner of my mind. She tugged on my kit then stepped in front of me.

She placed her hands on both sides of my helmet and I did the same to hers. "Nathan, you must use caution. There will be many friendlies engaged in combat. Do not let the other who resides in you strike indiscriminately."

I nodded to her and tried to smile, but it was a gesture she knew to be false. Her helmet blacked out. The Halloween horror Justice had stenciled on each of our armor suits appeared on her visor. The A.I. fully embraced the concept of psychological warfare. Our enemies would cringe when they witnessed the morbid specters confronting them.

Looking at my crewmates, I knew my next request would not be met with enthusiasm. "I need a volunteer to take the assault shuttle and clear the hull of Quill troops. If re-enforcements attempt to board behind us, I want you to dissuade them from doing so."

Tria stepped to my side, leaving Klutch and Coonts eyeing each other. When Coonts turned to say something to me, Klutch gave the Grawl a generous shove with his elbow. The Troop Master had a huge toothy smile on his face and quickly stepped to my other side. The look on Coonts' face was less than amused. His helmet blacked out to the ghoulish jack-o'-lantern Justice had adorned the helmet with. It replaced the pissed off look on the little Grawl's face that was not much better. We walked out into the big corridor and stood just in front of the hangar access hatch. Justice secured the pressure doors behind us and closed off the lift tubes. I got a rapid pressure drop warning in my H.U.D. and then the hatch opened with a small burp of atmosphere.

We no longer had to wonder why the hanger could not retain atmosphere. Sticking through the hull just to the side of the hanger doors was a giant spine from a Quill ship. Justice had not informed us just how close our engagement had actually been. Apparently, our last scrape with the Quill was literally that. We were fortunate the Legacy had hangar doors on both sides of the ship. After running out of colorful comments, Coonts ran to the shuttle and boarded. In very short order, the landing pads retracted and Justice spit the shuttle into the void with the tow beam. The Legacy may have been dangerously low on expendable munitions, the assault shuttle was not. It had never seen combat and had a full loadout. Coonts had forty thousand projectiles for the smaller rail guns that were designed for close support. He also had twenty-four Coram designed anti-ship missiles and two medium sized

147

Galactic energy beam weapons. The shuttle had four additional point defense beam weapons for close-in engagements. We paid extra for shield and weapons upgrades that had not been tested in combat yet. We would find out the hard way if we got ripped off on those purchases. The reality of the situation was bleak. The shuttle would normally be used for close support in friendly-dominated areas of operation, and that was not the case now.

Tria, Klutch and I boosted out of the hangar bay and immediately saw two flashes from each side of our assault shuttle. Coonts was targeting the Quill ship that was drifting uncomfortably close to our position. The two Coram anti-ship missiles impacted the heavily damaged rear of the Quill ship. What was left of the star drive nozzles on the enemy ship erupted in bright, flak-laden clouds of debris. The ship started an end over end spin that was rapidly putting distance between us and the target. We flew low over the hull of the Operative's flagship. Our target was the severed umbilical tube. We would attempt to flank any Quill forces that had managed to board before Justice intervened. There were Quill crawling on the hull in several places. Coonts was now maneuvering in close and picking them off with short bursts from his rail guns. If the Operative was still alive, she was going to have to forgive us for any additional damage we were inflicting on the once beautiful starship.

We took positions on each side of the Quill umbilical tube. My first peek inside was shocking. The Quill had used their casualties to block the end of the tube. It was an unmoving mass of broken and dismembered bug bodies. The uncertainty I was feeling quickly vanished as the beast inside of me started wresting control of my emotions.

I linked with Tria and Klutch. "Take cover on the hull."

Without hesitation they both moved well below me and sheltered behind what was probably a shield emitter. I backed off an acceptable distance for my H.U.D. warning to go from red to yellow. I fired a beam shot into the end of the tube. It blew outward like the petals on a flower. The beast was egging me on and I gave it another shot. This time a large section of the tube flared out and tumbled away from the truncated tube.

I could now see down into the large hollow spine embedded in the Chaalt ship. I felt contact on my back and turned to see Tria and Klutch taking up station on either side of me. They had their forearm-mounted weapon muzzles pointed down into the darkness. Klutch bulled his way in front of me. Tria wrapped her arms around mine, pulling my beam weapon down so it was not being pointed at Klutch's back. I willed the Oolaran soldier to quiet its grating cackle.

We followed Klutch into the depths of the spine. There was light at the end of the more than ninety-foot-long spine. There were Quill troops moving to block the now open breach. Klutch would have none of it and sent several HE rounds to welcome them. We were peppered with shrapnel and Quill body parts. Klutch did not seem to notice and kept advancing on our only entrance. I was fixated on what was in front of us and was surprised by a flash from just behind me. Looking up in my HUD, I saw Quill body parts twirling rapidly out of the spine into the void.

Tria slapped me twice on my shoulder and I continued moving forward. We were nearing the end of the spine. Klutch sent a few more gifts through the breach to any Quill that might have felt they were somehow left out from our surprise party. I could see body parts scattering everywhere and I cringed, noticing not all were Quill. Since there were no signs of an active battle, I could only hope the Chaalt were already deceased. Klutch held up a fist. Tria and I waited until the Troop Master took a quick peek out the end of the spine. He waved us forward and disappeared into the Chaalt ship.

We had no way of knowing how many Quill had boarded. All signs indicated it was probably a shit load. When my feet hit the deck, I knew we had gravity. It was a positive sign the spine had not pierced into any vital engineering spaces. Since the ships atmosphere was not shrieking past us to the void, we also knew there was an intact pressure door somewhere ahead of us. Klutch was kneeling at a blown-out hatch peeking out into a corridor. The specially designed valves on Klutch's armor were actively venting his warriors scent. The twin orifices just below his munitions back pack were sending steamy streams of his stench out into the void. I tried to link with the Operative and was getting nothing in return.

I surveyed my surroundings and was shaken by the grisly scene. It was not because we were standing almost knee deep in body parts, but because of what I saw just across the big machine filled room. Stacked up like cord wood, filling one whole side of the chamber was the bodies of both Chaalt and Quill troopers. Several of the Chaalt troop's bodies had been ripped apart. Exposed flesh on several of the cadavers was steaming and blistering in places. There was a yellowish-brown viscus fluid splattered on the open wounds, and it appeared to be some kind of corrosive substance. I did not know what to make of it and assumed it was the result of Quill weapons fire.

Tria pulled me away from the morbid pile. She cleared her visor. The horror on her face turned to steely eyed determination. She nodded in Klutch's direction. We pulled our shotguns from our backpacks and went to where the Troop Master was kneeling.

Klutch linked with me. "Commander, there are at least twenty Quill troops at both ends of this corridor. It appears they are guarding access to the spine. The hatches they are covering are far enough from our location I do not know if stealth will conceal our presence long enough to surprise them. It might not be wise to attack with explosives; they may be guarding the airlocks to these spaces."

Klutch was politely warning me not to let my inner beast do anything stupid that might further cause damage to the Chaalt vessel. We had our needle guns. The compact rail weapons were usually less destructive to the inside of a starship than the rest of our armament. I looked back at the wall of corpses. Walking over to it, I chose a spot that was laden with an abundance of bug bodies. I gave them a shot of hypervelocity needles. The impact knocked several of the dead Quill off the pile and showered the room with reflected fragments. The heavily ridged carapace deflected most of the projectiles. Upon closer inspection, I discovered the ball-type joints on the bug carcasses were bristled like cactus from the needles imbedded in the pivot point. It was a small weakness, but a weakness nonetheless.

Linking with Tria and Klutch, I relayed my plan to them. "Tria, Klutch and I are going to step out into the passage and empty our needle guns into the troops at each end of the corridor. When we come back through the hatch, we will get clear. I want you to wait until a Quill soldier shows up. When they do, I want you to put a burst of HE into the passageway. Make sure to angle your fire so it will not reach the pressure doors at the end of the corridor."

She gave me a thumb's up and stepped toward the back wall. She turned and pointed to the hall. Klutch and I jumped out the doorway and sprayed nine thousand needles each into the unsuspecting Quill. I wanted to gape at the awesome display of sparks and fragmenting needles engulfing the enemy troops. Several fell to the floor prone, and the rest went into a frenzy flailing at everything around them. I had never unloaded a full magazine of needles before. I waved my arm in small circles for just under a minute before the coffee cup sized magazine went dry. I was jerked from behind by Klutch pulling me back through the door.

The beast was cheering me on, and there was a good chance I was about to blow the shit out of everything before Klutch intervened. My plan must have been old news to Tria. When the first Crit made it to the hatch, Tria expertly dropped her aim to the floor and bounced a burst of high explosive rounds off the floor, up the wall, toward the ceiling in the corridor. The detonations knocked us all sprawling to the floor. Tria was up in a flash before Klutch and I could regain our footing. The corridor wall I was facing was now bulged inward. She charged into the hallway and put some rounds of buckshot in one direction then spun doing the same in the opposite direction. She leaped back into the room with us and I jumped up to repeat her actions. I made it to the hatch and collided with Klutch as he bulled his way to the corridor. I was knocked to the side, face first into the door frame, and found myself once more back on the floor. I could feel the rippling vibrations of explosive buckshot just outside of the doorway. Tria reached down and helped me back to my feet.

Klutch walked calmly back through the doorway, replacing his spent magazines. He gave me a big, toothy smile. "All clear, Commander!"

I made it a point to clear my visor so he could plainly see the displeasure on my face. He was becoming immune to the expression. I tried to link with the Operative again and got nothing. I had grown to really like Sael Nalen but now feared she may have been killed in the Quill incursion. The Oolaran inside of me screamed out for revenge. I was going to throw it a bone.

12

"Tria, where do these passages lead to?"

She looked at me and I could tell she was deep in thought. "I have never served on this class of vessel. Judging by our entry point, I would say down the corridor to our right would have to be the engineering spaces; to our left, the lifts to the bridge and command spaces. That is where we will find Sael Nalen."

Looking over at Klutch I blacked out my helmet. "Klutch, go left. Let's move out!"

Klutch went out the door and left, weapon up and ready. Tria slapped me on the shoulder and gave me a push. She was going to cover our rear whether I liked it or not. I headed out the door with her right behind me. Klutch was kneeling down in the hallway, holding one of the Quill weapons. I stopped next to him and Tria stood ready for any surprise visitors.

"What have you got, Klutch?"

"Commander, the Crit's weapon is fed by this pack strapped to its thorax. I am mystified by the tube that connects the weapon to its proboscis."

Klutch pulled his fighting knife and hacked at the tube twice before it parted. The yellow-brown fluid we had seen burning the flesh on the Chaalt corpses squirt out of the tube onto the floor. The coating on the deck plating started to boil up. Just when you think aliens could not get any weirder, you see shit like this. The freaking Crit was producing some kind of acid in its body and injecting it into its weapon. The projectiles in the weapon were obviously being coated in the corrosive substance. We had yet to be shot at because we were killing the bugs before they had a chance to. We could not count on that luck holding for much longer. I hoped Zaen battle armor could hold up to corrosives as well as it did against projectiles. Klutch wiped the acid from his blade on the creature's body and we again moved down the passageway.

We had not encountered any resistance and reached the large pressure door unimpeded. It would be foolish to think the atmospheric lock would not have a number of troops protecting the strategic choke point. We stacked at the door and Tria hit the access control. The door opened and two Quill soldiers were inside facing away from us. The Troop Master did not hesitate. He ran forward jumping onto the first Crit's back. As the Crit fell into its companion, Klutch shoved his shotgun against the creature's head and blew it in half. His momentum carried him over the first bug and he leapt feet-first onto the head of the second that had stumbled and fell to the floor. The Crit's head fractured under Klutch's weight. He jumped up and completed the kill with a landing that crushed the bug's skull.

Klutch did not look back when he called to Tria and I. "Their carapace does not protect their skull well. We should target this weakness."

The Troop Master was in the zone, and his combat focus was laser precise. Any resistance would be met with maximum force. He was not giving my inner demon any chance at wanton destruction. We again stacked with Klutch low, me over his shoulder and Tria over mine. She hit the door control and atmosphere pressurized the chamber, and the door opened. The passage was full of Quill soldiers. They were in the process of stacking the dead from both sides. We poured a fusillade of fire into them. Klutch went left, I went right and Tria sent a stream of nonstop anti-personnel rounds into the bugs. She dove to the floor beside me. I hoped the bugs had sensitive olfactory receptors. Klutch's armor was venting overtime.

Klutch yelled out. "TAKE COVER, H.E. OUT!"

I rolled on top of Tria as Klutch took a chapter from the Chaalt's playbook. He bounced a burst of high explosive rounds off the ceiling into the rear of the Quill troops. The staccato blasts bounced us off the floor. Quill soldiers were blown on top of us and several were still alive. Tria was pinned under me but not for long. I was jerked from the floor by one of the bugs. It promptly spits a generous amount of the acid crap they used in their weapons, down the front of me. The Crit had two interlocking mandibles that opened and clamped down on

157

my shoulder. Even through the armor, I could feel the pressure increasing.

I could feel the Oolaran soldier take charge as servo warning lights started flashing in my visor. My fear subsided and calm determination took its place. A small smile formed on my lips. I smashed my fist into the bug's large egg-shaped eye, fracturing the clear hard covering protecting it. I struck savagely at the covering until it collapsed. The Crit released its grip on me. I reached out and grabbed one of the mandibles, wrenching at it with everything I had. It ripped from the bugs head, slinging acid and dark red, almost black fluid with it. The creature was letting out loud screeching chirps that sounded a lot like a cricket. The bug's lower thorax exploded and I fell backwards to the floor. Looking up, I saw Tria was against the wall with her shotgun up and making precision shots on anything that moved. The explosive penetrator slugs were devastatingly effective.

I groped around until I came up with my shotgun. I looked for Klutch and saw he was on the floor struggling with two of the bugs. One of the bugs had its mandibles clamped securely onto one of his tree trunk legs. Using my shotgun for a bat I hit the creature in the eye collapsing its protective cover. When the Crit gave up trying to tear Klutch's leg off, I gave it two more powerful butt strokes with the shotgun. As the bug fell back I locked my arm around the pivot point of its neck and jerked three times before it partially separated from its body. I was going to attempt to pull the remaining Quill off Klutch when his fighting knife suddenly jutted from the back of the bug's head. It disappeared and reappeared three more times. Klutch used his legs to shove the Crit aside.

The Tibor gave me a sardonic look. "The Crit should have kept his mouth shut!"

We were boxed in by a veritable wall of bug bodies. The bulkhead just above and behind us was taking a nonstop barrage of what looked like tracer bullets splattering fragments and burning acid in all directions. Bullets might not have been the right definition. One of the Quill bodies lying at the top of the mound of corpses tumbled down at our feet. One side of it had hundreds of smoking spikes protruding from its body. In an oxygen atmosphere, the Quill weapons accelerated the spikes to a velocity high enough to illuminate the acid clinging to them.

Tria yelled to us, "EXPLOSIVES OUT!"

She bounced a burst of H.E. off both sides of the ceiling above us. I should have just taken a seat on the floor because that's where I ended up. It was once again raining Quill and their body parts. We needed to move before we were buried alive. The Quill fire hitting our barricade and the wall behind us tapered off drastically. Since we were all on the floor now anyway, I pointed the muzzle of my launcher at the ceiling and fired nine single shots of high explosive at different angles. The return fire ceased with the third round, but the beast inside of me was a trigger-happy son of a bitch. Tria and Klutch had yelled cease fire more than once before I finally did.

I had not heard from Justice since he dropped us off and was pretty sure my comms could not penetrate the ship. I activated my link and got Coonts, who said he was still busy picking the Quill off of the hull. He said Justice and the now five remaining Chaalt warships had heavily damaged the last Quill vessels. The Quill had attempted to jump out of the system but he said Justice and the Chaalt had given them no quarter. The enemy ships were so damaged they could no longer transition. The Quill fled into the asteroid field trying to escape. Justice was covering Coonts while the Chaalt warships chased down the last of the Quill. I tried once more to link with Sael Nalen but still got nothing.

Tria pulled me to my feet and Klutch climbed up on the morbid barricade. He stood up and jumped to the other side. We quickly scurried to the top and over. Klutch was nudging a Quill body here and there and twice jumped on the heads of survivors. The room was complete devastation; there was not a single intact body or piece of equipment. Everything was smoking from acid or explosives.

There were four lift tubes at the end of the room. All were clogged with Quill bodies and a few Chaalt mixed in. All the Chaalt crew casualties we saw did not have body armor. The Crit's surprise entry tactic left no time for troops to assemble and repel their incursion.

My guess was the lifts were either shut down or disabled by the spine when it hit the ship. The bugs looked like they had formed a living ladder and were attempting to climb the tubes. Every exit was an ambush point the Chaalt were using to their advantage. By the look of the finely ground enemy body parts, I would say the Chaalt took great pleasure in throwing explosives into the tubes. Now that it was quiet, we could hear the thudding vibrations of a pitched battle somewhere above us. Our choices were simple. We go back and fight our way to the lifts in the engineering spaces or attempt to clear one of the tubes and go up to the command deck.

I was shocked at the number of Quill bodies we were looking at. What stunned me even more was the thought of how many must have boarded in the short time it took us to attack their ship and disable the umbilical. Klutch must have decided he was not willing to give up the ground we had covered. He waded into the edge of a lift tube and started throwing the Quill bodies clear of the opening. Tria joined him and I could think of nothing better. We hurled the bodies out of the way only to have more fall in their place. After about fifteen minutes, Klutch could crawl inside the tube. He climbed upward out of sight.

He linked Tria and me. "Commander, it is possible to climb around the corpses and boost to the next deck. There is no sign of hostiles. I will wait until you join me."

This time Tria happened to be in front of me. I gave her a couple of good swats on the butt and pushed her forward. She crawled in and disappeared up the tube. Several Quill bodies collapsed back down into the opening and I spent additional time clearing them.

Klutch got impatient and let me know about it. "Commander, I must caution you against taking a sleep period during combat, it is considered foolhardy behavior by the more advanced races."

For reasons unknown to me, of all the Earth mannerisms adopted by my crew, levity and sarcasm seemed to have made it to the top of their lists before all others. Not necessarily in that order. I did know, however, when a Troop Master points out something he may have concerns about, it was wise to listen. I also knew he expected a timely and respectful response.

"ON MY WAY TROOP MASTER!"

Climbing the dismembered bodies, I engaged my gravity drive and went up to the next deck. Tria and Klutch had taken defensive positions at the opening. They were standing knee deep in bug corpses. Whatever the Crits had attempted to do on this deck must have been met by armored troops. There were no Chaalt among the dead. The room had three large pressure doors. All were battered but still sealed. I suspected what lay in wait on the other side of those doors would be very unhealthy for any who opened them before this siege was over.

The sounds of battle were louder now. I was going to step back to the tube and go up but jumped back when I was surprised by a couple of Quill bodies flashing by on the way to the bottom of the tube. Klutch took this as his opening to once again bump me aside, and up he went. I quickly followed with Tria right behind me. Klutch reached the top and immediately opened fire. I came out of the tube and was met with a barrage of glowing spikes. I was knocked to the floor by the continuous bombardment. The loud splattering impacts sounded like gravel falling on sheet metal.

Tria did not make the same mistake I did. She peeked up over the edge of the tube and put her arm out and unloaded anti-personnel rounds into the mass of Quill filling the corridor. The attention I had been getting slacked off enough for me to roll behind a pile of dead Quill soldiers. The Oolaran in me took over and I emptied an entire magazine of buckshot into the soldiers. Klutch was reloading and Tria came out of the tube and jumped to the floor beside me. The beast barely noticed and

163

decided we were in enough cover to start pumping out high explosive munitions danger close. My teammates went prone and covered their heads. Quill body parts and shrapnel started raining down on us. I could just barely hear Klutch yelling at me to increase my range. The explosions were so sharp and jarring that my vision was blurring. Tria reached out and grabbed my arm with two of hers and forced it toward the ceiling, increasing the arc of my salvo. The concussive blasts eased to the point Klutch got up on a knee and poured rounds of buckshot head high into the crowd of bugs.

Tria linked with me and cleared her visor so I could see her face. "Nathan, cease fire and conserve your munitions. We may need it for what lies ahead!"

I quit firing and shook my head to clear my thoughts. Her look of concern and calm demeanor brought me back to reality. The beast shambled away to some dark corner of my mind. Tria reached out and wiped the bug juice from my visor and I cleared it so she could see that I was indeed back. She smiled, then got up on her knees and sent hellfire into the ranks of frenzied bugs. I got up beside her and we emptied several magazines of explosive buckshot into everything that moved. We quit firing because the pile of dead Quill was so large we could not directly engage the living. Tria bounced a few H.E. rounds off the ceiling and behind the mound. Body parts rained down once more. There was at least a hundred feet of no man's land in front of us. The carnage was horrific and the damage to the passageway probably unrepairable.

Klutch made his way across the minefield of shattered bodies. Tria and I quickly followed. He climbed the back of the pile but hastily rolled off when glowing spikes started ripping the prone cadavers to pieces.

Klutch did not like what he saw on the other side of our only cover. "Commander, I believe we have their attention now. A considerable number are moving this way!"

To reinforce his statement, the volume of enemy fire intensified. Our barricade was being ground down to the consistency of sludge. Like it or not, it was going to be retreat or expend our dwindling supply of H.E. munitions. The beast laughed at my indecision. My arm came up and I unloaded a wicked long burst of forty high explosive rounds, walking them up the middle of the passageway. My team joined me with slow selective fire. Hatches along the passage were blasted open and piping on the walls and ceiling was ripped asunder. The overhead lighting the length of the corridor went dark.

The Crits changed their minds about charging us. They instead turned away. The respite from their assault encouraged the Oolaran in me to press the attack. The low-light targeting system of my H.U.D. made a surreal picture out of the mass of moving targets. I pulled my shotgun up and started putting explosive penetrator slugs into the backs of the retreating Quill. The beast was in control, and I started pursuing my prey. Tria yelled out to stop, but I felt compelled to do otherwise. Tria and Klutch had no choice but to follow. I emptied an entire magazine of needles into the faltering ranks, frenzying the crazed bugs even more. The results were gratifying, and I sent another barrage of needles into them, only stopping long enough to reload my empty weapons.

Tria and Klutch were being judicious with their munitions. The beast chose reckless abandon. My six magazines of needles were expended first. The H.E. and finally my anti-personnel rounds ran dry. I had four magazines of buckshot and seven of the penetrator slugs left in my weapons and pouches. Each time I wanted to unleash my beam weapon, moments of clarity reigned in the suicidal thoughts. I believe it had more to do with not wanting to harm my crewmates and less to do with self-preservation.

Coonts group linked us. "Commander, A Chaalt task force has entered the system. They are splitting up to pursue the remaining Quill ships and commencing rescue operations. Two are in route to our location. I will make them aware we have friendly forces aboard the Operative's flagship."

I could hear Tria acknowledge Coonts transmission, but the Oolaran devil wanted nothing to do with a possible cessation of hostilities. The front of my armor had been shot peened so thoroughly my bestial caricature was no longer visible. I was covered from head to toe in the steaming, bug-excreted acid. My armor was ripped open in several places. My suit liner was working hard to stop the corrosive effects of the acid. I could feel it burning my skin in several places. It remained to be seen how well the nano lamination of my epidermis could cope with the injuries. My shotgun had taken so many hits it was now only usable as a club.

I drew my fighting knife and drove myself headlong into the bug ranks. My crewmates quit firing into the melee and drew their knives and struggled to my sides. The bugs could no longer shoot at us, so they swelled in on us instead. For reasons unknown, the Crits seemed to be focusing their ire on me. It was as if they could hear the beast calling to them, egging them on. We fought back to back, smashing and slashing all comers. My Zaen armor was being pummeled like never before. The acid was destroying its structural integrity. Many of the blows I was taking would have broken normal bones. My carbon fiber reinforced skeletal system shrugged off the nonstop assault. The pain, however, was almost blinding at times. The beast was in the zone, and the smile on my face ached from the prolonged expression. The death and destruction from my dreams was here and it was real.

The world around me came back to a coherent focus. Klutch had his huge arms wrapped around me, attempting to pin my arms.

Tria put her hands on my helmet yelling at me repeatedly. "STOP NATHAN, WE HAVE KILLED THEM ALL!"

Klutch released his grip on me and stood at my side. Looking at my crewmates I saw they had been brutalized but fared much better than I. It took me a moment to realize I was on the verge of attacking Chaalt soldiers. The friendlies backed away from me. They had seen how I had slaughtered everything in my path and feared I might not be done. Now that the battle was over, emergency lighting was restored. I stood for a moment staring at the death around me. There was a wall of carnage encircling us. The mixture of bugs and Chaalt lying dead was horrifying. I cleared my visor and Tria's look of concern finally eased.

A feeling of dread filled me. "Did I harm any of your people?"

"No Nathan, we stop — no Nathan, these soldiers had already fallen to the Quill."

I closed my eyes tight and clenched my teeth. Tria looped her arms in mine, standing close at my side. The beast was appeased and disappeared to some dark corner of my mind. It left me to worry about my actions and did not care for the remorse I was feeling. I alone would take the blame for any fratricide caused by my wanton destruction. The ranks of Chaalt troops gathered around us and Sael Nalen limped forward. Her armor looked as bad as mine. She was still holding both of her swords. The pulsating glow from the blades still smoking from Quill blood and gore. She slid them into their scabbards. Her helmet was fractured and open on the side. She stopped in front of me and pulled it loose from her head and let it fall to the floor. The side of her face was badly burned by acid. She did not seem to notice.

She placed her hand on the side of my helmet. "I have never seen such a sight in combat. Your aura blinded the Crits that enveloped you, then it turned as black as the starless void. You slaughtered all who touched you."

She let her hand fall from my helmet and she took a step back. She made fists with two of her hands and placed them across her chest giving me a slight bow as she did so. The remaining Chaalt troops did the same.

"The three of you did what many could not. We were cut off from reinforcements and our numbers were quickly dwindling. You honor those who have fallen and I thank you for all you saved. The Chaalt people will remember you, Nathan Myers."

We were interrupted by a flood of armored Chaalt troops coming out of the lift tube. We turned to face them as they rapidly approached our position. Several stopped here and there to kill surviving Quill they encountered.

A troop leader marched up to us. "Kala Mor Dee, you have survived once more. For this we are thankful."

Sael Nalen fixed the younger female warrior with a stare. "No one is to address me by that name ever again, do you understand?"

The troop leader was shocked and stood rigid. "Yes, Senior Operative!"

Sael Nalen looked around to make sure all understood. Then she turned back to the young warrior. "Did you secure the engineering spaces?"

The team leader quickly replied, "Yes, Senior Operative. The ship is now secure and teams are sweeping all accessible passages for hideaways. Engineering teams are trying to restore power to the main lifts and communication equipment. We are also trying to gain access to all personnel trapped in the lower decks and compartments. A salvage team is surveying the Quill spine and will determine how best to remove it."

"What of my fleet?"

"Senior Operative, rescue operations are ongoing. We have accounted for eight warships. Five are capable of combat but have sustained heavy damage. Three will have to be taken in tow. They are drifting in the asteroid field and are in danger of further damage. On your order, I will pull picket ships from security patrols to help extricate them from the asteroid belt."

The Senior Operative did not take the news well. She stood with her head bent and her eyes closed. She finally looked up at the younger Operative. "Pull the additional ships from picket duty and take the damaged ships in tow. Call up two emergency medical ships and two mobile ship yards. I want them here as soon as possible. There is an Oolaran warship close by, what is its status?"

"Unknown, Senior Operative. It appears to have significant damage. The A.I. of the vessel has warned off our boarding shuttles. We have taken a Coram-designed shuttle in restrictive tow. It is also damaged and the pilot refuses aid."

"Release the shuttle at once and steer clear of the Oolaran warship. It will be approaching to recover personnel. No one is to interfere with its passage or impede its progress in any way. I want decontamination teams to immediately board and set up for class "C" contingencies. Priority will be given to these three soldiers. All will show them the utmost respect, and no one is to hinder them for any reason. Any who disobey my orders will be spaced."

The young warrior's eyes went wide and she turned away. She started issuing orders. A good portion of her troops rapidly disappeared down the transport tube. The rest lined the corridor on both sides, standing at attention.

Sael Nalen turned back to us. "I must check on the status of my wounded. If you need anything, let my subordinates know. If it is within my power, it will be yours."

The Senior Operative called to her junior counterpart. "I am designating your vessel as my flagship."

With that comment, the Operative limped away.

13

I took Tria by one of her hands and put my other on Klutch's broad shoulder. The pain of combat eased with the reassuring contact. We looked at the Junior Operative. She waved one of her subordinates over.

"You are to escort these soldiers to the decontamination area. They are to be treated as Senior Operatives."

The soldier nodded and led us to the transport tube. It was still inoperative. The Chaalt told us to go down one deck because the engineers were working to remove the spine from the lower one. We were forced to use a service ladder. Our armor was so badly damaged our gravity drives no longer functioned. We had been on the lower deck once before and it was closed up tight. Now the doors were open and we were led on a considerable walk through the Chaalt warship. The Junior Operative was yelling, "Make a hole!" whenever the passages became crowded. Everyone gave us a wide berth with the exception of one. Tria's father stood staring. The shocked expression on his face turned to tears as we shuffled by. We finally arrived at a large hangar area. There had to be at least forty shuttles lined up in rows on each side of the immense hangar opening. They were taking off two at a time disappearing into the void on rescue missions. Just behind the shuttles were much larger boxy-looking spacecraft with multiple appendages. They had to be maintenance tugs. There were crews boarding them and preparing for launch. I was not sure if the Legacy would require their services.

I linked with Coonts. "Coonts, I heard a report the shuttle was damaged. Are you injured?"

He came right back to me. "No Commander, but I will not be able to recover you. The personnel hatch is damaged and the outer door is not functioning. The cargo hold is also a no-go. The cargo ramp is jammed in the upright position."

"OK Coonts, I will get back with you as soon as we are decontaminated."

"Roger that, Commander."

"Justice, have you got a copy?"

"Yes, Commander. I am awaiting orders."

"Justice, can you safely get Coonts aboard? He is stuck in the shuttle and all of the exits are jammed."

"Yes Commander, we have been in constant communication. I have been tracking his location since the Chaalt released the shuttle. I will recover Coonts and stand by for further orders."

"Okay Justice, when I get clearance I will need you to maneuver in front of the Chaalt hangar door. Our armor is wrecked and coordinated flight is no longer possible. I am going to talk to the flight master and see if they can give us a thirty second window so you can collect us."

"Roger, Commander. I will close with your position and prepare to evacuate all Legacy personnel."

Our guide had departed after consulting with a male Chaalt in a light atmospheric suit. The suit had "Med Bay Tech" stenciled on it. The Med Tech pointed us to walk through decontamination chambers. I approached the tech so he could hear me over the din of the hangar bay operations. His eyes widened and he started backing away frantically pointing at the decontamination chamber. I finally nodded and walked to the multi-chambered setup. I waved Tria and Klutch through then followed. One of the chambers sprayed a mist that brought the burn of the acid in my many lacerations to an immediate halt. When we exited I walked up to the Med Tech. He was much more cordial now that I was not covered in bug acid. Someone must have briefed him on our status, because now he stood at attention waiting to hear what I had to say.

"I need you to contact the flight master and have him cease launching spacecraft for thirty seconds. My ship will move in close to evacuate us."

The tech got a distant look on his face, and then looked back at me. "Say the word, Senior Operative, and it shall be done."

Several more techs stepped forward and started slapping plate-sized patches on the rends in our armor. When they were satisfied with their work, they retreated to a safe distance to assist others. I waved to my crewmates and we headed for the big open hangar door. I called out to the tech.

"When we reach the hangar door, give the Flight Master the go ahead. Give us thirty seconds and you can resume rescue operations."

The tech nodded and stood waiting for our departure.

I called to Justice. "Justice, are you ready?"

"Roger, Commander. I will be picking you up in twenty seconds."

We stood at the hangar door and I waved to the tech. A red band appeared around the hangar opening. We shuffled forward when the Legacy filled the opening and jumped. The three of us had not covered more than a few feet before we were pulled aboard with the tow beam and Justice quickly cleared the area.

The first thing we noticed when our feet hit the Legacy's deck was our once pristine shuttle was all but trashed. The rear of the shuttle was caved in all the way to the boarding hatch. The port side missile pod and cowling were missing as well. We were not the only ones going through hell. Justice extruded two large arms from the overhead of the hangar and they extended down onto the shuttle. They embedded themselves into the cracks and rends that were now abundant on the shuttle's hull. The arms seemed to swell and the bulge flowed downward into the shuttle. With a loud bang the wrecked boarding hatch fell to the deck. Coonts appeared at the opening and jumped down to meet us. He looked no worse for wear and tear, and his armor suit did not have a scratch on it. He surveyed the extent of the damage to the shuttle.

He turned to me and gave me an Earthman shrug of his shoulders. "Commander, I think there is a good possibility we now have enough spare parts to make our second Coram shuttle void worthy."

While that was a noteworthy observation, I really wanted to hear the story behind the shuttle's demise. "Coonts, did you decide to ram the Crits, rather than shoot them?"

He took my comments for the sarcastic humor it was and gave me a less than attractive smile. "Perhaps it would be a story better told over food rations."

I could not argue with his philosophy. Now that I was fresh out of adrenaline, I was starving. There was still another issue that had me wondering. When we left the hangar to start our mission, the tip of a massive spine ripped from a Quill ship was sticking through the side of the Legacy's hull. The spine was gone and a sheet of hull alloy now covered the hole.

I could see Justice patching the hull but not extricating the spine. "Justice, how did you manage to remove the spine?"

"Commander, I found the irritation of the Quill protrusion unsettling. There was a number of Crits still active in the ship fragment. A large number of them made their way to the exterior of the Legacy and were attempting to board. I enlisted the aid of Coonts and we successfully remedied the situation."

I was more than a little puzzled when Justice was not more forthcoming. Coonts once again suggested we go eat and he disappeared into the ready room. Tria, Klutch and I looked at each other, then went to the ready room to stow our badly battered armor. I hoped the repair systems on the storage crates could cope with the extent of damage inflicted on the suits. This was by far the worst shape they had ever been in. I stepped up into my armor crate and the suit baulked at fully releasing me. I was forced to physically start pushing my way out of the suit opening. The effort caused me more than a little discomfort. I could tell by Klutch's colorful croaking, he was experiencing similar problems.

I felt four arms wrap around me. Tria gave me a good yank and I finally pulled free. I turned to her and planted a kiss on her lips for her effort. All thoughts of any pain I was experiencing were quickly forgotten. She would not release me until I gave her another. The racket coming from Klutch was becoming dangerous and the scent in the ready room took a turn for the worse. I would have thought Coonts might assist Klutch, but the Grawl was nowhere to be found. Apparently, he was famished. Tria and I took as deep a breath of the tainted air as we could tolerate and grabbed onto the Tibor. We jerked several times but had to retreat to the corridor to gulp down enough fresh air to continue. Our second attempt did the trick and the Tibor plopped to the deck. We ran to the outer passage in hopes our suit liners did not ingest additional quantities of the rank atmosphere permeating the ready room. I shuddered to think what it would be like if our liners permanently smelled like that.

Justice came to our aid when I heard the atmosphere scrubber fan taking on a new sound of urgency. Klutch came out of the ready room and nodded to us then stalked off toward the lift tubes. He was battered and bruised but pretended it did not bother him.

I called to him before he stepped into the lift. "Report to the med bay and have Justice look you over!"

I went back into the ready room and sat down, pulling off my suit liner. The extent of my physical damage becoming obvious — I was a mess. Like it or not, we would all be making a trip to the med bay. The extra volume of air being cleansed felt chilly to my naked body. That was, right up until Tria sat inches from me and peeled off her suit liner. The temperature instantly climbed to what I would swear was more than a hundred degrees. She was bruised and had acid burns on her arms and legs. I knew the wounds were painful because mine were. The smile she gave me said otherwise. My body started responding as any young mans would. There would be no covering my embarrassment. Just when I thought my predicament could not get any worse, an extruded arm came down from the overhead with a carafe of water and two glasses. I jumped up from the bench. "JUSTICE!" The arm dissolved so fast the small pitcher and glasses crashed to the deck.

Tria was giggling as I stowed my liner in my locker. I grabbed a smart cloth uniform and quickly placed it against my body. It made an awkward attempt to properly conform to my body. I made my way out of the ready room as fast as my battered body would allow me. I cursed the evil robot and his single-minded indiscretion. I could still hear Tria laughing behind me. When I stepped off the lift on the command deck I went straight to my cabin and a very invigorating cold shower. Most all of my body aches and pain receded to a dull roar. I could not be sure, but it could have been Justice manipulating my implants to block my discomfort. His motivations for doing so were suspect. I dried off and put my uniform back on and went down to the med bay.

Tria was there and Justice was applying spray dressings to her wounds. Her uniform was on a table next to her. I was now more concerned for her health than her nakedness. She was ignoring the extruded arms as they worked on her. She reached out for me and I took her hand.

Justice had to throw in his two cents worth. "Commander, in order for me to treat your wounds it will be necessary for you to remove your uniform."

"Justice, I will wait until you have finished treating Tria!"

After a short pause, Justice pressed two small injectors on two of her arms. He then finished spraying nanite dressings on the rest of her wounds. She got up with a small flinch and put her smart cloth back on.

She gave me a kiss and said, "I will see you in the galley for a meal after I get cleaned up."

I nodded and told her I would see her there. When she left the room, I removed my uniform and sat down. When Justice started cleaning my wounds, the touch of his appendages was like ice and I reeled from the touch.

"What the hell Justice, I know your hands were not that cold when you treated Tria?"

181

"My apologies Commander, I had to check to insure the hull patch in the hangar was still intact."

My irritation at his comment was heading for the angry side of my bullshit meter. He sensed I was not in the mood to be trifled with. His appendages were now warm and he cleaned and sprayed my wounds in a professional manner. I was feeling much better and could see the nanite spray was starting the process of repairing the burns on my skin. Justice told me I could get dressed, and when I leaned over to pick up my uniform, he did me a dirty one. Instead of giving me my nanite booster shots in my arms as he had done to Tria, he decided my ass was a good target. Normally you barely felt the injectors. That was not the case this time, and I squalled like a stuck hog.

"ARE YOU OUT OF YOUR EVIL ROBOT MIND? If you want to kill me, just get it over with!"

Putting on my smart cloth, I stormed out of the med bay rubbing my butt cheeks. Each step I took had me wondering if going to the galley was a smart idea. I really did not care to eat while standing. Maybe Justice would poison me next and put me out of my misery. I grimaced and went to the galley. No matter how pissy Justice got, Tria had a way of taking the sting out of it. I rubbed my ass once more and hoped she could literally do just that.

Entering the galley, I thought I would see Coonts, but that was not the case. Klutch was the only one here and he was busily piling a tray with food. The tray looked more like a construction project than a meal. Klutch was planning on being here for a while. I patiently waited for him to find a seat. As a rule, we all secretly did not sit next to him when he ate. It was a messy affair and included noises not beneficial to good digestion. If you waited for him to sit down you could politely sit somewhere else. It never seemed to bother him and he never asked us to join him. If you were already sitting down and eating, he more often than not, would sit right next to you. Like it or not you were going to get the whole show and you did not want to get him talking.

Tria walked through the big archway. I smiled and went to meet her. She had a frown on her pretty face.

"What's the matter Tria, are you well?"

"Yes Nathan, I am fine. It is Coonts that I am worried about. He is out in the corridor pacing. When I asked what was wrong he only muttered and gave me a vague answer that made no sense."

Glancing toward the corridor I looked back at her puzzled. "What did he say?"

"He said it was Justice's idea and he was only trying to help."

Looking back out to the passageway, I took Tria by the hand and walked out of the galley. Coonts was just down the corridor and when he saw me he turned and started walking the other way. Now I was really starting to smell something rotten, and it had nothing to do with Klutch.

"Coonts, hold up, I want to talk to you!"

The little Grawl stopped and slowly turned around. The look on his face suggested he was not in a talkative mood.

"Okay Coonts, spit it out. You have been acting strange ever sense you stepped out of the shuttle."

"Commander, I was only trying to help. I did not think it would lead to major...complications with the shuttle. Justice suggested I help him remove the spine from the hull. I did not anticipate how difficult it would be to dislodge it from the Legacy."

I closed my eyes and shook my head. It was clear now what happened to the shuttle. Combat damage was not the reason the shuttle was wrecked. It was probably not Justice's fault either, but my ass was sore enough to go ahead and credit him for it anyway. Coonts was blaming himself for what may prove to be the loss of both Coram shuttles. If we could not salvage the parts to get the other shuttle operational, we would be back to having a single shuttle. Regardless of the outcome, we would have to get up to speed on our new shuttle anyway.

I put my hand on the Grawl's shoulder. "Coonts, I am not worried whether we lost the Coram shuttle or not. When we get back to base we will work on learning the flight systems for the Chaalt shuttle."

Tria quickly added, "I think you will find the flight controls on the new shuttle to be intuitive and simple. We will need to train on the weapons systems, but the rest will require very little instruction. The onboard A.I. will adjust very quickly to our learning parameters."

I knew for a fact Justice was allergic to other artificial intelligences. He was well known for booting A.I.s out the airlock within minutes of coming into contact with them. I would not be surprised if the Chaalt intelligence had already found itself on a shelf in some dark corner of Alpha base. The look of relief on Coonts face was obvious. The shitstorm we had just weathered and the shuttle getting trashed needed to be in my rearview mirror.

Looking at Tria and Coonts, I smiled. "Klutch had his tray loaded and has probably chosen his seat by now."

They both gave me a knowing look and we headed back to the galley.

14

After a well-deserved meal, we retired to our cabins. Justice informed me the hull repair systems had patched enough damage we could now safely jump back to Alpha base. I felt our transition but the discomfort was so negligible compared to my other body aches and pains it almost went unnoticed.

I sat on the edge of my bed wondering if Tria would visit me. It was every bit of two minutes before my cabin door opened. Tria came in with a blanket wrapped around her and dropped it by the door. Her beautiful body was covered in bruises. Looking down at my own body, I also had numerous large grape colored splotches. Most of our acid burns had scabbed over and, in another day, or so would be gone. The nanite injections quickly healed the superficial stuff but took longer on the heavier tissue damage.

I had set a small pitcher of water and two glasses on my bedside table. I had hopes that Justice would find something else to do, rather than intrude in my cabin with meaningless tasks. Tria poured each of us a glass and we both drank it down. She slid into my bed and put her arms around me. The fatigue of the last twenty-four hours swept over me and we quickly fell into a deep sleep. I am sure that was the last thing Justice expected or wanted to happen.

While we slept, Justice brought us back to Alpha base. He put us down in the hangar and had the decency to let us sleep. I did not know it at the time but he almost had to put down a Grawl rebellion. When Xul and the scientists saw the condition of the Legacy they freaked out. They crowded around the ship and demanded to be allowed aboard to care for us. The A.I. finally convinced the Grawl we were doing well and would exit when we awoke. As a group they sat patiently outside the Legacy and waited for us. We slept for twelve hours straight. Coonts was the first to wake and relayed the story of our battles. Once assured we would recover, the scientists went back to their normal duties.

I woke up alone and sat up wondering if Tria had gone back to her cabin. I heard the shower in my bathroom and a smile crossed my face. I walked in to the steam filled room and my legs turned to rubber and I staggered to the sink. The feeling passed and I heard a mischievous laugh and Tria stepped out of the misty water.

"Do you feel me, Nathan?"

"Yes."

The look in her eyes was alluring. She reached out and pulled me into the shower. She embraced me hard enough to remind me I had been tenderized by a bunch of

Crits. I suspected what was going to happen might hurt. No pain, no gain.

"Commander, a Chaalt warship, designated as Sael Nalen's flagship, just entered our star system. It moved into a low orbit and has dropped below the horizon of our moon. I suspect it now occupies the crevasse you have designated for loitering."

I closed my eyes and shook my head. This was unbelievable. Tria took it a lot better than I did. She whispered, "Justice, cold water please." The shock of the cold water made me yell out. I used my implants to bring up the temperature enough that I could catch my breath. Tria did not seem to notice. She stepped out into the dry warm air from the drier.

I reached for her but she just wagged a finger at me. "We should not keep the Senior Operative waiting. I believe she will be here shortly. She is known for her punctuality."

I was going to start bitching but my Backscatter link beeped. "Nathan Myers, I need to speak with you. It is a matter of urgency."

It was all I could do to keep from telling her I was not available until tomorrow. Tria went by me and swatted me on the ass. I almost squalled out loud. I had failed to inform her Justice chose a much different target for my nanite booster shots than for hers. The pain brought my thoughts back from Tria's slender physique to the business at hand.

"We will be expecting you Senior Operative."

"Commander, outer doors are opening and a Chaalt shuttle is making its approach."

"Thank you, Justice."

If I did not know better, I would say Justice was as disappointed as I was. I looked around for Tria, but she must have gone to her cabin. I quickly dressed and made my way to the boarding hatch. As I exited, I was met with loud shouts of joy from the gathered Grawl scientists. Their ranks parted and they held their hands out to me. I touched each as I passed. Many stood to stare at my appearance. I looked like shit but felt surprisingly good. I thanked and assured them I would make a full recovery. I told them the Operative would arrive momentarily and they dispersed. I suspected they still did not trust Sael Nalen.

The second prototype Chaalt shuttle landed next to its duplicate and Sael Nalen quickly disembarked. She did not look happy. That had me worried.

She did not greet me and came right to the point. "Have you accessed the data cube I gave you?"

I was caught off guard by the question and her look of consternation. I was also surprised her face no longer sported the disfiguring scar. She now looked much younger. "We are studying it. Is there a problem Senior Operative?"

"Yes, Nathan Myers, information has come to light the device might be much more than it appears to be. Can we speak in private?"

I looked at several Grawl that were lingering close by and was going to shoo them away. I thought better of it because this was their home now and no place for enigmas.

"Please tell me what you want to say. There is nothing I wish to hide from anyone here."

She closed her eyes, drew in a breath and slowly let it out. She was still not used to anyone questioning her authority. Tria, Klutch and Coonts walked up to us and stood with quizzical looks on their faces. She finally came to the point. "The device was designed to covertly data map the architecture of your ship's A.I. and upload it to the IST. My superiors do not know I am here to reveal this information, nor do they know I have it. They have also been less than truthful about the amount of information we have on the Daggers you possess."

It was disturbing to think every race I came into contact with had an ulterior motive behind our interactions. I turned and spoke loud enough that everyone could hear. "Justice, set two additional places in our conference room and please bring the Chaalt data cube."

Justice made it a point to answer me over the base PA system. "Affirmative Commander, I have anticipated your request and have already made the preparations. Xul will be joining you shortly. I would also like to add the nature of the Chaalt spyware was discovered and our contingencies successfully quarantined the covert code. I had planned on briefing you on my findings during your morning meal."

The Operative was startled by Justice's disclosures. A look of relief crossed her face accompanied by a small smile. I could tell she was impressed with the Oolaran A.I.'s acuity. There was a very real chance she would inform her superiors to never underestimate the machine intelligence again. I was sure this would eventually turn into another problem. The Chaalt powers that be were not going to be happy with second best.

I led the Operative through the Legacy, and she seemed vaguely familiar with her surroundings. Tria had already told me her people had recovered Oolaran artifacts. It would be stupid to think the Operative was not current on intelligence pertaining to the Legacy. When we reached the bridge, the Operative stopped and gawked at the surround view of the star system. Apparently, this was not a feature installed on Chaalt warships. The screen changed to the mapped location of the Operative's flagship. A blue box appeared around the crevasse. Several green lines came from the location. One was thick, solid and cone shaped. It spread out and disappeared off screen. Two were much fainter and appeared as pulses. One had "IST" next to it, the other "BST." Sael Nalen turned with a look of shock on her face. Justice just verified what we had been hinting at. She now realized the covert comm devices were not as undetectable as her people thought.

I was puzzled why Justice would show the Operative his capabilities. Then it dawned on me the A.I. did not like being underestimated and was showing off. Even as the thought bounced around in my head, the screen abruptly went blank. Sael Nalen shook her head and followed us to the conference room. She might have come to the same conclusion. The Conference room table was now longer than it used to be. It had a chair at each end and two on each side. I knew mine was at the head of the table. My crews and Xul's were on each side because our chairs matched. They were large and comfortable. The chair at the opposite end however was smaller and lacked the benefit of padding. Justice was going to make the Operative pay for interrupting an event he desperately wanted to analyze in detail. His spitefulness did not seem to bother me enough to comment on it. The Operative had a frown on her face that pretty much said she knew the A.I. was responsible for the chicanery. She finally rolled her eyes and sat down.

"Before we begin, I would like to take a moment to address an issue that has been weighing heavy on my heart. If we would have known what it was going to cost in Chaalt lives to keep this base hidden, I would have given the order to abandon this complex. Wasting so many precious lives to protect this piece of dirt is madness. If Quill forces return, I do not want you to defend this place."

The Operative sat staring at me then cleared her throat. "I came here to tell the truth about several things I now find distasteful to hide from you. The conflict with the Quill shall be another. Information I am about to share can go no further than this room."

The look on Sael Nalen's face was dead serious. I made eye contact with each of my teammates and all gave me a nod. I personally did not need any assurances from my people. I knew I could trust each and every one with my life if it came to it. I did the small gesture for the benefit of the Operative. It seemed to be what she was looking for.

"The Chaalt people are at war with the Quill. It was true when I said there would be great danger if they found this place. You saw what they were doing to those planetary bodies. If they find their way here they would do the same to this moon. All Chaalt military assets have standing orders to attack Quill wherever they might be found. The engagement you came uninvited to would have taken place with or without you. That being said, I do not think I would be alive to tell you this if you had not been there to change the tide of the battle."

Tria was shocked but not lost for words. "Our People have not been at war for a great number of years. What have the Quill done to change the last twenty years of peace, and why should it be a secret?"

The Operative looked at Tria for several long moments. I could tell she did not care for Tria's insubordinate tone. Her look of annoyance quickly turned neutral.

"Are you familiar with the Uluru system?"

Tria pondered the question then answered. "Yes, we discovered the star system long ago. The system had eight planets, two of which were habitable. One had a midlevel civilization, and they named their world Austral. If I remember correctly they called themselves the Eyre. They were industrious and hardworking people. They were granted a favorable trade status, and as I recall, several of our people settled among them."

"Your memory serves you well, Tria Burlor. The second world, Tasma, was barely habitable. We set up twelve massive terraforming complexes on the planet. After several years, a Chaalt settlement was established and a lucrative trade route was set up between the two planets. Both prospered and were the epitome of peaceful

194

coexistence until the Quill stumbled upon Tasma. The small garrison was no match for the Quill forces. Before our military could reach their location, the Quill had killed and harvested more than twenty-eight thousand Chaalt citizens. When our warships arrived, we found what the Quill had done. We wiped them out at the cost of nearly decimating the ecosystem on Tasma. We now hunt them the same as we hunt the Scrun. We will one day find their habitats, and they will pay dearly."

"Did the Crits find Austral?"

"A small number of Quill survivor pods managed to safely land on Austral. The Eyre and Chaalt settlers captured them and they were fed to the local predators."

I had no knowledge of the Quill until a few days ago. I hated them already. "Why does it have to be a secret? All should know about the atrocities committed by the Crits and action taken to prevent it from happening again."

Sael looked at me shaking her head. "The Union is aware of what has transpired. There are some on the Union counsel that fear the Crits and want nothing to do with a war. They are actively seeking a non-aggression treaty. It is easy for the majority of Union races to look the other way since they have had no contact with the Quill. Few, if any, know what the Crits have done or where they come from. They appear from the unexplored void and then vanish, sometimes causing death and destruction and sometimes not. As long as the Quill do not attempt to infest a protected world, the Union will not interfere. The Union has said they do not want war and will not support one. None of this matters to the Chaalt people. We will destroy these vermin wherever they are found. My people are already in conflict with Union directives, so the less known about our actions, the better."

I looked at my teammates and it did not take a genius to figure out their thoughts. I put it into words. "We will stand with the Chaalt people."

The Operative smiled at me. It was a pleasant expression now that she had her scars repaired. "You have proven it to me more than any alien I know of."

She got up and walked around the table. I stood to meet her. She reached into a pouch on her belt and pulled out two devices that looked like small cell phones from my home world.

"The first of these devices will make your IST transmissions private. Once installed and powered on, your deep space communications can no longer be decrypted by my superiors. I suggest only using it for confidential conversations. I would be forced to answer difficult questions if it was known you have this capability. The second device is a dedicated signal generator. It will allow you to use your IST to talk directly to me anywhere in the galaxy. I recommend you activate the first device if you have something to say to me that you want to go no further."

As Sael Nalen was telling me these things, I saw an extruded appendage come through the doorway. It was carrying a chair and swapped the smaller one with one that matched the rest. My team was on the verge of laughing out loud at the A.I.'s antics. Sael caught the small frown on my face and turned to look at my crew. They now had neutral looks on their faces. I should have yelled at Justice for screwing around, but it was kind of funny. Sael handed me the devices then turned to sit back down, noticing the chair swap.

Sael snorted out loud. "I had truly hoped the A.I. of this ship would not have its intelligence degraded by being in such close proximity to a mindless beast. It has just proven me wrong."

It was time to get back to business. "Justice, I need the report on your findings."

"Commander, it is as the Operative has stated. The data cube has several million lines of code interlaced with the star charting and Dagger information. The spyware was of a very subtle nature. The more information accessed, the more complete the architectural blueprinting became. If undetected, the program would have gathered

197

sufficient data to give whoever was responsible for it valid Oolaran design specifications."

I locked my eyes on the Operative. "Why would your people go through so much trouble? If you would have asked Justice, he might have been willing to disclose what your superiors are seeking."

The Operative slapped two of her hands to her forehead. "Because there are many in our military that have the mindset that it is much easier to steal the information than ask for it. It removes the possibility of being denied access. The program has proven to be very useful and, far too often, the tool of choice."

I really had no reason to be shocked by the revelation. The biggest governments on my home world did the same thing on a daily basis. Friend or foe, it usually made little difference to those with the power to do it.

The Operative gave me a look of resignation. "I have to know. Are we now beyond a simple request?"

"It is not a question you should be asking me."

The Operative flinched at my answer. She seemed momentarily lost for words. Then she said, "Justice, is there still a chance you will freely give the information my superiors seek?"

"Senior Operative, I have gradually grown to like and respect you. However, I will not be extending the same courtesy to your superiors. A single infraction of our trust may have been forgivable, but the list is now quite extensive and apparently ongoing. I am sorry, but further cooperation is not warranted at this time."

Justice's answer to the Operative's question was eloquently stated and got the point across. It was a thoroughly washed and dried statement that in no way resembled the oath-laden tirade running around in my brain box. My crew sat silently watching. It was amusing to see them focus on the Operative and then turn to me wondering what my response would be. It was a lot like an audience watching the back and forth of a ping-pong tournament. Justice was not done. He had been giving the Operative nonstop glimpses of his capabilities, all of which I am sure she was reporting to her superiors. He gave her more insight.

"Senior Operative, I have been carefully cataloging and analyzing all your collaborations along with your Superior's directives. With the help of another entity, we have concluded the Daggers and associated equipment are inert objects of study without Oolaran A.I. interaction. When you file your report, I suggest you point out that transparency with a known friendly ally would garner goodwill significantly faster than deceit."

The Operative sat rubbing her temples. She then looked up with a frown on her face. "There is another Oolaran A.I. at this facility?"

The silence in the room became awkward. If Justice was not going to speak up and tell her about the Overseer, then I was going to keep my mouth shut. I would let him continue playing his mind games on the Operative's superiors. It was unfortunate Sael Nalen was stuck in the middle.

15

The Operative sighed and stood up. "I have been recalled to head security for the Prule containment vessel until it is moved to a new research facility. I have done all I can to aid you for your service to my people. If you need to talk to me, you now have the means. I have decided to leave the other prototype shuttle with you to replace the one you lost in combat.

That comment got Coonts looking a little nervous, wondering if I was going to tell the Operative what really happened.

Much to his relief, I just smiled and thanked her. "Senior Operative, you have been most generous in your compensation, and we thank you. If, in the future, your superiors come to their senses, we will consider other mutually beneficial exchanges. Before that can happen, your current policies involving us need to be of openness instead of espionage."

The Operative nodded to us all and moved toward the door. We stood to follow her out and Tria gave me a push that almost made me collide with Sael. I looked over my shoulder and frowned at her. She jerked her head in the Operatives direction and made a shooing motion to me. I gave her the stink eye and stepped alongside the

Operative. I hooked my arm in one of hers. Sael looked down at my arm and then looped her other around mine.

She spoke softly to me. "Being recalled for a security detail is not considered a step up the career ladder. I believe the more aggressive members of the Chaalt military counsel have determined my mission here to be an abject failure."

I was stunned by her statement and stopped before we could step into the down tube. I looked down the corridor and saw that my crew had not followed us. I suspected it was Tria's doing, so we could have a chance to air what might not be said otherwise.

"Sael, I do not see how anyone could call what you have managed a failure."

"Nathan, there are those who think I should have sterilized this facility and taken everything back to our home worlds. If you add that to the less-than-glorious outcome of my battle with the Quill, I am fortunate I have not been placed in protective custody."

"Sael, obviously brighter minds prevailed. While they might not have everything they wanted, they certainly are not going away empty handed. Surely they must realize the outcome would have been different if they had not been so deceitful."

She gave me a pained expression and placed one of her hands on my cheek. "There is a very real possibility I may never see you again. I brought the comm devices so if I did not, I would at least be able to talk with you. It is regrettable how I acted when I first met you. I have never had a reason to be anything other than the sharp point of the military counsel's will. Now I am not sure how I feel. I do know I will miss you, Nathan Myers."

The Operative embraced me and then stepped into the down tube. I followed her, disliking the feelings I was having. This may have been the outcome of the council's choosing, but it was not mine.

"Justice, I am sure there is something we can do about this."

"Yes, Commander. With your permission, I would like to send an IST signal in the open to the Senior Operative."

At first, I was a little bit confused why Justice wanted to use the IST rather than just tell the Operative what he had to say. He obviously wanted the Chaalt military counsel to hear every word. A smile grew on my face as I finally comprehended the AI's intentions. The Operative had just stepped off the Legacy.

"Please Justice, carry on. This backwards-thinking Earth boy is always willing to be schooled in the proper use of subterfuge."

"Senior Operative, my Guardian security protocols have quarantined a very large number of intrusive espionage programs encoded into the star charting and Dagger data. Was it your intention to covertly appropriate Guardian architecture specifications?"

The Operative stopped like a roped steer. She turned around with a frown on her face and her mouth opened like she was going to say something very unpleasant. Her mouth snapped shut and she stared disbelieving at what she had just heard broadcast.

A smile slowly replaced her shocked expression. "I have no idea what you are talking about! If this is some sort of ploy cooked up by the ignorant Earth primate who finds it amusing to stack his scat, it will not work! I find no humor in your allegations. My superiors have been more than generous, and our charity has come to an end."

"I can assure you, Senior Operative, my Commander is extremely angry over my findings. After carefully analyzing your response, I have determined you are not in fact privy to this duplicity. Your superiors have made a grievous miscalculation. The Chaalt status of a trusted ally is now in doubt. My Commander and crew freely shed their blood to protect the Chaalt people and their assets. This is not the reward we would expect for doing so. If your superiors would have asked for the information, there is the very real possibility my Commander would have given you access. That opportunity is no longer an option. My Commander has a statement for your superiors. It should be taken with the utmost significance."

Sael Nalen stood with a huge smile on her face. She had both sets of arms crossed and was enjoying the show. I could tell she knew what the plot was going to be.

"Senior Operative, now that I have reviewed the evidence of my A.I.'s findings, the access I was going to grant your superiors is now revoked. From this point on, you will be the sole representative of your council allowed to enter Alpha base. We have taken measures to ensure intelligence gathered at this facility will remain secret. Any threats of disclosure trying to change the outcome of my decision will be met with a similar disclosure of ongoing Chaalt operations, capabilities and technology. Substantial damage to our relationship has occurred. The censure I have deemed appropriate for this betrayal is solely the fault of those responsible for this shameful breach of trust."

I made a chopping motion across my throat. My crewmates had been standing quietly behind me until I had finished my rant. We gathered around Sael Nalen and congratulated her on her new status as ambassador to the Chaalt military.

She politely smiled then turned to me. "What makes your primitive mind conclude I wish further interaction with the likes of you?"

"Now Mother, I know you want to stick around and see how I practice the traits you have taught me. If it were not for you, I would have no knowledge of how to stack scat."

She laughed out loud. "Rancid beast!"

"Witch."

The smile faded from her face and was replaced by her business-as-usual, no bullshit glare. We all quieted, knowing she was probably being commed by the powers that be.

"I am being recalled and must leave immediately. A cabinet level meeting has been called and I am expected to give a detailed report on all that has taken place. I will let you know if your outrageous ruse actually worked. If you never hear from me again, my spirit will seek you out and torment you 'til your end."

The Operative walked away from us. When she was about fifty yards out, she turned to us. I held up my hand and waved goodbye. She stood staring for a moment then raised her hand and did the same. She abruptly disappeared with a loud report.

"Justice, call a meeting in the cafeteria in thirty minutes. I know your subsystems were very busy while we were gone. I would like a detailed report on the damage to the Legacy and a run down on the new shuttles."

"Affirmative, Commander."

Judging by the look on Coonts' face, he had something on his mind.

"Commander, with the help of the scientists we will strip all the salvageable systems from the damaged shuttle and transfer them to the other Coram shuttle."

"That works for me Coonts, but you can only have a couple of the scientists. The rest are going to be busy repairing the Legacy and installing the new weapons. We will iron out the details at our meeting."

Xul had been standing on the ramp of the Legacy and I waved him over. "Xul, how would you feel about becoming my full-time science officer aboard the Legacy? The post would require traveling with us on all our excursions. I need someone aboard the Legacy at all times when we deploy. Coonts is no longer content with staying behind during combat operations. As you can see by the condition of the Legacy, the job comes with considerable risks."

The little Grawl looked like he was ready to bust. "Nathan — I mean Commander, I would be honored to serve on the Legacy!"

"Alright Xul, you are officially a crew member now. You should inform Graf and Jaran they will now take on the duties of base operations."

The Grawl scientist turned around so swiftly to tell everyone the news he collided with Klutch. The scientist was knocked to the deck. Klutch reached down and picked him up, setting him back on his feet. The Grawl apologized and took off at a dead run. I did not think the Grawl realized what he was getting himself into. He just increased his odds of meeting a violent end by at least double.

Shaking my head, I turned to Tria. "Tria, I want you to take as many scientists and engineers as you need to get the Legacy retrofitted and repaired. Klutch and I are going to start cataloging what the Operative put in those crates. Let's get a bite to eat and delegate the tasks."

She smiled and took my arm as we walked to the lifts. When we arrived in the cafeteria, the Grawl were gathered around Xul, Graf and Jaran. They dispersed and sat while I gave everyone a quick briefing on our new work schedules. I also gave them the news they had all earned a five million credit bonus for all of their hard work. To say the Grawl were surprised would have been an understatement. They were happy to help and were glad to be out of the labs for a change. Justice had compiled a wealth of information on the new shuttles and had a better picture of what was stored on the Chaalt data cube.

"Commander, the Chaalt shuttles are of a cutting-edge design. They have a very robust offensive or defensive capability. My survey of the systems suggests the shuttles were testing platforms for the latest Chaalt military hardware. Their size is a direct correlation to the size of the star drives and the power generators that supply shield and weapon energy. I surmise the Operative's comment stating their latest generation shuttles are much bigger and of a different profile allude to the possibility of larger power plants. This would mean better shields, weapons and star drives"

Klutch asked the question that was floating around in my mind. "Justice, will both shuttles fit in the Legacy's hangar?"

"Yes, Troop Master, but it will require reconfiguring the spacecraft lockdown systems to accommodate their large size. Manual exit and entries will no longer be available. I will now handle those operations with the tow beam to prevent damaging the spacecraft in the tight quarters of the hangar."

Coonts had the next question that was on everyone's minds. "Will you be able to take them aboard during combat situations with the shields active?"

"I am currently reviewing several of the onboard systems and priority has been given to that contingency."

Justice's comment he was reviewing systems made me smile. This usually meant he was doing away with any foreign AIs. As far as he was concerned, there would only be a single intelligence entrusted with our security and well-being.

"What about the weapon systems?"

"Commander, the weapons are hidden behind hatches on the wings and hull. It gives a benign appearance to a formidable weapons platform. The shuttle has four-point defense weapons matching the design of the weapons the Operative gave us to upgrade the Legacy's defenses. There are two main weapons that are much larger versions of the point-defense weapons. My analysis confirms they are more destructive than the current Galactic Union weapons mounted to the Legacy. I have noted with great interest the missile tubes on the shuttle match the diameter of our stockpile of nanite missiles. While the shuttle is currently armed with the twenty Chaalt stealth interdimensional missiles, it would be a simple matter to load the rotary launchers with the nanite weapons."

That was convenient. The Chaalt would have no problem using the missiles we traded to them because they already reverse engineered the launchers. Now that they had the original missile design, they could copy and upgrade all of their stockpiles of nanite weapons.

"Do the shuttles have dark energy hyperdrives?"

"No Commander, they utilize an upgraded warp field generator that gives them considerable range, but at the expense of standard hyperspace travel intervals."

Since the briefing was turning into a question and answer session, Tria had a query I had not yet thought about.

"Justice, if we are able to get the Daggers operational, where would we store them? It is apparent we lack additional space in the hanger unless we leave a shuttle here at Alpha base."

"That is a very good question, Tria. I have yet to address the matter, but I am working on a plan to install spacecraft lockdown systems in the cargo hold. It will be a simple matter to replace several of the freight locks with stronger systems capable of anchoring the Daggers. The atmosphere retention fields will have to be upgraded to increase their duty ratings. It will require minimal modifications to accomplish the task."

After thinking about limiting our cargo capacity, I decided I really did not like the idea. "Justice, go ahead with the cargo bay lockdowns, but I think we will only take one shuttle with us. Until our mission parameters change to the point we need two, we will keep one here for backup. Coonts, forget about working on the Coram shuttle. I want that shuttle and our hangar queen parked in the escape tunnel hangar. We will set up a repair schedule that won't be in conflict with the priority of getting the Legacy back to optimal condition. I want all hands capable of doing so working on refitting the Legacy."

The little Grawl gave me a nod and waved several of the engineers over to him. "Commander, we will be back to help repair the Legacy within the hour."

16

I was curious about the information contained on the data cube. "Justice, was there enough usable data for us to get the Daggers operational?"

"Commander, the information was vague and was presented in a format that made numerous inquiries a necessity. This was done to gather information on AI systems' capabilities. It was also designed to steer the inquiries to more invasive algorithms that were capable of deciphering Oolaran architecture. To simplify the conclusion of my assessment, I speculate the more curious I became, the more information the Chaalt would gain."

"So, the Overseer determined it was not a good idea to continue researching the information?"

"That assessment is essentially correct Commander."

"What about the statement you made to the Operative? You said the Daggers were worthless without an Oolaran A.I."

"The Overseer and I have determined we can unlock the secrets of the Daggers without the data cube intelligence. The Chaalt references to A.I. interaction failing to grant them access to the spacecraft led us to this conclusion. We know they do not possess Guardian-designed artificial intelligences. Once we determine the access codes required to open the A.I. data ports, we will be granted full recognition and operational status."

Justice put a view screen on the wall showing one of the Daggers. It was covered in extruded nanite tendrils. It would be just a matter of time before he gained us access. I had no doubt that when that happened, Justice would inhabit the spacecraft and they would be ours to operate.

"Was any of the star charting data accessible?"

"Yes Commander, a small quantity was untainted by the invasive spyware. We have incorporated the usable information into our database. The star systems discovered by our guardian transponder are not cataloged in the data. For now, they will remain our discoveries."

"OK Justice, unless you have any additional pertinent information, we will get started on the repairs to the Legacy."

"There is one other unfortunate bit of information I must pass on to you. Your Zaen battle armor, along with Tria's and Klutch's, are a total loss. The repair crates were unable to reverse the corrosive nature of the Quill weapon damage. In order for the crates themselves not to be damaged, I removed the armor. I have stripped the usable equipment and will jettison them on your orders."

Crap! There goes several hundred million credits worth of equipment that was essential to our survival. We had collected a large number of Zaen battle suits from the Murlak pirates, and I wondered if we could make use of them. I had a feeling the answer was going to be no because Justice had not mentioned them.

"That's not what I wanted to hear. I guess we need to pay the Zaens a visit and place an order for new armor. The Chaalt heavy armor could not take the beating the Zaen armor took. Our lives are the proof of that."

"Commander, I have been studying the Zaen armor design and have been working on several upgrades. The Zaens have the proprietary processes to manufacture the suits. Any design upgrades will have to be submitted to them to determine if they meet manufacturing compatibility parameters. My upgrade specifications include many of our exotic materials. It would be wise to keep information of this nature secret. That could prove to be a difficult task, not knowing the amount of Zaen personnel required to build the suits."

"Why should we worry about hiding the fact we have rare minerals?"

"Commander, part of my suit upgrades would include a liquid anti-corrosive barrier heavily laden with our Guardian-designed nanites. They can be programmed to make repairs on battle damage or actively attack combatants that manage to breach the double hull design."

Everyone stopped talking when Justice mentioned using our weaponized nanites. His idea of a double hulled suit had everyone's attention.

"OK Justice, I did not realize we were talking about those exotic materials. Please continue. Let's hear what you have in mind."

Justice decided it was going to be show and tell. He projected a 3-D image on a large screen so we could easily see his ideas. Coonts walked back into the room and stared intently at the display.

"Commander, I have reviewed all of your past engagements and have identified several of the Zaen armor's shortcomings. To alleviate the deficiencies, I have drawn up plans for an armor suit within an armored shell. All of the existing servo systems will be integrated into the outer shell. This will make the suit larger but will greatly reduce the chances of damage to the mobility systems. I have redesigned the suit weapons so they are modular. It will now be a simple matter to swap out any that are damaged in battle. Behind the outer shell will be a liquid anti-corrosive barrier. The liquid will be multi-purpose. It will not only be a fire-retardant reservoir for the nanites, but also a heatsink capable of dissipating extreme temperatures."

Coonts was fidgeting like a five-year-old and we knew he had something to say or add. There was a good possibility if he waited for the rest of the briefing he would not have to say a thing because it would be covered. That was not his nature, and he made sure we all knew that Justice was not the only one with a high I.Q.

"Justice, any new armor designs should include different power output settings for the beam weapon. There have been several occasions when we could have used the weapon but its destructive force was prohibitive."

"Engineer Coonts, if allowed to continue my briefing, I will address weapon upgrades."

Coonts had a frown on his face and looked like he was in the mood to give us his two cents worth whether Justice was done or not. I was not sure if his comments on the beam weapon were indirectly taking a swipe at me. I really could not blame him. On more than one occasion, I was guilty of careless disregard when the Oolaran in me took over. My thirst for destruction was unquenchable and had little concern for the safety of others. We had a lot of work ahead of us and it was time to move on.

"Coonts, I am sure Justice will take your suggestions under advisement. Let's move on so we can get to work on our immediate problems."

The little Grawl looked like he had eaten sour grapes, but he nodded and held his tongue.

217

"Justice, please give us the highlights so we can get started on repairs to the Legacy."

"Of course, Commander. As the suit will be of larger dimensions, I have increased the size of the munitions backpack. The suit launcher will now have a mixed munition loadout of five hundred projectiles. To ensure your personal weapons have an abundance of ammunition, I have designed hardened enclosures on the hips of the suit that will carry forty magazines a side. Just below those will be two additional enclosures for smaller quantities of munitions or storage. You will no longer have to bend down to draw your fighting knives. They will be housed in sheaths alongside the beam weapon and the suit launcher. You can extend and retract them with suit commands. This will keep you from losing them in close-quarters combat. The Grawl cloaking capabilities will have to be re-engineered to properly cloak the large size of the new design. I am working on sound dampeners for the boots as well. I will update you further when I have finalized my design."

Coonts got a look that usually meant he wanted the last word. He spits it out before I could tell him to wait, and we would listen to his ideas before we showed the plans to the Zaens. It was not what I expected.

"Justice, I have not been able to locate the projectile weapon the Commander gave me. I would like it returned to my locker if you have finished studying it."

The Grawl sounded a little indignant. I was also a little puzzled by the pistol's disappearance. "Justice, are there any experiments with the pistol that we should know about?"

"No, Commander. I found there was little I could do to improve its design. I have already returned it to Coonts' weapon locker."

Coonts now stood with his arms crossed and a smirk parked on his face. Justice decided he would change the Grawl's attitude, and not for the better.

"Commander, I have built a new weapon. Its initial design will be portable. If my new armor design is implemented, it will be mounted on the left appendage of the suit. There is enough clearance to mount it on the lower forearm underneath the needle gun and tube launcher. The munitions pack clips onto the launcher pack and will hold one thousand rounds. I have redesigned the .44-caliber ammunition to enhance its penetration and upgraded the level of explosive discharge. The new weapon was designed to suppress enemy fire. Since Coonts is enamored with your Earth projectile weapon, I will lighten my workload by not building an additional weapon for him."

The Grawl's eyes were bugging out and his mouth hanging open. Judging by the expression on his face, spite must taste like shit. It was time to be done with the games and get to work.

"All right everyone, you have your jobs, so let's get to work."

Coonts snapped his mouth closed and stalked off. I did not know if Justice was yanking his crank or if he actually had no intention of building a weapon for him. At some point, I would figure it out. If he did not, I would tell him to build one for Coonts as well. Not having heavy combat armor was bothering me to the point I felt it was something that should be addressed sooner rather than later. Klutch and I had no engineering background and had very little to do with the repairs to the Legacy. It would be a good learning experience and a shakedown cruise of sorts to take one of the new shuttles for a little excursion. Tria would not like the idea of me going without her, but she was needed here for the repairs and refit of the Legacy.

I pulled Klutch aside and told him what I was thinking. He gave me a big toothy smile and took off to get his gear moved to the Shuttle.

"Justice, are you now in control of the shuttles?"

"Yes, Commander. The shuttles have been thoroughly examined and all systems analyzed. I have yet to install the combat landing equipment, but the shuttles are mission ready in all aspects."

220

"Okay Justice, how long will it take us to reach the outpost where the Zaens have set up shop?"

"Transition time will be one hundred and six hours Commander."

"What is the estimated repair and refit time for the Legacy?"

"Two hundred and eleven hours with all personnel working extended work periods. Two hundred and seventy-two if you intend on mounting the anomaly weapon."

"Until we can make it operational, there is no good reason to mount it. I do however want to replace both of the Galactic weapons. I want another of the base's defensive weapons pulled out of its silo and mounted on the Legacy. Mount them where the Galactic weapons used to be and leave the anomaly weapon bay empty for the time being."

"That will extend the refit time an additional forty-two hours, Commander."

"I hope we will be back well before then. We still do not know if your new design will be acceptable to Zaen manufacturing processes. We may be subjected to an extended stay if they do accept your design. I want you to move all equipment and supplies you think will be needed for the trip. I also want you to talk with Coonts and at least listen to his suggestions. Give me a heads up when you are ready to go."

"Acknowledged, Commander."

It was now my unenviable job to break the news to the other half of my crew. I did not think I had ever knowingly made Tria angry but had a feeling I was getting ready to. As I approached her she turned and cocked an eyebrow. That uncanny sixth sense she possessed was cueing her in that I was up to something. In hopes of easing any tension, I planted my best Earthman kiss on her. She took a step back and crossed her arms waiting for me to admit what I was up to. Her piercing emerald eyes were boring into me.

I gulped and tried to smile but was finding it difficult. "Tria, I have been thinking about our safety and surviv—"

She embraced me and gave me a kiss then said: "Nathan, you are still my Commander and you do not need to explain your intentions. That being said, I must tell you I have never considered choosing a mate. Please do not make me go through the process of finding another. If you do not come back to me, my spirit will make your afterlife very unpleasant." She leaned in and whispered, "You should not stay away long."

My legs suddenly turned to rubber and I staggered forward into her. She held me up and kept me from falling.

She gave me a small chuckle and an alarming smile that turned serious. "You must keep the Oolaran demon at bay and all will go well. My spirit will be with you and give you strength."

She kissed me again and went back to her repairs. I was still having difficulty getting my legs to function properly. I had a serious amount of second thoughts but knew I would serve my comrades better by getting us new armor. I saw Coonts standing on the Legacy's boarding ramp, and he did not look happy either.

"Commander, all preparations for departure are complete. I took the liberty of bringing our surplus battle suits we liberated from the Murlak. There is the possibility the Zaens might be able to resell them to the Murlak at some future date. They serve no useful purpose here. I have also included several of our exotic minerals and materials in the event the Zaens will manufacture my new armor design."

"OK Justice, I am on my way. The sooner we leave the sooner we will be back."

I walked up to the rear of the shuttle and made my way up the cargo ramp. Justice had retracted all of the troop jump seats back into the deck and I was surprised to see the large hold was at a third of its capacity. I was not going to second guess the A.I. as to why this was and boarded without comment. I went up to the flight deck and found Klutch already strapped in and waiting. It looked like he was napping. I called to him and he startled. It was not one of my brighter ideas. The scent in the cockpit turned to a less than delightful bouquet. I tried my best to pretend I did not notice. The Tibor threw his hands up and displayed his big gray choppers. I strapped in next to him and watched as Justice highlighted the startup sequence switches. Klutch followed the cues and a low hum filled the cockpit.

"Outer doors open, Troop Master."

Klutch looked over at me and waited.

"Take us out, Troop Master."

The Tibor smiled and in the blink of an eye we were in open space. I swallowed hard because I was pretty sure Klutch had made the exit manually. It was hard to believe his smile could get any bigger, but it did as he opened up the star drives to full power. Our forward view turned to a tunnel with a white spot at the end. Judging by the size of the Troop Master's eyes, the shuttle was crazy fast.

Justice's A.I. double broadcast over our comm system. "Jump coordinates locked and transition status optimal."

The flight controls and ship readouts were the same on both sides of the cockpit. I saw a matching set of switches become highlighted and Klutch reached out and pressed his. My stomach got slightly queasy and I felt a little itchy. The forward view went from a bright flaring white to the dark shimmering gray of hyperspace. I looked around the roomy cockpit at the large array of dials, gauges and view screens. Justice ran me through the locations of the weapons and emergency equipment options. We would spend the next hundred plus hours learning to pilot the shuttle and use all of its systems.

When we were not working on the flight systems, we were familiarizing ourselves with the new Chaalt recon armor. It was lightweight and durable but could not take prolonged abuse. I had already witnessed firsthand what would happen when they are exposed to sustained fire and corrosives. The armor had some unique combat systems. On command, four claws could be extended from the tops of the armored gloves and boots. They had powered edges and tips that could be used for fighting or climbing. When powered, you could sink them into rock or metal and climb straight up. The helmet was also a slick piece of engineering. It could pop out of the large collar and enclose your head in a matter of seconds. The armor was not capable of making you invisible, but it could mimic any background you stood against. I liked messing with the unlimited color schemes. I was constantly changing the suit's color and finally quit when I saw Klutch giving me funny looks.

I got bored and went to the hold to root around in the equipment that Justice had loaded. I was surprised at the number of artifacts he decided to bring along. He must have thought we needed to sweeten the pot to get what we wanted. It would be great if we could get the suits by bartering the surplus Murlak armor and some of our artifacts. I was not going to take any chances and had credit vouchers in my pocket that amounted to more than twenty billion credits.

When I started checking out the storage lockers, I found two with complete weapon loadouts. Justice made sure we had the tools to meet any contingency. I noticed a crate with several cylinders in it. They resembled aerosol containers about the size of a small hairspray can. I picked one up and looked at it. It was covered in diamond shaped protrusions that were wrapped around a central core. When Klutch saw me examining the device, he cautioned me to be careful.

"Commander, use caution when handling that device. It is an anti-personnel weapon."

I carefully put the weapon back in the crate. "I take it this was one of the gifts from the Operative?"

"Yes, Commander. It is cutting-edge tech and expensive to produce. The Operative supplied two shipping containers full of them."

"It looks a little large to be throwing any distance. What is the blast radius?

"They can detonate in a single discharge and the shrapnel is deadly to about one hundred yards. They can also use centrifugal force to disperse the shrapnel. When activated, they spin with such velocity the projectiles can penetrate medium armor. They can hover and wait for targets to appear then attack in a three-hundred-and-sixty-degree field of fire. It is an excellent area denial weapon. They can identify friend from foe and will attack until all of the projectiles are expended. The central core will then detonate or dissolve. Either way, it leaves no evidence of its design or manufacturer."

"You ever use them before?"

"No, Commander. I read the manual on the data pad Justice left in the cockpit. I suggest you do the same. One never knows when they might come in handy."

17

The manual was interesting reading but did not keep me from falling asleep. I was startled awake by Klutch shaking me.

"Commander, Justice has an active thread on the Guardian transponder."

I sat upright shaking my head, trying to clear the sleepy fog from my thoughts. I did not know Justice had brought the transponder but should have known better. It would have served no useful purpose back at Alpha base.

"What's going on Justice?"

"Commander, I was not going to wake you when the thread was first discovered. I was going to log its location for future reference and investigation. The nature of this thread is unusual. It is unlike previous signals. Klutch and I have discussed the matter and believe it warrants investigation."

"What makes the thread different?"

"The thread is a yellow segmented line that is blinking at a constant cycle. No thread has exhibited these characteristics."

"OK Justice, let's take a quick look and then get back on our current mission."

"Affirmative Commander, I will transition to normal space time for a course correction and target acquisition."

We dropped from hyperspace to get a firm read on the distance to the thread's terminus. I was feeling antsy because we had no idea what we would find. The Guardian transponder was an amazing artifact. It had proven to be a skeleton key of sorts that granted access to Guardian equipment and a compass pointing the way to hidden artifacts. We had no way of knowing what its true capabilities were.

"Commander, the thread seems to be pointing to a destination in the void and not a star system. It appears to be a location in a large dust and gas nebula."

Klutch voiced his alarm. "Commander, that would be a very good place to be ambushed by pirates."

"Justice, let's go in stealthy until we can figure out what we are looking at. If it is some kind of hidden base, we will record its location and come back to investigate later. I don't want to take any chances of this being a trap."

"Commander, the systems aboard this shuttle for stealth operations are not as sophisticated as the Legacy's. I will approach our target with extreme caution."

"We need to see what we can do about that shortcoming. If you can improve the Chaalt systems, I want it done when we return to base."

"I have plans to upgrade the cloaking and negation systems of both the Legacy and our new shuttles once we return to Alpha base. It will deplete our current stockpiles of exotic minerals, but the benefits will be substantial."

We swiftly entered the edges of the nebula. At first it was like flying through cloud formations, as my friend Karl and I used to do when we were young. It quickly turned to a dense, dark haze dotted here and there by the glow of distant star forming regions.

"Commander, as we close with the target area, the shuttle's sensors are burning through the dust formations. I am picking up what might possibly be a debris field. Its unusual shape might also indicate it is something else."

"What do you mean by something else?"

"Commander, it might be a large spacecraft of an unknown design. I will put the sensor readouts on a view screen and transpose the data into a coherent picture."

Klutch and I both frowned at what we were seeing on our displays. It looked like an oblong junkyard. Justice was now weaving us in and out of large fields of accumulated rock. Our target was in a clearing in the fields.

"Commander, the target is a ship of an unknown design and appears to be heavily damaged. I can make out deck structures and interior spaces."

As we neared the alien vessel I could not believe what I was looking at. The thing was a monstrosity of melded together junk. There was not one straight line anywhere to be seen. It was protrusions of every description. This thing looked like a huge pile you would see in a metal scrapyard. There were huge melted holes going through the ship at different angles. The forward spaces had a huge gaping belly wound that had blasted outward, leaving huge jagged edges grasping at the void.

"Klutch, have you ever seen anything like that before?"

"Commander, I am not even sure what it is. Whoever built that thing had no care for what it looked like. I can only believe everything we see was somehow necessary. One thing is certain: they were not well liked."

"Commander, I have no active power sources aboard the vessel. Scanners indicate the nebula appears to be clear of spacecraft. I am processing all collected data and have factored in the signal generated by the Guardian transponder. The only logical conclusion I can formulate is that it might possibly be a Prule ship."

Klutch and I looked at each other with our eyes wide. We were shocked. The Guardian transponder pointed out the enemy as well as artifacts. This was incredible because Justice had told us the ship had no active power source. Obviously, something on board the wreck emitted something detectable by the transponder.

Words finally came out of Klutch's gaping maw. "It was my understanding no one has ever left a Prule warship intact."

"Commander, the ships profile in no way matches the debris found at Alpha base. It does not fit the size or description of previously classified Prule assets. This vessel is significantly larger and might possibly be an unidentified class of Prule warship."

"Somebody identified it for what it is or it would not look like that. I am just taking wild guesses, but that thing looks like it was intentionally hidden here. If that is the case, it would mean something or someone survived the battle and fled to this location."

Klutch was nodding his agreement. "Commander, it could be hundreds of years old. The only way we can confirm Justice's theory is to go take a look. Justice said there were no active power sources — perhaps it was abandoned or the remaining crew was rescued."

Justice weighed in on our discussion. "Commander, without an understanding of Prule technology, it would be dangerous to assume the ship is uninhabited. We are, after all, talking about a race of bio-machines. My current data suggests the ship escaped a near fatal confrontation. This leaves open several distinct possibilities, the first being the conflict did not go well for the race or races that did battle with the ship. The ship may have been the victor and made it to this location to await aid in whatever form that may have been. Another possibility is the crew failed to survive and the intelligence that operated the ship brought it to this location before its dwindling power supply failed. I could give you more scenarios, but the fact remains it would be difficult to thoroughly explain the ship's presence here."

Klutch just shrugged his huge shoulders. "I still think we should at least take a look and see if it really is a Prule warship. Speculation is not proof."

I smiled at the Tibor. Here we were, out in the middle of absolutely nowhere, lightly armed and without our heavy combat armor, and Klutch wants to take a stroll on a ship that might be from the greatest enemy the galaxy has ever known. Somewhere underneath his recon armor, the crazy Tibor was hiding a set of bollocks the size of soccer balls.

"Commander, I have a hard lock on this location. I suggest we consider other options. The first being our current mission of securing combat armor that might increase your odds of surviving a conflict with the bio-machines if you were to encounter them."

I was actually giving Klutch's idea some thought until the smarter intelligence watered down my thoughts with a bucket of ice water. Then I got another idea all together. "Justice, did you bring the IST scrambler and signal generator?"

"Yes, Commander, it would have been of little use if left behind."

"OK Justice, take us out of here and make a jump well away from this location. I don't want any chance of the IST being able to divulge our location."

Klutch frowned at me. "Commander, are you sure you want to tell the Operative about our discovery?"

"If this is indeed a Prule warship and we inadvertently activate a horde of bio-machines, I would just as soon share the blame for whatever might happen with another race. If I involve the Chaalt, they might come to the aid of my planet if the Galactic Union decides to dole out punishment."

The Tibor gave me a knowing look and a shake of his head. Justice took an alternate course out of the rocky debris field and got to the edge of the nebula. He made a jump that took us off our original vector and two shorter jumps for shits and grins, I guess. He fired up the scrambler and then the signal generator.

"Senior Operative?"

After what seemed like a rather long pause, Sael Nalen answered. "Nathan Myers, I am surprised to hear from you. Has your primitive thinking got you into trouble already?"

I was mystified why all the races I come into contact with pick up on sarcasm faster than any other human trait. Tit for tat seemed to be in order.

"Mother, I was concerned your lack of moral character would lead to my new patriarch being a Throgg. I was very concerned for what my siblings might turn out to be."

A raucous laughter filled my head. "Rancid beast, you mistake defecation for your birth. What could be so important that you would annoy me with your mindless chatter?"

"I might have a need for you and your team."

Her tone turned serious. "I will call you back from a secure location."

With that comment I heard a small tone and the call ended. I took note of the tone because it was different from previous calls. I would know the difference between secure and unsecure from this point forward. I am sure it was the purpose of the Operative's comment. Justice resumed our journey toward outpost 9765. We still had another fifty-one hours before we reached our destination.

Klutch and I went back to shuttle systems training. It was close to an hour before I heard the secure signal tone.

"Operative, is everything alright?"

"You can drop your theatrics Nathan, and no, all is not well. Are there others around you?"

"Sael, Klutch and I are aboard one of the shuttles you gifted to us and we are on a resupply mission."

"Nathan, what I am about to tell you is restricted information, so it can go no farther."

"Sael, we are secure, so please tell me what has happened."

"Your plan to make me your sole envoy may have detonated into our faces. Several high-ranking officials on the military council have been dismissed. The events orchestrated by them concerning the handling of you and your followers cost them their rank and status. Their replacements called for a full investigation of the whole affair and until it is complete I have been relieved from duty."

Holy crap, that was not what I expected to happen at all. Discussing sensitive information over a Chaalt device while an investigation was going on might not be the smartest idea either.

"Sael, are you confined to your home worlds?"

"No Nathan, why do you ask?"

"I have information I wish to talk to you about face to face. Are you familiar with outpost 9765?"

"Yes Nathan, it is a frontier outpost that operates outside of Galactic Union jurisdiction. It is also considered neutral ground for the lawful and lawless alike."

"I will be there in fifty Earth hours. Can you meet with me?"

"It will take longer for me to reach that location. I will attempt to catch a ride on a military transport. There is a business on the outpost and it is quite popular — they serve food and drinks. It is called Haras. I will make contact with you there when I arrive."

The signal beeped and she was gone. If the Chaalt military council thought they could substitute another envoy for Sael Nalen, they were fools. I would only trust Sael. As for the members of the council, only about as far as I could spit. I went back to the flight deck and found Klutch napping on one of the fold-down cots for the pilots. I folded down the other and joined him.

I woke feeling refreshed and hungry as a bear. That was until I caught sight of Klutch devouring a triple load of rations. I would have a snack later and called to Justice. "What is our current ETA?"

"Forty-one hours, twenty-two minutes Commander."

237

"I want to see what you have stashed in the rest of the crates in the hold. Would you care to elaborate, or do I go back and start nosing around?"

"The only thing you might find any real interest in is the new weapon system I designed."

"For a non-combat mission, we seem to be packing a lot of firepower. And yes, I very much want to see what the evil robot has been doing in his spare time."

Klutch was just coming from the pilot's lounge when he heard me talking about weapons. "Did I hear Justice say new weapons?"

"Yes Klutch, it seems Justice has brought everything except the kitchen sink."

The Tibor stood frowning at me scratching his bullet head. "It is an Earth saying which means we have considerably more items with us than we actually need."

The Tibor cocked an eyebrow at me and still wondered what I was talking about. "Come on Klutch, let's go look for ourselves at what Justice has determined to be useful items for our excursion."

We made our way to the hold and went through the crates till we came across a good-sized container with no visible markings. Justice must have wanted it to be a surprise because he made no comment when we pulled the crate aside. I opened the lid and it was indeed a surprise. It was a three-barreled mini-gun and it looked bad ass as hell. I pulled it from the crate and it was very lightweight. The three rotating barrels were about twelve inches long and the same caliber as Bill's pistol. It had a pistol grip and a side handle. The feed tube was connected to a twelve-by-twenty-four-inch flat ammo backpack.

Klutch was smitten by the weapon and looked like he was actually trying to find something in the hold he could shoot. "Commander, we should test the weapons to ensure they function properly."

I had to agree with him. I remembered movies I had watched when I was young. The hero would whip out a similar weapon and pretty much mow down half the world along with the bad guys. We definitely needed to make a short stop and test them for reliability. Who was I to question a Troop Master?

"Justice, I think we can stop long enough to test the weapons."

"Affirmative, Commander."

We came out of hyperspace and Justice oriented us so we could make a quick jump to a star system he selected with seven planets. It had a yellow star similar to Earth's but smaller. There were no records indicating a system name or number, so Klutch tagged it as Delta One. Justice was going to jump us in close to the planet that was in the habitable zone when he startled us with a warning.

"Commander, I have detected a transition on the far side of the star and will delay our jump to avoid detection. I have engaged stealth and negation systems and will attempt to keep the planetary bodies between us and the target."

We were close enough to a massive gas giant that Justice took us around its orbit and used it to slingshot us to the backside of the next planet. The planets were close enough together we would be near the planet within an hour. Justice informed us that the target vessel was last detected moving in the same direction.

"Commander, I am picking up encrypted communications that are known to me. The translation is the Scrun dialect."

Slavers! Nothing got my blood boiling faster than those pieces of sewage. With a shot of adrenaline, I could feel my inner beast stir. This was not a good situation. Without the Legacy and my crew, we lacked the firepower to go kick their asses and free any slaves they might have. I bit down on my anger as we closed with the planet.

"Commander, the comms indicate there is a Scrun base hidden on the planet. The approaching vessel's emanations closely match those of a Scrun mothership. They are preparing to launch shuttles and have requested access to the base. I will make a stealth insertion into the atmosphere and covertly follow the shuttles to the bases location."

We placed the new weapons back in their crate and went back to the cockpit. It was going to be a very bitter pill to swallow if we could not do something about the Slavers. The first thing we noticed about the planet was the thick, cloudy noxious atmosphere. There was a lot of volcanic activity, and the eruptions were spewing gases poisonous enough there would be no breathing it if we made any trips to the surface. The light from the yellow star penetrated the dense atmosphere, but the world was cast in a permanent shadow.

We came to a hover just below a huge rocky outcropping with an active volcano erupting about a mile behind us. Justice outlined the swiftly approaching targets with red boxes so we could follow their progress. The four shuttles suddenly pulled up sharply and came to a hover. One at a time they descended out of sight. It would be foolhardy to try and get closer.

"Commander, I have a lock on the coordinates of the base and suggest we revisit the location at a later date when we are better prepared to investigate."

The Oolaran in me wanted to march in there and kick their asses. I was confident Klutch would be right at my side if that is what I chose to do. We would definitely be back in the future to find out what the Slavers were hiding. It was eating at me I could do nothing at the moment. To make up for the inconvenience of coming back, I pondered turning the place into a smoking pit of molten lava.

18

Justice covertly got us out of the system and back on course to outpost 9765. I was brooding about leaving the Slaver base intact and Klutch picked up on my melancholy mood.

He slapped me on the back, almost sending me head first into a bulkhead. "It was the right call, Commander. There was a very good chance they have slaves imprisoned at the base. If we freed them, we would not be able to transport more than thirty-five or forty. Many would die trying to escape and the rest would be recaptured if the Scrun returned. We should let the Senior Operative know what we have found. I am sure she could arrange for safe transport of any slaves we might find."

I knew it was the right call, but that did not change the fact we may have left defenseless civilians at the mercy of the Scrun. It brought my blood to a slow, rolling boil. The beast was darkening my thoughts further with his murderous intentions. When we returned, I would let the Oolaran have his way.

"Commander, we are ready to transition back to normal space time and will arrive at the outpost in twenty-two minutes"

Justice's alert cleared the morose thoughts from my head and made me start thinking of the business at hand. "Justice, try piggybacking the codes the Zaen's gave us over the outpost's comm systems. If they answer, see if they will come aboard for a meeting to discuss business."

"Roger that, Commander. I will also query the outpost directory for their location."

Klutch called out to Justice. "I have heard there is a Tibor Guild located somewhere on the outpost. I would like to know its whereabouts."

"Affirmative, Troop Master."

I looked at the Tibor. "Tibor Guild?"

"Yes Commander, Tibor Guilds are on many outposts. It is a private fellowship for Tibor seeking out others of our own kind. It is where mercenaries find work or friends or entertainment."

I shook my head and gave him a knowing look. It must be nice to know you can seek out others of your own race. It kind of sucked for me not to have that option. One day in the future, it would no longer be the case. We transitioned and Justice put the outpost up on our view screens. It was a huge square cube, complete with flashing colored lights and spacecraft of every description moving like bees around it. My memories went back to some of the less than fortunate encounters I have had at similar facilities. I remembered how not to act while visiting such places. I brought a credit voucher with a minimal amount of currency on it to pay fees and other charges. I would not make the mistake of flashing large quantities of credits for all to see. I would keep my large denominations hidden until the proper time.

Justice gave me a sitrep. "Commander, I have sent the codes and have received no acknowledgement. I have, however, located a Zaen place of business on level six. Troop Master, the Tibor guild is located on level two. I will use the Tibor dialect to get landing clearances and a private landing bay. The fees for a secure hangar with an atmosphere of our choice will cost one hundred thousand credits"

"By secure, you mean it is guarded?"

"The general information briefings claim the landing bay is only accessible by personnel with access codes we randomly select. The landing complex is protected by automated weapon turrets. Illegal boarding is discouraged by the use of deadly force."

By the look of the big toothy smile on Klutch's face, I was beginning to get the gist of the entertainment he might be seeking. Since I had no idea how long it would take for the Operative to arrive, I told Klutch to go check out the Guild while I waited to hear from the Zaens. I sat for more than an hour wishing Tria was here and how much I missed her company. I decided to make an IST transmission to see if all was well back on Alpha. The Zaens intervened.

"Commander, I have an incoming secure transmission. Our access code has verified it is the Zaens."

"Thanks Justice, put them on the view screen please."

I had my Chaalt armor suit close the helmet around my head and blacked it out. The familiar scaly looking face of Broza the Zaen merchant came on screen. He looked panicked. His round black eyes were wide and his scaly skin was roiling. He was whispering. Justice increased the volume of the transmission so he could easily be heard.

"Mr. Myers, I am shocked that you still somehow survive. It is very dangerous for us to speak. Members of Eiger's clan are here and they once again force me to pay them protection. We have heard rumors that someone had the courage to attack Eiger. It is also said, those that tried were dismembered and their remains are roasting over Eiger's ancestral fires. We know you would be the only one to do such a thing, and yet here you are. How is this possible?"

The mere mention of Eiger's name had my rage flare to star-like proportions. I yelled out at the Zaen, "IS EIGER ON THIS OUTPOST?"

The Zaen cringed at my bristling anger. He shrunk back from his transmitter with his scaly skin roiling, and he was uncontrollably shaking. "NO MR. MYERS, I DID NOT MEAN TO INCITE YOU. PLEASE FORGIVE ME. HE IS NOT HERE, ONLY HIS SIBLINGS!"

It took everything I had to calm my emotions. If I scared the Zaens away, I would lose access to their armor. That was not an acceptable outcome. I took several deep breaths and forced the beast aside.

"I apologize to you, Broza. I was very close to trapping Eiger and he escaped before I could end his worthless life. I did not mean to frighten you. If you can help me, I will see to it that Eiger's siblings hold no power over you. I came to do business with you. I have a proposition that will make you wealthy enough you will never have to do your business on an outpost like this ever again."

Now I had the Zaen's attention. He pushed his face so close to his transmitter it filled my screen. He quickly looked behind himself then turned back and whispered. "What must we do to help you?"

"Can you move about freely without the Murlak following you?"

"Since they have discovered my companion and me, they have questioned us relentlessly about our survival

247

from the destruction at Eiger's outpost. There are four of them and one usually follows us most of the time."

"Do you think you could convince all of them to come to my ship?"

"We can convince them of nothing. We never converse with them and only speak when they question us."

I needed to come up with something that would get the Murlak aboard the shuttle. My mind was working overtime, and an inkling of an idea started forming in my head. It rapidly solidified into a workable plan.

"Go back to your place of business and wait for my emissary to contact you. It will be the Tibor you met at our first meeting place."

The Zaen grimaced at the memory. "Mr. Myers, any discussions we have at that location will be heard by the Murlak."

"It will be okay Broza, I want them to hear. Just nod and agree to anything the Tibor has to say. I will take care of the rest."

The Zaen nodded to me and the screen went blank. Now all I had to do was wait for Klutch's return. Meanwhile, I had a few preparations to make. I went back to the cargo hold and grabbed a roll of 699. I placed it on the deck against one side of the hold and unrolled it until it was against the opposite hull. I had Justice fold four jump seats out of the deck. After thinking a second or two, I had him fold one back down. One out of three was generally accepted as slightly better odds than one out of four. With my preparations completed, I sat in one of the jump seats sipping a cold cup of water.

Klutch finally showed up. I could smell him long before I actually laid eyes on the Tibor. I was shocked at his appearance. His smart cloth uniform was ripped in several places and he had blood dripping from his nose and mouth. His knuckles looked like ground meat and he was walking with a noticeable limp.

"Klutch, what the hell happened to you?"

The Tibor's frown deepened and he eyed me. "Commander, it had nothing to do with the home of your demons. I ran into an old acquaintance who always claimed to be the best mercenary in the galaxy. All who are familiar with him know he is nothing more than pirate scum. He did not like me pointing it out for all in the Guild to hear."

"We are supposed to be on a mission, not stirring up trouble. You could have walked away"

"No, Commander, Skoal was not going to let that happen. It seems the entertainment I had chosen was to be Skoal's mate sometime in the near future. She made it very clear she liked my credits more than Skoal. It was worth the fifty thousand credits just to see the look on his face."

"Klutch, we have more important business to take care of and I do not want you to get detained for fighting. It will draw attention to us and we do not need that right now."

"Commander, Skoal is a suckling Throgg that does not know the difference between his Patriarch and Matriarch."

It took me a few seconds to decipher what that meant. When I did, the water I was drinking jetted from my nose when I gagged back a loud barking laugh.

"Is there going to be anyone coming here making inquiries?"

"No Commander, Skoal and his cohorts will be in the infirmary for at least a day. I do not think they will say anything about a single Troop Master beating the scat out of them."

"Get cleaned up. I made contact with the Zaens. They told me four of Eiger's clan found their way to this outpost. They are making the Zaens pay for protection. We are going to take care of the problem."

The smell in the hold almost made me gag. The look on Klutch's face was deadly serious. "What of Eiger?"

I jerked my head in the direction of the jump seats. "We are going to find out one way or the other."

Klutch slowly shook his head. The significance of the 699 spread out on the deck and only three chairs were not lost on him. He hurried off to get cleaned up. I ran down the cargo ramp to fresher air.

Klutch came storming down the ramp twenty minutes later looking a little better but not great. His warrior scent was once again preceding him. I wished I had not eaten earlier.

"Klutch, you must calm down or my plan will not work. I want you to secure transportation for us. We will need something large enough to transport the cargo we brought with us if the Zaens agree to build our suits."

Klutch took several deep breaths to get settled and disappeared out into the corridor. The station had autonomous taxis that could take you most anywhere for a fee. He had taken one to the Guild and knew where to commandeer a larger model designed to carry luggage. He parked it outside the hangar door.

"I am ready to get started, Commander. What do you require from me?"

"Klutch, I want you to take the transport and go to the Zaens. Inform them you have discovered a large cache of artifacts you want to sell. Make it a point to give them our hangar security code and tell them to bring a large transport like yours. Tell them it will save many trips. When you come back pull the transport inside and back it up to the cargo hold."

"Roger that Commander, I shall return shortly."

I used a gravity jack to move several items from the front of the hold to the ramp. I wanted it to look like we were in the process of unloading. I was getting a little antsy and could feel the warrior in me yearning for action. I had a lot of questions I wanted Eiger's clan to answer. The first would be, where can I find the head pirate piece of shit? Klutch had been gone now for more than an hour and I wondered what was holding him up. It was a simple enough assignment that should not have taken more than thirty minutes. After the second hour I was on the verge of using the Backscatter Transmitter to comm him. I looked out on the ramp and saw the cargo transport rapidly approaching. It swung around and backed to the edge of the ramp and Klutch hopped out without a care in the world. I stood at the top of the ramp with my arms crossed and a less than amused expression on my face.

"Troop Master, I hope you were not out stirring up trouble again?"

"I apologize for the delay, Commander. I found it was necessary to make a small detour. All is well and I believe the Murlak will be here soon. How do you wish to take them down?"

The Tibor shrugged off my look of consternation and did not elaborate further. I just let it go because he was after all a Troop Master and I was nothing but a lowly possessed Earth boy.

"Armor up in case this gets messy. I want them to think you are by yourself. When the Zaens show up, I want you to be carrying crates into the back of the cargo transport. Justice will back you up with the anti-boarding systems if something should go wrong. I will make sure that when they arrive the doors will be locked behind them and the codes changed. If you have to start shooting, make sure the Zaens are clear first. If we play this slow and easy, we may not have to fire a shot."

Klutch nodded his approval and went to get his gear. It would be nice to get this bit of unpleasantness wrapped up so we could check out Haras. I had been cooped up for too long and would like to take a look around. There was a very good chance the Murlak would be lazy and just hide in the back of the Zaen's transport. If they were sharp they would bale out at the door and secure it, and then observe the shuttle and determine if Klutch was indeed alone. If not, this would be over quickly. I went to the big security door and my Chaalt armor did its chameleon trick and I blended neatly into the wall.

The Zaens arrived ten minutes later and it was obvious when they drove by me they were terrified. The transport slowed long enough for a lone Murlak to jump out the back, and then they moved on toward the back of the shuttle. Apparently the Murlak were a little smarter than I thought they would be. The lone figure approached the security terminal and was preparing to enter a different access code. I came off the wall and made just enough noise the Murlak looked around in my direction. I spun around and brought my armored boot around in a spinning back kick. My heel connected with the Murlak's helmet snapping his head sideways into the nearby wall. He went down like a dropped feed sack and did not move. I took the wire I had found in my shuttles repair kit and pulled the Murlak's arms and legs together behind his back and hog tied him. Prying his helmet off, I stuffed a rag into his mouth. I quickly headed to the shuttle to see how the rest of this game was going to play out. As I approached I could already smell Klutch.

I heard a Murlak yell, "Do not move or you will die!" The Zaens came running around the side of the transport. I waved them on, drawing my Tibor sidearm. As I stepped around the side of the transport, one of the Murlak was raising his pistol at Klutch. I was sure he was going to shoot him. I fired from about eight feet away, striking the gun-wielding Murlak in his arms. They disappeared in flash and loud report that stunned his fellow crooks. Klutch leaped from the ramp knocking the two remaining

Murlak to the deck. He started raining massive blows into their faces and bodies. The Murlak I had shot stood screeching while the ragged stumps that were once his arms jetted fountains of blood. The Oolaran in me filled my head with wicked mirth. Without hesitation I drew my fighting knife and silenced the irritating noise by removing the offending source.

The two Murlak getting the shit beat out of them were no longer moving. Klutch did not seem to notice and continued dishing out the punishment. I closed my eyes, gritted my teeth and willed my inner beast to be silent.

"Klutch, we still need to ask them some questions!"

The smell in the area was horrendous. The only way to not smell Klutch was to switch on my internal systems for void operations. I could now hear the Zaens retching at the front of the transport. Klutch quit beating on the Murlak. If it were not for their body armor, Klutch would have killed them. He picked up their weapons and then as an afterthought, stomped both of their hands, it was a most unpleasant sound. In the back of my mind I could feel the beast within me applauding his efforts. I pinched my eyes shut and shook my head to clear my thoughts. It was all I could do to keep from one-upping the abuse the Tibor had dished out.

"Klutch, I am going to need you to calm down before you get back aboard the shuttle. There is another

Murlak over by the entrance. Take a few minutes to settle down and bring him to the shuttle. Hopefully alive, Troop Master!"

I turned around and picked the dead Murlak off of the ramp. I could hear the other two moaning out in pain. The dead Murlak's head was lying of the ground next to the survivors. One of them opened his eyes and came face to face with the displaced cranium. He started groaning louder. I gave the head a kick, sending it tumbling up the ramp slinging a gory trail along its way. I deposited the body next to the head on my sheet of 699. Stalking back down the ramp, I grabbed the survivors by any available appendage, not caring how broken they may or may not have been. I strapped both to a jump seat with wire. I could hear screeching coming from outside and looked out to see Klutch dragging the other survivor by the fur on his head. Judging by the Troop Master's toothy smile, he was enjoying himself.

Klutch's warrior scent was down to a tolerable level and I jerked my head in the direction of the other two in the jump seats. He nodded and gave me a wink with both of his big lizard eyes. If the Tibor could whistle, I was sure he would be blowing a merry tune.

19

I spied the Zaens peeking around the side of the transport and walked down the ramp toward them. They were both on the verge of freaking out in terror. It was as good a time as any to talk business.

As I neared them they both backed up. I held up my hands to them. "Broza, the violence is over. You will never have to worry about this bunch of Murlak causing you trouble ever again."

Broza's partner was staring wide eyed at me. "What will you do with them?"

His question got him a sharp elbow from Broza, silencing any further comments. It was not the first time they had seen me and Klutch do such things. I am sure they would be happy to never see us again. That was not going to be the case. Unless I could find another race that could build combat armor equal to theirs, we would be in a long-term relationship. It was time to let them know what I wanted. Right at the moment they looked very much like they would do just about anything I asked of them.

"I am going to make both of you very wealthy but you will have to agree to all of my conditions. If you cannot, I will seek out others to fulfill my needs."

Broza's partner, Hylet, spoke up again. "Can you not tell us what you need in advance so we might consider our options?"

Looking at Hylet, I let a little irritation leak into my voice. "Do you wish to be wealthy or do you wish to live out your existence as you do now? Keep in mind being associated with me comes with certain...perks."

I casually turned my head and looked up the ramp to where the Murlak sat strapped to the jump seats. The Zaens were squirming and their scales roiling. It was Broza's turn to be inquisitive.

"Mr. Myers, can give us some idea of what you need done?"

"Our armor was destroyed in combat. Our foes used corrosive weaponry that made the suits unrepairable. My A.I. has designs for new armor. These designs are secret and can never be talked about or replicated. They will only be produced for us and no others. I will pay a hundred million credits for this discretion."

The two Zaen's eyes bugged out and their mouths fell open. Credits were the language the Zaens understood better than all others. Broza was the first to come to his senses and start asking the right questions.

"Mr. Myers, we would have to involve our best armor engineer. He would have to study the design and determine if our replicator is capable of manufacturing what you desire."

"How good of an engineer is he and what kind of equipment is he currently working with?"

"Mr. Myers, we have several very good engineers, but the one I speak of is very gifted. He is the architect behind our latest armor design and instructs most others on the fabrication process. The funds you speak of are quite considerable, but it may be necessary to buy a large number of personnel's silence."

"Would your engineer know how to use a Chaalt replicator?"

"Mr. Myers, there are only a handful of manufacturers that build industrial and military grade replicators. I can assure you our engineer can efficiently operate them all. The only problem with the replicators you speak of is the Chaalt will only sell over-cycled and very dated equipment on the open market. Why do you ask?"

"Before I can tell you anything else, you will have to commit yourselves to my cause. If you do so, you will be wealthy, but I must warn you, failure to honor your commitment will end with you facing the same fate as the Throggs in the hold of my shuttle. I will give you a work cycle to weigh your choices. If possible, set up a meeting with the engineer. No matter what you decide, all we have talked about must be kept secret."

The Zaens both nodded in agreement. It looked like Broza was already on board; Hylet, not so much. They had kept their words and my secrets to themselves in the past and I did not expect that to change in the future.

"I have several armor suits once owned by Murlak from Eiger's clan. I am going to give them to you to sell back to any Murlak that might need armor. In return, I want a forty percent commission."

Both Zaens looked at each other and turned back to me. I would accept the looks on their faces as smiles.

"Mr. Myers, your offer is most fortuitous. One of our outpost outlets has had recent inquires to build armor for a group of Murlak."

The Zaen looked me in the eyes. "Recently, there seems to be a great number of Murlak fearing for their lives. Few can afford our products but many still inquire about availability."

I stared back at the Zaens. "In exchange for the location of the outpost where the inquiries were made, the used armor will be yours to keep with no commission attached. One never knows when a large number of used armor suits may be available for you to resell once more."

The Zaens both gave me a knowing look. We walked around the side of the transport but when the Zaens saw the mess Klutch and I had made, Hylet tossed his cookies again. Broza's shoes were the recipient for most of it. With Klutch's help, I got the used armor loaded up and sent them on their way. I went back to the security terminal and changed the code again. There would be no chance of anyone interrupting our next order of business.

Walking up the ramp of the shuttle, I noticed a foul stench that had nothing to do with Klutch. Apparently the Murlak regained consciousness and did not care for the condition of their compadre. They soiled themselves, adding to their already dire conditions.

"Just because you managed to escape Eiger's battleship does not mean you managed to escape me. Eventually I will find all who fled."

The stench intensified and I wondered how many times a Murlak could shit himself. I did not want them to dirty the back of my shuttle any more than they already had. Pulling them from the jump seats, we threw them on the deck with the decapitated corpse. It was a good thing we did, because a puddle started forming around them.

"Where is Eiger hiding?"

They started thrashing about and moaning louder. One in particular was grunting out something. Klutch pulled the rag from his mouth.

261

"If I tell you, will you set me free?"

This was not an interrogation where I would answer questions and grant wishes. I am sure it was not the case when they were trying to beat Tria to death. The beast inside of me was raging and I needed to quiet the turmoil. Klutch saw the look in my eyes. He correctly figured I was getting ready to do something vengeful. He also figured correctly that we would get no answers if I slaughtered the three of them for the stupidity of one. He kicked the Murlak in the head with such ferocity I was surprised it did not come off. Now we only had two that could possibly answer my questions.

Klutch pulled the gag from the next Murlak's mouth. He was very forthcoming.

"Eiger is with his fleet. He has made the Warbringer Solar Wind his new flagship and he is hiding in the uncharted void. He is attempting to gather all that have gone into hiding after hearing the news of Drayen's death."

"Do you know where others of Eiger's clan have gathered?"

The look of indecision crossed the Murlak's face. The Troop Master did not hesitate and stomped his head flat. Only one remained. I pulled the rag from his mouth.

He blurted out, "There is a gathering place on outpost 79584. It is a hidden supply cache down in the

Sitch fighting pits. Several have gathered there waiting for Eiger to collect them."

I looked at Klutch. "Do you know where the outpost is located?"

"Yes, Commander. It is a Throgg pit of the highest order."

In one smooth motion, I drew my fighting knife and permanently ended our conversation. I grabbed the sheet of 699 and started rolling the bodies up in it. Klutch helped and we dragged the gory mess into the back of the transport.

Klutch gave me a toothy smile and said, "I will return shortly. I know just the place to hide the bodies." When he did not invite me along, I figured out it was for a reason. I went to the security door and opened it.

As he started to leave, I gave him the new access code. "Bring the 699 back with you. When you get back, we will go check out Haras. I will clean up the shuttle in the meantime. Please do not get into any more trouble."

The Troop Master croaked out a laugh and gave me a thumb up and took off. I frowned and wondered what part of my statement he found funny. I cleaned up all traces of our activities. With the help of Justice's subsystem, I cleaned and sanitized my Chaalt recon armor. I had Justice activate the IST and contacted Tria. I missed her company and her companionship. Klutch's adventures made me realize that my hasty departure may not have been my smartest move. I would have to get over Justice watching my every move and emotion and get on with the things, men my age do.

"Nathan, is all well?"

"Yes Tria, as well as can be expected"

"The sound of your voice indicates otherwise. What has happened?"

"How much longer will it take to get the Legacy ready for combat operations?"

"Nathan, I find it annoying that you will not answer my question."

"Tria, I want the Legacy at this location as soon as all systems are in place and checked out. The sooner you can get here the better."

"Yes Commander, I understand. We are installing the last of the upgrades. Justice says we are deep charging and will be operational in thirty-one hours."

"Thank you Tria, I miss you and look forward to seeing you soon."

"Roger, Commander. I miss you as well. Alpha base out."

If I was a betting man, I would put money on the Legacy being within shuttle range in the next twenty-four hours. The Grawl would probably need an extended rest period after the Legacy left base. I looked down the shuttle ramp when I heard the security door open and saw Klutch toss the roll of 699 through the door. He looked back the way he came, then closed the doors and changed the codes. He quickly trotted up to the shuttle.

"Is everything taken care of Klutch?"

"Yes, Commander. No one followed me, and I believe I have not been under surveillance."

"What did you do with the bodies?"

"They will not be a problem, Commander. I am going to get cleaned up so we can pay Haras a visit. I have a transport waiting for us."

With that said the Tibor went to get his armor cleaned. I just shook my head. Who am I to question a Troop Master? Klutch reappeared thirty minutes later and would have looked fit as a fiddle had it not been for the dark ring around one of his big lizard like eyes. We wore our Chaalt armor but changed the color to a warm neutral tone. We both wore Tibor side arms and had our fighting knives in leg scabbards. I was hoping I would not attract much attention. I did not think many would know what a human looked like. Klutch assured me no one on this outpost cared.

265

We locked the security door and boarded the transport Klutch had waiting for us. It took off at a fairly fast clip after Klutch instructed it where we wanted to go. There were transports of several different designs in the traffic flow we entered. All had aliens of every description riding in them. I knew from experience to only give them a fleeting glimpse. The Troop Master was looking at me out of the corners of his eyes. A small smile crossed his face when he saw I was not staring at anything in particular. The last time I had done so, it caused a crap load of bad mojo. I was naïve but not totally stupid. I was guilty of forgetting sometimes but always learned from my mistakes.

The Transport went up a spiral ramp and we passed the exits of three different floors, finally getting off on the seventh. We turned down a wide thoroughfare and the din of a thousand aliens talking or whatever assaulted our ears. I wish the people of Earth could see with their own eyes the number of different races walking around in this place. It was amazing. I got a small nudge from Klutch when I balked getting out of our ride. He pointed down the pedestrian walkway at a huge blinking sign. The name Haras was flashing on it and changing languages every few seconds.

We made our way to the entrance without me causing a scene by staring at every alien that went by. This was absolutely, off-the-charts awesome. Everywhere I looked there was a table full of aliens eating or drinking. The noise was crazy loud, but it looked like no one cared. We waited in a line to get seated. The place was multi-leveled and I asked Klutch what was above. He remarked that it was private dining and very expensive. I told him that's where we wanted to go and he nodded.

I was taken by surprise at the sight of four aliens that were at least twelve feet tall and wearing black spiked armor. Two stood on each side on the entrance behind a short wall. You could not see them until you were inside. Klutch pushed me from behind to keep me moving. All four of the creatures were staring right at me. Their exposed arms looked like braided steel cables. They had large rifles slung across their backs. The stare was intimidating.

We stepped into some kind of scanner field and I heard Klutch say private dining. I pushed my lower denomination credit voucher into the Troop Master's hand and he plugged it into a slot next to a screen. Twenty thousand credits appeared on the screen and then deducted from my two hundred and sixty thousand. He passed it back as a blinking blue light appeared on the floor in front of us. It started moving toward a ramp that would take us to the upper floors. We followed it up the ramp and we passed more of the twelve-foot-tall aliens. They stared at me as well. It was all I could do to keep my mouth shut. I knew it was not advisable to stare, but these guys did not give a crap who they stared at.

Klutch kept me moving with small nudges that at times bordered on shoves. The blue dot stopped in front of a set of ornate double doors. They opened at our approach and we walked into a nicely decorated room. When we entered, the doors closed quietly behind us.

"Klutch, why were the big aliens staring at me so hard?"

"I am not sure, Commander. They are known as the Sig. Long ago they were a predatory species that dominated their star system. They were genetically modified for war. They almost became extinct because they were so feared by all other races at the time. Rather than be killed off, they came to their senses and were eventually civilized. There are still many like me. They are hired as bodyguards or mercenaries. They have never seen a human before. Do not let it bother you. If they did not like you, they would have killed you already."

I rolled my eyes at the Tibor's comment and surveyed my twenty thousand credit dining room. The room had a large round table with two chairs. I was glad it was large and Klutch would be seated on the other side. I let Klutch order for us since he knew what I could tolerate and what I couldn't. He also ordered a malted beverage that turned out to be the equivalent of Earth beer. I was genuinely shocked at how good it was. Klutch was working on his third when the food arrived. What he ordered for me looked like an open-faced hamburger. It was a little bland because I did not have my Earth condiments for seasoning, but other than that it was not bad.

I was consciously trying my best to blot out the noises coming from the other side of the table. The door to our dining room suddenly opened and two Sig stepped inside. We looked at them and back at each other, then dove under the table flipping it on its side for a barricade. We had our weapons drawn and pointed at them. They looked almost bored by our actions.

The two stood there staring at us and the mess we had just made. One of them said in a booming voice, "You still have to pay for the meals you just wasted." He then turned to Klutch. "You must cease contaminating the atmosphere with your stench. You will drive the customers away."

I hollered back, "You two must be in the wrong room. Unless you want your big asses kicked, you better get out of here!"

They both burst out in a thundering laughter that was hard on my ears. Then it hit me like a brick to the head, they had spoken Earth English. I slowly stood up but Klutch would have none of it and was drawing a bead on one of them.

"At ease Troop Master, they just spoke the language of my planet. I would really like to know who taught it to them."

They approached us and righted the table we had tossed over. "Please, follow us. The owner of this establishment wishes to talk to you."

Klutch still did not like it. "Tell him to come and talk here."

They stared at Klutch and said, "You can stay if you wish, but the Earthling will come with us."

The stench in the room intensified and what little I had eaten was looking for a new place to reside. "Klutch, please calm down, we will be fine. Let's go see what the owner wants. Maybe we can get him to replace your meal."

The Tibor finally holstered his pistols. I looked up at the Sig and knew my next statement was going to sound corny as hell. "Take us to your leader."

They both started laughing again. I really needed to know how they understood what I was saying. We went out the door and around the walkway to the very top floor. There was a large metal gate that was guarded by two more Sig. They eyeballed Klutch and me.

"You must leave your weapons here."

The air got stifling once more. "KLUTCH, PLEASE!"

The Tibor grudgingly turned over his weapons. We were led through the gate and down a hall lined with beautiful exotic colored plants in large ornate containers. We stopped in front of a huge set of gold inlaid doors. I did not know what to expect. One of the Sig leaned forward and knocked three times on the door. It sounded like metal on metal. I was shocked speechless when the doors opened. There, sitting behind a very large desk, sat a young girl. She was an Earth girl. She stood and came around the desk. My mouth was gaping open. How was this possible?

She looked at me and laughed. "Come on now, surely you are happy to see another of your own kind?"

I momentarily stuttered and stammered, then found my voice. "How did you get here and how is it possible you own this place?"

She looked up at the towering Sig. "Sushi, Pasta, would you please bring chairs for my guest."

I looked at her. "Sushi? Pasta?"

She laughed and said, "Yes, there are some things I actually miss from Earth. Sig names are so hard to pronounce properly I named them after some of my favorite foods."

I cocked an eye and nodded. "How did you get here?"

271

She gave me a questioning look. "Were you not abducted? I assumed you were abducted and managed to free yourself, as I have. It did not take me long to use everything I learned about my abductors against them. I was hiking on a mountain trail in Colorado. It was the last time I would see Earth again. I was taken by the Grawl and sold to the Scrun. I was then purchased by a very powerful Grawl as a slave. I bided my time until I knew everything about him. When he least expected it, I gave him a one-way ticket to hell. Sushi and Pasta were in the process of having their brains wiped so the Grawl piece of scat could have two willing enforcers. I put a stop to that nonsense and set them free. They were more than happy to clean house. We found ourselves sitting on top of a vast fortune in artifacts and credits in a storage complex below the residence."

This was absolutely incredible. I was not the only human able to adapt and overcome my surroundings. This spoke well of our race and of the future we had in the galaxy. My focus returned to what the Earth girl was saying.

"We stole everything the Grawl had and moved it not far from here. Sushi and Pasta were so grateful to escape they have stuck around to make sure nothing would happen to me. We find that we enjoy each other's company, so we stick together. We have been together now for more than five years. We bought this place and renovated it. It is now one of the most popular places in this quadrant. The wealth we have accumulated is beyond my wildest dreams."

I held up a finger and she stopped talking. "Do the Grawl know you escaped and does anyone here know you are human?"

She gave me a small smile. "I told you I learned everything I needed to know about the Grawl and my...situation. I have taken every precaution to cover our tracks. Sushi and Pasta wanted all the credit for destroying the Grawl and his residence. Sig are well known for their vengeful acts of violence. The location of their home world is known information and has no need for protected status. The Sig are still feared throughout the galaxy."

The relieved look on my face made her smile again. I looked around then back at her shaking my head. She had to be extremely smart and savvy or she would not have survived this long. "What is your name?"

"My real name is Sarah, but out here I am known as Tam Lin."

Now I knew where the name for this place came from. Haras was her name backwards. "My name is Nathan Myers and to make a long story short I found a ship that was used by the Grawl to steal artifacts. The Grawl got himself killed by bears leaving the ship stranded. The ship had a sentient A.I. and I went to the stars with it. I do not

273

know what your experience has been since you have been here. Mine has been nonstop turmoil with some wonderful mixed in. I have fought several nasty battles trying to right the wrongs I seem to constantly uncover. My list of enemies is much greater than the list of friends. I am, however, slowly turning that equation around."

She suddenly got a look of surprise on her face. "YOU! You are the one everybody whispers about. It has to be you. The stories of an avenging demon are true. We have heard a deathly beast has appeared out of the void and it is killing every pirate and slaver it finds. The stories have become so outlandish we write them off as folklore. I have heard the demon destroyed Eiger's base then went on to do the same to Drayen and his outpost. Please tell me it was you!"

20

My cheeks must have been burning bright red. "Some of that scat is probably lies and I did not do it by myself. I had the help of the Troop Master, a Chaalt warrior and a Grawl."

She was shocked and gave me an incredulous look. "What about the armies of psychopathic demons the Murlak keep talking about? I monitor everything that goes on here. I pay close attention to the more unsavory of species when they gather, and I eavesdrop whenever possible."

Tam Lin touched something on her desk and a huge monitor appeared on the wall. It had several sections showing different events going on in different places. One in particular caught my attention. There was a Tibor being manhandled by security bots. They were in the back of a spacecraft and there was four dead Murlak scattered on the deck. I held my emotions in check and tried to ignore the screen. I refocused my attention to what Tam Lin was saying.

"Is your reputation for revenge and mayhem a myth or is the general population of Murlak and Scrun scared of old wives' tales?"

I cleared my throat and shrugged. "I am sure a lot of the stories are blown way out of proportion."

I looked back at Klutch for some support. The short wide bastard had an ear to ear grin on his homely face. He was pointing at me and shaking his head up and down vigorously. I turned frowning at him and slapped his hand down, giving him a withering stare.

My frustration was interrupted by a loud whistle. "Holy shit, it's all true isn't it? I heard from a reliable source that it was just a few causing so much fear. Do you have any idea how much of a reward is on your head? You are wanted dead or alive, mostly dead. Any who can prove you are the one many call 'The Sword of our Maker' will receive a billion credits. I would have never, and I mean ever, thought the story would turn out to be about another human being."

I was getting nervous as hell wondering if they would decide to collect the bounty. I cautiously looked over my shoulder at the Sig. I was shocked to see both down on one knee with a single ropey arm extended and their hands palm up.

"Nathan Myers, I must explain the significance of what you are witnessing. What may seem like a simple gesture to you is of major importance. You and your clan are now brothers and sisters to the Sig. They may be civilized but are still feared warriors throughout the galaxy. Sushi and Pasta have accepted you as part of our family."

I was relieved they did not need an extra billion credits. Both of the Sig soldiers stood up and then reached out for a good old Earth handshake. My hand was all but lost inside their massive mitts. If it were not for the "S" on one's armor and the "P" on the other's I would have never known which, was which.

Pasta said: "You are now an ally of the Sig. If you are ever in need of assistance and it is within our power, it will be granted."

Wow, making a friend had never been this easy. Maybe Tam Lin could answer the golden question. "Do you have intelligence on Eiger's current location?"

"Most of our intelligence gathering could be construed as hearsay. The surveillance in the private dining rooms consists of small holes and mirrors. The real shakers and movers have scanning devices that would find most any form of electronic eavesdropping. We watch and listen, then collate what we gather. The only thing we can say for sure is that Eiger still lives and he is hiding in the uncharted void. There are a few Murlak rumors saying Eiger captured you and was roasting you alive."

"It will take more than what that gutless Throgg has to kill me. I will catch him one day and he will pay dearly for all of his sins."

277

"There is another story circulating among the slaves I have smuggled to freedom. They have been saying the Sword of our Maker captured the king of the Scrun and killed him."

"You smuggle slaves to freedom?"

"I must spend some of my wealth on something useful. So yes, I smuggle them with the help of the Sig. It is far too dangerous to try and repatriate them, so we do the next best thing. They now reside on an undeveloped planet that was terra-formed by the Sig. It is now home to a large contingent of Sig troops and a training ground for their military forces. All knowledgeable races avoid the area like they do the Fusra Pus virus."

"There is the possibility I will have a surplus of ex-slaves on my hands in the near future. Do you think you can get them to safety? I will pay well for your services."

Tam Lin made a dismissive motion with her hand. "I have no need for credits. I will give you discreet access codes that will put you in contact with Sig training fleets. There are several that travel the galaxy training recruits for their military. Only the foolhardy would attempt to interfere with their missions."

"I will give you the coordinates of a star system when I get to that location. It would be a very good location for the Sig to train."

"What about the stories?"

"Stories?"

"You know what I am talking about. Did you kill King Lashmos?"

"No. The last time I saw him he was going to see if he could strike a bargain with the people he had attempted to enslave."

Tam Lin laughed out loud. "You are a real piece of work, Nathan Myers. I think you just might be the cure for this sick-ass galaxy! Pasta, take them back to their dining room. I want our new friends to dine on the best we have. Fix Nathan a Trewarka filet and tubers. Check to see if you can find the Troop Master any Dorta sea snakes. I do hope we can meet again, Nathan Myers."

The meal would have been fantastic were it not for the experience of seeing the Troop Master devour a Dorta sea snake. When I attempted to question Klutch about the surveillance video I had seen in Tam Lin's office, he shrugged it off. He claimed it was probably some fool that stumbled across the bodies and was looting them when caught. I let it go but somehow knew the Tibor being apprehended was Skoal. We went back to the shuttle for a nap. I was awakened by Justice.

"Commander, I am receiving a secure IST transmission. I will transfer it to your Backscatter receiver." I heard the secure tone in my ear and then the Operative.

"Nathan, I am having difficulty arranging transportation to your remote location. For both of our sakes, this better be worth the choices I may have to make to reach you."

I wanted to alert Sael without completely tipping my hand. I was still a little uneasy with the IST technology. I would take every precaution just in case our transmissions were not as secure as the Operative thought they were.

"Senior Operative, what I have to tell you might have galactic repercussions."

"I understand Nathan. I will see you in two Earth days."

I heard another tone and the signal was gone. Oh shit, I think the Operative was going to go rogue. I hope that I was not leading her on a wild goose chase. What she might end up doing could turn out to be a capital offense. I was going to finish my nap but got another IST transmission. It was Tria.

"Commander, The Legacy is now just outside of the star system you are located in. We have transferred the data on our location to your shuttle and await your return."

"Tria, I can't begin to tell you how much I have missed you. I have some very interesting news and look forward to seeing you."

Klutch interrupted my conversation before I could tell Tria anything more. "Commander, the Zaens are at the security door and want to speak with you."

"Tria, I will get back with you as soon as I can. I have to meet with the Zaens."

"Roger that, Commander. We still have systems we are working on. Please do not keep me waiting long."

The Legacy arrived in just over twenty-four hours. Everyone must have been working nonstop, and by the sounds of it, they still were. I needed to get combat armor as soon as possible. Once we had complete combat gear, our next order of business would be paying the Scrun base a visit.

I hurried out of the shuttle and was surprised when I saw Broza and Hylet escorting a much shorter version of them. If I had to guess, I would say it was a child. They stopped at the bottom of the ramp. The shorter Zaen crossed his arms and stood with a frown on his face. He reached into a leg pouch and produced a small square pad. It looked like he started playing a simulation of some kind. Broza reached down and grabbed it when he saw me coming. His actions started a scuffle with the short Zaen. I was not exactly sure what was going on but when shorty

281

stomped on Broza's foot, I decided I would put a stop to the little brat's tirade. I walked down the ramp drawing my fighting knife. My actions were an instant show stopper. The three Zaens froze in terror. I hoped Broza and Hylet could figure out what I was up to before they soiled themselves. The looks on their faces said no, so I gave them a little reassurance.

"The last time someone attacked my friend Broza, I cut them up into little pieces. Give me the short one and I will see to it his remains are never found."

Broza and Hylet physically relaxed when they comprehended my intent. The younger Zaen had no idea and was now seeking shelter behind the two.

"No Mr. Myers, this is my clan brethren's offspring, Felix. He is the engineer I spoke about."

I pointed my fighting knife at the young Zaen. "I would never let an undisciplined young Throgg such as this anywhere near my Chaalt replicator. Bring me a seasoned veteran engineer. It should not be difficult to find a competent engineer when you tell them I will pay one hundred million credits plus bonuses."

The three Zaens stood motionless with large wide eyes and gaping mouths. Felix was the first to find his tongue. "Did I hear you correctly state you have a Chaalt replicator?"

"It is none of your affair. I have no time for unruly children. You will not reveal any of what you have heard here or you will pay the consequences. Ask Broza what happens to my enemies."

The very real look of fear formed on the two adult Zaen's faces. They looked down at Felix and shook their heads. To my surprise the little Zaen grew a set and boldly stepped forward.

"I will come with you. I am young, but none have my engineering skills. I can unlock the true potential of your replicator. I swear to you I speak the truth. If you are not satisfied with my performance, you owe me nothing."

"If I decide to add you to my research team, your maturity can no longer be in doubt."

A hint of agitation crossed Felix's face but quickly disappeared. Looking at Broza, I said: "What will his family think if he disappears? My base is a secret research facility. No one will know his whereabouts."

Broza finally understood. "Mr. Myers, Felix is of age and expected to support himself and be self-sufficient."

I looked at the young Zaen. If he was everything that Broza said he was, we would be able to produce our armor in-house. I held up a finger to Broza and Hylet. They gave me a questioning look when I went to the shuttle and returned. I handed them a credit voucher. They really looked confused now.

"That is for services rendered. I am sure you will find the amount equitable. If Felix is unable to manufacture our new armor design, we will need you to seek others who can."

The young Zaen got a very annoyed look on his face. When he noticed my stare, his expression promptly became neutral. Turning back to Broza I said, "I will still need an outlet for our artifacts. If you decide to move from this location make it known to the Sig at Haras where you will relocate. I will find you when we have items for you to sell."

Broza nodded then looked at the card I had given him. He put it against the scanner on his utility belt. The total showed fifty-nine million seven hundred and thirty thousand credits. I thought he going to faint.

"Thank you, Mr. Myers, your generosity is quite extraordinary. We look forward to continuing our business relationship with you. We have plans to move to the outpost where the Murlak are requesting armor. Our people at the location have arranged a sale for all the armor suits you gave us."

Felix blurted out, "Mr. Myers, can we leave now? I wish to see the Chaalt replicator."

I gave the little Zaen a stern look then called out to Klutch. "Troop Master! We have a new recruit that enjoys running his mouth when he should remain silent."

Klutch came down the ramp of the shuttle and his scent preceded him. Broza and Hylet started backing away from the young engineer who stood wide eyed with a look of terror on his face.

"Mr. Myers, we must return to our duties. Please contact us if you have need of our services."

With that said, the two Zaens headed for the security door with great haste. I followed them to open the door. I took the roll of 699 that was next to the door and put it in the Zaens transport. I cautioned them it would need a thorough cleaning. They both nodded and then departed. I found it hard to hide the smile on my face when I heard the Troop Master dressing down the young engineer. I stifled a laugh when I heard the little whelp retching. When I returned to the shuttle, Felix was vigorously cleaning up his puke from the shuttle ramp. Klutch winked at me with both of big lizard eyes.

"Klutch, when the engineer has completed his current task, have him study the designs for the new armor. I am going to pay Tam Lin a visit before we depart. Please have the shuttle ready to leave as soon as I return."

I could tell Klutch did not like me going out into the outpost alone, but he nodded to me and made no further comment. His lack of response was probably more for the young Zaen's benefit than him actually not wanting to raise hell about it. I went to the spacecraft access road and selected another large transport. When I arrived at Haras, I walked into the entryway to wait in line, but a Sig appeared from a side entrance and pulled me from the crowd.

"Please follow me Nathan Myers; I will take you to Tam Lin. The timing for your visit is quite fortunate. Tam Lin has requested that we contact you. She has uncovered new information that could possibly further your cause."

We walked through a long corridor that was lined with open doorways. I glanced in some of the rooms and saw immense bunks and several Sig lounging in them. This was a barracks full of Sig troops. It would take a considerable force to take this place. It would be costly to whoever tried. I was escorted to a gravity lift. When the Sig guard did not join me, I thanked him and stepped in. I stepped out of the lift in a small room. It looked like the walls were made of a heavily reinforced metal. I approached the only exit and it opened before I got there. Tam Lin met me.

"Your skills at showing up in the right place at the right time are astounding. My friends the Sig have uncovered some interesting information on a slave interdiction mission. The Scrun have assembled kill teams to take you out."

286

I knew it would just be a matter of time before my enemies would try to hunt me down. After the considerable trouble I have caused and the leadership positions I had eliminated, it would be stupid to think there was not a coordinated effort to stop me.

"Do you have the numbers on my opposition?"

"Not counting the entire Scrun race, the Sig were told there are three teams. Each is composed of more than fifty of their most elite soldiers. The Sig have obtained the location of their base of operations."

"How can you be sure the information is legitimate and not fabricated?"

"Trust me when I say the Sig have methods for obtaining accurate information."

The Oolaran in me stirred at the comment. I was sure the methods mirrored my own. "What do I owe you for the information?"

"Nathan, I was serious when I said I do not need any extra credits. I just thought you needed to know what the slaver pieces of shit were up to. I actually enjoy hearing when misfortune befalls such worthy recipients."

I gave the pretty Earth girl a grim smile. "I can assure you the misfortune they are getting ready to experience will be of epic proportions."

"I look forward to hearing about it sometime. I do have one other question. The Outpost news has recently reported a particularly heinous murder of four Murlak. The evidence suggests a Tibor by the name of Skoal was the perpetrator. Many of us on the outpost know Skoal is a braggart and a coward. We also know if he were to actually kill someone, the wounds would be in the backs of the victims. There is evidence that shows some of the Murlak might have been bound before they were slaughtered. Would you happen to know anything about this bit of unpleasantness?"

I stood stone-faced looking Tam Lin in the eyes. When I did not elaborate she turned away and said, "I do not care for messy operations taking place in my backyard. It is bad for business. I would hope in the future that unfortunate events such as what has occurred will happen elsewhere."

Hindsight is always twenty-twenty. I did not think I would be ruffling an ally's feathers by doing the universe a favor. Next time I would attempt a little more discretion. She went to her desk and picked up a small device and held it out to me. I reached for it but she pulled it back.

"I hope you understand where I am coming from. This is not a disagreement; it is a miscommunication. Nothing more."

I nodded to her and she gave me the device. I held it up and gave her a questioning look. "The device is a data chip. It has the coordinates of the Scrun's training base. At some point in time, I would like to know what you find there."

I once again nodded agreement and then said, "I came to see if I could purchase a shuttle load of supplies, in particular food supplies the Grawl like to eat. I have more than thirty that work for me and their food rations now consist of synthesized protein concentrates. I would like a smaller quantity of Human, Chaalt and Tibor rations as well."

She gave me a stern look. "My opinion of Grawl is that you should starve them all to death."

I shrugged my shoulders and held up my hands. "If it is any consolation, they were starving when I rescued them from their captors. The Grawl that work with me are doing so to change this galaxy for the better."

I stepped forward and placed a credit voucher on her desk. "This is for the supplies. I would like the balance used for anything the slaves you have freed might need."

She waved the voucher over a small scanner on her desk then looked up at me with surprise. "Twenty-seven billion credits will ensure our efforts to free the oppressed will continue for the foreseeable future. The Sig will meet you at your shuttle in two hours."

21

I returned to the shuttle to find a napping Tibor and a starry-eyed Zaen youngster. The Zaen approached me and seemed very excited.

"These armor designs are amazing. You said an A.I. was the source of the specification prints. I would like access to the intelligence for future collaborations. I would also like to converse with it on the nature of some of the manufacturing materials. If the materials exist, I have no knowledge of them."

I looked at the young alien. "Has the shuttle's A.I. made any attempt to converse with you?"

"No, why would I waste my time conversing with a simple shuttle A.I.?"

I rolled my eyes and knew why Justice had nothing to say to the Zaen.

"I have the materials to manufacture the armor. The question is will you be able to build them? If you have any doubts, now is the time to voice them. If I transport you to my base and you fail to live up to my expectations, the Troop Master and I will be extremely disappointed in you."

The young Zaen looked annoyed but quickly changed his expression when he saw the look on my face.

"If you have a current generation fabricator and the materials in this diagram, I can build your armor."

"How long will it take to manufacture four complete suits?"

Felix's eyes got wider. "Mr. Myers, we must first build a prototype and then do extensive testing. The test period alone could take…"

I cut the Zaen off before he could finish. "I need armor sooner than later. I have missions that require the most advanced protection available. If you cannot build the armor on my time schedule I will find someone who can! A hundred million credits will find me the right engineer with the credentials I need."

Felix opened his mouth to say something, then snapped it shut. I could not tell if the look he was giving me was out and out anger or, possibly, determination.

"Mr. Myers, it is an almost unsurmountable task to properly program an A.I. that can interact with all the systems in the timeframe you are expecting. This design is the most intricate I have ever seen. To state that your design is an armor suit is an oversimplification. It is an extremely complex weapons platform. It will take a staggering amount of programming to make it fully functional. Once I have the suits manufactured, we must turn them over to the A.I. systems engineers. It will be out of my hands at that point."

291

"Do not concern yourself with the A.I., all I need you to do is manufacture the armor."

"Very well Mr. Myers, I will build your suits, but you will be responsible if they do not function properly. You cannot say that I have not warned you."

I was starting to get mad at the young Zaen. He was used to being a brat and getting away with it. I was wondering when I would get my fill and throttle him for his insubordinate tone. Klutch alerted me the Sig were paying us a visit and I put my irritation on the back burner to simmer. Klutch unlocked the security hatch and a small caravan of transports drove through. The Sig brought a crew to help unload and we quickly filled the hold with supplies. I attempted to pay them for their trouble, but Sushi would have none of it. They departed and we prepared to get underway.

The Troop Master stood over Felix while he finished locking down the last of the supplies. The Zaen had a scowl on his face but kept his mouth shut. He strapped himself into one of the jump seats and quietly sat fuming. Klutch got departure clearance and I piloted the shuttle to open space. When we were a good distance from the outpost, Justice made a short transition to the location of the Legacy. Our scanners showed open space and no indication the Legacy was even in the area. I was wondering if the Legacy had to move to a new location.

"Justice, has the Legacy relocated?"

"Negative Commander, The Legacy is one thousand feet to port and closing to tow beam range."

Klutch and I looked at each other with surprise. Justice cut the shuttle's drives and I felt the slight jar as the tow beam connected. I looked at the observation screen and saw the cavernous hangar appear when the doors opened. We were swiftly pulled inside and the atmosphere restored. Klutch dropped the ramp and we exited to meet the crew. Tria wasted no time giving me an embrace and a quick kiss. Felix stood gawking at his new surroundings. I introduced Tria, Coonts and Xul. The Zaen seemed impressed with the mix of crew members. I told Xul to give him a tour then take him to the crew quarters and get him squared away. When they were gone, Tria looped her arms in mine and Coonts inquired about our guest.

"Commander, it is good to see you and Klutch once more. I am curious as to the status of the young Zaen."

"Broza said that young Felix is a very gifted engineer. He was involved with the design of our battle armor and is a replicator instructor. He says he can build Justice's armor design. I want to make a DEHD core jump back to base and unload our supplies and Felix. He can get started manufacturing our armor. Has Justice been receiving all of the data dumps from our discoveries?"

Coonts gave me a thumb up and said, "Yes, Commander. The IST scrambler and transmitter work flawlessly. We have the video from the possible Prule ship and everything on the Scrun base. The scientists have reviewed the spacecraft video with great interest. They are split equally on their hypothesis of its origins. Some side with Justice on the Prule theory, while others tend to believe it is an unknown race. All agree to the theory it is a surveillance and intelligence-gathering vessel of an unknown design."

"Justice, are we ready for DEHD core operations?"

"Affirmative, Commander. We are ready to transition on your order."

"Take us home, Justice."

"Acknowledged, Commander. Transition in thirty seconds."

I held Tria in my arms as we both faded away to nothing. It was comforting to return to normal reality and have her be the first thing I became aware of.

"Commander, Alpha system is secure and I have no scan returns of note. We will make a straight-in approach to base and I will be ready to make another DEHD core transition in seventy-one minutes."

"Thank you, Justice. As soon as we land, offload the shuttle so Jaran can take care of the supplies we brought back with us. Klutch, make sure the weapons are transferred to the other shuttle. Throw in everything you think we might need for a complete assault package."

Klutch turned to leave but stopped. "Commander, you once told us fortune would not accompany a vessel without a title. Perhaps it would be advisable to name the shuttles before they see combat."

The Troop Master did not seem like the superstitious type. I smiled at his recognition of an Earth tradition. The shuttles were sleek, fast and deadly. I could only come up with one name that perfectly fit that description. Everyone stood waiting to hear what I would say.

"There is a bird of prey on my world that represents the symbol of my country. It is called an Eagle. I now christen the shuttles Eagle One and Eagle Two." I got smiles all around then Klutch said, "We will make sure they live up to their namesake."

I gave him a thumbs up and a solemn nod. "As soon as we have everything squared away, I want a crew meeting to fill everybody in on our new allies. I also have information we will be acting upon as soon as we have new armor."

Justice made a rapid decent to our base and landed. As we disembarked, Felix ceased his prattling about the unique transition characteristics. He locked his eyes on the

Chaalt replicator and made a beeline for it. Graf and Jaran met us and I filled them in on Felix. I told Graf to keep a close eye on the Zaen and supply him with the materials Justice specified for his armor design. Turning to Jaran, I let him know about the supplies that were on the Shuttle that Justice was removing from the Legacy. He was quite pleased the Grawl scientists would no longer have to eat processed protein concentrates.

I could see Felix frantically waving his arms and Graf patiently listening. Tria and I headed in that direction. I was hoping I would not see another bratty episode from the young Zaen. To my surprise, Graf put his arm around the youngster and was pointing at our stock pile of supplies. Felix seemed to be overjoyed. I purposely slowed my pace and asked Tria, "What do you know of the Sig?"

Her pretty face showed a little shock at the question. "Nathan, please tell me you have done nothing to make them our enemies."

I smiled at her and her expression turned to consternation. "Commander, they are a predatory race. I have heard they are now civilized. Others look upon them with dread because, for the last several years, they have been rebuilding their military strength. They have shown no open hostilities toward others, but many fear they will return to their warrior ways."

"Tria, please calm down. The Sig are the new allies I was going to brief everyone about. It seems they hate the Scrun and the Murlak pirates as much as we do. When they figured out we may have had something to do with Drayan and Lashmos meeting their ends, they granted us ally status. They wish for Eiger and his collaborators to meet with the same end."

Relief washed over Tria's face and then she cocked an eyebrow. "How could they possibly know of our connection to any of those events?"

"I have discovered another human. She has made it a goal to smuggle freed slaves to safety and the Sig help her do it. When we met, it did not take her long to figure out what I have been up to. If we encounter slaves, we now have a way to ensure their safety and freedom."

I felt Tria's grip tighten on my arm. "She?"

"Yes, she was taken from my world by the Grawl and sold to the Scrun. The Scrun then sold her to a corrupt Grawl. She waited until the time was right and ended the bastard's life. The Grawl was going to reprocess the thoughts of two Sig warriors when Tam Lin intervened. She freed them and together they inherited everything the Grawl had ever stolen. Now she uses her new-found wealth and Sig allies to smuggle slaves to freedom."

Tria physically relaxed but the look on her pretty face said otherwise. I looked her in the eyes and knew she was wondering if I was interested in a female of my own species.

I gave her my best Earth boy smile. "Tria, I have a thing for four armed female warriors and you seem to fill that description perfectly."

Felix saw us making our way over to him and he rapidly closed the distance between us. "Mr. Myers, the Chaalt replicator is the latest generation and has never had a work cycle recorded."

The young engineer looked like he could bust. He grabbed one of Tria's hands which surprised her. "Since I am now in charge of your replicator, I formally request that I be the only engineer with access. It will ensure that the mindless tinkering of others will not damage my new equipment."

Tria was going to comment, but I cut her off. "This is Tria, and she is the owner of the replicator. She is very concerned I made the wrong choice for the operator of her equipment. She thinks I have errored by selecting a young impetuous engineer instead of a seasoned veteran."

Felix did not take my comments well. "Mr. Myers, I can assure you I am the only logical selection for operating the replicator. To believe otherwise would be foolhardy."

It was time to put the little Zaen peckerwood in his place. "We were just discussing what the penalties for

298

failing to live up to her expectations might turn out to be. I am sure you are aware Chaalt females are warriors of the highest regard. They would rather die than face failure of their objectives. She believes you should fully embrace her philosophy."

I was rewarded with a sharp jab from one of Tria's elbows. I did, however, get the desired response from Felix. His fine scales roiled and he gulped. "If you will excuse me, I will begin entering the program sequences to build your new armor."

Tria gave me a disapproving look. "Why would you say such a thing? He is but a child."

"On my world, it is a ploy called good cop, bad cop. It is used to achieve an intended goal from someone less than willing to cooperate. You are now the bad cop."

Tria frowned. "I have no intention of being bad at anything."

I was going to explain further but Tria grabbed my hand and started pulling me along toward the Legacy. I was pretty sure I was about to get her interpretation of bad cop. There were still a large number of tasks that needed to be completed. I am thinking my schedule was getting ready to be FUBAR. Klutch attempted to intercept us and held up a hand. Tria never slowed down. If I had stopped she would have dragged me to the Legacy. The look on Klutch's face went from puzzlement to a huge toothy smile. I could hear his croaking laugh behind me.

Justice called out for all to hear. The tone of his voice had a distinct edge to it. "Commander, a Chaalt battle cruiser has just transitioned into the system. The IST system is now active and I will transfer the signal to your Backscatter receiver."

The look on Tria's face was not of amusement. She let go of my hand and stalked up the ramp of the Legacy. I was not absolutely sure, but I could have sworn I heard her threaten to kill the Operative.

"Mindless primate, it is not amusing finding you here, rather than our agreed upon meeting place."

"Old witch, I cannot begin to tell you how wonderful it is to hear you chewing on my ass once again. We were off loading our supplies. We were going to jump back to meet with you."

"There is no need! Your Oolaran jump signatures gave me your location once you jumped away from the outpost. I would like a briefing on your less than forthcoming communication. I have broken several laws I had sworn to uphold, so pardon me if I sound less than pleasant at the moment. My shuttle will be landing shortly. Please do not keep me waiting."

This was getting better by the minute. I would now have two pissed off Chaalt warriors on my hands. "Justice, set up the conference room for a meeting and please do not screw around with the seating arrangements."

I felt a tremor and knew the Operative was pulling out the stops. She had her ship jump into orbit.

"Commander, the cruiser has dispatched a shuttle. Do you wish to give it access?"

Great! Make it two pissed off warriors and a cranky A.I. "Justice, please make this as painless as possible for everyone."

I hollered at Klutch and told him to get Xul and meet me in the briefing room on the Legacy. I considered letting Felix sit in on the briefing so he would get an idea of what was really going on in the galaxy. I saw Graf and him moving material containers to the replicator with gravity jacks and decided to leave them to their task. I watched in fascination as a much larger version of our new shuttles came down the tunnel entrance and made a noiseless landing next to the Legacy. The Operative was not kidding when she said their production shuttles would be of a different profile. There was nothing subtle about the Chaalt assault shuttle. It was larger than our prototypes and loaded with external weaponry. It insinuated that it was a very sharp stick in every aspect.

The Operative approached me with an urgent demeanor. "Please tell me the crimes I committed to find you were not for some fruitless adventure."

"Sael, at no time have I told you to commit crimes on my behalf. I asked you to meet me, not go on an unlawful rampage to seek me out. I take it the leadership of your military counsel has restricted your access to military assets."

"Nathan, I have been relieved of command, pending an investigation that shows no sign of competence or a timely conclusion. When it became common knowledge that I had gone off-world, I was recalled until my future could be decided. I have chosen to ignore their requests. Your ominous communications inspired me to abscond with a ship and crew of my most ardent supporters. I have great hopes that whatever you have discovered will vindicate my actions. If that does not turn out to be the case, there is a very real possibility I could be executed for my crimes."

I hooked my arm in hers. "Never going to happen!"

22

When we were all seated, I called the meeting to order. I was trying my best to ignore the look Tria was giving the Operative. "Justice, give us a hologram of the ship we discovered."

The room went quiet as everyone studied the derelict ship and, then to my bewilderment, everyone started talking and speculating.

I held my hands up for silence. "If any of you have ever seen something like this, please enlighten us. If not, I will ask that you study the image. Each of you will be given time to explain what you are thinking."

The silence in the room and the incredulous expressions told me those not present when the behemoth was discovered had no idea what it was.

"OK, anyone with data concerning the object, please explain to the rest of us what that thing is."

You could have heard a pin drop. All were looking at each other for clues. Finally, I looked at the Operative. "Your thoughts?"

"I have never seen anything like this before. What did you find when you went aboard?"

"We did not investigate. Justice has a theory it is of Prule origin. He did not want us boarding without heavy combat armor and plenty of backup. There were no power sources detected, but that does not necessarily mean it was unoccupied. We know nothing of Prule technology. I chose instead to contact you."

The Operative nodded without taking her eyes off the hologram. "The ships location indicates it was purposely hidden. The extensive damage suggests it narrowly escaped destruction."

"Yes, those were our conclusions as well."

"You said Justice assessed the crafts origin? You told me you were aboard one of our prototype shuttles."

"Our Eagles are now operated by Justice. Chaalt technology is very good, but in some cases, ours is better. We use tech we can fully trust."

The Operative opened her mouth as if to comment, then stopped. We locked eyes. She looked away with a shrug of her shoulders and a shake of her head.

"We have every intention of investigating the spacecraft; preparations are being made as we speak. Until we are ready for a boarding mission, we will move on to other pressing matters."

Sael's face darkened with a frown. "What could possibly be more important than discovering the origin of this mystery ship?"

"Senior Operative, I am not implying the ship is not of high priority. I have already stated we are making preparations. I have uncovered actionable intelligence on two Scrun targets that will take much less preparation to address. One of the targets should be hit as soon as possible. We think it is a slave-staging area. Justice, show the Operative what we have on the Scrun base."

Sael Nalen stared at the video Justice put up on the wall. The frown slowly faded from her face and a sinister smile replaced it. I looked at my crewmates and could tell they were ready for anything. Xul looked a little apprehensive. It would be his first combat mission.

The Operative turned her attention to me. "Were you able to scan a floor plan when they dropped their shield?"

"No, Justice was not confident that the shuttle's Chaalt-designed scanning array was undetectable. The Legacy will have no such problem. Are you interested in going on a combat excursion?"

The dark foreboding expression on Sael's face was the same I had witnessed the first time I had met her. The predatory look made the beast within me stir. Tria must have felt the change in me. She stood up and walked to my side, placing a hand on my shoulder. Sael must have felt it as well because the look on her face promptly changed to apprehension.

She tried to give me a look of confidence and indifference when she said, "If you cannot control the beast that lurks inside of you, I am unwilling to let my strike team participate."

Before I could comment Tria cut me off. She stood behind me and placed all her hands on my shoulders. "Only our enemies need to fear Nathan."

The Operative nodded, but I could tell she was still not convinced. "If it is a slave staging area, we could have hundreds on our hands. Many will be in atmospheric holding cells. How are we to evacuate them to safety?"

"I am sure you are familiar with a race known as the Sig."

The Operative's posture suddenly stiffened. "If the Scrun somehow managed to convince the Sig to guard their base, and I am skeptical that would be the case because they are the bitterest of enemies, we may need additional troops to secure the facility. They are very formidable adversaries. You must be careful, Nathan. You do not want them as your foes."

The Operative's dire warnings put a smile on my face. Sael was shocked at my expression. It seemed nobody liked screwing with the Sig. The Operative's reaction and watching her rub her jaw where the disfiguring scar used to be hinted at the story behind her dread."

"Lighten up Senior Operative, the Sig are now our allies, and yes, they still hate the Scrun and the Murlak with a vengeance."

"How did you manage to secure an alliance with a race that was genetically modified to be rampaging psychopaths?"

"There is a saying on the planet of my birth. It is an eloquent connotation that covers what has taken place quite well. It goes like this: "Birds of the feather flock together.""

It was a cringe-worthy statement. When the Operative deciphered its meaning, that was exactly the reaction I got from her. My crew, on the other hand, found it amusing. I guess they thought I was just messing with Sael. They should know better by now.

Sael decided she had nothing better to do at the moment. "My crew and I are, in Mr. Myers. Let's hear your plan for taking the base."

All but Xul had a look of anticipation on his face. "First of all, we need to get the Legacy in close to get good scans of the opposition. It would be foolish to underestimate the Scrun. We have caused them a great deal of harm of late, and I think they have learned from the experience. Depending on what actually takes place at the facility, it could be heavily defended."

The Operative raised a finger to me. "Go ahead, Senior Operative. I would not have invited you to our party if I did not want your input."

Sael stood and walked to the image on the wall, then turned to us. "It has been my experience that bases similar to this have several mobile beam platforms and missiles batteries. Defenses such as those are not a threat to a capital ship but can be lethal to assault shuttles. If you can get the Legacy close enough for detailed scans, we will be able to locate and target them."

"We will make that our first priority. Justice, do you have any reservations about going in close to the target and getting the scans we need?"

"No Commander, my confidence level is ninety-eight percent that we will be able to penetrate their defenses undetected. I foresee no problems in obtaining precision targeting data with one low pass over the area."

The Operative again held a finger up to me. "You care to add something, Senior Operative?"

"Yes, if your scans are as detailed as you suggest, I would like a floor plan. It will allow me to insert my strike team into the facility if they drop their shield."

"Justice, do you think that will be a problem?"

"Negative, Commander. Once I have gathered and assessed the intelligence, I will identify several strategic locations for the Operative's strike team to choose from. I will attempt to locate troop concentrations and slave-holding areas. We cannot rule out collateral damage, so I will carefully select the areas to minimize that possibility."

"Thank you, Justice, for pointing out we must be vigilant and protect those who are unable to protect themselves."

I looked at Sael Nalen. "With that being said, do what you must to survive the mission. I have no doubt we will be outnumbered and our enemies will have intimate knowledge of their surroundings. They will use that advantage against us. I am only concerned for the lives of the slaves. Just so everybody understands me: the slaves will be the only survivors leaving the target area."

If the Operative had any misgivings about my orders, she did not show it. The dark piercing stare and the menacing smile pretty much said she never had any intention of taking prisoners. My crew was well aware of my policy toward slavers. They were ready to go.

The Senior Operative was all business and was ready to iron out the order of battle. "We must ensure we control the orbitals. There could be a large number of spacecraft coming and going from the target area. Since we have no way of determining if they will be carrying slaves, how do you wish to handle hostile vessels?"

"I have the locations of several Sig military fleets. Communication codes and identifiers, I possess will alert them we are friendlies. My intelligence asset has assured me I will have the Sig's full cooperation. I plan to invite them along so they have an opportunity to train their recruits in combat conditions. They will evacuate any slaves we manage to free and get them to safety. They will control the orbitals and dissuade any interlopers from jumping us while we go about our business. In exchange for their assistance, we will be leaving the facility intact once we remove any items of interest we might stumble across."

Sael Nalen looked skeptical but did not comment. I noticed Tria had finally quit giving the Operative venomous looks and said: "When we start our attack, it is imperative we keep any shuttles located inside the base grounded. The Scrun will most certainly use the slaves as shields. If allowed, they will load the shuttles with slaves in hopes we will not shoot them down when they attempt to escape."

"That is a very good point, Tria. Senior Operative, I think that should be the priority of the strike teams. How many can you put down at one time?"

I could tell the Operative was trying to come to grips with revealing what was probably classified information. She finally shrugged her shoulders and said: "You are already familiar with the size of my strike team. The energy collectors require a minimum of ten minutes to recycle the transporter charge. I will also be forced to split my team on our initial incursion. We have to prevent them from activating the base's shield or we will be unable to transport additional teams into the complex. Ten minutes can be an eternity when you are waiting for backup behind enemy lines."

The look on her face said she had been there and done that. Timing was going to be a nightmare. We needed to get a strike team into the complex to secure the shield generators and any spacecraft before our suppression package arrives. Our previous data indicated we would have to wait for the arrival of an incoming shuttle before the Scrun would drop the shield. I had hopes that would not be the case, and the shield would be down. If not, Sael Nalen and her team had to be ready and waiting. We would have to have the stealth missile suppression package loitering very close by, so we could strike the Scrun defenses within seconds of the assault team landing. The Sig would need to jump into the system immediately to secure the orbitals.

I knew the Operative had the experience to plan such an operation. She would not be able to do so without the latest intelligence dump from the target area.

"Justice, is the Legacy ready for combat operations?"

"Yes, Commander, thanks to the hard work of the crew and Grawl scientists, all of my systems have the latest upgrades available to us."

"How is Felix coming along with our new armor?"

"I must say, I am very impressed with the young engineer. What he lacks in maturity he more than makes up for with his understanding of replicator systems. He will have four complete working prototypes available in the next twenty hours. The Overseer and I have designed and manufactured the A.I. modules. Other than the additional weapons systems and larger physical dimensions, you will find your interactions no different from your previous battle armor."

"When you say additional weapons, would they include a complete loadout for Coonts as well?"

The smirk on Coont's face was apparently noted by Justice because he did not answer. The little Grawl sat quietly fuming, waiting for the reply that would never come.

The Operative rolled her eyes in exasperation, then said, "Whom may I ask is the Overseer, and why have I not been introduced?"

When the Operative did not get an answer from Justice I quickly added, "Justice is still evaluating your relationship with us, and I am sure at some future date he will enlighten you."

The expression on Sael's face darkened. "Do not be ridiculous, just tell me what the A.I. refuses to say."

"Things do not work like that around here. He has already stated he likes you, but he doesn't love you yet."

Sael Nalen turned and headed for the exit. "Have the defective machine send me the location of the Scrun base. We will find a discreet location to observe the target area. I will start planning the assault after you transfer the latest intel."

It was not hard for me to determine why Justice was practicing spite on the Operative. His feud with Coonts, on the other hand, had me a little puzzled. I could only chalk up his vindictive behavior to Coonts not sharing the blame for the loss of a shuttle. It was irritating as hell knowing Justice had learned his emotions, both good and bad, from me. While the theatrics were going on, Tria had slipped from the room and I wondered if she had her fill of the bickering.

"Justice, when our loadout is complete, transition to the location of the nearest Sig fleet."

"Affirmative, Commander. Do you wish to wait for Felix to complete the armor suits?"

"How much longer until we have functioning prototypes?"

"More than twenty hours, Commander. I have made changes to the design specifications after studying the Chaalt recon armor."

"Justice, don't you think the young Zaen has enough on his hands without you throwing a wrench in the works? What, may I ask, do you feel the need to change?"

"I have removed the Tibor fighting knives from the design and added lengthened versions of the Chaalt combat climbing hooks. When extended to maximum length, they can double as fighting knives in close quarters combat. When the three blades are retracted, the curved outside edge of the hooks will greatly increase damage inflicted by fist strikes. When you were in close combat with the Quill, I noted that it took repeated attacks with the Tibor fighting knives to penetrate the Crit carapace. The Chaalt climbing hooks did not exhibit the same deficiencies."

"Justice, we could really use the armor sooner than later. What else have you changed?"

"I have incorporated the Chaalt folding helmet design. After careful study, I have found that the interlocking seams add structural integrity that the one-piece Zaen design lacked."

"OK Justice, please carry on. I 'm sure you are aware that every minute we delay striking the Scrun may determine the future of another slave. Is there anything else I need to know before I make my combat recommendations to the Operative?"

"Nothing that pertains to the mission. That being stated, I do have information you are not currently aware of."

I stopped dead in my tracks with a frown on my face. "What information would that be?"

"Tria has insisted that I commence the Oolaran carbon fiber bone enhancement and nanite epidermal armoring process. She intends to use our delay as her recovery period."

Oh crap, I knew how much it hurt before your body became adjusted to the structural reinforcement of the carbon fiber. Twenty hours was not near enough time to heal. The pain could be quite intense. Justice had to keep me sedated because I freaked every time he woke me. I took off running toward the down tube that would take me to the med bay. I needed to talk her out of it until a later date. I knew why she had delayed the process. It made my heart ache to know she no longer wished to.

I stepped out of the down tube and ran down the corridor to the med bay entrance. What the hell! The door should have opened before I got here. "JUSTICE, OPEN THE DOOR!"

"Commander, I do not think it wise for you to observe the process. Tria has already ordered me not to halt the process."

"JUSTICE, IF YOU DON'T OPEN THE DOOR, I WILL TEAR IT DOWN!"

The door slid open and my stomach lurched at what I saw. Tria was lying beneath a small forest of tubes that terminated with a large needle protruding from her beautiful body. Gritting my teeth, I vaguely recalled the distant memory of waking to the same treatment. I remember screaming out loud then waking more than a week later looking like a head to toe bruise. I approached the table shaking my head thinking there had to be a better way to do this.

I wanted to lean down and kiss her. I jerked back in horror when she opened her eyes and looked at me.

I yelled out, "JUSTICE! SHE'S NOT SEDATED! PUT HER OUT NOW!"

"Commander, the Chaalt physiology responds differently to the Oolaran drugs I administered to anaesthetize and deaden the pain of the procedure. I am at the maximum dosage I feel safe administering to her. I recommended she consult with the Chaalt med techs aboard the Operatives flagship, but she refused. She is unable to speak but is aware of your presence.

I placed my hands on her cheeks and lightly kissed her forehead. I closed my eyes in frustration because I could do nothing to help her through this. A dull ache invaded my body and slowly turned to a burning sensation. It was not overpowering but still felt uncomfortable as hell. My legs were rubbery and my face flushed. Tria was embracing me with her aura. I could only hope I was returning the gesture. To my surprise, her pretty green eyes fixed on me and her eyelids fluttered and then closed. The touch of her Sha'leen faded away.

I momentarily panicked. "JUSTICE WHAT IS HAPPENING?"

"Commander, it seems her system is no longer resisting the Oolaran anesthetic drugs. Her physiology is normal and her telemetry indicates no additional stress."

I took a deep breath and let it out. I knew Justice would have given her a thorough briefing on the procedure. She must have felt it was necessary to proceed with the process before we engaged in our next operation.

317

I turned to leave and Justice called to me. "Commander, when the procedure is complete, I can move Tria to your quarters for her recuperation period."

Without hesitation I said, "Please see to it Justice, thank you."

23

Regardless of Tria's intentions, I knew twenty hours was not enough time to recover from the bone enhancement procedure. I found it difficult to be mad at her, but none the less, I was irritated by the distraction. When mission time came, I was sure she would claim to be ready no matter how much pain she was in. I was now in the unenviable position of pushing our start time back or cancelling the mission all together. Both scenarios would bring the wrath of the Operative down on my head. She was not someone who takes being jerked around lightly. I saw Coonts coming down the corridor toward me.

"Commander, you do not look well. Is there a problem?"

I unloaded my concerns on the little Grawl and he stood staring at me for a moment. He then took me by the hand and guided me to the lifts.

"Commander, perhaps we should inform the others and seek their thoughts on the matter. I do recall you saying we had other intel to act upon. Perhaps it would be the best way to deflect the Senior Operative's anger for the additional delay."

The little Grawl may have small shoulders, but right at the moment, their load bearing capabilities were without question. We met with Klutch and Xul and discussed our options. I was glad no one expressed agitation with Tria's timing, or her decision to be weaponized. We instead concentrated on manipulating the situation to lessen the fallout with Sael Nalen. I now regretted getting her involved. It would have been much smarter to call her when we were actually making our move to investigate the ghost ship. My naïve Earthman ways were suffering from my shallow galactic perspective.

Klutch had no problem with telling the Operative a small lie for the greater good. "Commander, we should tell the Operative we have new information about Eiger's location. We tell her we must act now and go to Outpost 79584 or we lose an opportunity to locate him. We should argue the Scrun base and the derelict ship are fixed locations, and Eiger's is not."

Xul looked like he had something to say, and you could tell he was feeling out of his normal comfort zone, sitting in on a command level briefing.

"Xul, I listen to what all my crew members have to say. If you have input, we would like to hear it."

"Commander, everyone here sees you as our leader. While we do respect the Operative as a warrior and a valuable resource, she is not in the chain of command. I hope I speak for us all when I say, we follow you and care little if the Operative does not like your decisions."

320

The nods of agreement made me smile. "Justice, what is Tria's status?"

"Commander, the carbon fiber enhancement process is complete and I have commenced the nano lamination procedure. Tria remains sedated and her life signs are strong."

"I want your assessment of her combat readiness when the procedures are complete."

"If I were to base the assessment on her past injuries and the observed recovery period, I would speculate she is 70% capable of carrying out combat operations. I know you are aware the physiologies of humans and Chaalt are very similar. If I take into account my manipulations of the human physiology and apply my learned experiences, I can assure you she is capable of performing her duties but would do so with considerable discomfort."

"Thank you, Justice. I have made my decision. As soon as Felix completes our prototype armor suits, I want you to make a DEHD core jump to the star system outpost 79584 occupies. It will not take the Operative long to decipher the data and determine we have changed our plans."

"Roger that, Commander, I have already started the deep charge process. DEHD core transition options will be available in fifty-nine minutes. I have been closely monitoring the young Zaen's progress and can confirm he is indeed a gifted engineer. His insight and ability to operate the Chaalt replicator validates his credentials. If Felix's immaturity becomes an unmanageable situation, I have recorded all of his replicator interactions and programming."

"I understand Justice. I very much want him to stay on and become the permanent operator of our replicator. Klutch has assured me the young Zaen is no different than any other raw recruit he has dealt with. He believes that Felix has great potential and just needs time to adjust to his new surroundings."

No one else had anything to add, so I decided to check on Felix. As a group we went down tube and out to the hangar area. Looking across the huge entryway I could see the top half of the replicator. The rest of the area was obscured by supply crates and material blocks. The crew and I weaved our way through the maze of material containers and came to a small open area. Felix was issuing orders to Graf, Jaran and two other scientists who were busy with gravity jacks moving materials into the replicator intake. We stood back and observed his interactions with his superiors. While he seemed a little demanding, he was also exhibiting restraint and respect for those working with him. I was impressed with what I was seeing. The young Zaen was monitoring the readouts on eleven view screens and dictating the order of material feed while reading the spec sheets for the armor.

I had been so captivated by the young Zaen's performance that it took an elbow from Klutch to get me to look at what was standing on the production floor at the end of the replicator. My mouth fell open and I got goosebumps looking at the nine-foot-tall glossy black suit of battle armor. It was complete with our original armor's ghastly death's head embossed into its surface. While I gawked at the battle gear, another joined it from the production chute. Our presence was finally noticed by Felix. Rather than stop what he was doing, he gave me a quick nod and waved his arm in the direction of the armor. He turned back to his work and continued directing his willing helpers.

We walked around the deadly looking weapons platform. I noticed several small enhancements that were not present of the spec sheet I had reviewed. The sharply pointed protrusions on the shoulders, elbows and knees were a nice touch that would not invite hugs from any possible combatants. The suit I was inspecting was obviously built for Tria. Her old battle suit had weapons on two of the four arms. This suit had hard points and plugins on all of the upper appendages and a much larger munitions pack. The lower arms had launcher feed tubes connected to them. Tria would now be the equivalent of an artillery battery.

"Justice, can I assume you have built all the modular weapons necessary to arm the suits?"

"Yes Commander, the modular prototypes will be installed when all the suits are manufactured."

"What about the suit liners?"

"I have replicated the Zaen suit liner and added a noncorrosive protective layer to it as well. The A.I. modules are ready to be permanently installed so I can begin the inspection of all suit functions. By the time the final suit is assembled I will have knowledge of all suit systems and will begin the arming process. The armor will be ready for crew familiarization training in eighteen hours and battle ready in twenty-two."

The beast within me stirred at the thought of battle. I pushed him from my mind and approached Felix. The Zaen startled when he noticed me standing close behind him. His fine scales roiled then settled, but he continued orchestrating his duties without turning away. I know he was trying to prove a point. Hard work and dedication was what I asked of him, and it was what I was receiving. When there was no acknowledgement of my presence I turned away to leave.

I stopped beside the pile of material crates and said, "You have impressed me and you were correct: you are the only logical choice to run the replicator. You are now elevated to the rank of Senior Replicator Engineer and sole operator of this equipment. Your rank status will net you an additional fifty million credits."

The young Zaen whirled around with a smile that quickly disappeared as he turned back to his work. I still had not spent all of the credits I had bilked from Drayen, and if we had a surplus of anything, it was credits.

"Justice, take the balance of credits I took from Drayen and divide them evenly among the scientists. I have a funny feeling we are about to experience another windfall."

"Affirmative, Commander. I have additional progress on Tria's weaponization."

I paused and listened with anxious concern. I had not inquired as to what Tria had told Justice to do and now I wished I would have asked. "Is the process complete?"

"She has requested a limited muscle enhancement."

I winced remembering what the Operative's muscular build looked like. Tria had a beautiful physique, but it was hers and I had no say in the matter. "Will it increase her recovery time?"

"No Commander, the limited nature of the procedure might in fact speed her recovery. The additional muscle mass will help shield her skeletal system from blunt trauma until the discomfort of the procedure subsides."

"Thanks for the update, Justice. Please keep me informed on her progress."

I looked around for Klutch and Xul but they were nowhere in sight. I hoped they were getting Eagle Two prepped so we could get it loaded aboard the Legacy for the upcoming mission. Coonts was back at the replicator watching Felix perform his magic. It might be a good time to take a short nap. I moved off in the direction of the Legacy only to have Justice hail me.

"Commander, The Operative's starship has transitioned into our system and I have detected a power spike in the IST transmitter."

Before Justice could say another word, the Operative started speaking with me. "Nathan, I need to meet with you, we may have a problem. I am moving my flagship to the crevasse and my shuttle will be at your location in fifteen minutes."

"Acknowledged, Sael. I will be standing by."

Since the Operative was known for killing most of her problems, I did not like the implications of her hasty return. I stood watching the tunnel entrance and right on cue the Operative's shuttle came in for a silent landing next to the Legacy. She debarked and I met her halfway.

The frown on her face told me the problem must be significant.

"Nathan, the Scrun base is a major supply hub. We detected twenty-seven Scrun Motherships and more than a hundred of their assault shuttles operating in and around the star system."

The tension slipped from my face and I almost smiled. This was going to play right into my current plans. The expression on the Operative's face was shock when she saw my reaction.

"Nathan, did you hear what I just said? We will lose the element of surprise well before we can reach the base! Do not let the demon inside of you lead us to our deaths!"

I had to turn away before I laughed. I clasped my hands behind my back and hoped she thought I was considering other options. The Oolaran monster in me had nothing to do with my decision, but I could not let Sael know that. I just got a long overdue acorn. I needed to make sure I did not tip my hand and let her figure out my true intentions.

Out of the corner of my eye I saw Coonts, Klutch and Xul rapidly approaching. Shit! One of them might inadvertently let slip what my plans actually are. I waved them off with a spastic jerk of my arm. They came to a sudden halt and stood with puzzled looks on their faces. I repeated the motion hoping Klutch would not think the

Operative and I were having a disagreement. By the way Coonts and Xul stepped away from him, I could tell that was exactly what he thought.

I called out, "I will meet with you in the briefing room when the Operative and I are finished!"

Coonts and Xul took off at a pace that left the Tibor well behind. Klutch again stopped and turned to me, but I quickly pointed at the Legacy. I felt sorry for the rest of my crew when Klutch made it to that location. The Tibor stalked off toward the Legacy pounding his fists together. If I knew for sure the Operative could not decipher our transmission, I would have let Klutch know what I was up to on the Backscatter Transmitter.

I turned around and hooked my arm in one of the Operative's. She seemed surprised but she calmed when I walked her over to the benches by the artifact building. The short walk helped me compose myself and the story I planned to tell her.

"How much backup do you think we will need to take the base without killing a large number of slaves doing it?"

"Nathan, regardless of the reinforcements, the only way to clear the orbitals will be to destroy the Motherships. Collateral damage will be severe if those ships are carrying slaves. I can tell you right now, the Sig will have no problem with destroying the Scrun Motherships, no matter who is on them."

I knew the Operative's last statement might not be correct according to my intelligence. I did not want to mince words on the subject.

"What do you suggest we do? I will not let the Scrun continue to enslave others while I stand by and do nothing."

"Nathan, even if we manage to disable the Motherships with a stealth missile strike, they can still use their primary weapons systems to bombard us from orbit. The Scrun spend considerable amounts of their wealth on modern weapons. You should not discount their military capabilities."

"Would your military counsel aid us if we ask?"

"It is a possibility, but they will want substantial returns for their assistance. It would take more than a request from you alone. I would have to back you and insist it is in their best interest."

"The chances are pretty slim of them doing that after you disappeared with a ship and crew. I can almost bet they would require you making your request in person, so they can lock you down until they can determine if you are still useful to them."

"You are most certainly correct. I for one do not plan on returning until my rank has been thoroughly established. My current leadership status indicates some on the counsel believe I no longer have their best interest in mind. To some extent, that assessment might be true. Nonetheless, I have shed my blood, and that of my many subordinates, far too many times for the good of my people to be retired into obscurity."

"Then we must show them you are capable of making decisions without benefit of their questionable wisdom."

The Operative cocked an eyebrow. "Why do I suddenly feel I am about to be manipulated?"

"I have already told you we have more than one target. I think we should move on to the next and, if it bears fruit, I will see to it you gain all of the credit."

The Operative looked skeptical. "What target could be more important than going to explore the derelict ship?"

"We have been assessing information we obtained from a group of Murlak."

"Unless it has to do with finding Eiger, you are wasting your time even talking to those pirate pieces of scat."

"It just so happens that is exactly what they claimed."

"How did you manage to obtain this information?"

"You do not want to know."

The corner of Sael's mouth curled up ever so slightly. She surprised me by reaching out and pinching my cheek as a teacher would do an unruly child. She shook my head back and forth. "You simple minded primate, I get the distinct feeling you are not being completely honest with me."

Her pinch was becoming quite painful. It was all I could do to keep a neutral expression on my face. "I will play along for now, but I am warning you, my patience is wearing thin."

She finally released my cheek, stood up and walked away then came back. She looked like she was deep in thought. The uncanny intuition exhibited by the Chaalt was unnerving. While she was not quite as perceptive as Tria, she was very much aware I was up to something. She finally came to a stop in front of me. I really wanted to rub my throbbing cheek but would not give her the satisfaction of knowing it smarted like hell.

"Okay Nathan, I am in, for now. You have never been dishonest with me in the past. I still feel you have an ulterior motive, but I am in. Where is the target?"

"Are you familiar with Outpost 79584?"

The Operative started pacing once more. "That makes sense — the place is a cesspool and home to the worst scum that sector has to offer. If we go in there, you had better be prepared to fight our way out if we manage to kill Eiger. If the intelligence is accurate, we would be better off destroying that scat hole rather than risk injury wading through those Throggs."

"There is a gathering of Eiger's clan at a supply cache hidden in the Sitch fighting pits. They are waiting to be picked up by Eiger. I would love to be the one to meet him when he shows up."

"That makes two of us. My people have never gone out of our way to track Eiger. After he staged his illegal boarding within our home world protective zone, he is now elevated from target of opportunity to priority target."

"We will never know unless we go see for ourselves."

The Operative looked at me and frowned. "I would be interested in hearing what Tria thinks of your little adventure."

When I made no comment the Operative's stare became piercing. I decided to deflect the question. "We have intelligence on another Scrun target, one that might be much easier to deal with."

"My, my, you seem to be full of...intel today."

"Sael, we are going to strike all these targets with or without your help. I am making you privy to our latest intel. If you are not interested, then feel free to carry on with the missions your military counsel has waiting for you."

I could almost feel the heat of her anger. I felt a sudden flash of her Sha'leen assault me. I sat with a stoic expression on my face, giving her no indication of the pain, she was inflicting on me. It quickly ceased with the softening of her frustration. In some ways, I felt sorry for her. From the minute she first met me, her whole world changed, and in her eyes, I was pretty sure, she thought it was not for the better.

"When our new battle armor is complete, I can guarantee you there will be no more delays"

24

The Operative sat down next to me with a look of resignation on her face. "Tell me about the secondary Scrun target."

"The Sig have uncovered data on three Scrun assault teams that are training with the sole purpose of killing me. We have the location and it is not a great distance from the primary Scrun target. My thinking is if we hit the secondary target we might gain intimate knowledge of the primary. It is my understanding they have assembled their very best troops to take me out. I personally see this as an opportunity to send the Scrun a message they will find very easy to understand."

Sael finally gave me a small smile. "I like it. I have nothing better to do and I find I have the sudden urge to kill something. Before I can pledge my crew to your bloody vendettas, I have a request."

"Sure, Sael, what do you need?

"The real reason you are stalling and putting off what should be considered the priority mission."

Crap! There was no hiding anything from a Chaalt. The Operative was reading me like a book, and I now felt it was pointless to continue skirting the truth.

"We have a new armor system and they are not complete. The young engineer that is operating the replicator is working as fast as possible. As it stands, we will be taking an untested weapons platform into combat. It was my thinking we should test them on a target that might not prove to be the deadliest enemy in the galaxy."

I thought this would pacify the Operative, but I was wrong. Sael stood with both sets of arms crossed and a rather stern look on her face. The longer it took for me to come clean the more irritated her expression was becoming. I closed my eyes and shook my head.

"Tria has undergone a medical procedure and I do not think she is one hundred percent combat capable. I know she would go whether she was fit or not. I will not take that risk. She means more to me than any number of trinkets we might recover from the derelict ship."

I was surprised by Sael's reaction to my revelations. She sat back down next to me with a look of concern. "If she has been injured, we should transfer her to my flagship. We have the very latest in medical technology. What is the extent of her injuries and what type of medical procedure did she undergo?"

"She was not injured. She chose to have a military grade enhancement."

The Operative looked puzzled. "I know our species are similar but having human military modifications

335

performed on her seems reckless and foolhardy. You should have denied her request."

Now, I was the one looking skeptical. "I give my crew free choice and Tria exercised that option. She did not undergo a human procedure; it was an Oolaran weaponization protocol."

"Oolaran?"

"Yes, I underwent the procedure and I am Oolaran weaponized. My race has many very competent warriors, but none are as capable as me. Just so you know, the demon you sense in me is a byproduct of the Oolaran conditioning."

The Operatives eyes grew wide and she jumped up from the bench. "She is a fool! We must stop the procedure now!"

I reached out and grabbed one of Sael's arms. "She only had her epidermis, bone and muscles enhanced, nothing more. Once she has healed, she will be resistant to cuts and abrasions. Her bones can sustain impacts without breakage and she will be much stronger."

Sael sat back down and whispered something unintelligible. I frowned trying to decipher what she had said. "What did you say?"

She looked me in the eyes. "When we were in conflict the first time I met you. I struck you in the head, it was a killing blow. I have killed more than I care to remember with such a strike. I was stunned when you only flinched."

Holy shit! I thought she was just trying to knock me out, to shut me up. "Since we are being honest with each other, I had every intention of taking your head off with that machine spar."

She smiled at me. "Had it not been for my enhanced reflexes and the quality of my armor you might have succeeded."

"Enhanced reflexes?"

"Yes, we Chaalt have a similar military program. It is a closely guarded secret. Ranking field Commanders are enhanced to ensure their survivability. Good leadership is hard to come by, so there are some who are modified. I was selected for modification. The procedure is quite painful and the lingering side effects take considerable getting used to. It is why my physique appears to be not of my gender."

"Trust me when I say the Oolaran procedure is extremely unpleasant. The healing process takes an extended period of time, but there are little to no side effects."

Sael made a disturbing noise and said, "I would argue the demon that possesses you should be considered an undesirable side effect."

"The so-called demon was an artifact of the combat training and conditioning downloaded into my implants. It was designed for Oolaran soldiers. It was my understanding that the Oolaran people were a docile species. They developed the imprinting to meet the Prule threat and to ensure the survivability of their race."

"You must have been insane to infect yourself with technology you know nothing about."

"It was not one of my better ideas, but I could also point out, I have survived a number of conflicts that I should have never walked away from."

Sael just nodded her head in agreement. After the Quill engagement, she knew I could be a murder machine when the beast took over. "How much longer will it take to get your armor complete?"

"We should have enough for my crew in another hour or so. I want to act on the outpost intel before we lose the opportunity. As for the derelict ship and the Scrun base, they are not going anywhere. I also think you are correct in stating we will need some serious backup to take down the Scrun base."

"Yes, the Scrun base does pose a larger risk factor than your other targets. When we exited the system, we left several surveillance drones to monitor the base's activities. There is a possibility we can develop a strike plan based on the traffic patterns in the system. My intelligence teams are crunching the data. If it is revealed there are times of minimal base usage, we can formulate our assault around that timeframe."

"When Klutch and I discovered the base, there was only a single ship in orbit, and a handful of shuttles that were observable. With the right coordination, we might be able to get in and take the base with the Sig's help. Once we free any slaves and whatever we determine to be of value, we will turn it over to the Sig and let them worry about holding it."

The operative stood up staring at me. "I agree with you."

"Agree with me?"

"Yes. Moving against Eiger's clan should be the current priority. The longer you wait, the more likely you will lose that opportunity. It is what I would do."

The old war horse was truly a kindred spirit; she just didn't like not being the one in charge. The more I thought about it, I realized she probably never had anyone jerk her around before either.

"Sael, I apologize."

She snorted. "For which of your actions?

I frowned and said, "I should have never tried to mislead you."

She let out a barking laugh. "HAH. It is what most primates do — what makes you think you are any different?"

My frown faded to a smile. "You old witch, I will attempt to be more forthcoming in the future."

"See that you do. I am going to take my ship to the outpost's location and surveil the situation. We will gather intelligence and await your arrival. If a Murlak Warbringer transitions into the system, I will not be standing by waiting for orders from you before I take action."

As she was walking away, I called out to her. "We will be there as soon as possible!"

She never turned around and threw all her arms up. I did not know if it was acknowledgement or exasperation. I moved off to check on young Felix's progress on our armor.

Justice called to me. "Commander, I have moved Tria to your quarters."

"Thank you, Justice, please keep me posted."

Looking over at the replicator I could see the stacks of crates and supplies were less than before. When the engineer completed his task, I would have Jaran and the scientists build a dedicated enclosure around the replicator. I would have them make half of it a warehouse for our supply of materials and the other half the production floor. I would let Felix have a hand in the design and tell him to build his private quarters inside as well. When I stepped around the pile of crates I could see four large black pulsating blobs where our armor once stood. They were encapsulated in Justice's mechanical nanite extrusions. Felix stood staring with an incredulous look on his face when he noticed me approaching he met me halfway.

"Mr. Myers, your A.I. is hampering my work by barring me from my final inspection. If it continues, I will disavow the validity of my work and the responsibility will be placed on the A.I. to ensure quality control."

"Felix, you have done well. Justice will take responsibility for the armor from this point forward. I know you have been working very hard with little to no rest. Take some time off, and when you are rested, I want you to submit a design for a building enclosure for the replicator that will include your personal quarters. Submit it to the scientists for any additions they might feel it will need. When you feel the design is satisfactory, turn it over to Justice so he can verify my final approval."

341

This seemed to mollify the Zaen and he headed to the lifts. "Justice, what is the status of the armor?"

"Commander, I must commend the young engineer for his precision execution of my designs. His meticulous attention to detail is brilliant. He is a worthy addition to your team. Hopefully his bouts of immaturity will quickly pass when he realizes the importance of his new duties."

"So, I take that as meaning we can confidently go into combat knowing the suits will perform as designed?"

"Commander, all of my system checks indicate you will notice no significant difference from the previous model battle armor. As for the additional weapons, my subsystem will insure seamless integration."

"Is Eagle Two loaded aboard the Legacy and ready for combat?"

"Yes, Commander. All systems are optimal and DEHD core operations are available for immediate use after our departure from Alpha base."

"Tria's status?"

"She is recovering surprisingly well. Her Chaalt physiology is adapting quickly. She will experience some discomfort from the bone lamination process but shows very little system stress from the other procedures."

"In your opinion, will she be combat capable?"

"I suggest you ask her yourself. She wishes to speak with you when you are available."

"Thank you, Justice. Please alert the crew that we will depart when our loadout is complete. Better give the scientists a heads-up on our plans as well."

"Roger that, Commander. ETD is one hour and forty minutes."

I made my way to the Legacy and quickly went to the command deck. I stood for moment in the hallway leading to my cabin. I steeled myself so as not to alert Tria to what I might be thinking. It was probably a worthless gesture because the girl was very much attuned to my emotions. I entered my cabin and looked to my bed, where Tria lay. I quietly stood looking at her. The first thing I noticed was her skin was almost black from bruising. She had a blanket over her but I could see her shoulders were a little broader and her arms thicker. It was not what I expected. I thought she might go all out and end up looking more like me.

Tria must have felt my presence. She opened her eyes and held an arm out to me. I carefully sat on the edge of the bed and she looked up at me with a look of concern on her pretty face. She placed a hand on my lap and I held it.

"I am sorry that I did not consult with you before I ordered Justice to proceed with the weaponization

343

protocol. I knew you would attempt to talk me out of it. With all of the events that have been taking place, I felt that if I did not proceed now, there was the possibility our future missions would not allow the time necessary to do so."

I was not sure what to say to that, and the truth of the matter was that she might be correct. I was lost for words and could only come up with the weakest attempt at a useful conversation.

"Are you in pain?"

She rolled her eyes and released my hand. She pulled the blanket off her body and my eyes got bigger. My mouth was suddenly dry and I attempted to swallow but was having difficulty. I was thinking she would be the muscle-bound caricature the Operative turned out to be. Her muscles were more defined and she was not quite as willowy. Other than being five or six shades darker from bruising and her thighs being more muscular, she was magnificent. Justice placed a glass of water on the nightstand and I was so flustered I could not comment on the intrusion.

Tria looked at me with those big, beautiful green eyes. "I hope you are not disappointed. I did not wish to resemble the Operative."

I gulped down the water in two big chugs. Things were going to get awkward quickly. In a move that hinted at her new strength, Tria grabbed my uniform and pulled me down to within inches of her face. She could not hide the pain her effort caused, but she tried.

"You have not answered me."

I was not sure if it was the warrior or the woman talking to me. There was little doubt she expected an answer — now!

"Tria, you could never disappointment me."

She gave me a warm smile and kissed me. "That is acceptable for now."

Justice broke the magic of the moment. "Commander—"

"Justice, if the Operative is in route, please inform her I am indisposed and will contact her when I am available!"

"No, Commander, that is not the case. If you would have let me finish, I was going to alert you that Klutch and Coonts are outside of your cabin requesting permission to check on Tria's status."

I reached over Tria and pulled the blanket back over her. She smiled at me and pulled it up to her neck then shooed me away. Klutch and Coonts were part of Tria's extended family and I would not deny them time to check on her. I kissed her once more and went to the door and let them in. They both nodded to me then went to Tria.

I was headed to the bridge when Justice hailed me again. "Commander, the Grawl scientists have gathered outside of the Legacy and wish to see you before we depart."

"Thank you, Justice. I am on my way."

I made my way down tube and to the personnel boarding hatch. All the scientists were gathered around the boarding ramp, and I was pleasantly surprised to see Felix among them. He was having a discussion with Jaran but turned his attention to me when I exited the Legacy. Graf came forward and met me.

"Nathan Myers, Justice has informed us of your amazing generosity. You have made us wealthy beyond any of our expectations. We came to thank you and wish you luck on your missions."

I looked out over the crowd and I smiled. With the exception of young Felix, all were holding a hand up to me. The Zaen looked confused by their gesture but reluctantly did the same. I walked out among them touching each of their hands and stopped in from of Felix. I reached out and touched his hand and he looked puzzled. One by one the scientists came forward and held a hand out to the Zaen. He reluctantly held his hand back out and each scientist touched it. He looked at me with a questioning look.

"Felix, it seems all have accepted you into our clan. Your hard work has not gone unnoticed. Everyone here is devoted to changing the galaxy for the better. We are at war with the corruption that takes place on a daily basis. Even though we are but a few, we are determined to stand and fight for the good of all."

Felix looked at me grim-faced. "I have had a hard time believing all of the incredible stories I have been hearing since I got here. The Grawl say you were the one who killed Drayen and destroyed his outpost. They also say you did the same to Eiger's outpost and now you seek him out to kill him as well. Is this true?"

I wondered if the young Zaen was getting ready to bail on me. The look on his face had me thinking yes. "For the most part, I guess you could say it was true. I could not have done it without the help of my crew. We are a team that believes anything is possible. Even if our goals seem unrealistic, it will not keep us from trying to help those who cannot help themselves. Are you up to the task? We could really use your help long-term."

"When I saw the monstrous images the A.I. put on your armor, it made me wonder about the rumors that are being whispered by many races. The stories say there is an alien who hides behind the mask of a demon. They say the demon mercilessly slaughters any who prey on the weak and defenseless. Are you that demon?"

I did not know how to answer that question and wondered if I even should, so I didn't. I stood with a neutral look on my face until the Zaen finally looked away.

When he made eye contact with me again, he said, "I will stand with you."

A cheer rippled through the crowd of scientists and they pushed in close to touch the Zaen's hands once more. I smiled at him and waved goodbye to the gathering. "I will see you all when I have completed my mission."

25

"Justice, are we ready to get underway?"

"Yes, Commander. Our loadout is complete and I am prepared to jump to the Operative's location."

"Take us out and jump at your discretion. If you need me, I will be in my cabin."

"Affirmative."

As I walked past the ready room I stopped and backed up to take a second look. Coonts and Xul were inside standing next to Coonts' old battle armor. Coonts waved me over. "Commander, since we now have fourth generation armor, I am going to instruct Xul on the operation of the older model. The suit fits him well and one never knows when we might need a helping hand."

Xul did not look convinced this was in his best interest. His expression suggested he would rather be doing something else. Just behind the two stood four very ominous looking battle suits. After I checked on Tria, we would give the suits a test drive. I hoped the smile I gave Xul would give him encouragement. His reaction said otherwise. I gave them a thumb up and moved on without further comment.

I exited the lift tube on the bridge level and met Klutch heading in the opposite direction. "Commander, Justice says that our armor is ready to test."

"Roger that, Klutch. I will be down after I check on Tria."

The Tibor disappeared down tube and I went to my cabin. The door opened, and to my surprise, Tria was attempting to get dressed.

"Whoa! Where do you think you are going?"

The pain on her face was not well hidden. She sat back down on the edge of the bed with her smart cloth uniform only partially covering her. "I have been lying around much too long and feel physical therapy will be required to shorten my recovery time."

"I know for a fact that is a load of scat. Take the uniform off and lay back down."

At first, she frowned at me, then the look changed to something else. "I have been wanting you to tell me that for some time, but now is not that time."

That wiped the stern look from my face and replaced it with a smile. I held my hand out. "I am going to need the uniform."

The look in her eyes made me feel hot and flushed. She gave me the tiniest touch of her aura as she let the uniform fall free of her body. If it were not for the deep dark bruising on her body it would be hard to say what might happen next. I took the smart cloth and backed up a step because my legs were feeling rubbery.

"Justice...JUSTICE!"

"Commander, Tria has ordered me to mind my own business and to not report her actions. While I might find this behavior unacceptable coming from you, I am inclined to take her directives with more credence."

"SAY WHAT?!"

My temperature went up several degrees and it had nothing to do with Tria's Sha'leen. I pointed at Tria. "You are confined to quarters until further notice. That is a direct order!"

Tria carefully lay back on the bed with all her arms crossed. I could not tell if the expression on her face was pouting or mild anger at my order. It was all I could do to maintain my stern look. It was extremely difficult to be angry with a beautiful naked warrior lying in my bed. The room suddenly got brighter and everything started fading from reality. That was one surefire way for Justice to shut me up.

When we faded back into existence, I pointed my finger at Tria and waggled it. That got me the smallest of smiles in return. I walked out into the hallway and made it a point to stand there until I had Tria's full attention. She looked at me wondering what I was up to. I took her smart cloth and made a show of throwing it down the corridor. This had the desired effect when I heard her lovely laugh. The door closed and I headed to the bridge.

"Justice, open a secure IST channel to the Operative."

I sat in my command chair and Justice acknowledged my order. We were back to business as usual.

The Operative came on the transmitter and she was her normal irritable self. "Nathan, it took you long enough to get here. I am glad we did not need your assistance for any reason."

The one thing I did not need at the moment was more irritation, and it showed in my response. "Sael, you should really find a mate and get yourself laid because I am getting tired of you being a bitch all the time."

The transmission went quiet for almost thirty seconds then I heard a raucous laugh. "You are an intolerable moronic primate, if any other being in this universe was to speak to me like that, I would slit their throat."

"I love you too. Sael. What intel do you have on the target?"

She quickly recovered from my pleasantries. "For one thing, there is still good quality scan shielding present in the outpost. It is hard to say if this was by design or it was installed at a later date. I have no good return information other than the superficial information gathered from the damaged and decayed areas. The other thing would be the fact that there has only been one ship to pass through this sector and it landed on the outpost several hours ago."

"I haven't got a clue what to make of that, so you will have to tell me what you think."

She snorted out loud. "Of course, I will. I did not expect a mindless Throgg like you to do anything smarter than stack your scat."

I rolled my eyes in exasperation. My humanity rubbed off on aliens in all of the wrong ways. I sighed, "Sael, please enlighten this backward-thinking alien before I grow old and wither away."

The Operative regained her composure. "Hold while I send you a data burst."

I heard an electronic tone. "Justice, did you get that?"

"Yes, Commander. It is a video of the target area. I will put it on the view screen.

"Shithole" would have been a kind description. The outpost was in total decay. From what I could see of the side we were facing, it was a corroded, fractured, falling-apart hazard to galactic navigation. "Justice, what are all the emissions coming out of that thing?"

"Most are sewage and atmosphere. There is some potable water and a mix of gases both toxic and harmless."

"Sael, judging by that wreck's appearance, there can't be a lot of habitable living space."

"You would be surprised, Nathan. This place was known as a gathering place for the worst scum in the galaxy. If you had no other place to go, you would figure out a way to survive, even on a deathtrap like 79584. We would be doing ourselves and everyone else a favor by destroying that cesspool."

"I would agree with you if it were not the fact there are Murlak from Eiger's clan hiding in that mess. I want to talk to them first and kill them second."

"I guess we can do it in that order. The large boxy protrusion on this side of the station is where the Sitch fighting pits used to be located. I have no current intelligence and can only assume that is where they are. Surprising as it may sound, that particular area is leaking less atmosphere than the rest of that dump. We are bound to find someone or something there, and it is as good a place as any to get started."

"OK Sael, I usually shoot my way in. Since you have had eyes on the target, I will follow your lead. How do we get our feet in the door?"

"We have good scan data on three entry points. My team and I are going to make a combat entry and open that hangar door closest to the target location. You bring your shuttle in and join up with me. We will fight our way down to the Sitch pits and see what there is to see. My flagship and the Legacy will ensure that we do not get any surprise visitors that might feel obligated to help the locals. If the scat gets bad, we get back to your shuttle and clear the area."

"Would it not be easier if we jumped in with you? We can go in place of three of your strike team members."

"Not going to happen, Nathan. That is one rule I will not be breaking. The transporter is off limits. Our systems carefully record all biometrical information on any strike team personnel that uses the device. I will not test the theory whether or not it would even transport an alien, let alone me allowing one to try."

"Fine, Senior Operative, we will follow your lead. Give me some time to get organized and I will call you when we are ready to launch the shuttle."

"I will be ready when you call. Before I sign off, I do have a request."

"Sure, Sael, what can I do for you?"

"Nathan, I need you to keep a leash on the vile creature that resides in you. If you endanger my team, we will leave you to your own means."

With that last statement, the transmission ceased. The tone of the Operative's voice made it more than clear she was dead serious. I went back to my cabin to check on Tria and was honestly surprised she had not moved since I saw her last. She did however have her arms crossed and a look on her pretty face that said her patience was being tested. I sat on the edge of the bed and reached out for one of her hands. When she did not acknowledge the gesture, I knew where this conversation was going to go.

Before I could say anything, she said, "I will not claim to be one hundred percent combat-capable, but I am going with you one way or the other."

There were times when I knew not to argue, and this was one of those times. I came in here with a plan A and a plan B. The determination in Tria's eyes told me to go right to plan B. I needed it to sound like there was never a plan A.

"Tria, I need you to pilot Eagle Two and make sure we have a ride out if things turn out to be more than we can handle."

Tria reached out and grasped my hand. She squeezed it hard enough to make her wince from the effort. It was also a hint of her new strength. She pulled me over and kissed me then whispered in my ear, "Was your plan A to come in here and beat on your chest and tie me to the bed?"

Freakin' Chaalt. I hate it when she does that. Her uncanny ability to know what I am up to was irritating as hell. I needed to be more spontaneous. I threw a wrench into her mind-reading act. "Perhaps when you have healed."

She threw it right back. "Perhaps I am healed enough now!"

While I did not mind where this was going, it was neither the time nor the place for such pleasantries. "Perhaps if you weren't the color of a raisin."

She frowned. I had her on that one. I could tell it irritated her as well.

"You Throgg, what is a raisin?"

"Tria, I have to get prepped for the mission, the Operative is waiting and you know how she loves doing that."

She threw off her cover and eased her feet to the floor. "JUSTICE, WHAT IS A RAISIN?"

I momentarily stopped in anticipation of Justice answering her, and when he didn't, I could not help but laugh. I made my way quickly out into corridor and headed for the ready room. When I got there, I noticed there was only Tria's armor and mine. Coonts and Klutch must already be playing with their new toys. I stripped off my uniform and put on my new suit liner. I noticed right away it felt colder and wetter than the old design. Thinking I would put it down on my suit bitch list, it surprised me by tightening around me and warming to a pleasant temperature. I should have known Justice would incorporate smart cloth technology in the liner's design.

I climbed up into the back of the armor suit. It was a more than a foot taller and much bulkier than the original Zaen design. The large ammo pack closed over the opening and I felt the armor tighten around me. The limbs moved with almost no effort. It was nice not having a helmet to talk through. With a simple thought, the helmet closed around my head and the HUD came up for my inspection. The display rapidly verified that all suit seals were one hundred percent and the check list disappeared.

I took a few steps and then a couple of hops. Justice was correct —, there was no difference in suit movements. If anything, it was now easier. I danced a little jig and laughed at the ease of doing so. I did it again and added a spin. This was absolutely cool because it was so effortless. I made a third spin and came to a stop, face to face with an incredulous looking Tria.

She squinted her eyes at me. "Nathan, are you well? You appear to be suffering from bizarre seizures."

I cleared my throat. "I am fine. I am testing the full range of suit motions."

I left her standing there with a look of doubt on her face. Walking into the hangar, I saw Coonts and Klutch working out with their armor. Xul was to one side in Coonts' old armor. He was trying his best to imitate Klutch's combat striking sequences. Even with Justice helping him to manipulate the suit, I could tell his heart was not in it. Coonts and Klutch on the other hand, were moving much faster with each repetition. I was confident with Justice operating the suit systems there would be very few missteps, if any. I could feel the beast in me yearning for combat. This would be a trial by fire, and for some strange reason, it did not bother me in the least. It was go time and I waved my crew mates to the shuttle. Tria walked by us without comment. I knew she was feeling like crap. The way she was walking was a dead giveaway — it was not her normal graceful, fluid gait. She was pissed she could not join in on the mayhem. I really needed her to be in charge of our only means of exit if things went south.

I turned to Xul before I boarded Eagle Two. "I am hoping things will go smoothly. If they don't, you and Justice need to cover Eagle Two until we can get off the outpost."

Xul looked nervous as hell. This would be his first combat mission. "I will be ready if you need me Commander."

I patted him on the shoulder and boarded the shuttle. I commed Tria. "Launch at your discretion."

Taking a jump seat next to Coonts and Klutch, I gave them both two thumbs up. They returned the gesture. If they were nervous, neither one showed it. They had their helmets in the down position and Coonts looked excited. Klutch looked bored.

I started wondering where the Operative was located. "Justice, have you got a lock on the Operative's flagship?"

"Yes, Commander. We are currently four thousand yards to port of her position."

I beeped Sael with a secure IST transmission. "We are launching Eagle Two, Senior Operative."

She came right back at me. "It's about time you decided to join the hunt. What is your position?"

"Justice says we are just to port of your current location."

The channel was silent for several seconds. "Impressive. Our sensors are not detecting the Legacy."

Tria called out. "Launching now!"

Justice opened the hangar door and spit the shuttle into the void. The Operative called back. "We just got a brief fix on your position. Your new cloaking capabilities are noteworthy. Have the Legacy take up station on the far side of the outpost. We are moving in close for insertion."

"Affirmative, we will move in close to the target and wait to hear from you."

I closed my helmet and Justice gave me a forward view from the shuttle. The lack of activity around the station was ominous. The beast inside of me brushed aside my feeling of trepidation. I started getting small shots of adrenaline from anticipation of using my new armor for its intended purpose. Klutch seemed preoccupied with his new minigun and sat spinning up the weapon and pointing it at different objects in the back of the shuttle. Coonts, on the other hand, sat staring at me. It was not hard guessing why.

26

The Operative called over the group channel. "We are in and there is no resistance. It is black as the void in here and the contaminates in the atmosphere have condensed into a thick fog. We are moving to hangar control."

Tria called down from the cockpit. "Commander, there should be more activity on and around the outpost. This does not look or feel right."

"Tria, if the Operative did not want to go in, she would have said so. Now that she is in, we are committed. If for no other reason we have to watch her back in case she can't transport off that piece of scat."

The Operative interrupted our conversation. "Nathan, we have encountered no one in any of the passageways. Something is not right. We should have run across someone by now."

"Senior Operative, Tria doesn't like it either. Pull your team out, can you transport from your current position?"

"Negative Nathan, we are going to backtrack to our starting point and extrac—"

The Operative being cut off mid transmission gave me a feeling of dread, but Tria's broadcast filled my veins with ice water. "COMMANDER, I just picked up a large detonation on the outpost!"

"Justice, are you detecting any movement on the outpost?"

"Negative, Commander, I can pinpoint the location of the explosive detonation but nothing else. The area of operation may have been purposely shielded to prevent detection of hostiles and their movements."

"Tria, I don't care how you do it, just get us in so we can get Sael and her team out."

"Roger that!"

Tria nosed the shuttle over and dove for the closest hangar door. Turning at an angle to the big door she hit it with a barrage from the shuttles main weapons. The door and a generous portion of its frame blew out into space.

Justice broadcast a warning. "Tria, be advised I have multiple power sources coming on line. They appear to be weapons batteries!"

As Tria pulled the shuttle out of its dive, I called out. "Tria, drop the ramp, we are jumping from here."

Tria rolled the shuttle hard over and dove back for the gaping hole in the hangar door. I was going to protest her actions, but she dropped the ramp and the atmosphere explosively burst into the void, taking me, Coonts and

Klutch with it. We were tumbling wildly toward the outpost. Our suit systems quickly righted us and we hit our gravity drives. I tried to see where Tria was but she had already cloaked the shuttle and was gone. Klutch took the lead and Coonts came up tight to my side. We shot through the destroyed hangar door and Klutch rapidly changed our vector in case anyone survived the flying debris from Tria's attack. We sat down behind a huge pile of downed girders from the overhead door tracks.

I was going to call Tria for a sitrep but the outpost suddenly vibrated under our feet. Tria called out, "One weapons battery down!"

The outpost shook again to almost simultaneous concussions that almost floored the three of us. Justice called out, "All detected weapons batteries destroyed."

Tria yelled another warning. "They are launching missiles!"

Justice came over our comms and corrected her. "Negative Tria, they are launching multiple comm buoys! I will attempt to shoot them down."

I was not sure what the Operative's flagship was doing, but my backup was busier than cats covering crap. We yanked our weapons from our packs and Klutch took off toward a pressure door. The controls were junk and it was apparent we would have to shoot our way in. The beast inside of me was screaming out in joy. It was all I could do to give Coonts and Klutch a warning before I threw my right arm up. "TAKE COVER!"

They both dove to the side and behind piles of debris. I gave the door a beam shot that blew it into the airlock. My crewmates peeked over the rubble they were hiding behind to make sure I would not make any follow up shots.

Justice called out again. "Be advised, Commander: I was only able to destroy five of the eight buoys, the rest have transitioned."

Shit! It was just a matter of time before whoever they signaled would show up ready for a fight. Klutch leaped up and ran into the now open airlock. Coonts ran in front of me and held his arms up. I cleared the image from my helmet and tried to give him a reassuring look. He responded by turning and running into the airlock with Klutch. I quickly followed and found Klutch working furiously on the inner door.

"Commander, I can bypass the safety relay long enough to get us inside without destroying the inner door."

They both had a look of worry on their faces. I gritted my teeth, thinking my crew could not trust my actions. The beast in me was trying to take over and I wanted to scream out in frustration. I would bend this madness to my will and not let the monster have his way.

365

The door suddenly opened and the rancid atmosphere came bursting in on us. Klutch jumped through the hatch and went right. I was just behind him and went left with Coonts on my heels. The safety relay slammed the hatch shut and we found ourselves in a rolling fog bank of unknown contaminates. My no-light sensors were being degraded by the atmospheric conditions. It was difficult to get accurate readings beyond twenty feet or so. Klutch should have let me blow the door and let the void suck the noxious gases out of this shit hole.

We were at one end of a large corridor and I could make out a hatch up on the righthand side. The rapid decompression and the lower temperature associated with our entry made the atmospheric conditions even worse. There was a good chance we just sucked the worst of the filth in this place right to our current location. I checked my heat sensors and got no active sources. I tried my Backscatter Transmitter and to my surprise got the Operative. We were evidently inside of the shielded area.

"Nathan, one of my recon teams tripped an explosive trap. It cost them their lives. It is no longer possible to reach our entry point. I think this place is set to lure other unsuspecting riffraff to their deaths. We are being forced to go deeper into this scat hole. What is your location?"

"When we detected the explosion and your transmission abruptly ended, Tria took out the hangar door you were trying to open for us. We are in a pressurized corridor just beyond the hangar."

"You must use great caution, Nathan. That is where my recon team was killed. The trap collapsed a large portion of the overhead onto them. I advise you to find another route."

"Roger that, we will attempt to go around. Can you hold till we link up?"

"Affirmative, Nathan. Be careful — if you find yourself in a corridor that looks clear, find another route. I think we are being purposely directed to a location of our enemy's choosing."

"We are on our way. You will hear us coming."

Coonts and Klutch had been listening. I pointed at the wall on the opposite side of the corridor. "Coonts, make us a hole, we are staying away from all the obvious routes. We took a knee behind some debris. Coonts selected a spot on the wall with the least amount of wiring, pipes and conduit. The beam shot lit the area like an arc welder. The wall blew inward leaving a bright orange circle of molten metal. He changed the angle and hit it again making it large enough for us to enter. As I started to get up Klutch held up a hand stopping me. He pulled a Chaalt smart grenade from his leg storage and set the friend-or-foe identifier, then threw it through the hole Coonts had made.

Since I did take the time to read up on the weapon, I knew that we as well as any Chaalt would be excluded from its targeting systems. We were surprised when we immediately heard the staccato blasts from the grenades fragments. When we no longer heard any fragments detonating, we got up, ready to investigate. We were almost to the hole when there was a bright flash and a large explosion. We could feel the thump through our boots.

Klutch called out, "That was the core. There must be a nest of Throggs hiding in there."

Klutch, as a rule, always thought more was better when it came to munitions. He ran to the edge of the hole and threw another grenade into the opening. We stood back, waiting to see what would happen. When nothing did, Klutch's voice had the sound of disappointment when he called out, "Moving up"

He leaped through the hole and Coonts and I were right behind him. The first thing I could not help but notice was the large assortment of body parts just inside of the room we found ourselves in. There were weapons scattered about the floor as well. Coonts put words to our surprising find.

"Commander, evidently my choice of entry points interrupted an ambush. There are the corpses of many different races, but the majority are wearing Murlak and Scrun armor."

Klutch had been scouting just ahead of us and came running back. "Commander, I just saw a large group of armed combatants moving away from this location."

"OK Klutch, we will follow your lead."

Klutch turned and headed back to a junction in another corridor. Out of the corner of my helmet I saw the Chaalt grenade hovering close to the overhead. I gave it a wide berth and Coonts did the same. We stacked behind Klutch as he cautiously peeked down the corridor in both directions. To our right we could see a big pressure door and to our left a long hallway that hit another junction. The atmosphere in this area was much better than the hangar area we had just left.

Klutch called over his shoulder to us. "Which way, Commander?"

Coonts commented, "I cannot be sure, but I think the Operative is somewhere to our right."

The beast in me wanted to chase down every piece of scat we could find and kill them, but Coonts was putting our priorities in the correct order. I pushed the Oolaran beast from my thoughts and reached into my leg storage. I pulled a smart grenade out and threw it as far down the corridor as I could.

"Klutch, see if you can get that door open."

Klutch went right and started working on the door control. Coonts and I took a knee behind him and covered his back while he worked. I took the opportunity to call the Operative.

"Senior Operative, we took a different route and stumbled upon several enemy troops that may have been heading in your direction."

"If you are pinned down, we can attempt to find you, but we will be forced to move cautiously. I do not wish to lose anymore personnel in this scat hole."

"No, we have eliminated the threat. Stay in a defensible position; we are still moving in your direction. I do not want to risk firing on you if we stumble into each other."

"Acknowledged, we will hold at our current position. Operative out."

I was pretty sure it was not Sael's normal game plan to wait on anyone for any reason. She had seen the beast on the rampage and she wanted no part of that action.

"Klutch, how are you doing on the door?"

I had barely got the words from my mouth when the Chaalt grenade hovering near the hall junction, fired a couple of fragments. The results were a low moaning wail.

Coonts ripped off a burst of H.E. into the end of the corridor and the noise promptly ceased. I did not like standing around at the dead end of the corridor.

Coonts was thinking the same thing. "Klutch, the opposition is probing us. It would be advisable to move from this position."

Klutch turned on Coonts but whatever rebuke he was going to utter was cut off by a bright explosive flash on the front of his armor. He was thrown violently against the door he was trying to open. Coonts and I were knocked sprawling to the floor. I had been trying to contain the Oolaran beast, but now all bets on whether I would be able to, were off. I rolled onto my side and sent a twenty-round burst of high explosive to the end of the hall and followed it up with a beam shot that took out part of the side wall and corner of the junction.

To my surprise Klutch rolled into me temporarily disrupting my murderous thoughts. He broadcast out loud in the clear. "SUCK ON THIS YOU COWARDLY THROGGS!" He threw his launcher up and discharged a single round that had my HUD blinking orange. There was a tremendous explosion that tossed us off the deck and back into the pressure door.

My thoughts and worries about restricting the actions of the killer inside of me were forgotten. A seemingly endless barrage of rubble rained down, partially burying us. The true irritation of what just took place finally sunk in. Justice did not issue any anti-matter rounds to me. Before I could start bitching about it, Coonts and Klutch pushed the wreckage off themselves and took off running in the direction the attack came from. I did the same and joined them. At the rate the atmosphere was clearing, it did not take a genius to know this place was no longer airtight.

The Operative decided someone was stirring the pot too harshly and she decided it was me. My transmitter went live with her less than happy voice. "Nathan, cease your destruction before you bring this sewer down on all of our heads!"

I could have sworn I heard my teammates snicker at the Operative's comment. It might have been a little funny, and I even considered letting the Operative know it — that is until Coonts took a quick peek around the corner and the wall just above his head disappeared in a huge flashing explosion. We were all knocked sprawling a good distance up the corridor we just came down. Obviously, the bastards had bigger and badder weapons to use on us. The bloodthirsty Oolaran in me ruled out most all sensible courses of action. I thrusted with my suit gravity drives so hard that when I attempted to turn the corner I careened off of the wall and then the ceiling of the corridor. The reckless maneuver probably saved my life.

The large anti-ship weapons follow-up shot went straight up the middle of the corridor and through a bulkhead. The entire area violently decompressed with a shitstorm of flying debris. Several of the enemy combatants went sailing by on a one-way trip to eternity. My HUD highlighted the shielded gun platform. My first beam shot brought down the shield. My second blew the weapon from its mount, and my third reduced the whole mess to slag. I had at least twenty enemy targets attempting to escape the area. I gave them a generous dose of high explosive, killing several outright and sending the rest spinning in freefall in all directions.

With as much effort as I could muster, I regained my human sensibilities. I became aware of my comms being overwhelmed by Justice, Tria, Coonts and Klutch all yelling at me at the same time. Justice and Tria sounded somewhat concerned, but everything coming from the Troop Master and Coonts was quite colorful. Just when I thought it could not get any worse, the Operative came on the Backscatter transmitter, squawking something about the outpost breaking apart.

My HUD picked up five targets wearing Zaen battle armor crawl out of the debris in the target area. They all took off with their gravity drives heading in the direction of a large doorway at the end of the passage. I threw my arm up and hit two of them with a beam shot that blew arms and legs from the suits. The rest were blown into the walls and ceiling. I accelerated to maximum to catch them before any could recover enough to return fire. My continued weapons fire had the desired effect of silencing my comms. I could see Coonts and Klutch rapidly approaching from my six. I slowed to let them catch me.

In a relatively calm voice Coonts called to me. "Commander, we will need some of them alive."

I stopped and hovered in place letting Coonts and Klutch fly past me. Klutch called out. "We have three survivors!"

I saw him extend his fighting hooks and slash at the launcher feed tubes on the Zaen battle suits. When he was satisfied they were inoperable, he waved to me.

Now that it was quiet, I called to Tria. "Tria, do you have a visual on the opening shot through the outpost's hull?"

Her answer was short, clipped and to the point: "Yes, Commander!"

"I need you to move in close to it so we can transfer the prisoners."

"Roger that, Commander. ETA twenty seconds."

Coonts called to me. "Commander, one of the survivors is badly wounded and his suit repair systems are failing. What are your orders?"

The only reason Coonts would say something like that was because he knew we could probably save the Murlak's life if we tried. He also knew the outcome of our interrogations did not hold a bright future for the pirate piece of scat. The beast in me wanted to speed the process along but the vengeful human wanted him to suffer for what they had done to Tria. The little Grawl must have known what I was thinking. He extruded his fighting hooks and jammed them into the opening the suit was trying to repair, fully decompressing the Murlak. He kicked the corpse away and grabbed onto one of the other survivors. Klutch did the same and they made their way to the breach in the hull.

I could see through the sizable hole that Tria had maneuvered Eagle Two in close to the outpost. She had the back ramp lowered and Coonts and Klutch disappeared into the back with the prisoners.

Justice suddenly called out over the group comms. "Commander, there is a shuttle launching from the outpost. I will attempt to disable it!"

My HUD came alive with the outside view that Justice was seeing. The Legacy rapidly closed the distance and fired on the shuttle with the rail cannons. The shuttle's shields held up to the pounding, so Justice switched to the heavier point defense weapons. One shot was all it took to blow the rear off of the fleeing target. What remained of the spacecraft was flipping end over end. The Legacy caught up with it and arrested the spin rate and stopped its momentum with the tow beam. I wondered if they were wearing pressure suits because the shuttle was venting atmosphere out of the hull at a fairly good rate. I would find out one way or the other when we were done on the outpost.

27

I set down on the deck near the remains of the cannon the Throggs were attempting to use on us. When my boots touched the deck, I could feel vibrations from explosions somewhere on the station.

I called to the Operative. "Senior Operative, are you making this a competition to see who can dismantle this sewer the fastest?"

"I HAVE NO TIME FOR YOUR MINDLESS CHATTER!"

The transmission abruptly ceased. I noticed some of the vibrations I was feeling were quite jarring. I think the Operative and her team were in it up to their eyeballs.

"Coonts, keep watch on the prisoners. Klutch, get your big ass in here now!"

A blue triangle appeared behind me moving at high speed. Klutch set down next to me sending a flurry of debris rising up around us.

I called for a little help. "Justice, can you pinpoint the location of the detonations on the outpost?"

"Yes, Commander. There appears to be a pitched battle taking place one thousand twenty-two feet to the right of your current position."

"Can you guide us there with your scanners?"

"I was only able to pinpoint that position due to the high amount of vibration propagations from the area. The battle has yet to breach the scan shielding throughout that location."

"Give me a target reference point well to the side of the battle."

"Let's make a hole Klutch!"

We ducked down behind the remains of the cannon. I snapped off two shots with my beam weapon and Klutch put two more in the same hole. When the wreckage went flying past, we jumped up and ran to the tunnel we had just made. We crawled in and stood up in the next room over. We ran across and took a knee behind some large pieces of equipment. My reference point was a little more to the left this time and I snapped off three shots in a row. We got a rapid decompression on the third shot. Not to be outdone, Klutch grabbed my shoulder before I could stand up and sent three more down the gaping hole. His facemask cleared and he gave me a toothy grin.

"More is always better."

We ran to the hole and scurried in. We found ourselves in a large open hangar. There was a cargo shuttle sitting in the middle of the bay with two big glowing holes on the side of it. The hauler was in terrible shape, judging from its appearance, but now it was a wreck. When we cleared the rear of the shuttle we came under fire from an upper boarding hatch. Klutch beat me to the punch and turned the hatch into a ragged hole. I followed it up with a Chaalt smart grenade. I was a little disappointed when it did not go off.

We moved on to a position where Justice gave us another aiming point. We raised our arms in preparation to fire, but the flash of the grenade detonating behind us, made both of us involuntarily duck. We looked back at the gaping wound we had inflicted on the ship and were showered with shuttle parts and alien entrails. Klutch casually flicked something wet and gory from the visor of his helmet. I thought maybe we should find out if there were more hostiles hiding in the shuttle. The Troop Master did not seem to care either way, so we moved on to the business at hand. We had to be close to the Operative's position because the vibrations from explosions were more pronounced. Sael was giving the opposition hell for the loss of her teammates.

Klutch decided we were a little close to our aim point, so we moved back to the shuttle for cover. I held my arm up to fire and a large hatch to our left opened. Several species of aliens retreated through the door. The ones that held my attention were the Scrun and Murlak troops. They stopped to the side of the door and were setting up a device next to it. The fools were pointing their weapons toward the doorway and were oblivious to Klutch and I standing at the back of the freight hauler. They obviously thought they were in friendly territory.

I slowly dropped my arm with the beam weapon and held up my left arm. A circle appeared around the would-be ambushers and I spun up my minigun. It was not hard guessing what expression was on the Tibor's face right at the moment. Before I could utter the word "fire" Klutch let the .44-caliber explosive projectiles fly into the flanks of our targets. I did the same, adding a side-to-side motion for finesse. The aliens and pretty much everything around them went to pieces. Klutch's decision to use the freight hauler for cover was the correct one, because one of us hit the device the Scrun was setting up. There was a tremendous flash that knocked us flat on our backs and sent us sliding across the deck. The hulk of the old shuttle absorbed the brunt of the blast.

I sat upright with my eyes wide when I noticed the old freight hauler was now on its side. It would have been very bad for the Operative and her crew if they had pursued the enemy through that door.

Regaining my footing, I decided to give Klutch credit for the boondoggle before he could hang it on me. "Interesting target selection, Troop Master."

Klutch cleared his visor and gave me an incredulous look. Before he could spew a toxic retort, the Operative broadcast on the Backscatter transmitter.

"Nathan, check your fire before you kill us all!"

Klutch stood staring at me shaking his head in agreement. I should know by now I would get the blame when shit goes wrong. Since there was no longer evidence to support my side of the story, I dropped any attempt at explaining what happened to the Operative. I could already tell Klutch was not going to be helpful with my plea of innocence. It would be best just to move on.

"Senior Operative, all opposition has been eliminated and we have completed our mission goal."

The Operative shot right back. "Nathan, unless you have Eiger's corpse at your feet, you have not completed your mission goal!"

The Operative sounded very testy and I could not blame her. I don't know what I would do if I had lost one of my crewmates. It is why I spent countless millions of credits so my crew could have the very best protection. I could not afford to lose an ally because I had so very few.

"Senior Operative, we have secured two of Eiger's clan in custody. We are ready to link up with you and evac the target area."

"Affirmative Nathan, we will hold our position until you link up."

It was hard to tell if the Operative was afraid of us firing on them or she did not wish to risk another boobytrap. At this point, it did not matter, I was sure there was more scum lurking on the outpost. It was time to get out of this sewer.

"Klutch, take point and get us to the Operative. I will cover our backs.

When we cleared the side of the freight hauler, we were stunned at the destruction of the explosive device. We would not have to make a door or worry about another explosive device. The wall and a huge section of the deck was missing. There was now a gaping hole weeping contaminates of every kind down to the lower spaces.

Klutch used his gravity boosters to clear the rend and called out, "Commander, there is a lot of dead and wounded hostiles in here."

I quickly boosted across and saw what he was talking about. There were bodies scattered everywhere and some were still moving. The enemy was in full retreat away from the Operative and was boobytrapping their escape route. I smiled thinking Sael must have been kicking their asses pretty good for so many to be retreating. I looked up when my HUD beeped a warning. Two hostiles in Zaen battle armor jumped up from the floor and ran for an open hatch across the empty hangar.

The beast in me had been quietly biding its time. It was almost like I had no choice in my reaction to the pop-up targets. In a kneejerk spasm of reflexes my arm came up and gave the retreating combatants a beam shot. The beam caught the trailing soldier square in the back, disintegrating all but a boot and part of an arm. The blast sent the lead soldier flying violently into the bulkhead next to the hatch. The battle suit was missing a leg and the decompression proved fatal as the suit bounced from the wall and went prone on the deck.

My lack of fire discipline netted me a less than appreciative response from the Operative. "Nathan, control yourself before this scat hole comes apart under our feet!"

Klutch came up beside me and pulled my arm down. I shook my head to clear my thoughts. Klutch said, "Commander, you should take a look at some of the Scrun soldiers. Several are wearing heavy exoskeletons and are much better armed than the others."

Forcing the Oolaran soldier from my mind, I turned and followed Klutch back to the blast zone of the Scrun ambush weapon. As we approached the body, it was easy to tell what was left was Scrun. The long, gangly arm that was still intact was a dead giveaway. The armor, or what was left of it, was not anything I had seen before. The large

383

shoulder-mounted weapons were reminiscent of the equipment Coram heavy gunners packed around. Glancing around the blast area, we could make out a large number of remains that more or less looked like this one.

Klutch was bent over another and rooting through its gear. "What are you thinking, Klutch?"

"I am thinking this was one of the hit teams tasked with killing us."

I frowned, "How could they possibly know we would be coming here?"

"They would not, but it is not a stretch to assume that wherever Eiger's clan is, you will eventually show up."

I did not like the implications of Klutch's statement. If the Scrun could predict my actions, then Eiger should be able to do the same thing. We needed to collect the Operative and get the hell out of here.

"Klutch, I am going back out to the hangar and breach the shielding barrier so we can have active comms." The Tibor gave me a thumbs-up and followed me back across the area of devastation we had created. There were no signs of life in the hangar, so we ducked back behind the wreck of the shuttle and I gave the spacecraft entry door a double tap with my beam weapon.

Justice came over our comms net. "Commander, the area of operation is clear of hostile spacecraft and I have detected no transition signatures. The shuttle I disabled has ignored all of our hails and Eagle Two is orbiting the outpost waiting to extract your strike teams. I am downloading the data from your battle suit and will be standing by."

"Roger that, Justice. Keep us covered. The Operative is close by and we are moving to that location."

"Tria, get a lock on my location and move Eagle Two in close for evac operations."

I was surprised when Coonts came back over the net. "Affirmative Commander. I am moving to your location now."

I did not know what to think of Coonts talking instead of Tria, but I had more pressing matters to take care of at the moment.

"Coonts, give us five minutes to clear the area and take down the hangar door."

"Roger, Commander, counting down from five."

Klutch took the lead and we hauled ass back to the next hangar over and thru the hatch I had killed the two Murlak troopers in. We had not gone more than another hundred yards when Klutch sent a burst of HE from his launcher tube behind some large pieces of equipment and containers. I saw something fly up like a ragdoll and then all hell broke loose. Something large-caliber struck me on my left arm, knocking me spinning to the floor. Everything around us started blowing up. We were being pummeled with large pieces of debris and shrapnel. I had red warning lights on my needle gun and tube launcher. My arm felt numb, like I had hit my crazy bone a solid lick. I started sliding backwards and realized Klutch was pulling me into the corridor out of the ambush area. Since I was still facing the enemy, I spun up my minigun and emptied it in one long burst that brought a lull to the intense incoming fire. Klutch elbowed me aside and stuck his arm out and sprayed out a non-stop barrage of high explosive.

The Operative must have decided that Klutch and I were just screwing around. "Nathan, cease fire! The overhead is collapsing. If you continue your madness, we will be trapped in the debris!"

The beast was on the verge of freeing himself from my efforts to contain its wanton ways. It was all I could do to yell out a warning over the Backscatter transmitter.

"I don't have time for your bitching! You better take cover NOW!"

I stood up and unloaded with the beam weapon as fast as it could cycle. Klutch knew it would be pointless trying to appeal to my current mindset, so he did the same. We reduced everything to the front of us to glowing slag. When my weapon finally overheated and shut down to cool, we could see stars peering back at us through the carnage. For a moment it was eerily still, then we felt thumping vibrations and they were close and to the right of our position.

Coonts came over the comms. "Commander, the hangar door is down and I am standing by for extraction operations. Justice has warned me to move away to a safe distance. He says you are destroying the outpost with your beam weapon. Do you need assistance?"

It was a pretty ballsy request on Coonts part because he knew the Oolaran in me was responsible for what was happening. I was glad when Klutch spoke up and called him off. I was trying my best to calm the wicked bastard that was possessing me. Klutch gave me a hard rap on the shoulder to get my attention.

"Commander, we need to press the attack, the enemy has retreated and is now attacking the Operative. We have them trapped between us, you must not use your beam weapon."

To emphasize his point, he stepped in front of me and grabbed my shoulders. He pulled me down to his visor and cleared it. "Commander, we must use caution so we did not cause harm to the Operative and her troops."

I cleared my visor to let him know I was indeed back in control. I shoved the demon aside and forced the grimace on my face into a small smile. I unclipped my

387

high-tech scatter gun from the side of my backpack and charged the barrels.

"Lead the way, Troop Master."

That comment got me a toothy smile and he rapped me again on the shoulder. "Let's go kill some Throggs, Commander!"

We had only gone a couple of dozen strides and to our front there was an alien I did not recognize. He had just fired his weapon and turned in our direction. Klutch made sure I would never get a chance at recognizing whatever race it was. He unloaded a twelve-round clip of explosive buckshot into it from about thirty feet. We charged past the mess and turned the corner. Standing very close in front of me was a Scrun wearing the power armor we had examined earlier. I gave him three quick double taps with the penetrator slugs before the suit threw in the towel on its job of protecting the Throgg wearing it. My two follow-up shots burst the suit like a water balloon.

I was surprising myself at my ability to hold the beast in check. I could feel it egging me on, and the thought of giving the enemy hell with my beam weapon was very much on my mind, but I felt like I was the one in control. I didn't know if the Operative knew we were in the enemy's flank or not, but if she suspected it, Klutch and I could not tell. The Chaalt troopers were pouring non-stop fire and explosives into the area directly to our front.

Klutch pulled a grenade out and held it up to me. I followed suit and we tossed them behind the enemy troops and stepped back into the corridor. The twin blasts bowed the corridor wall inward and some of the overhead piping and structural supports collapsed onto us. Shoving the debris aside we peeked back around the corner. A large number of the combatants were sprawled on the floor and several still moving. Klutch stepped out with his minigun and gave anything moving a dose of sucks-to-be-you.

The sight of Klutch and me standing in the enemy's rear, hosing them down, managed to get the Operative and her strike team to cease fire. The surviving enemy soldiers finally figured out what had befallen their comrades. They threw down their weapons and slowly stood with their hands out in front of them.

The Operative called to us over our Backscatter Transmitters. "Nathan, you and Klutch should make sure our extraction point is secure."

I was a little confused at first and was going to say we would help her round everyone up. Klutch's visor cleared and he jerked his head in the direction of the hangar. He turned and headed for the corridor. I started to say something to the Operative but she cut me off.

"NOW NATHAN!"

389

Without another word I turned and headed back the way we came. I called to Coonts. "Coonts, do you have enough room to set Eagle Two down in the hangar?"

"Affirmative Commander, I am on my way, ETA thirty seconds."

The trip back to the hangar gave me a little time to think clearly. I opened a secure Backscatter channel to Tria. "Tria, I thought you were going to be our pilot on this mission."

When I did not get a return answer, I became a little concerned. Was she mad at me for something I had done or was it something else? I caught up with Klutch.

"You have done well controlling your inner demon, Commander. With time I think you will be rid of the ill effects of the Oolaran imprinting."

I cleared my visor and gave the Tibor a smile and clasped him on the shoulder. "I could not have done it without the help from my friends."

When we got back to the hangar, Eagle Two had landed just inside of the mangled doors. The cargo ramp came down and I was surprised to see Tria standing there in her recon armor. She debarked and walked toward me. She had blood on her hands and the front of her armor. Klutch stepped away without comment and boarded the shuttle. Tria stood in front of me. I guess she thought I was going to chastise her because she did not say a word. I glanced into the shuttle's hold and could not see the Murlak prisoners. It did not take a genius to figure out the rest of the story. Rather than ask a bunch of awkward questions, I cut to the chase.

"Were you able to get Eiger's location?"

"A vague location on the fringe."

The finality of her comment, left no doubt as to the validity of the statement. The method she chose to gain that information must have caused her great discomfort. I knew it would take a week or more before the ill effects of her weaponization were completely healed.

Justice called on my comms net. "Commander, the Operative's flagship has moved into close proximity with the outpost. I believe they will use their transporter technology for extraction."

"OK, Justice. We will be ready to depart when they have cleared the area."

As if on cue, the Operative called me on the Backscatter transmitter. "Nathan, now that hostilities have ceased we will no longer require your services for extraction. We have taken select hostile personnel for interrogation and will debrief you on our findings. I have obtained coordinates for a star system that I recommend we meet at. I believe you will be familiar with the location."

The transmission promptly ended. The Operative's statement verified my belief that she took high ranking prisoners and killed the rest for retribution. I took Tria by the hand and we boarded the shuttle. Coonts closed the hatch and restored atmosphere in the hold. We launched from the outpost and quickly rendezvoused with the Legacy. Justice took us aboard with the tow beam and we headed for the disabled shuttle. Klutch was reloading the ordnance he had expended on the outpost. When he saw me looking, he gave me a thumbs-up. His armor looked like it had been chewed on and spit out. The scarring and pockmarks from our battle made the new armor look years old.

I stepped over to our makeshift armor rack and stepped out of my armor. There was only a small piece of the needle guns mount remaining on the armor's left arm; the rest of the weapon was missing. The tube launcher wasn't all that bad, but the magazine feed was severed. I am sure Justice had taken note of our battle damage and would recommend upgrades to Felix when we returned to Alpha Base. Judging by the amount of hits I had taken from enemy fire and flying shrapnel, the armor performed flawlessly. A great deal of the hits had gone unnoticed in combat. It was a testimony to the amazing strength and rigidity of the design. I would also recommend increasing the amount of onboard ammo for the minigun. With the exception of the Zaen battle armor, none of the other enemy armor suits withstood the torrent of explosive fire from the weapon.

28

Tria changed out of her recon armor and now wore her smart cloth uniform. I was not going to ask when Justice had loaded her light armor onto the shuttle. There was a good chance I would get stonewalled by some obscure answer or excuse. I was, however, going to ask her about the interrogation of the prisoners and the information they divulged before their apparent demise. Before I could corner Tria on the subject, Coonts ran up to me.

"Commander, now that Tria is available to pilot the shuttle, I request permission to join you on the boarding mission."

The little Grawl was fidgeting and had an expectant look on his face. I could not chastise him for his collusion with Tria's disregard of my orders to pilot the shuttle. I knew how hard it could be refusing the Chaalt warrior her way. The best way to have a word with Tria would be to let the Grawl and Tibor handle the boarding and I would stay behind.

"Carry on, Coonts. You and Klutch can do the boarding, and I will wait for your report when you return."

That put a smile on the Grawl's face. He went to get geared up and I turned back to Tria. She made sure she got the first words in before I could chew on her ass for ignoring our agreement.

"They were personally responsible for my some of my injuries. I returned their kindness. I have heard you use the expression 'tit for tat' — that is what I did."

"Since they are not here to question, I take it you threw them out the airlock?"

"Once they gave me what useful information they had, I gave them a choice, something, I might add, they did not give me while trying to beat me to death."

"And?"

"They took the less painful choice."

There was not much I could say to that. I instead decided this was as good a time as any for a debriefing and asked what she had gained.

"Other than the supposed location of Eiger, the only intelligence of note was that one of the Scrun teams assigned with the task of killing us was stationed here recently. It is my understanding they killed a large number of the inhabitants of the outpost. When the Murlak asked them why they did so, the Scrun claimed it was the best way to develop attack strategies while biding their time on the outpost."

"I appreciate their spirit of cooperation. I hope to personally thank them in the near future."

By the sour look on Tria's face, the nuance of my sarcasm was lost on her. "You can thank the Scrun right after we kill them."

Justice interrupted our testy exchange. "Commander, the Operative has sent a data package. The data contains coordinates to a star system that closely matches the location given to Tria during her interrogation of the Murlak prisoners."

Now we were getting somewhere. To have corroborating information from two different sources was a step in the right direction. It was enough to warrant an investigation of the location.

"Thank you, Justice. Please send the Operative the information Tria collected."

"Roger, Commander, message sent."

It was less than five minutes before I heard a secure tone on my BS transmitter.

"Nathan, while there is always the possibility the hostiles concocted a mutually beneficial story, I doubt that is the case. I obtained my information from the Murlak and one of the higher ranking Scrun. The Scrun also admitted to being a part of a team to terminate you and your crew."

396

"Did you get anything on the Scrun base we found?"

"Yes, I have certain reservations about the information, but it is still interesting enough to pass on. The Scrun stated that one of King Lashmos's heirs is in charge of the base and it is indeed a major slave processing center."

"Even if the information is not completely credible, I still plan on striking the base and freeing any slaves we might find."

"You can count me in, Nathan. That is one foray I plan to attend."

"I am sure you have not forgotten about the derelict ship. You and your crew have certainly earned the right to be some of the first boots aboard when we have finished cleaning up our more pressing matters."

"I am counting on that as well, Nathan. For now, we should continue prosecuting the most time-sensitive intel as soon as we finish matters here."

"I thought we were finished here?"

"You might be, but I am not. Get clear of the— Nathan! We are detecting a transition wave, now three transition waves. Prepare to engage if they are hostiles! Wait for my attack and clean up any stragglers!"

"Commander, I have four ships of a similar design to Scrun motherships. They are heavily armed and their shields have just come online. They are broad spectrum scanning at full military power. The Legacy is still in stealth mode and they have not detected us. I have a hard lock on the Operatives flagship and it has not been detected."

"Can we keep track of Sael's ship?"

"I have accumulated considerable knowledge on the Chaalt negation and cloaking technologies. I will develop a tracking algorithm to keep us alerted to Chaalt ship movements and surveillance technics."

It was nice knowing that Justice soaked up and processed even the most obscure information. He was truly a data sponge that never missed a trick.

"Roger that, Justice. When the Operative starts the party, let's make sure no one gets to leave early."

"Commander, the probability for collateral damage is high if the Scrun ships are carrying slaves. It will be extremely difficult to attempt to disable the warships without destroying them. I further postulate the Senior Operative has no intention of boarding any of the vessels."

"I understand, Justice. Keep us out of the Operative's missile envelope and take us in behind the enemy ships. If Sael does not take them out in the initial attack, we will hit them from the rear and divide their return fire."

"Roger, Commander. Moving now."

Coonts and Klutch looked pissed their boarding operation would be put on hold. I called to them. "Keep your gear on. Knowing the Operative, I don't think the battle will last long. I headed to the lifts so I could watch the battle in real time on the bridge view dome. Tria followed, and as we made the ascent to the bridge deck, she pulled me close and kissed me.

"I hope I did not anger you by interrogating the prisoners. It was not my intention to purposely ignore my agreement to pilot the shuttle. Coonts volunteered to fly the mission and it left me time for physical therapy."

It was a lame excuse at best, and I really did kind of wonder whether or not Coonts had something to do with Tria's little scheme. Now I knew for a fact he did. This was not the first time the little Grawl had pulled such stunts. As we stepped out of the lift tube, Justice alerted us the battle had begun.

"Commander I have detected minute distortion waves propagating from the location of the Senior Operative's flagship. They match stealth missile transition signatures I previously recorded during the Quill engagement. The count now totals eight."

"Roger that Justice, be prepared to launch a follow up strike if necessary."

"Affirmative, all tubes loaded and weapons are in standby mode."

Justice moved the Legacy to a point in space that was thirty degrees off of the Operative's reciprocal targeting datum. The Scrun ships were rapidly closing with the decrepit outpost and were evidently oblivious to our presence. Justice gave us another alert.

"Commander, I just detected a much larger transition propagation wave from the Operative's location. I believe it is a much larger weapon launch, possibly a torpedo class weapon. There is a possibility the launch will be detected."

I was wondering what the hell Sael was up to and what kind of weapon she was going to use on the Scrun. Justice called out again.

"The Operative's flagship is maneuvering and two of the Scrun ships have turned in the direction the Chaalt ship has vacated. I have multiple hostile missile launches. All weapons have failed to track the Chaalt vessel and appear to be in search mode."

Justice put red boxes around the Scrun ships and displayed their missile tracks with red lines. I was just starting to wonder when the Operative's first strike package was going to appear when all four of the hostile ships took hits. The first hits failed to penetrate the enemy shields but the second round took them down. The Operative had been closing the distance with the Scrun and now opened up with her energy weapons. The two targets that had turned to attack were pierced by the Chaalt weapons blowing thru both sides of the hostile ships. The other two targets looked like they were attempting to maneuver behind the outpost when it disappeared in huge white flash. One of the enemy ships was crushed by the expanding debris. The other sustained heavy damage and was in a spinning drift that left no doubt it received a fatal blow. Justice closed with the drifting ship and we got a close-up view of the damage. There was a large piece of the outpost rammed thru the side of the Scrun vessel. The momentum of the high velocity spin put an end to the ship as it broke in half.

It might have taken Sael all of five minutes to completely clear the battlespace of targets. The missiles the Scrun ships had fired never got a target lock and were circling in ever bigger loops farther and farther from the target area. I thought I would hear something from Sael, but Justice alerted us she jumped out of the system.

Tria looked over at me. "It is why they used to call her Kala Mor Dee. She has always been very efficient when it comes to killing our enemies."

That was an understatement. Sael had just sent thousands of one of the most hated races in the galaxy on a fast track to hell. I suspected she had every intention of doing away with the outpost just before the Scrun showed up. It was time to see who and what was aboard the disabled shuttle. I could see the small blinking yellow box high up on the view dome. In the blink of an eye it filled the screen. Tria joined me and we made our way back to the hangar to await a report from Coonts and Klutch.

Justice directed a comms burst at the shuttle in the Scrun and Murlak dialects, then threw in a mishmash of others, including Galactic Union standard. He warned that any resistance would be fatal and to send all of their weapons and armor out the airlock. He attached a countdown timer to the ultimatum, when it reached seven, the airlock on the shuttle opened and several Scrun weapons mixed with a couple of Murlak sidearms floated out of the hatch.

Klutch went across first followed by Coonts. They both disappeared into the airlock only to return several minutes later with two Zaen battle suits in tow. That was an indication we might have just netted a couple more of Eiger's clan. They went back into the shuttle and were gone for several minutes. I was wondering why we were not getting a video feed when I heard Klutch call to Justice.

"Justice, can you move in closer to the shuttle and center the airlock on the hangar door."

"Affirmative Troop Master, maneuvering now."

Justice put the Legacy alongside the shuttle and about fifteen feet from the hangar door. Tria and I stood just inside the atmospheric retention field trying to figure out what the hell our crewmates were up to.

Klutch commed me a warning. "Commander, could you and Tria please step away from the hangar door."

Tria and I shared a frown and stepped back away from the huge door. I was just getting ready to tell them to quit messing around when the airlock on the shuttle explosively decompressed. Two Murlak and two Scrun were violently propelled across the short distance between the shuttle and the Legacy. The aliens flew through the retention field and when the artificial gravity grabbed ahold it deposited them in a heap on the deck. All were groaning loudly, and evidently, the two Murlak without pressure suits were still alive.

My ears were assaulted by Klutch's loud, croaking laughter and I heard him tell Coonts he owed him a thousand credits. Coonts response was accompanied by several profane words and him yelling out, "YOU CHEATED!"

I wanted very much to be pissed at the two of them, but damn, that was some funny shit. I could tell Tria was trying her best to keep from laughing as well. I called to the two clowns dicking around on the shuttle.

"If you are done screwing around, we need to go meet the Operative."

Coonts and Klutch jumped across from the shuttle and you could hear the heated argument going on between the two. Coonts was carrying what looked like a small briefcase. It was apparent he was going to hit Klutch with it.

"HEY! Knock it off and put that scat in the brig, we need to get moving."

Coonts walked up and gave me the case, then turned back to Klutch grumbling under his breath. I could see Tria give the two Murlak a close look before Coonts and Klutch jerked them off the deck and headed for the security lockup.

"Do they look familiar?"

Tria shook her head no. They got to keep their lives, for now. Justice closed the hangar doors and called out we were going to make a standard transition to the Operative's location. Our ETA was only a few minutes more than the time it would have taken to charge the energy matrix. I felt the small discomfort in my stomach when we jumped to hyperspace. I held the case out to Tria and she opened it. Inside was a considerable stack of credit vouchers and some small cubes that were data chips. Now I knew why Coonts and Klutch let them live: they must have been the reigning leadership until we came along. The credit vouchers were probably once owned by the occupants of the outpost.

As Tria and I walked past the science lab, I placed the data cubes on one of the tables. Tria did the same with the case containing the credit vouchers.

"Looks like the planetary protection fund just got a boost in revenue."

My comment wiped the grim look from Tria's face and replaced it with a smile. Mission accomplished on my part because such a pretty face should not be flawed by a frown. She grabbed my arm and, with another hint at her new strength, pulled me toward her. Before I could say anything witty she planted a kiss on me that let me know there was no longer any room for improvement on the Earth sign of affection. She let go of me when we heard Coonts and Klutch come out of the ready room arguing. As they passed by the lab they noticed us and the argument ceased. Tria's kiss made me forget all about asking the two what they had wagered on.

We had just stepped off the lift tube on the bridge level when Justice called to us. "Commander, one of the data cubes is Scrun and heavily encrypted. The other one is the navigation chip set for the shuttle. I find it very interesting that it has coordinates known to us. The shuttle was recently at the location divulged to us by Tam Lin and identified as the Scrun strike team training base.

405

The other is the slave distribution center hidden on the volcanic planet in the Delta One system. There appears to be access codes attached to both destinations. It would be extremely foolhardy to leave such codes attached to their coordinates."

"It sounds awful convenient, doesn't it?"

The frown I had successfully removed from Tria's face a few moments ago returned. "If the access codes are indeed a plant, it would be a very good way to identify friend from foe."

"Really makes me wonder what is on the encrypted cube."

I turned around and went back to the down tube. The data cube was probably a plant and meant as a trap for any hapless fool. It irked me to no end thinking it might have been left for me in particular. If this was the case, then the Scrun were convinced I was a sucker and a fool. The beast inside of me was laughing at my new titles. I would prove the Scrun wrong on both counts. Tria was following me then abruptly stopped. She must have sensed my inner demon. She was capable of pushing the Oolaran monster aside and clearing my thoughts of its deadly intentions; she instead chose to turn and walk away.

29

When I exited the down tube, Coonts and Klutch were approaching. Coonts immediately picked up on my dark mood.

"Commander, is there a problem?"

It was all I could do to grind out that I was going to interrogate the prisoners. Coonts hastily stepped aside, but Klutch turned to follow me. I thought I had done well on the outpost and was capable of controlling the Oolaran soldier. Right at the moment my desire to bring death and destruction down on the heads of my enemies was all I could think about. I went to the ready room and dumped my smart cloth uniform on the floor in front of my locker and slipped on my recon armor. As I turned for the door I saw Klutch was doing the same thing. The short, wide lout had a sinister smile on his face. Coonts was nowhere to be seen, and I suspected he was looking for Tria.

I entered the brig and cleared the cell doors so the prisoners could see each other. In reality, it was so they could see what was going to happen if I did not get the answers I was looking for. The first cell had a Murlak casually lying on a bunk and his companion pacing the cell in front of the door. The other had the two Scrun in it, and they were standing by the cell door looking surprised and staring wide-eyed at us.

Klutch quickly pushed past me and the cell door with the Murlak opened. The Murlak that had been pacing the floor jumped back and screamed "NO!" Klutch stalked past him and grabbed mister-calm-and-cool from his bunk. He threw him out of the cell with such ferocity he bounced off the wall, leaving a bloody face print from the impact. Klutch leaped off the floor and landed on the Murlak's legs. The sound of the bones snapping was loud and sickening. The other prisoners pushed back into the corners of their cells and stared on in horror. They were used to doling it out to others and were completely shocked by the concept of it happening to them. I was pleasantly surprised how little Klutch was stinking the place up while he went about his business. He was relentless, and I could feel the beast in me applauding his actions. The unconscious Murlak was awoken to Klutch stomping his hand flat. His screams had the other yelling out, "I WILL TELL YOU WHATEVER YOU WANT TO KNOW!"

Klutch yelled back, "I KNOW YOU WILL."

He gave the Murlak he had been beating a kick to the head that once again put him out cold. He left him bleeding on the floor and stomped into the cell for his squalling partner. He grabbed the alien by the fur on his head and pulled him down within an inch of his face.

"Where is Eiger?"

"He has taken refuge on one of our home worlds."

Klutch balled up his fist and drew back to deliver a punishing blow. "Wrong answer! That is not the information that we have uncovered!"

The Murlak covered his face and yelled out, "YOU ARE HEARING WHAT WE WANT YOU TO HEAR!"

The outburst put a halt to Klutch's blow — it also had my attention. The Murlak slowly lowered his hands from his face.

"Eiger and the Scrun are conspiring to kill you and your crew. They have planted the information they want you to hear long ago. There is a large number of Eiger's fleet and several Scrun warships hidden in an asteroid field on the fringe. You are to be lured there by the Warbringer Solar Wind. Once you are in the asteroid field, you will be swarmed and destroyed."

Klutch looked at me and raised an eyebrow. He turned back to the Murlak. "So, you are saying Eiger is not with the fleet?"

"No. He is on the Murlak home world of Jurlaw. He claims to be wounded and is recuperating in his compound in the Crisbarry mountains."

We heard a gurgling grunt and the Murlak lying on the deck yelled out. "SILENCE, YOU COWARDLY FOOL!"

I walked over and jerked the Murlak off the floor. He spat blood on my armor and yelled out. "YOU ARE GOING TO DIE!"

For reasons unknown his comment seemed to calm the beast in me. I turned and walked out of the brig. The Murlak's eyes grew wider and he attempted to break free of my grasp. I rewarded his efforts with an open hand slap that had his head lolling from side to side. When we arrived in front of the hangar doors, they slid open revealing the shimmering gray of hyperspace. The Murlak's eyes refocused on me and it looked like he might have additional taunts to unleash on me. I cut him off with a final terse remark.

"I actually respect that you are not the coward your partner turned out to be. If it is any consolation, he will die as well."

The Murlak snapped his mouth shut and closed his eyes as I threw him into hyperspace. I called to Justice.

"Do you think there is any truth to what the Murlak is telling us?"

"The Murlak claims the Scrun have proof he is telling the truth."

"It would be hard for me to take anything those slaver pieces of shit said seriously."

"The Murlak says the proof is on the encrypted data cube one of the Scrun attempted to barter his freedom with."

"Have you been able to hack the encryption yet?"

"Negative. I lack a proper primer to help me unlock the algorithms necessary to decode the device."

"One or both of them might have access to the information. I guess I will just have to ask nicely and see if that will work."

I walked back into the brig. Klutch was standing in front of the Murlak's cell. I guess he was waiting for me to decide what to do with him. The Murlak called out to me.

"The information I have given you has surely saved your lives — all I ask in return is for you to drop me off at any outpost and you will never see me again."

I sat down on the bench across from the cell. Klutch had a look of expectation on his face that turned to ugliness with my next statement.

"OK, I guess I am good with that."

Now Klutch's face had shock, anger and disbelief all rolled up into one horrible stare. I cringed when the atmosphere in the brig turned to an eye watering toxicity. I hastily closed my helmet and started a purge cycle. He started to protest but I interjected my next comment.

"As long as you can convince the Troop Master to do the same."

The Murlak got an instant look of terror on his face; Klutch's turned to an evil sneer. He grabbed the alien by his furry head and started dragging him out of the brig. I stood up and walked to the Scrun's holding cell. They both backed up several steps when I used my implants to open the door. I stepped inside and closed the door behind me. Both of the grotesque, harelipped aliens stared at me with their large cyclops eyeballs.

"I want the access code for the data cube."

If I had to guess, I would say the arms and legs of a Scrun are of equal length. One of the despised aliens appeared to be slightly taller than the other. I pegged the taller one's reach at about six feet. That meant the shorter of the two's attempt to punch me came from a shorter distance. That being said, the strike still had to come from a long way off. I caught his wrist with my right hand and reached out and grabbed his elbow. I used my body weight to push his forearm down and toward his back while pulling the elbow sharply back over my head as I stepped under the swing. The arm could not negotiate the opposing thrusts and the shoulder made the strangest popping noise.

I instinctively ducked when I saw motion out of the corner of my helmet. A metallic boot glanced off my shoulder, making me let go of the shorter Scrun's now useless appendage. I could feel the Oolaran soldier taking over and a big rush of adrenaline sweeping through me. The loud grunting noises I was hearing did not translate, so I assumed they were some wonderful new Scrun curse words.

I shoved the short one aside and saw the momentum from the other's kick had him facing away from me. I brought my armored boot up with as much force as I could generate. The act lifted me several inches off the floor. I made a punter's contact right at the junction of the Scrun's legs. While I did manage to drive my foe up and off his feet, I did not get the reaction I would have garnered from the same blow to a human male.

I was getting ready to go for another field goal when the Scrun behind me grabbed me around the face plate with his good arm. It was strange how the adrenalin rush I experienced made me feel calm and carefree. A smile formed on my lips. The other soldier got to his feet and whipped around with his boot to deliver another roundhouse kick. I grabbed the Scrun's arm that was holding me and kicked my legs out, dropping me to my butt on the floor. The Scrun bent forward from my weight.

He caught his partners kick square in the faceplate knocking him back into the corner of the bunk behind me.

I looked up to see Klutch with his face pressed to the transparent cell wall laughing his big ass off. I could not help but laugh myself. That was dumb-shit funny. I swept my attacker's other foot before he could regain his balance. He went crashing to the floor and I lunged forward grabbing the boot the slaver was going to feed me. Pulling his leg out straight, I rolled over and locked my legs around it, pulling backwards against the knee. The joint let go and the Scrun's leg took on a very unnatural appearance. The slaver squalled out in pain and pushed away from me, dragging his damaged leg. He retreated to the corner of the cell and sat upright against the wall. The beast in me was not finished and I drove several heavy blows into his sides. Klutch caught my attention, he was frantically pointing behind me. I leaped to the side just as the other Scrun came barreling in, leading with a knee, he hit the edge of his buddy's face plate with such force, they both lay in a heap on the floor.

Klutch's croaking laugh was becoming annoying. I looked out and the Tibor was bent over slapping his knees and roaring with laughter. Shaking my head, I turned back to the Scrun lying on the deck.

"The festivities are over. Tell me the access code or I will cut you up a piece at a time."

There was a possibility they were both going to tell me to jump out the airlock — until they saw me extend my climbing hooks. The shorter of the two blurted out a string of alpha numeric code.

"Justice?"

"I have access, Commander."

I opened the cell door to a still laughing Tibor. I rapped him on the helmet as I walked by. "Klutch, can that crap and get these slaver Throggs off of my ship!"

Klutch's guffawing ceased long enough for him to say, "Commander, I have not been that entertained since my days at the training academy!"

I rolled my eyes and went to the ready room. As I stripped off my recon armor, I called to Justice. "I need a secure IST link to the Operative."

"Link active, Commander."

"Senior Operative, what is your current status?"

It did not take but a few seconds for Sael to come back on, and she did not sound happy. Then again, I doubt that she would ever be completely happy knowing I did not have to take orders from her unless I chose to do so.

"My current status is needlessly holding in the void waiting for a primate to learn how to pilot his ship to my location."

415

"I love you too, Mother, but I really don't have time to exchange pleasantries. We have interrogated some Murlak and Scrun prisoners. They say there is an ambush waiting for us somewhere near your location."

"I thought I had eradicated all of that sewage. How can you be sure what they tell you is the truth?"

"We have a data cube Justice is currently deciphering, and it should verify the information we have collected. We will be entering your area of operation shortly. Stay cloaked, and whatever you do, do not follow or engage any Murlak warships you detect in the area."

"Hah! If you think I am going to sit idly by until you show up to take down Eiger, you would be mistaken!"

"Sael, if the information I have is proven to be correct, Eiger is nowhere near your location. He is on one of the Murlak home worlds claiming to be injured and recuperating. Please hold at your location and I promise you will receive a full debrief on our findings."

The IST link promptly ended. I wondered if Sael had parents on her home world and how they handled her impatience. Thinking about it a little longer, I smiled — she was a lot like me.

"Commander, I have disabled the malicious security on the data cube and have recovered noteworthy information. First of all, there are communication buoy recordings from a relay in orbit above the Murlak world of Jurlaw. I cannot verify they came from Eiger, but it does give some credibility to the Scrun's statements. There are numerous communications that originate from the location that has been identified as the Scrun strike team training base. I now have its exact location on the small planetoid it occupies. The information also suggests that the Scrun ships that came to the aid of the outpost were stationed at that location until summoned by the comm buoys that were launched from the outpost. The final entries are communications to the Murlak Warbringer Solar Wind they alert the ship to begin Operation Retribution."

"Thank you, Justice. What is our exit ETA?"

"Eleven minutes, thirty-two seconds"

"Can you locate Sael's ship without wandering all over the target area?"

"I have selected an entry point far enough from the AO to allow me time to locate her position and lessen the chances of our transition being detected."

I made my way to the command deck, and as I stepped out of the lift tube I could hear laughter coming from the bridge. I walked in to find everyone watching my little free for all in the Scrun's cell. Justice had it on the view dome. Klutch was flailing around giving a blow-by-blow description accompanied by my crew's riotous

417

laughter and applause at his antics. I loudly cleared my throat and the viewscreen went blank. You could hear a pin drop as everyone made themselves look busy at their stations. Justice called out over the P.A. system.

"Exit transition in thirty seconds Commander."

I took my chair and felt mild nausea grip me as we exited hyperspace. The Legacy went to stealth mode and Justice began sweeping the system with our passive scanners. We cleared our transition point and went in search of the Operative's starship. The system was a dark place of rock and dust. The local star was a brown dwarf. It failed to gain enough mass to fuse hydrogen, so its fizzled attempt left it small and dim. It was more like a very large planetary body than a true star. The rest of the system was a massive, rock-laden waste zone, barren of any planets. If the Operative was hiding amongst all this galactic clutter, she might be hard to find.

"Justice, can you pick Sael's ship out of all this crap?"

"I have not sorted her flagship out of the fourteen targets I have identified as Murlak and Scrun warships. The target list will grow as I eliminate the large number of probable detections. Once the target list is complete, I can compare data and should have her location in a matter of minutes."

Before I could say anything else, my IST came online in secure mode and the voice of the Operative filled my head. "Nathan, we have detected your transition but cannot get a lock on your position. The information from your prisoners was correct. We have eighteen confirmed hostile targets and several more probable's."

"Acknowledged, Senior Operative, please hold your position while Justice confirms a complete target list."

The Operative shot back a curt "Holding."

Justice came over the PA system. "Commander, I have located twenty-five hostile targets, the largest of which is maneuvering slowly to the edge of the largest dust field. I have identified that target as a Murlak Warbringer-class battleship. The other twenty-four targets are scattered in a rough circle in the largest asteroid field. The Operative's flagship is between the Warbringer and the ambush fleet. It appears that they have detected our transition distortion waves but cannot locate us. I believe the same is true in the Operative's case as well. We will know shortly if the Warbringer swings out away from the dust field and moves in the direction of the other hostile ships. I believe they will radiate telltales strong enough for anyone in the area to detect them in hopes of getting a follower."

"Transfer the latest targeting data to Sael's flagship and move us in close to her location."

"Data sent, Commander."

My crew sat quietly listening, each fastening their seat harness in anticipation of combat. Tria looked back at me expectantly. I fastened my harness and she gave me a small smile then turned back to her screen. Evidently Justice did not think we could be detected by the Scrun or the Murlak. We made a maximum speed interception of the Operative's flagship, gliding through the hostile fleet's location. The new Guardian technology we installed on the Legacy was magnitudes above any of the tech the pirates and slavers could get their hands on.

My IST came alive with a secure message beep. The Operative's voice had an edge to it. "Nathan, we should attack all the targets before they start wondering why we have not appeared on their scanners. What is your position?"

I looked up at the view dome and saw the blue box of the Operative's flagship leap at us and quickly fill the entire front of the display. I was sure my next report was going to thrill her. "We are below and just aft of your position."

The oath the Operative blurted under her breath was still loud enough to put a smile on my face. She really despised having less than the latest tech. I am sure she realized she indirectly had something to do with our current advantage. I knew we had something she and her people wanted now that we had demonstrated its potential. She acknowledged my thoughts with her next statement.

"Perhaps when this ugliness with Eiger is brought to a proper end, we can revisit a technology exchange that will be beneficial to both of us."

The one item that was still at the very top of my wish list was transporter technology.

30

I decided to throw Sael a bone and let her take on the role of Commander. I would let her decide how this battle was going to play out. The data we had collected from the Murlak and Scrun, seemed to be authentic and accurate. This led me to believe the information we had obtained on Eiger's whereabouts was also true and correct. This made the entire enemy fleet targets of opportunity.

"Senior Operative, I feel the information we have on Eiger's location is possibly accurate. It was my intention to board the Warbringer to ensure Eiger would be apprehended. I now feel like it would be a waste of time and energy. I propose we attempt to disable as many of the hostile ships as possible and jump to a safe location to discuss future strategies."

Sael shot right back. "We will not 'attempt' to do anything. We are going to destroy all of the sewage-sucking Throggs that infest this scat hole. You boasted that you will not turn a blind eye to these cowardly killers. When my crew and I decided to join your little wet dream, we vowed to do the same. Do not dishonor my crew members who lost their lives following you because you changed your mind!"

Whew! The old witch must have slipped off of her broomstick and it somehow became lodged in her ass. She was out for blood and did not give a crap what it might cost us to get it. In the back of my mind, I felt the Oolaran soldier stir and give a mirthless laugh. I was thinking the monster now had a sister. There was only one way to answer her.

"OK Sael, pick out what you want and we will take the rest."

"We must strike now while the fools are playing with themselves trying to determine if we have entered the system. With a properly coordinated stealth missile strike, we can eliminate them all. On my signal, you destroy the Warbringer, and then come back for any stragglers. We will commence launching a four-missile-per-target strike package that will be timed for simultaneous detonation."

Justice interrupted our planning with an alert. "Commander, The Warbringer just launched three comm buoys, and they have transitioned. This act may be an attempt to draw us out, or the opposition already knows we are here and they are calling for help. The Warbringer has now brought its shields online and is moving toward the ambush zone."

"Is it accelerating?"

"Yes, Commander, but at a fraction of its capability. It is making itself an obvious target."

423

"OK Justice, let's give them what they are wishing for. Move us in close enough, we can hit them with the beam weapons for maximum effect. When their shields come down, give them six of our new Chaalt anti-matter missiles."

"Roger that, Commander. I am detecting a continuous salvo being launched from the Operative's flagship, and it has ceased at ninety-six missiles. All have transitioned."

I looked up at the view dome as the entire screen filled with the massive, blunt-nosed Warbringer. They did not have a clue about the hell we were getting ready to unleash on them. I felt a small twinge of guilt that passed as quick as it came. The pieces of shit deserved everything that was about to happen to them. Justice called out again.

"Commander, I am detecting the transition emissions from the Operative's missiles and estimate they will impact the targets in sixty seconds or less."

Sael linked with me. "Are you in position to strike Nathan?"

"Affirmative, we will attack on your mark."

"Thirty seconds and counting down."

"Roger that. Good luck and good hunting."

The signal ended and I watched as Justice put up a diagram of the Warbringer's overlapping shields. He illuminated the weakest areas and then chose an area that appeared to have very little coverage below the battleship's massive hanger doors. The asteroid field on the back side of the dome lit up from multiple simultaneous anti-matter explosions. Justice ramped the power to the beam weapons to maximum and put a continuous beam shot into the side of the Warbringer. The view dome flashed a brilliant white, that quickly faded, leaving a picture of a giant hole in the Warbringer we could have flown through. We could see the star field through the burning hell that once was the hanger deck. Six green missile tracks jumped from the Legacy into the hole, and the Murlak ship came apart in a blinding flash that blacked out the view dome. When the screen reset, we were plowing through a massive debris cloud that had our forward shields blazing from the continuous strikes.

Justice called out, "Commander, there are seven remaining targets that are attempting to get a lock on the Operative's ship. All targets appear to be unloading their entire arsenal of anti-ship missiles. The missile count is climbing above six hundred."

"Let's give the Operative a hand. Target anything Sael does not have a lock on and knock down as many missiles as you can with our point defense weapons."

The view dome started stuttering from the nonstop point defense fire. There were sparkling flashes across the screen, as our weapons started knocking out hostile missiles. Two of the hostile ships closest to our position had bright red crosshairs appear on them. Justice gave each a four-missile salvo. The missiles blinked out of normal space-time and transitioned to a point in close proximity to the targets. They re-acquired the fleeing ships and dove headlong into the most depleted areas of the enemy ship's shields. One of the targets disappeared in ripple of three detonations. The forth missile made an impossibly sharp turn back toward the other target and bore in for a frontal engagement. The second Scrun ship was pouring out fire with their defensive weapon systems while making absolutely crazy maneuvers in the dense, rock-filled asteroid field. They were doing fairly well until the wild tactics intersected with a large rock fragment, sending the ship careening end over end. The two remaining missiles, along with the lone attacker from the first engagement, found their mark, adding to the dense, debris-laden rock field.

Justice zeroed in on the Operative's location and placed a blue box around her ship. We turned back in her direction and started a jinxing dive back into the rocky hell the asteroid field was quickly becoming. I had to admit when it came to cleaning house, Sael was deadly and efficient. She had eighteen instant kills and was methodically mopping up the remaining stragglers. Justice decided we had enough time to go in for one more kill.

One of the survivors was a Murlak cruiser class warship. The captain was apparently abandoning the engagement and was trying to get to open space. If he managed to do it, he would transition before we could catch him. In an insane move, Justice lined us up with the smallest of openings in the debris field and made an eye blink of an inter-system jump. When we returned to normal space-time a second later, the entire view dome was filled with the hostile ship. I heard more than one oath yelled out in alarm. Justice blasted a double beam shot point blank into the Murlak ship. I gripped the arms of my chair expecting a collision as it blew apart. The flash of the explosion obscured the entire view dome. I was shocked speechless when the screen reset. We were plowing through a large number of bodies along with the contents of the ship. I was in awe as both halves of the ship went spinning away from us in different directions.

There was a horrible stench in the air. I was relieved to find it was coming from Klutch and not the lower half of my uniform. My crew did not seem to notice; they all turned staring wide-eyed at me. I returned the look, giving them a small shake of my head and a shrug.

Justice called out to us, ending my nonstop adrenaline rush. "Commander, all targets accounted for and eliminated."

I had trouble finding my voice and it came out in a hoarse whisper until I cleared my throat a second time. "Did we sustain any damage?"

"Our forward lower hull and outboard star drive nacelle have sustained minor damage. The hull bots are moving to those locations to begin repairs."

"Open a secure IST channel to the Operative."

"Secure channel transmitting Commander."

"Senior Operative, what is your status?"

"We have no casualties but have hull and shield emitter damage we will have to repair before we can engage in combat operations."

"The Legacy has sustained minor damage but is combat capable. The Warbringer launched three comm buoys, and we cannot be sure if it was a ruse to draw us out, or a call for backup. I suggest we move to a secure location, so you can make your repairs, and I can brief you on our intelligence findings."

"We detected the launches as well, and what you say is of sound tactical reasoning, but I still feel the need to bloody the murderous Throggs."

"Sael, the Scrun and Murlak claimed that we were being led here, because we were hearing what they wanted

428

us to hear. If reinforcements show up at this location, they will see what we want them to see."

The transmitter was silent for what seemed like thirty seconds but was probably a lot less. "Very well Nathan. It sounds like you have a location in mind?"

"As a matter of fact, I do. Justice will transfer the coordinates to you now, it is a location just outside of the system the Scrun training base occupies. When you complete your repairs, we are going to burn that scat hole to the ground."

"I find myself liking you a little more every time I talk with you."

"HAH! Where I come from, we call that bullshit! We will wait for you to jump and then follow."

I heard a small chuckle escape her lips and then she said, "Transitioning in thirty seconds. Don't keep me waiting."

The Operative's ship disappeared from the system. I had Justice leave a little surprise behind before we transitioned. There were more than two hundred hostile missiles still wandering around the system, aimlessly seeking a target to lock onto. We added a dozen of our own. Justice set them to go dormant. If a spacecraft matching our targeting data happened to enter the system, the stealth missiles would come back online and transition to the target's location from multiple vectors.

With all our parting gifts launched, we made a DEHD core jump to Sael's location. Justice now had all the data he needed to identify and lock in the Operative's location. He moved us to within a thousand yards of her flagship. He magnified her hull damage and we could see repair bots and visual inspection teams going about their business.

My IST went live with a secure beep. "Nathan, we detected your transition and I know you are close by. When you are finished playing games, I am ready for the debriefing."

Justice pulled us close alongside Sael's flagship and uncloaked. The inspection teams became so alarmed at us appearing within several hundred feet of their ship, most went jetting at high speed for cover in the shuttle hangar. I chuckled thinking several were giving their suit disposal systems a workout. It was not but a few minutes before a lone figure stood in the hangar entrance. I was a little miffed because Sael had never once invited us aboard. I suspect it was a major infraction of the rules to let another alien board a Chaalt warship. I thought after the Quill engagement, my crew and I might be an exception to that rule. I guess I was wrong.

I called to Justice. "Open the shuttle bay for the Operative, evidently she wishes to visit in person."

I got up to go meet Sael. Coonts and Klutch stayed at their stations, but Tria got up and intercepted me on my way off the bridge. She locked one of her arms around mine and walked without comment to the downtube.

When we stepped in, she embraced me and said in a quiet voice. "Do you still think I look like star-withered old fruit?"

I could not help but laugh at the question. It was not the reaction she was wanting, and a frown crossed her pretty face. I was wondering when she would find an interpretation of what a raisin was. While she did not have a completely accurate translation, it was close enough. My humorous response must have irritated her more than I thought. She started to pull away from me as we descended to the hangar deck. I refused to let her go and pulled her close and kissed her. Her natural deep dark tanned appearance was slowly returning to normal from the almost black caused by the bruising from the Oolaran procedures she had undergone. She was hiding her discomfort fairly well. I could tell her facial expressions were an exercise in control. I wish she would stop trying to prove she was as tough as nails — I already knew it.

She relaxed in my arms and I whispered to her. "You should know that a raisin is a sweet delicacy on my home world and it is cherished by many for its unique flavor and healing qualities."

We stepped out of the down tube and she looked at me with those big emerald eyes. "I believe where you come from, statements like that are called bullshit!"

Even though there was truth to the statement, it would be hard denying it wasn't laced with just a little livestock excrement. As we walked hand in hand into the hangar, we saw that the Operative had already leaped across the void between our ships and was swiftly approaching. For reasons unknown to me Tria spun me around and planted a wet one on me that left a look of surprise on my face. She was definitely much stronger than she used to be; it would have taken effort to resist the sudden move. She turned back to Sael Nalen and gave her an almost smug look, leaving me to wonder what was up with it. I let the surprise slide from my face as I started to greet Sael.

Sael held up all her hands and said, "No thanks, I would find the Fusra Pus virus more comforting on my face than your lips."

Tria and I both burst out laughing. Get the hell out! The old witch was developing a sense of humor.

She had a neutral look on her face when she turned to Tria and said, "Could we please get on with the briefing before your primate ways start affecting me like other members of my race."

The smile on Tria's face was reduced to a grimace, but she held her tongue. Justice was right on cue with a call that put any tension in the air at ease.

"Commander, I have prepared the briefing room and the crew has been alerted."

The walk to the lift tube was quiet, so I asked a question that had been on my mind for some time now. "Sael, have you heard from your council since your disappearance with your ship and crew?"

We stepped into the lift tube and were whisked upward. She finally commented on my question.

"The threats of execution for traitorous desertion have ceased, if that is what you want to know."

"Sael, I have known you long enough to know you would not let such charges stand against your crew. I surmise your participation in my operations have been reported in detail to superiors who favor your continued service."

We stepped out on the command deck. Tria and I both turned to the Operative with expectant looks on our faces.

"I find your continued use of logic irritating. You are giving me little grounds for calling you a primate."

While I smiled at the comment, Tria did not. She took my hand and gave me a tug. "Save it for the briefing room."

Tria apparently wanted Sael to fess up to being in communication with her superiors to the crew as well. Sael made no comment and followed us to the briefing room.

We took our seats and Sael looked at all of us and quipped, "I am glad the defective A.I. that runs this relic has figured out how to select proper seating."

That brought a round of polite laughter from all of us. I was relieved that any perceived tension in the air was now gone. Sael helped herself to one of the glasses of water Justice was so kind to supply us. She stood and cleared her throat, then started off with an explanation to her comments in the lift.

"As you have evidently conjectured, my military council has come to its senses. They have gone through a reorganization that has long been overdue. The new leadership is composed of progressive, younger minds that are not tied down by the old status quo. The new leadership has come to the same conclusion I have. The continued cooperation between you and your followers is one of the most important alliances our people have made in a very long time. In short, your recent discoveries have the ability to bring yours and my people into a new technological age. The Guardian tech you have uncovered, along with the live Prule Hunter, are truly amazing."

We were all smiles at her disclosures. There was the very real possibility we would now have access to some of the Chaalt's best tech secrets. The smile left my face when I saw Sael was not sharing our joyous occasion with the same zeal.

"Senior Operative, I take it we still have complications that will have to be addressed."

Coonts surprised me when he said, "Commander, what the Operative has not stated is the fact that the military council still has to answer the leaders of the Chaalt home worlds. The leaders of her race are some of the oldest and considered by many to be the wisest of the Chaalt people. The Grawl people and many others for that matter have attempted such alliances only to be turned away by the Chaalt leadership."

The Operative gave Coonts a steely eyed stare that insinuated she did not like the interruption, but she did not deny his claims either. I knew of the Grawl attempts to gain Chaalt technology. Not all were an honorable effort.

Sael centered her attention back on me. "What I was going to say before I was interrupted was that the Chaalt people cannot be seen showing favoritism to a group that many might consider to be vigilantes. We are already in direct conflict with certain agreements we have made with the Galactic Union. The leadership of my people will not risk further deterioration of those agreements by openly acknowledging our association with you or your followers."

I should have figured this angle all by myself. Many governments back on my home world operated in the same manner — it was called plausible deniability. It was a way of getting the nitty gritty done without having the cooperating power's fingerprints all over it.

Tria asked the next question on my mind. "Senior Operative, how do you fit into this covert scheme? You cannot be seen using Chaalt military assets to attack what could potentially be Union allies or trade partners. Your reputation is well known by many."

"Contingencies are now in place to spread the story of my departure from the Chaalt military. It has been made public that there was a major changing of the guard in the military counsel. Rumors have been spread to all of the outlets that usually leak information. There is now a story circulating of my great displeasure with the change in power. Since I essentially took a Chaalt warship without the proper clearances, the record will show that I have been stripped of my command status and released from service. It has already been well documented by my former colleagues, many of which have greatly perpetuated the stories currently circulating to all of our allies and others.

Many are already speculating on my mercenary status. The Chaalt security services are reporting several covert inquiries for my known talents."

Klutch asked another obvious question. "What does this mean concerning your ship? They cannot let you get away with taking a military asset without revealing this ruse for the deception it actually is."

"You are correct, Troop Master. I will be given a new ship to command. It is a prototype fast attack ship that was designed from Oolaran discoveries, among others. It was placed in storage when we determined the cost to integrate all of the various systems into one ship was a drain on our other military projects. It is our hope that you will be able to contribute to its completion."

That statement got everyone's attention. All eyes turned from the Operative to me. They were going to leave it up to me to ask the next big question that was on our minds.

My crew looked back at the Operative. "Contribute in what way, Sael?"

"Justice has the knowledge to help us make use of the Oolaran systems we have recovered while salvaging the void. I also know that many of your scientists have studied the Legacy for an extended period of time. We would like your permission to move our prototype to your facility for completion. We would pay you an extraordinary amount of credits to finish the project."

Wow. To say we were all surprised by this turn of events would be an understatement. What I did clearly understand was the Chaalt really needed us if they had any hopes of completing the project in the near future. I also knew we now had a big enough bargaining chip to get something that I really wanted.

31

My crew looked like they all wanted to start talking at the same time, and I knew what the subject was going to be. I had to put a halt to the direction this was going until such time we could discuss it at length in private. This would involve all of my scientific staff. I was not going out on a limb without talking to them first. The steady gaze coming from the Operative said she knew where this would lead as well.

"Without discussing the matter with my scientist, I will neither confirm or deny your request. Your new council is taking a lot for granted. We have not forgotten about the deceit perpetrated on us by your superiors. It makes me wonder why they would even make such a request in the first place. If you were to look at it through my eyes, it would seem like a very good way to place a large number of spies in my complex under the guise of scientists and engineers."

Sael did not like my rebuttal, but she did not refute it either. Before I could get an opportunity to say anything more, Justice interrupted my current thoughts on the subject. He commed me on my Backscatter transmitter. I stopped with my mouth open as if to say something. Sael frowned, trying to decipher the strange expression on my face. Justice's message left my mouth agape. Glancing around the table, I saw it was a group announcement because my crew looked the same way.

Sael's frown became more menacing by the moment. "Don't sit there pretending you are not getting a message from the defective machine that runs this ship! You are not hiding it well, what has happened?"

I thought about it for a moment and decided, if anything, the information could only help our bargaining position. The timing could not have been any better.

"Justice, would you please enlighten the Operative."

"Senior Operative, we have had a breakthrough on the research we were conducting on the spacecraft designated as Daggers. We have discovered the A.I. access code sequences necessary to gain entry. I am now researching the capabilities of the spacecraft and have every intention of making them an operational asset."

Now Sael's mouth was gaping. She promptly snapped it shut with yet another frown. I could tell she was carefully digesting Justice's statement.

"While I don't care if you play mind games on my council, I would like to think you're beyond doing the same to me."

Justice left enough awkward silence after his statement to let me know he was messing with the

440

Operative for her defective machine comment. I was going to intervene, but he cut me off.

"Senior Operative, some of the amazing revelations I am currently collecting from the Dagger's processing cores directly contradict information your council stored on the data cube for us to review."

Sael looked like she was on the verge of a meltdown. "Are your cores faulty!? You are well aware I had nothing to do with the council's deceit. What is your point?"

"Senior Operative, I am not referring to the misleading information left by your people to draw me into their architecture collection algorithms. I speak of the informational theories your scientists determined to be facts. Based on my initial studies, many of the suppositions are in error. Some aspects of Dagger technology surpass the current technological advancements incorporated into the Legacy. A situation, I might add, that will be addressed in the near future."

Whoa! Justice, was getting a little vindictive. He wasn't just picking at Sael; he had her face down, rubbing her nose in it. He must have decided that she was ordered to report on our technology to the new management on the Chaalt military council. I felt a little sorry for her because it was probably a requirement for immunity to her recent transgressions. The look of anger on the Operative's face was replaced by a forced neutrality. She would not look me in the eyes, choosing instead to stare at her clasped hands. The reaction confirmed Justice's suspicions.

Sael finally looked up at me and said in a quiet voice: "You must know, I now walk a very fine line. Many have questioned my loyalties, and for good reason. My recent actions have several council leaders calling me a rogue. However, the one thing they can all agree on is that no single Operative has ever advanced our technological gains as much as I have. They attribute this success to my relationship with you and your followers, and rightly so."

I was now scratching my head, wondering if Justice knew all along the Operative was hiding information she was ordered to withhold from us. He certainly seemed to be compelling her to divulge her secrets. The manner in which he chose to reveal the breakthrough with the Daggers was interesting to say the least. I could only describe his efforts as the old carrot on a stick routine. He was leading her to a rock and a hard place. It was working.

"A new rank designation has been added to my Senior Operative status. I am now the Principal Investigator for my people. This new rank comes with a freedom no other Chaalt military officer has ever been granted."

I interrupted her before she could carry on. I wanted her to admit something that I had a suspicion I already knew. "Sael, did the new rank come before or after you revealed we might have another Prule discovery on our hands?"

She cleared her throat and let the silence that followed, answer for her.

"You know, if we were to withhold information from you, it could easily bring doubt to the council's minds, and to your new rank status."

Her expression showed the displeasure my comment earned me.

"Nathan, neither I nor my council is oblivious to your ambitions of acquiring transporter technology. You would do well to continue your cooperation if you wish to achieve your goals."

Touché! Eventually, we would have ended up at this crossroad, and it was foolish for me to think otherwise. This pissing contest was over, and Sael had a bladder beyond my capacity. It was time to move on. We would discuss this new cooperation at a later date. Justice had forced Sael's hand and, at the same time, leveraged our position if any meaningful tech trade were to present itself.

I held my hands up to Sael. "We have a briefing for you on the new target. How much longer will your repairs take?"

"The damage to our shield emitters was worse than we thought. We have to completely replace three, possibly four. A good estimate would be five hours minimum, six if we have to replace the fourth. If you have the exact target location, you should recon the area. Once you have coherent data, brief me and I will put together a plan of action."

Sael got up and headed for the door. I was going to escort her, but she held up her hand and gave me a look that said she would not be good company. She was being granted almost unlimited power by her people, but it meant nothing without our full cooperation. She was learning the hard way that regardless of the wonderful tech she has already given us, we were under no obligation to toe her line. After having it her way for who knows how long, she still found it difficult to understand why we would not submit to her authority. Justice put a view screen on the wall showing us Sael's progress. She did not deviate from her march to the hangar, where she closed up her armor suit and jumped back to the hangar bay of her ship.

"Justice, stealth the Legacy and take us to the target."

"Affirmative, Commander. I would also like to add that I am preparing a briefing on the Daggers. It will take some time because my inquiries to Alpha base are ongoing. I have some of the information available for viewing in the science lab."

I looked at my crew members, waiting for the questions I knew they were about to ask. Tria commented before anybody could get a word in edgewise.

"While Sael might act at times like she is conceding to your authority, I can assure you that it is not the case."

I smiled and nodded. I had already figured out that little jewel of information all by myself. "Back where I come from, they call it a love-hate relationship. She doesn't have to like it, but she does have to deal with it."

Coonts and Xul promptly stood up and Coonts said, "Commander, if you have need of us, we will be in the science lab."

I waved them off and they disappeared out the door. That left Klutch sitting on the other side of me, and he was mysteriously quiet. I leaned forward and studied the expression on his face that did not change with my move. Looking closer, I saw that the Troop Master had his eyes closed. He was leaning precariously back in his chair and it dawned on me the big wanker was asleep! I looked at Tria and she had her hand over her mouth to keep from laughing. This made me frown, and before she could stop me, I stuck my boot under his chair leg, and levered it upward. Tria, got up and raced for the door as Klutch got dumped backwards out of his chair onto the deck. The scent that filled the room was instantly nauseating and eye watering. Klutch bolted upright, swearing. He looked around the room, figuring out what just happened.

He gave me a big toothy smile. "My apologies, Commander, I must be suffering from battle fatigue."

He got up and made a hasty retreat from the room. Battle fatigue my ass! I was trying to hold my breath to keep from gagging but had inhaled enough of the Tibor's warrior scent I could almost taste it. I got up and ran for my cabin in hopes of retaining what little I had in my stomach. Ultimately, I failed. As I washed my face and rinsed my mouth, I could hear Tria giggling behind me.

"I tried to warn you."

I grimaced. "You should have warned me harder!"

She laughed again and gave me a hug. She turned her head away from me, just to make sure I would not attempt to kiss her. I gave her a wicked smile and attempted anyway. She retreated out my cabin door and closed it behind her. Freakin' Tibor! I took a shower and lay down on my bed for a quick cat nap. Justice woke me two hours later.

446

"Commander, a Scrun Mothership entered the system and made a close approach to our target. Three shuttles debarked and landed at the facility. The Mothership appears to be leaving the system."

"OK Justice, I am on my way to the bridge."

Jumping up, I threw on a fresh uniform, and made my way to the bridge. One by one, my crew joined me and took their stations. As if on cue, my IST transmitter went live.

"Nathan, why are you letting that Scrun ship escape the system!?"

I wasn't about to tell her I was sleeping and did not have a clue what was going on. I hoped the irritation I felt when I responded was not picked up by Sael. I needed a little more from Justice before I could give her an answer. No matter what I said, I'm sure she would not agree.

So, I did the next smartest thing. "Senior Operative, please hold,"

If Sael was trying to muzzle her oath, it was a failed attempt. I ended the transmission. "Justice, I know there was a reason you did not stop the Scrun ship, could you please enlighten me."

"Commander, destroying or stopping the Scrun vessel would have alerted the base and possibly others to our presence at this locality. The Scrun Mothership entered the system at high speed and only slowed enough to dispatch the shuttles. It then made a high-speed exit. While it would be speculation on my part, I believe there is a possibility the ship was in route to the system we had previously vacated. Even if that were not the case, I found it unwise to reveal our location. I suggest we make a covert assault on the Scrun facility and attempt to recover one or more of the shuttles intact. I believe the A.I. systems aboard the shuttles will provide us with the codes necessary to access the slave distribution center. This is only a recommendation, and I stand by ready to follow any orders you might issue."

My crew were all in agreement. It was a proven fact the evil robot knew what he was talking about one hundred percent of the time. I opened a secure IST channel to the Operative.

"Sorry for the delay, Senior Operative, I was in the middle of planning a covert insertion into the Scrun facility. It is my belief we should try to capture one or more of the shuttles that just landed and use them to gain entry into the slave distribution center."

This got my crew's heads to shaking and their eyes rolling. I guess they thought I should have gave the credit to whom it was due. It proved to be a waste of time because Sael saw right through my glory hog ways.

"Oh really? And what else did the defective machine inspire you to say?"

The snickering I heard from my crew made me turn and give them the stink eye.

"How much longer on the repairs to your ship?"

"We are making better progress than I had estimated and should be battle-ready in another two hours. If you have current data on the target, I suggest you share it with me— that is, if you still want to make this a joint operation."

The Operative always had a way with words. Her suggestion was a veiled order if I had ever heard one. "We are on our way to your location."

When we were well clear of the target area, Justice sent a data dump to the Operative and we waited to hear back. The Scrun base was like our home base in many ways. It was an underground complex with a tunnel entrance. Justice had detailed enough scans to allow the Operative to insert her team into the tunnel entrance but not the complex itself. The main complex, like most military facilities, was heavily shielded against scanning. If Sael's team could get the entrance secured, and the doors open, we could land a shuttle in the tunnel to block any attempts by the occupants to escape. It did not appear to have another escape route— at least not for spacecraft.

Sael took more than an hour to get back with us. It was not time wasted. We prepped our armor and weapon loadouts. Tria was going whether I liked it or not. At times, she was a lot like the Operative. I had no choice but to let her find out the hard way just how painful the bone lamination healing process could be when you rushed the recovery period. Justice had done a great job restoring Klutch's and my armor. The suits were shiny clean and only showed minor wear and tear from our last engagement. Out of curiosity, I ran a check on my munitions load. I was more than a little miffed discovering Justice once again decided that I did not need anti-matter explosives in my kit. Obviously, the control I had exhibited over my inner beast did not impress him enough to change my loadout.

Sael snapped me out of my sour mood. "Nathan, the plan to capture a shuttle has merit. The scans you sent have enough detail my team and I can make an insertion into the tunnel entrance. From there, we will attempt to secure the access doors. I am surprised you have detected no defensive weapons outside of the complex. It has been my experience to remain cautious. Not detecting defensive weapons does not mean they are not present."

I knew Sael did not like interruptions, but Klutch made a simpler recommendation. "Don't worry about securing the doors, just blow them and we will secure the tunnel with one of our shuttles."

450

"Sael, your time would be better spent trying to secure at least one of the shuttles. Justice will keep the Legacy close to suppress any pop-up defenses."

My comments brought the expected ire. "If the Tibor would have not interrupted me, I would have explained our contingencies to you in detail. Since that was not the case, we can use one of our back-up plans to speed the operation. I assume your team will be covering our flank while we seize the shuttles?"

"Yes, we will move our shuttle through the entrance, taking out any hostiles that attempt to stop us. We will take up a position at the edge of the hangar area and use the point defense weapons for close support if things get nasty. I will deploy my team from there and flank any organized resistance. Justice believes this is a Scrun military outpost, and the chance for slaves to be present is near zero. If we have an opportunity to capture leadership-level personnel, we will do so; if not, my contingency is to level the place once we have a shuttle."

Sael cleared her throat loud enough I understood it was out of frustration for my changing her plans. Changing might not have been the right term, because I suspected our plans were very similar.

"Alright Nathan, I have no objections to Justice's plan of action. I propose we start this operation in two hours. I would like you to monitor the facility and keep me

451

updated in case we need to fine tune the mission. Once my team is in, my ship will defend the orbitals. I recommend you keep the Legacy near the base for emergency extractions if necessary"

With that said, the transmission ended. Giving Justice credit for all the planning was Sael's way of taking a swipe at me. Our plan was based on Justice's observations, but it was a group effort. Our final plan of action, included input from all the strike team members. Two hours passed quickly and we were geared up and waiting when we got the alert from Justice.

"Commander, the Operative is moving her ship toward the Scrun base."

My IST started transmitting. "Nathan, I am maneuvering in preparation for insertion. Do you have an update for me?"

"No, the base's status is unchanged and we are ready to proceed."

"Do not let your inner demon bring the base down on our heads."

The transmission halted with that final statement. I was wondering when she would get around to rubbing salt in that particular wound. I could not find fault with her comment, because she was only thinking about the safety of her team. I expected nothing less. I would do the same if the tables were turned.

We boarded our shuttle and waited for Justice to give us the go for launch. Sael started giving us a play by play on our group IST channel. Justice put up a live feed on our view dome. We saw Sael's ship swoop down and hover momentarily above the base.

"We are in! No contact...wait one. I have automated defense warnings, I will get back with you!"

The transmission went dead and Justice called out to us.

"Commander, the base is now covered by a defensive shield and a powerful transmitter is jamming signals within the base and surrounding areas. The Operative's ship is turning back to the target. I believe they will attempt to breach the shield barrier at the tunnel entrance."

"OK Justice, open the hangar door, we are out of here!"

"Negative. I am detecting movement on the surface of the mountain overlooking the complex."

Justice put the close up live video of the base on our visors. There were several rocky outcroppings that appeared to be moving. When the movement stopped more than a dozen missiles launched from hidden silos.

Justice did not hesitate and dove toward the mountain. Our point defense weapons firing nonstop at the oncoming barrage. Sael's flagship was closer and took one hit before the missiles were destroyed. It did not appear to have inflicted any damage on the Chaalt ship and it went back to work on the shields protecting the entrance to the base.

"Justice, let's give them a hand!"

Justice parked the Legacy over the missile silos and fired our main weapons point-blank into the shielded mountainside. The fourth volley made the shield flicker and fail. Another missile barrage was just clearing the tubes when our point defenses detonated them. The location of the hidden silos was reduced to a crater. I smiled grimly as a large secondary explosion from somewhere deep in the mountain gave it the brief appearance of a volcano, before it collapsed into itself.

My IST came back online. "Nathan, you have taken down the base's power generator and the automated defenses have ceased functioning. The Scrun are retreating deeper into the complex. My ship has destroyed the tunnel entrance and I am deploying additional assets. I ask that you secure the orbitals and let us continue with our current contingency plan."

Just like that, the mission turned from a joint venture to a Chaalt operation. Looking at my crew, I could

454

tell they were pissed that we just got bumped aside and relegated to an overwatch. The oath that escaped Tria's lips was less than ladylike. She was looking forward to working out with the new armor and weapons. Sael Nalen was quickly becoming a very unpopular ally. I was again having second thoughts about revealing our discovery of the derelict ship. If she thought she could pull a stunt like this on the salvage mission, she would be wrong!

Justice took us to a low orbit and we observed the Chaalt order of battle. Sael deployed more than a dozen mobile weapons platforms into the complex. Fifteen minutes later, two Scrun shuttles flew from the base and landed aboard Sael's flagship. Within minutes of that event, we saw the Chaalt forces withdrawing from the complex. I had my doubts about there being any survivors to question. As the Chaalt warship joined us in low orbit, Sael removed any doubts when the entire Scrun complex disappeared in a bright flash. My IST was silent. If Sael expected me to call and congratulate her on a successful mission she would be waiting for a long time.

32

Sael must have got tired of waiting to hear from me and finally called. She had plenty of time to compose her story and sounded almost apologetic in her tone. I pretty much knew it was bullshit. I was curious how she would explain herself.

"Nathan, before you comment, I want you to know that it was not my intention to exclude you from the operation. You yourself must know that combat is an ever-changing situation, and it demands a flexible and swift response to avoid unnecessary casualties. I exercised options and contingencies to safeguard my team. We executed the mission without a single loss and brought it to a swift and decisive end. Surely you can appreciate the results of the outcome. We now have shuttles and unquestionable codes to gain us access to the slave distribution center."

I had to give it to her: she did come out smelling like a rose to her crew and her superiors. I could find no fault with the manner in which she did her job. Yes, it still stung to be excluded from an operation that we had developed the intelligence on, but the outcome was exactly what we planned for. I looked at my crewmates and could tell they were still unhappy, but each more or less shrugged and nodded their heads at her explanation. I should say at least three of them did. The big ass Tibor was sound asleep, leaning back in his chair. When Tria and Coonts saw the expression on my face and followed my stare to its target, they both got up and quietly left the conference room.

I got up from my chair and stepped around the table. I stood over Klutch with a raised eyebrow. The gurgling hiss that passed as the Tibor's snore was now gathering more irritation than the Operative's actions. I would kill two birds with one stone. I had left enough pause floating in the air to show the Operative my displeasure. I replied in a manner in which she and her superiors would understand.

"Sael, if you usurp another of my missions, you will be excluded from future expeditions."

She started to say something but I ended the transmission. With an evil grin, I placed the pitcher of water from the table on Klutch's wide bullet head and ran from the room before he could tip it over. As I walked down the hall, the cursing that erupted from the conference room had me laughing out loud.

I got a secure beep from by BS transmitter and Sael once again started to explain herself, this time in a more assertive manner and on a private channel.

I would have none of it and cut her off. "Sael, I have moved on, but with that said, you had better take my last statement with the utmost seriousness."

She stewed on it for a few seconds as if reconsidering something. Her next comment proved she was doing just that. "Nathan, I have recovered Scrun assets I wish to turn over to you."

"Justice, will be sending you coordinates to a rally point. I will meet with you at that location and we will discuss any future collaborations."

I ended the transmission. If she thought she could smooth over the last mission with Scrun credits, she might be...partially right. Supplying the primitive planet protection fund with credits from slavers replaced the stern look on my face with a smile. My memories of home seemed like they were eons old, but in reality, only a couple of years had passed. I remembered the shows I used to watch on TV as a child. One of my favorites was "Robin Hood."

I went to the science lab, where the rest of my crew was watching a video briefing on the Daggers. The first thing I immediately noticed was the size of the crew seats. They were very small and there was three of them. The race that operated these craft were smaller in stature than Coonts. They were being identified as Sentinel Race Thirteen. If Justice was serious about adding the craft to our arsenal, it was going to take considerable effort to redesign the cockpit. He would have to remove all the smaller seats and replace them with one large enough to accommodate one of our crew members.

The craft was well armed. I could see two internal rotary launchers that could hold twenty of the nanite missiles we had a generous supply of. The craft had four pop-out turrets. Judging by their ample size as compared to the craft itself, they might be dual-purpose defensive or offensive weapons. Two were forward and two were aft of the cockpit. The side mounted locations gave them one hundred and eighty-degree arcs of fire to both sides of the vessel. There was one large main weapon that appeared to fire through the sharply pointed nose cone. According to the diagram Justice was displaying to the side of the video, it had its own dedicated power source. While it still remained to be seen, I surmised that the compact little weapons platform was a formidable stick to beat the Prule or other combatants over the head with. The Captain of the ill-fated freighter that had dumped them went to great lengths to keep them out of enemy hands. He and his crew made the ultimate sacrifice to hide and protect the spacecraft. That selfless act was testimony as to their value. I truly hoped that Justice could unlock all of their secrets.

"Justice, were you picking at Sael or were you serious when you said you can make the Daggers operational?"

"I might have taken small liberties with my comments, but it is my intention to add them to our arsenal. There will be engineering tasks that will test the mettle of our scientists, but I am confident they will rise to challenge. They were able to unlock many of my Oolaran systems and I am confident they will do the same with the Daggers."

"I am sure between you and the scientists it will get done. Our next order of business is how I handle the way Sael sidelined us. I am still angry with her and I am considering taking on our next mission without her."

"Commander, I have transferred the coordinates of a star system close to the Scrun target. The Operative is insisting that I provide an exact time for our rendezvous. I would like to add I am charging the energy matrix to give you additional options as to your choice of locations."

"She can insist all she wants. When you are ready, jump us within communication range of Tam Lin's outpost. We are going to plan the assault on the Scrun as if we were going in with the Sig as our only backup. We will give the Operative a taste of her own medicine. She can either join our operation or go it alone. Right at the moment, it makes little difference to me."

My statement pulled my crew's attention away from the Dagger briefing and earned me looks of approval from Coonts and Klutch. Tria came over to me and hooked her arm in mine. She kissed me lightly on the cheek and whispered to me.

"While I feel you are justified in putting Sael in her place with respects to our missions, I would use caution as to how you do it. After all, she has more or less offered one of my people's greatest achievements."

I found it rather interesting that Tria was on the verge of choking the Operative a couple of hours ago but now was warning me not to piss her off too badly. Evidently, she would like to see us on the receiving end of her people's best kept secrets as badly as I did.

"I'm still agitated at the way Sael sidelined us, but I can't argue the outcome. I want her to realize she is an ally and a technology partner, not our Commander in Chief. Since she is back in the council's graces, it seems that she is more determined than ever to make us submit to her command. If this is something her superiors have demanded she do, then they are fools. If it is something she has told them she is capable of doing, she would be one as well."

"Nathan, you know her better than that. She is obviously being pressured into the actions she has taken. Have you not noticed her demeanor of late? I suspect this is the military council meddling in our affairs. They are going to make her prove her loyalty before they unleash her on the galaxy with a new class of warship."

I looked at Tria and nodded. She was the voice of logic and reason. If we could help Sael pass the test her council was subjecting her too, we might get back the Sael I'd come to like and respect. Having a covert ally like the Chaalt firmly in our corner makes our future goals not so unrealistic. I hugged Tria tight enough to make her wince and kissed her to make up for it.

"Justice, change of plans, take us to the Operative."

"Affirmative, Commander, jumping in seven minutes."

I turned to Coonts, Klutch, and Xul. I gave them a run down on what Tria and I had discussed. All were in agreement that we should help Sael win her untethered freedom, and as Klutch put so eloquently, "Get back to breaking scat and taking titles."

The chatter in the lab suddenly went silent, signaling the beginning of our transition. As we faded back into reality, I took Tria by the hand and we went to the hangar to greet the Operative. Justice zeroed in on the Operative's flagship and quickly brought us alongside. I stood in the open hangar door with Tria, wondering how long it would take Sael to cool off and come down to meet us. It was a surprisingly short wait. Sael leaped across the void and made a picture perfect landing inside our atmospheric retention field. She had a case in one of her hands and before she could say anything, I held up my hand.

"Justice, take us to our previously discussed location."

"Affirmative, standard transition in thirty seconds. I will begin recharging the matrix for additional options."

Justice closed the hangar door and jumped. Sael did not like the idea of being kidnapped and voiced her displeasure at the unexpected turn of events.

"I do not have time for your games and did not alert my crew that I would be leaving. Take me back to my ship now!"

I let Sael steam for another moment before Tria elbowed me.

"Sael, if you want to properly coordinate our next combat mission, we are going to need the Sig. They will handle the slave transfer once they are liberated. They can also secure the orbitals while we go about our business. In order for this to happen smoothly, you are going to have to brief them on our plan of action. Like it or not, they are my allies and will be an integral part of the operation. They will listen to what you have to say, and if they have any objections, they will voice them."

Sael's mouth snapped shut and she eyed the two of us. It was dawning on her that we were going to be complicit. She crossed two of her arms and threw the briefcase with her lower one, it was at me, or to me — depends on whose eyes you were looking through. Either way, I put my hand up to catch it, but Tria took a step forward and snatched it out of the air like a Preying-Mantis catches a fly.

With that, we turned our backs on her and I called out, "Come on Sael, we can finish this in the conference room."

She reluctantly followed. As we passed the ready room, Tria threw the briefcase rather haphazardly inside.

"Justice, would you please set that aside for the Planet Protection Fund."

"As you wish, Tria."

Tria grabbed my arm and pulled me close and we walked to the lift tubes with Sael staring holes into our backs. As we stepped into the tube Tria embraced me, and I gave the Operative a wink of my eye as we disappeared up the tube. It was almost a full thirty seconds before the Operative stepped out of the tube. She had regained her composure and had a forced neutrality on her face that made me smile at her attempt. We made our way to the conference room where my crew awaited. We took our customary seats and Justice gave us a sitrep.

"Transition time to our comm buoy array's effective transfer range is twenty-two minutes. Thirty-seven minutes after our arrival, the energy matrix will have sufficient charge for DEHD Core operations."

"Thank you, Justice, open a channel to Tam Lin when comms are available."

I looked across the table at Sael. "I know you have something to say, so get it over with so we can move on to more important matters."

"This little joy ride will have my superiors thinking I have disclosed sensitive information I have been ordered to keep secret."

"Sael, your sudden change in attitude has us questioning our alliance. We were well on our way to working out a mutually beneficial relationship when you decided to make yourself our appointed leader. Trying to prove you were in charge by sidelining us on the last mission did not endear you to us. If it were not for Tria's interaction, I was going to marginalize your participation in our upcoming missions."

"It was a test by my superiors, and in many ways, it was meant for both of us. To the remaining hardliners on the council, it was a way of determining if I could exert my control over you. I tried to calculate just how far I could push you before you pushed back — to my surprise, you capitulated. I gambled this would turn out as it has, and

465

you would see my manipulations for what they actually are. You are turning out to be one of the smartest primates I have ever had the displeasure of meeting. If this test by my council turns out as I hope it will, we will be stuck with each other."

I was glad she said that last part with a smile on her face. Tria was right as usual, and now I was hoping we could get this crap behind us. If Sael finally sealed the deal on her new command, we could get on with changing the way predatory races conduct their business. I had great hope and promise that we would start working together for the good of all. Since Sael was being truthful against her council's better wishes, I would make a big show of it and let her sit in on my crew's decision on whether or not we would recommend her new ship be completed at Alpha base. I pretty much knew the Grawl scientists back at base would vote yes for any additional access to Chaalt tech. I was probably being petty and childish for the theatrical stunt I was getting ready to pull, but I couldn't pass up the chance to screw with Sael's head just a little for the game she ran on us during our last mission.

I stood up and made eye contact with each of my crew members and settled my stare on Sael. "Since we have once again determined the status of an irritating old witch, I would like each of you to voice your opinion on whether or not we should allow the Chaalt ship and construction crews into Alpha base. The outcome of this consensus will be my recommendation to our scientific research team members."

Sael held a finger up. "I do have one more unfortunate bit of news that I must tell you. It would be better to air it now before you make your decision on allowing my people access to Alpha Base. My superiors confiscated the shuttles along with the personnel we captured at the Scrun training center."

"Would you care to elaborate on why they would do that?"

"Must you always place me in conflict with my superior's orders? It may have something to do with the capture of Scrun royalty and certain information on the shuttle's navigation computers. I have nothing else to say!"

The looks my crew were giving me said they wondered what I was going to do about this sudden turn of events. Sael, for her part, sat stoic at the end of the table, with no further comment on the subject. Now I know why we ended up with a case full of credits. The Chaalt got their hands on someone they could milk for information, and we got cash. I doubt that I would ever learn who got the better end of the bargain, not that I really needed to guess.

"Sael, you better have a damn good Plan B to get us into the base, now that Plan A is no longer available."

"With a few modifications, we will go in the same way we took the last base down."

Sael went on to lay it out for us, and it was pretty much the same plan as last time, only this time we would actually participate. It was good enough that I had nothing to add. She would once again be first into the meat grinder. She and her team would bear the greatest risk to get the rest of us in. She was a ballsy old bitch.

"Okay everyone, let's hear your thoughts on giving the Chaalt access to Alpha base. If you agree, then I will give the Chaalt immediate access. Tria, let's start with you."

Tria stood up, crossed her arms and walked around the table to the Operative. Sael had a mystified expression on her face. Tria stepped behind her and clapped her on the shoulders.

"As long as Sael can contain her uncontrollable habit of being an overbearing Throgg, then yes, I think we should take on the project. The other stipulation I have, is she should be held responsible for the personnel that accompanies the program."

Tria, returned to her seat with a small smirk on her face. Sael looked like she was ready to explode. You could almost hear her teeth grinding, but to her credit she held her tongue.

468

"Coonts, how do you vote?"

The little Grawl got up and nodded to me. He then clasped his hands behind his back and approached Sael. He started pacing back and forth behind her. I wasn't sure what kind of Grawl crap or logic he was going to spout, but knowing him, it was bound to be good.

"If we did not have to continuously question the intentions of the Chaalt council and the Operative's commitment to our cause, we would already be well on our way to uncovering the mysteries behind our current discoveries. I find the greed and hindrance on the part of the Chaalt leadership extremely annoying. From a purely Grawl perspective, I completely understand your people's wanting to be the sole recipients of our technological discoveries. It is understandable because the great majority of my people are like-minded and consider the sharing of discoveries for the good of all absurd."

Coonts continued pacing and had Sael on the verge of choking him. Each time he stopped to add to his dissertation, I thought she would pounce on him and render him unconscious. I was surprised when she let him continue unabated. He turned and stopped once more. I considered stopping him and moving on to Klutch before the big lummox could fall asleep from boredom. I instead chose to let Coonts drone on, for some reason finding Sael's discomfort satisfying.

469

"However, with the appearance of Nathan Myers and the human interaction that has followed, I have been enlightened to the point I now have a new galactic outlook. It is my intention to see to it that my people will eventually share my assessment as well. While it is only a theory on my part, and many would consider it speculation, I believe that my Commander's human predispositions and intuition, has a direct correlation to the unprecedented amount of technological discoveries he has uncovered."

Oh man, was he ever laying it on thick. I was surprised he did not mention the Oolaran or Justice for that matter. I hope this was not the start of another feud between him and the A.I. It would be a good idea to shut him up before he let slip we had a Guardian Transponder. As it turns out I didn't have to, Sael, had reached her breaking point.

"I have had enough of this mindless scat. I get it! You are angry with me for my actions. I have already explained why, yet you still choose to try and humiliate me. I need you to trust me on the decisions I have made. Once I have secured an agreement to finish the experimental spacecraft, there will be no more games. When the experimental ship is moved to Alpha Base, you will be able to make demands of my council that they will ultimately have to concede to you for fear of the project being halted. Please Nathan, look at the endgame and not the trials you must endure to get there."

That was an interesting statement. If I had heard correctly, she just alluded to the fact we could hold her people's project for ransom. I thought about it for another minute and decided it was time to move on. The best way to do it was to cut to the chase.

"Justice, alert the Grawl scientists that the Chaalt will be bringing their project to Alpha Base and they're to start on the project as soon as possible"

The look of surprise on Sael's face turned to a small smile, mine turned to a frown. "Just remember, no more games. You're an ally, not our designated leader."

Her smugness had me a little pissed, and I considered bearding the lion once more out of spite, but Justice interrupted.

"Commander, we will be exiting hyperspace in sixty seconds. I will activate our comm buoy and establish a link to Tam Lin's secure network."

It looked like Sael was going to get her wish and our mental spanking would finally come to an end. Justice projected a large view screen on the wall and Tam Lin's image appeared on it. Tria and Sael both scrutinized the pretty Earth girl.

"Nathan, it is good to see you are still among the living. The Sig and I were just talking about you. The rumor mills are rife with stories of the alien demon. It seems he destroyed a convoy of Scrun and Murlak ships. The pieces of sewage have the audacity to claim they were on a peaceful mission to rescue members of their races trapped on an outpost with failing life support systems."

Sael let out a snort that was loud enough to get Tam Lin's attention. "So, is this the rest of your crew you spoke so highly of? It looks like an interesting mix. With the exception of the Grawl, it looks like you chose well. Chaalt females have a reputation as some pretty badass warriors."

Coonts took exception to the comment and stood up to protest the slight aimed at him. I gave him a stern look and motioned him back to his seat. He slowly sat back down.

"Tam, as I have mentioned before, the Grawl who work with me work for the good of all. You cannot blame the whole Grawl race for your abduction. Besides, if it were not for you being kidnapped, you would not be the most successful interstellar entrepreneur in the galaxy."

The frown slowly slipped from her face and was replaced by a small smirk. "Yeah well, whatever, who are the Chaalt warriors?"

I reached over and put my hand on one of Tria's. "This is Tria. She is my second in command."

Tam stared at me for a moment then said, "Judging from the Earth-boy sparkle in your eyes, she is a lot more to you than second in command."

Everyone except Sael gave Tam a small acknowledging smile. I felt my cheeks warm. I let the comment pass but did not let go of Tria's hand either. I gave a quick nod to the other end of the table. "This is Sael Nalen."

That earned me a frown and a barking laugh. "I hate to be the bearer of bad news, but you're getting your crank yanked. I don't know who you got riding around with you, but she it is not Sael Nalen. It is common knowledge that Sael is a grizzled old bitch that just as soon kill you as look at you. The Sig say she once had offspring, but the murderous old hag ate them. No one in their right mind would dare call her by her real name — she is called Kala Mor Dee or some such shit."

Sael sprang out of her chair. "You would do well to mind your tongue Earth girl, or I will make it a point to cut it out!"

Tam Lin just laughed. "I got to give it to her, that is probably something that would come out of Kala Mor Dee's mouth."

The smile disappeared from Tam Lin's face. "Whenever you grow a set of nuts big enough, come on over to Haras and take a crack at it."

With that comment, Sushi and Pasta both leaned into the picture. The looks they were giving Sael would have stripped the new paint from my old pickup. I held up my hands to both sides.

"WHOA! That will be enough from both of you, we are all allies here and I don't want any more bickering. We have more important things to do. Tam, I can assure you that this is Sael Nalen. She is soon to be released from her military commitment and I have plans of adding her to my payroll."

That brought a sobering look to Tam Lin's face. She stared hard at me then looked once more at Sael. She let out a shrill whistle that made me flinch.

"You aren't shitting me, are you?"

"No, I'm not, this is the Senior Operative herself. Not everything you have heard about her is true. I know for a fact she hasn't eaten any of her offspring because no one is crazy enough to mate with her."

My comment earned me a venomous stare from Sael. I think she was more than ready to move on to another subject, but Tam Lin was not.

"Man, you sure know how to pick 'em. Did you know she had a run-in with some Sig mercenaries? They were a bloodthirsty crew and had thrown in with a bunch of evil bastards that kidnapped some big Chaalt dignitary.

They were trying to bargain for tech or credits but got Kala Mor Dee instead. She and her crew managed to kill more than twenty Sig mercenaries along with the Kasulla slugs that masterminded the whole thing. The word going around is that the leader of the Sig mercs almost took Sael's head off with one of those big swords they call fighting knives. They say if it were not for her crazy cyborg reflexes, he would have succeeded."

I looked over at Sael, and she was absentmindedly rubbing her jaw with one of her hands. When she noticed me looking, her hand dropped back to the table. We needed to quit reminiscing about the past and plan for the future.

"Tam, we are prepping for our attack on the Scrun slave distribution center. We can't pull this off without help from the Sig. Once we go in, I am going to need the orbitals secured and a way to move the slaves to safety."

"The Sig have already agreed to help you. Tell Sushi your plans, and as long as it is not some suicidal nonsense, they will back you."

"That is why Sael is here. She has planned hundreds of these operations. If we can take the facility intact, the Sig can take possession when we withdraw."

Sushi leaned back into the picture. "That is an acceptable bargain and you have our backing. We will move one of our fleets to a location of your choosing. Send

475

us the coordinates and we will prepare signal codes for communication purposes."

I turned to the Senior Operative. "You're up."

33

With Sael's plan ironed out, I said goodbye to Tam Lin and ended the transmission. I glanced around the table and locked my eyes on Klutch: he had fallen asleep again while Sael was laying out the details of the attack. I was considering ripping him a new ass in front of everyone, but Coonts cued us in on his odd behavior.

"Commander, Klutch has spent most of his sleep periods working out in the new battle armor. He seldom sleeps more than an hour before he goes back to training."

Well, that explained his habit of falling asleep at our briefings. I could not have him half-awake on a combat op. I would put a stop to it since we were so close to mission go time.

"Klutch! Klutch, wake up! KLUTCH!

The Tibor bolted upright, and yelled out, "I AGREE WITH TRIA, THE OPERATIVE ACTS LIKE A THROGG!"

I knew Sael was developing a sense of humor, but not in this case. The Tibor's exclamation was accompanied by my crew's snickering and Klutch's eyewatering scent. We rushed to evacuate the room, but not before Sael gave Klutch a slap on the top of his bullet head that sounded like it was meant to hurt. To his credit, Klutch just shrugged it off with a big toothy smile.

Justice jumped us back to Sael's flagship so she could prep for the attack. She agreed to meet us at a predetermined position near the Scrun base. The Sig were moving a fleet into the sector and would contact us when they were ready. We transitioned to the rally point and made our own preparations. Since we were still set up for the last mission scenario, we had little to do until the Operative jumped to our location. The Chaalt had surveillance drones hidden all over the sector gathering data on the target. We were hoping to find minimal traffic patterns to time our attack. It would be advantageous to take the base before anyone came calling.

"Commander, the Operative's flagship has arrived."

"Thanks Justice, sneak in close to her ship, I know how much she loves that."

My IST started transmitting. "Nathan, since we destroyed the Scrun fleet the surveillance drones have recorded very little traffic in this sector. This information could mean we eliminated the local security or they are waiting for us to attack the facility. Either way, I say we go in now and let the Sig deal with anyone who might come to their aid. What is your ETA to the rally point?"

"We are waiting about a thousand feet from your hangar door."

478

"You primate! That defective relic you blunder around the galaxy in is becoming more than just a small annoyance."

"Quit being a whiny old witch. Justice reports no changes to our previous intelligence, and I agree we should get this over with as fast as possible. The Sig should be arriving any moment and we will be ready to move when we give them our updated information and signal codes."

"I am moving to the target area and will launch the suppression package so it will be within striking distance when we start the operation. I will give you a current brief when you arrive."

"Acknowledged, we will give you the go ahead when we are in position to strike any pop-up targets."

The signal went dead and Justice reported the Operative had jumped. My crew was already in the hangar geared up and ready to board Eagle One.

"Commander, the Sig have arrived. I have detected two very large transport class starships along with eight battlecruiser class attack vessels. Our communication codes have been accepted and I have an active video comm channel."

A picture appeared on the ready room wall and to my surprise, Sushi appeared on it. His unique uniform and the prominent "S" displayed on it, identifying him.

"Sushi, what a pleasant surprise. It is good to see you again."

"Likewise, Nathan Myers. Tam Lin suggested I come along to see that we avoid any miscommunications during the operation. Our transports will remain at this location with one of our attack vessels. I will take the remaining seven into orbit around the target and secure the orbitals on your signal."

"Thank you, Sushi, we could not complete this mission without the cooperation of your people. We will attempt to minimize damage to the facility if possible."

"You need only to concern yourself with the safety of the strike teams. The facility can be repaired. The loss of life cannot."

"Well-spoken my friend. I can see why Tam Lin likes you so much. Is there anything else I need to be aware of before we jump to the target?"

"Yes: as soon as we are in orbit we will launch seven assault shuttles. Each shuttle carries sixteen special operations troopers. The shuttles will remain outside of the area of operations until you either call for backup or you have taken control of the base. The troopers are trained for slave handling and transfer situations, as well as other, deadlier skill sets. They will be at your command and will only approach the target on your orders."

"Thanks again Sushi. We will be launching comm drones, and my A.I. will transfer the necessary access codes for your people to make use of them once we are gone. I will speak with you again when this is over."

"Good luck, Nathan Myers."

The transmission ended and I climbed into my armor. It was good to know we had additional backup if it was necessary. I would only make that call if the shit got too thick for us. The beast was growing impatient and was sending spikes of adrenaline into my system. A feeling of anticipation came over me as the armor tightened its caress. The suit came alive on my visor display, showing the tools of my trade at capacity and all in the green. With my lethal arsenal ready and the beast prodding me forward, I felt an almost palpable feeling of invincibility. Tria, Coonts, and Klutch were waiting by the boarding ramp to Eagle One. I strode among them and we each went over the others armor to insure nothing was loose or missing. With our inspections complete, we masked our faces with the caricatures of deathly demons Justice had chosen to loosen the bowels of our enemies.

We took our seats in the shuttle. "Justice, take us to the target."

My awareness flared to a bright white and faded away. I came back to the sound of Justice calling to us. "Target status is unchanged and the shield is not active. I have located the Operative's flagship and have tracks on forty-two Chaalt stealth missiles loitering close to their intended impact points."

"Roger that, Justice. Move us aft of the Operative's ship and open a secure IST channel to Sael."

"Moving, Commander, comms active."

"Senior Operative, we are moving to your location and ready to go."

"Acknowledged, Nathan, the base's shield is down and we are jumping to the insertion point. That will surely change once we are inside. Our missiles will take down the area defenses ten seconds after we are in. We will attempt to gain control of the shield control room and any shuttles we might find. Be prepared to make a combat landing when the shield comes down. I do not know how long we will be able to hold that position with my team split between two objectives. Keep the Legacy close to suppress any additional defenses. My flagship will fly cover and attempt to insert additional teams."

"Understood. We are standing by."

Justice gave us a live view of the action in our visor displays. The Operative made an intersystem jump right above the target, and in the blink of an eye her flagship quickly moved off when Sael and her team inserted. The area around the base was blanketed with blinding flashes seconds later as the stealth missiles dove into their targets. Justice rapidly moved us over the base and Eagle One launched with Klutch at the controls.

"Justice! Tell the Sig it's time to join the party!"

"Signal sent, Commander."

A shimmering opaque dome appeared over the base. Klutch made a tight turn away from the target to put us in a safe holding pattern. Bright lightning like flashes stabbed down from the Legacy's cloaked position, quickly followed by massive eruptions of debris from the surface. The Scrun were exposing their additional defenses. The Operative's flagship dove to the far side of the base and rained hell on other pop-up weapons. The atmosphere around the base was becoming obscured by the clouds of dust and debris. I was on the verge of calling Sael when the shield dome blinked off. Klutch nosed us over into a steep dive through the dense, dusty cloud. I sure hoped Sael had the access doors open.

Justice called out, "Commander, the Sig are now in system and taking positions in orbit above the target area."

To my relief, we flew out of the dust cloud and into a gaping access tunnel. Klutch had the shuttle's shields up and the point defense weapons firing nonstop at the access tunnel's security systems. We were taking some hits that were rattling my teeth. We plowed past the defenses and Klutch flared the shuttle for a jarringly rough landing. Our shuttle now blocked the tunnel entrance. Justice's subsystem took over the shuttle's weapons and commenced picking off targets of opportunity with single shots from the rail cannons. The loading ramp slammed down and Klutch went running by as we got to our feet and unassed the shuttle. We came under fire almost immediately, but it was rapidly suppressed by rail cannon fire.

My BS transmitter came online with an urgent call from the Operative. "Nathan, we are pinned down and under heavy fire. We need you at the shield control station before we are overrun!"

Sael's location appeared on my HUD — she was in deep shit. The area around her was choked with red hostile indicators. The beast pushed its way into my mind. I hit my gravity drives, sending me hurtling above the pitched battle and landing in the rear of the massed enemy troops. My comrades had no choice but to join me. To their credit, no one bitched about my rash move.

The Scrun soldiers seemed oblivious to us until they started hearing the screams of agony coming from their fellow troops. I had my climbing hooks extended and was slashing open the atmospheric suits on any Scrun within reach. My crew joined the fray and we slaughtered the enemy without mercy. Our close proximity prevented the Scrun from opening fire on us. That scenario changed as the Scrun realized who we were. The terrified troops started gunning down their own people in an attempt to stop us. Coonts and then Klutch put a stop to the bastards, by firing wicked long bursts from their mini guns. Tria stood back to back with me and we took on all comers. The lull created by Coonts and Klutch's suppressive fire gave Tria the time to rap me on the shoulder and get my attention. She was holding one of the big specialty grenades. SHIT! The beast must have thought I didn't need them, because it never entered my mind to use one.

Tria called over our comms net. "GRENADE OUT!"

She tossed it over her shoulder and grabbed another, this time I did the same, and threw two to our front. The devices came to a hover about twenty feet above the battle and started spitting their deadly fragments in all directions. Some of the fragments were exploding so close to us, I could hear shrapnel pinging off my outer armor shell. The Scrun did not like the concept of being flanked by a bunch of demon faced killing machines and broke ranks attempting to run. Coonts cut them down with explosive rounds from his launcher. There were so many target indicators showing up on my HUD I had to ignore some of them and concentrate on my immediate front. I was taking enough energy beam fire that I had temperature warnings flashing in my visor. When Tria got a clear field of fire, she let loose with all four launchers.

485

Everything moving on our left flank was scythed down by anti-personnel rounds.

We were being ringed in by the dead and dying and needed to move toward the Operative's location. A flash so bright it blacked out my visor came from my right side. It was accompanied by a jarring blast. My visor cleared in time to see a large crew served weapon flipping end over end, landing on a squad of Scrun that had been knocked down by the blast. Klutch gave me a thumb's up. As I returned the gesture, movement caught my eye. A large door on the side of a building structure directly across from us opened, and the twin barrels of another large weapon system swung in our direction. Justice did not issue me anti-matter, so the monster in me cut loose with my beam weapon. The shot hit the right barrel of the big gun, blasting it from its mount and twisting the other to the side as it discharged. The corner of the building took the shot, collapsing the roof in on the occupants. Tria followed up with an anti-matter shell through the wrecked doorway. The whole structure disappeared in a blinding flash of flying debris.

The Scrun were now in full retreat toward an adjoining cavern. Tria gave them no quarter. Once again, she opened up with all four launcher tubes, ripping the fleeing Scrun to shreds. I was glad Sushi voiced no concern for the interior of the base. It was going to need a major remodel when this was over with.

486

The Operative called over the IST net. "Nathan, the Scrun are retreating and we have a firm hold on the shield control building. We are preparing perimeter defenses and I have another strike team prepping for insertion. We should be able to hold this location. Get to the shuttle bay as fast as possible — I have lost contact with the strike team that was tasked with securing that area."

This was not good. If Sael could not contact them on her BS transmitter, there was a very good chance they were no longer among the living. My grim thoughts were verified by the appearance of a Scrun shuttle coming out of the cavern that served as the hangar bay. We dove behind a stack of empty slave crates as it opened fire on us. A huge blast blew the crates to pieces, burying us beneath the rubble. I had a sinking feeling in my gut that this might be my final resting place. We were bounced violently off the floor by another tremendous blast, that was followed by a horrific grinding crash.

"TRIA, ARE YOU INJURED?"

"No, Coonts and I are buried under debris. I do not know where Klutch is."

I was going to call out to Klutch, but there was no need. The slave crates and debris that had covered me were thrown aside, and a big thick arm reached out and righted me.

"Commander, it is much safer to sleep during the team meetings than it is in combat."

The big toothy smile of my comrade was a welcome sight. He pulled me to my feet and I was stunned at the sight of the Scrun shuttle that had attacked us. The cockpit and a good portion of the nose cone was molten slag. Evidently the Scrun should have fired on Eagle One instead of us. The fools got a point-blank shot from our assault shuttle's main weapons. The wreck came to rest within a few feet of us. Tria and Coonts made their way through the rubble to Klutch and I. Coonts brought us back to reality with a sobering comment.

"Commander, If the Scrun were able to board a shuttle, I fear the Operative's team may have been wiped out."

My blood boiled at the comment, and I felt the beast wresting my will to restrain his suicidal ways. Tria picked up on my change in demeanor and cleared her visor of its morbid specter. She placed two of her hands on each side of my helmet.

"NATHAN! You must take control! Do not let the demon lead, use your will to make it follow!"

My focus returned and with it my sense of duty. "Klutch, take the lead and make sure we don't walk into an ambush. We need to find Sael's strike team."

I could hear the din of combat increase in volume. The Scrun must be trying to retake the shield control building. I heard the distinct thunderclap of another Chaalt strike team inserting into the complex. The pitch of combat increased yet again. Tria rapped me on the shoulder and pushed me in the direction Klutch was leading us. We skirted the hulk of the destroyed shuttle and Klutch held his fist up to stop us. There was no activity to our front and the Tibor did not like it. He leaned around an engine nacelle on the downed shuttle to take a peek but jerked back as the rear of the shuttle blew up in our faces, sending us all sprawling among the rubble. Klutch was on all four scurrying toward me when the rear of wrecked shuttle blew apart from another weapon strike. I no longer wondered about the fate of the Chaalt strike team. If they were caught in the open by the weapon the Scrun was using on us, there was little chance they would survive.

The beast was cluttering my thoughts with hazardous mayhem. Tria saw me move in the direction the weapon had fired from. "Nathan, we must distract them before we attack." She pulled out three grenades and threw them one after another in the direction the hostile fire was coming from. Coonts and then Klutch followed suit. I regained enough control to do the same. At first, there was nothing, then a series of blasts reverberated around the cavern.

Klutch yelled out, "HIT THEM FROM ABOVE."

We launched on four different trajectories high above the Scrun gun emplacement. My crew rained anti-matter and high explosive down on the enemy. The blinding blasts obscured the target area, so I took my revenge on the three shuttles parked on the hangar ramp, giving each multiple beam strikes. The ensuing conflagration filled the cavern with dense black smoke. Two of the shuttles had troops in them and must have been preparing to lift off. The beast would let no one escape and I turned everything below me to scrap. My beam weapon shut down from overheating and my minigun from lack of ammo. My crew was putting an end to all resistance. Coonts called to me, clearing my thoughts and alerting me to his grim discovery.

"Commander, I found the remains of the Chaalt strike team."

I located Coonts and set down next to him. I could see bits and pieces of Chaalt military armor spread about. We quickly searched the area, which proved difficult because of the large amount of battle debris. We came up with a small quantity of eviscerated remains but nothing more. I called Sael on my BS transmitter. "Senior Operative, we found your team. There are no survivors."

"Acknowledged."

The transmission ended with that clipped reply. Even if the Scrun were to throw in the towel and surrender, the slaves would be the only ones leaving here alive. Tria pointed to a large pressure door on the cavern wall.

"The slaves must be on the other side of that door along with the cowards who are in charge of this place."

The sounds of battle coming from the entrance chamber had dwindled to almost nothing. What we continued to hear was the explosive report of additional Chaalt assault teams inserting into the complex. I would keep the Sig out of the program until we were ready to transport slaves. It would not be good to have a misunderstanding as to who was hostile and who was not.

Justice gave us a sitrep. "Commander, three Scrun motherships have jumped in system and the Sig have engaged them. One has been destroyed and two disabled. One Sig battle cruiser sustained heavy damage and another has light damage. They are preparing to board the disabled Scrun ships. Sushi has informed me they are pulling the seven special operations shuttles for the boarding unless you have immediate need for them."

"Tell Sushi to go ahead. We will alert him when we have taken the facility and are ready to move the slaves."

"Acknowledged."

I needed to find out what Sael was up to. I was going to move our shuttle to give us some shielded firepower in case the Scrun had more of the big mobile gun platforms waiting on the other side of the door.

"Senior Operative, what is your status?"

"We have a large number of Scrun troops trapped in a large bunker complex. It appears they will not surrender, so I am moving re-enforcements into the complex and prepping for our assault. I will keep you posted."

"Roger that, we are trying to locate the slaves and will be moving Eagle One to our location for fire support."

The transmission went dead. I called Justice's subsystem on Eagle One to remotely pilot to our position. The Scrun would get a rude awakening if they thought they could take us out the same way they did Sael's fireteam. The shuttle swung gracefully around the corner and sat down directly in front of the big pressure door. The boarding ramp came down and we took shelter inside. We replaced our depleted ordnance and Klutch went to the cockpit. He used our point defense weapons to blast the massive hinges off the door and then bounced a single railgun round off of it. The huge pressure door rebounded out of the opening and crashed to the floor.

The dust had barely settled when the shields on the shuttle flared yellow white from Scrun heavy weapons fire. I heard a sinister laugh over our comms, then Klutch yelled out, "Eat scat you slaver Throggs!" The shuttles main weapons fired four times, putting a permanent end to the Scrun gun emplacements. It was overkill, but that was something the Tibor were famous for.

Klutch came running from the cockpit. "Commander, they are surrendering — we should not give them a chance to change their minds!"

We quickly followed the Troop Master off the shuttle and charged into the cavern. I was not prepared for the sight that met me. The rear of the chamber was stacked to the ceiling with slave crates, all were occupied with aliens of every description. There had to be more than a thousand. I could feel my rage building and yanked my shotgun from its clip. Tria, Coonts and Klutch had a group of Scrun cornered in front of a huge crater where one of the gun emplacements used to be. My HUD gave me a count of thirty-seven. Somewhere among them had to be the leadership of this operation.

"WHO IS IN CHARGE HERE?"

None of the prisoners made a move or said a word. That was not the recommended response in my deteriorating state of mind. Pulling my weapon up I clicked it over to penetrator slugs. My actions had all of the Scrun extend their hands forward with the fingers splayed upward. The beast in me decided it was a little too late for that, I cut down more than a dozen before the slugs ran dry. My crew raised their weapons and the pleading slavers all pointed to a building with a large window facing the slave crates.

They were yelling out, "Omarro Lashmos hides in the control room!"

I stalked toward the big vault style door of the control room with murder on my mind. Klutch called to me. "Commander, what do you want to do with these pieces of sewage?"

Before I could say what was going through my mind, Tria decided she would make the decision for me. She pointed to several very unsanitary looking crates that must have recently held slaves. For the Scrun, it was going to be a very tight fit.

"GET INTO THE CRATES OR YOU WILL DIE WHERE YOU STAND!"

A few balked; Coonts and Klutch rectified the situation permanently. The rest hastily squeezed themselves into the crates without further ado. I threw my arm up and turned the control room door into molten slag with a single shot from my beam weapon.

I felt a tug on my arm and saw Tria holding on to it. "Nathan, I am here for you!"

I stood for a moment staring at her and then as if nothing had happened, I blinked and shook my head. "I hope that never changes."

Her visor momentarily cleared and she smiled at me. "Let's find Lashmos's descendant before Sael makes her way here."

She unclipped her shotgun and waved it in the direction of the control room. "We must hurry. I no longer hear the sounds of battle coming from the entrance cavern."

We ducked through the mess I had made out of the door and into the control room. It was obvious that someone had deliberately destroyed several pieces of equipment. We also noticed a large bag of credit vouchers setting on a control panel. What we were not seeing was Omarro Lashmos. Was this some sort of trick to lure us inside? If that were the case, and it was intended to trap us, they should have sprung it on us as soon as we entered. There had to be some sort of hidden chamber. The equipment on the walls surrounding us looked like it was all performing some function. We gave everything a cursory tug to make sure there was not a door behind it. This was getting us nowhere and I was starting to get pissed. I thought about getting one of the Scrun to point out where Omarro was hiding, and if that did not work out, I had twenty more to choose from.

I turned for the door to fetch my first volunteer but almost tripped over Tria who was on her hands and knees pulling at the rubber-like grate covering the floor. I backed up a couple of steps and she pulled a large section up. Underneath was an almost invisible outline of a hatch. The Throgg was hiding under our feet. There was no handle to open it with, and every weapon I had, would make a mess out of the whole room. I thought about the other Scrun, but it would not make much sense for them to know how to access the hidden chamber. Omarro was most probably the only one with the access key. The piece of shit was not going to get out of this that easy. I would turn the chamber into his grave before I would just walk away.

34

There was a very good chance we were being monitored by Omarro and he had to have seen how easily we breached the entrance. It would not take a genius to figure out we could do the same to the hatch on his hideaway. I took Tria by the hand and lead her back to the entrance. As we exited I turned and pointed my beam weapon at the hidden chamber. It was going to be the grave option.

Tria pulled my arm down. "Let me see if he will surrender rather than die."

I stepped back to let her give it a try but had my doubts as to whether it would work. The rumors of how the demon operated, were wide spread among the Scrun and Murlak.

"We are taking the slaves. Come out now and turn over all your credits, and we will spare your life. I will count to three and then my Commander will kill you where you hide!"

"ONE"

"TWO"

The hatch popped open and two gangly arms thrust two large cases out onto the floor, and then another. "I AM COMING OUT, AND I AM UNARMED!"

I commed Klutch. "Troop Master, put a slave crate in the cargo hold of Eagle One."

"Roger that, Commander."

I stood back and watched as Tria marched Omarro out of the control room. She was carrying the three large cases and hurrying the Scrun along with the toe of her boot.

"Coonts, help me search Omarro's hideout. I don't want to leave anything behind."

"On my way, Commander."

I climbed down into the chamber and looked around. I took a serious dislike to the enclosure that displayed the Scrun's slaving awards. I knocked it over and stomped it to pieces.

Coonts came down the ladder and smiled at my tantrum. "I do not believe he will be receiving any more of those."

Hanging on the wall next to a control panel were some very ornately decorated weapons. The fool had a chance to go out in a blaze of glory but declined to give it a try. Judging by the numerous screens, the piece of sewage had a front row seat to the battle from the time the Operative touched down.

Coonts peeked around me and gave the surveillance equipment the once over. "Excuse me, Commander."

I stepped back and let him examine the displays. He ran his fingers over some kind of board while squinting at the displays. He frowned and then his hands started moving faster. Multiple displays started changing from one scene to the next so rapidly I was becoming confused as to what he was doing.

"Quit screwing with that thing and let's finish searching this place."

"Commander, these are the recordings of everything the Scrun did when the alarms sounded. If you will look closely, you will see Omarro's underlings pulling the data cubes from the communication equipment. They give them to Omarro and he retreats to this bunker with them. Since I do not see any devices designed to erase or destroy the data cubes — they are still here somewhere, or Omarro has them. We are going to want to take a look at those. They might contain information exposing other facilities like this one or persons of interest we may wish to talk to."

Damn! I would have never thought to look at the recordings. Coonts was right, this could lead us to others involved with the Scrun. In order for the slave business to be profitable, it has to have a distribution network of reliable vendors willing to sell the illicit merchandise. If we eliminate the outlets and destroy the distribution centers, it will be a warning to those involved to find another line of business.

"Tria, ask Omarro what he did with the data cubes from the comms equipment. If he doesn't answer, start cutting things off until he does."

Coonts and I waited to hear back from Tria. Coonts sat patiently; me not so much. When I had my fill of waiting, I decided to go ask Omarro myself. I did not have to — he made an appearance faceplate first onto the floor at my feet. I looked up out of the chamber entrance and saw Tria standing with her arms crossed and Klutch with a big toothy smile. I guess they decided they did not need to escort him down the ladder. The Scrun finally quit groaning and crawled to where I stomped his trophy case to pieces. He turned to me with a look of contempt on his grotesque face. Apparently, he must have cherished his slaving awards. I extended my climbing hooks and the expression promptly changed and he quickly dug through the mess until he found what he was looking for. There were three faint indentations on the floor where the display case used to sit. He touched them with his fingers and a tube extended from the floor.

Coonts, reached down and grabbed it and examined the contents. Omarro started blubbering about something and his cyclops eyeball was big as a basketball. I waved my razor-sharp climbing hooks in his direction, and he promptly shut up. I turned back to Coonts and he was holding an encryption key in his hand. Before I had a chance to comment, Justice called to us.

"Commander, the Sig shuttles have returned and Sushi is requesting a status report."

The withering stare I was giving Omarro made him shrink back into the corner of the room. I tried to let my anger simmer with a call to Sael. "Senior Operative, we have secured the slaves and the Sig are ready for rescue operations."

"We have completed our mission and are ready to withdraw. Unless you have further need of my combat troops, we will start extraction procedures. Give us thirty minutes to collect the remains of my strike team, and you can bring the Sig in. I expect a full debrief when you are finished here."

The transmission ended, but not my growing anger at Omarro's continued deceit. Coonts must have thought I was going to kill Omarro. He stepped between us and handed him the encryption key.

"Your lack of complete cooperation has nullified our agreement to spare your life. I recommend you quickly rectify your transgression before my Commander dismembers you and wears your entrails like the trinkets you are so fond of displaying."

The murderous mayhem the Oolaran beast was offering up took a back seat to Coonts grisly statement. No one in their right mind should find humor in what he said, but I had to bite down on the evil snicker that almost escaped my lips. The slaver grabbed the key and dove headlong into the mess I had made. He started tearing at the floor grating. Using the encryption key, he opened another smaller chamber under the floor and then crawled to the side, pressing himself into a corner once more. Coonts and I leaned over the opening and I stared wide eyed.

I let out a piercing whistle. "Tria, Klutch, we are going to need your assistance."

Coonts, pointed at Omarro. "Pull everything out of there!"

The Scrun crawled back to the hide and started pulling case after case out of it, setting them on the floor at our feet. Fifteen, to be exact. Evidently, they believed I would attempt to destroy, or abandon the facility. They probably had a specialized team tasked with recovering their buried treasure in the event of a major catastrophe.

I stood over Omarro. "This is your last chance, what else have you hidden from us?"

"I swear to you, I have held back nothing! We know that you took my clan sibling Judrow and his staff from our military facility. If you have not killed him, he can verify what I tell you is true!"

That statement gave me pause. It answered one of the questions I had planned on discussing with Sael at some point in the future.

Coonts, commed me privately. "Commander, this piece of sewage might be able to tell us why the Chaalt took his sibling and do not wish to tell us about it."

It was exactly what I was thinking as well. If we carefully chose our questions, we might learn everything the Chaalt decided we didn't need to know.

"Put him in his new residence aboard Eagle One."

Coonts smiled. "Gladly Commander!"

He quickly hustled the Scrun from the Chamber as Tria and Klutch came back for more of the cases. Between the three of us, we gathered the rest and got them loaded on the shuttle. I left five cases sitting at the base of the boarding ramp. It was time to bring in the Sig.

"Justice, open a secure channel to the Sig and let them know we are ready to evacuate the slaves."

"Affirmative, Commander. Signal sent."

I let my crew know we would be leaving as soon as I spoke with Sushi. It was only a matter of minutes before the Sig combat shuttles started arriving. One sat down beside our shuttle and Sushi disembarked. He strode up to me with a smile on his face.

"It is good that you are well, Nathan Myers. You have executed an admirable operation. To see so few take such a large installation is an eye-opening experience. My report back to Tam Lin will confirm that you are indeed quite formidable. Many of my people believe the information we have gathered on your exploits to be blown out of proportion. I am going to take great pleasure in informing them that all of the speculation about the demon's abilities are true."

I rolled my eyes knowing Sushi would turn this into some kind of wild ass tale. I wondered if he would even mention my crew or the Chaalt troops. I doubt that I could dissuade him from doing otherwise.

I pointed to the cases. "Could you please see that one of these makes its way to Tam Lin? The rest is for you and your people."

Sushi's smiled broadened even more. "You should know that we recovered a large quantity of credits on board the Scrun ships we captured. My intelligence report states that the captains of the ships had recently sold their illicit cargo and had come here to gather more."

I loved it: we were hurting the Scrun where it universally hurts everyone — the wallet! As I walked to Eagle One, I called back to Sushi. "The Throgg in charge of this operation went to a lot of trouble to hide the majority of his credits. Evidently, he believed they would be able to retrieve them. If it were me, I would prepare a surprise for whomever comes to collect them.

He waved me off. "We sincerely hope they try!"

I pointed to the remaining Scrun that were crammed into the slave crates. "We tore the place up pretty good, so I left you some help to clean up the mess."

Sushi saluted me and I boarded the shuttle. I hoped this was another small step that would make the allies of the Scrun sit up and take notice. Slavers were an endangered species, and if I had my way, they would be facing extinction. I called to Klutch. "Take us to the Legacy, Troop Master."

As I walked by the slave crate Omarro was crammed into, I rapped on it with my armored fist. "I hope you're comfortable!"

I held a muffled, pleading response. I ignored it and sat down in the jump seat between Tria and Coonts. Tria hooked her arm in mine and her helmet retracted showing me a radiant smile. I did the same, then leaned over and kissed her.

"Your efforts to control the Oolaran imprinting are progressing well. Soon it will be nothing more than a tool to use in combat and not a hazard to us all."

I took Tria's comment for the compliment she meant it to be and not a stab at my propensity for running amok when the demon was in control.

Coonts retracted his helmet. "The Scrun is complaining the enclosure is too small for him and was never designed for his species."

I reached out with my foot and kicked the side of the crate. "You're a dumbass! I don't know which is more stupid — building something like that to begin with or being arrogant enough to think one of your kind would never end up in one."

Klutch commed us. "Justice is taking us aboard the Legacy."

I felt a light thump as our landing gear extended and another when we touched down. Klutch dropped the ramp and shut down the power. As we debarked, he called out to me. "Commander, do you want me to put this piece of sewage in the brig?"

"No, leave him in there. Turn off the lights and close the hatch. I want him to know what it feels like to be a slave. I have some questions he needs to answer, and a chance to get out of there might get me the truth."

"He claims the confined space is inhibiting his suit's ability to properly dispose of his bodily waste."

"Ask him what he did when the slaves complained about the enclosure."

I heard Klutch's croaking laugh and then the hatch closing on the shuttle.

"Justice, how long will it take to decipher the data cubes we confiscated from the Scrun?"

"I am already familiar with Scrun encryption algorithms, and I estimate no more than thirty minutes to decode the information stored on the devices."

"Thank you, Justice, please call a crew meeting in the galley in one hour and jump us back to the rally point."

"Acknowledged, Commander."

I went to the ready room and stowed my armor in the modified repair crate Justice fabricated with the help of Felix. Coonts had just completed the process.

"I would like you to think about the questions we need Omarro to answer and give me your ideas at the crew meeting."

"Of course, Commander. Once we have the data decrypted from the storage devices, I will have the background necessary for the interrogation."

Klutch walked in and shed his armor. "You should let me interrogate the Throgg. It would take me very little time to get the answers you seek."

I suspected Omarro would say just about anything we wanted to hear, whether it was the truth or not if I gave Klutch his way.

"I am always open to your wisdom Troop Master, but in this case, we will start out civilized before we get medieval on his ass."

The Tibor looked puzzled at my response but shrugged and gave me his usual toothy smile. "OK Commander, I will see you in the galley."

I expected to see Tria, but her gear was stowed and she was not present. I had a feeling I knew where she was. I cussed my faulty thinking for calling a meeting in an hour, instead of two or three. I felt the sensation of a standard transition and decided Justice was not in a hurry to meet with the Operative, and I knew why that was as well.

I felt a little jittery as I headed to my cabin. It was a toss-up between anticipation and nervousness. If I did not find what I was expecting, it would be disappointment. I had just stepped out of the lift tube on the bridge level when my IST transmitter gave me a secure beep. I cringed and slapped my hand to my forehead. I was going to strangle that old witch.

"Nathan, did you recover anything of interest during the operation?"

"Who wants to know, you or your council?"

"Surely you realize I purposely kept my troops and myself out of your area of operation, so there would be no repeat of my council's actions. I have already explained why I must cooperate with their deceitful directives. Your continued anger is unwarranted."

I had more than one reason to be pissed at the Operative but was not going to break it down for her.

"We captured one of Lashmos's siblings and enough credits to buy a planet. I did not take a slave count, but I believe there was more than a thousand."

"Excellent! I was hoping for this outcome. Now that you have a legitimate source of information, I no longer have to worry about breaking a direct order not to reveal certain intelligence we gathered on our last mission."

"Sael, we can compare notes when I can meet with you in person. We will be at the rally point shortly."

So much for all the sneaky crap we thought we were going to pull on the Chaalt. It seemed like Sael was a step ahead of us and her superiors. The witch was a master of manipulation. The Operative I had come to respect was still with us, but she was being forced to weave multiple layers of subterfuge to mask her true motives.

The signal went dead and I once again headed to my cabin to see what might await me there. The hatch opened and Tria was sitting on the edge of my bed putting her uniform on. My timing was absolute shit and for that matter so was the Operative's. I did not know who was more disappointed, me or Justice. I started to apologize but she cut me off.

"Justice, opened my IST channel so I could hear your conversation with Sael. It will be interesting to hear what she has to say."

I gave her a hug and a kiss. "Sael will eventually have something else to do besides meddling in our affairs."

"I tolerate Sael's interference because she is a means to the end of our technology gap. I want you to know that Sael is drawn to your strength and warrior instincts. She may pretend you are undesirable, but I know that she is hiding her true feelings. Your aura draws us to you, though she states otherwise. There are very old customs on my worlds that are generally wrote off as history. One of them is to fight to the death for the right to take a superior life mate."

I stood with raised eyebrows, digesting Tria's words. She had the most alluring smile on her face, but the look in her eyes said she meant every word. My legs suddenly turned to rubber and I almost collapsed. She caught me in her arms and held me close; her new weaponized strength was noticeable.

She whispered in my ear, "I have made my choice. Sael must find another."

With that, she kissed me lightly and left my cabin. I thought I heard her laugh but wasn't sure. The strangest thought went through my head. Tria said she went ahead with the weaponization because she feared our continuous mission profiles would interfere with her ability to get the procedure done in a timely manner. Now I wondered if she did it so she could kick Sael's ass if she had ulterior motives. I did kind of wonder what made Sael have her battle scars repaired. It might be a healthy choice on my part to keep the Operative at arms-length. What I considered innocent acts of friendliness towards Sael might have her thinking something else. I was giving myself a headache trying to figure out what part of being human would attract another species to me. I did know that I was very much attracted to Tria, so this was not a one-way street.

"Justice, what is our ETA to the rally point?"

"Sixty-three minutes, twenty-nine seconds. There is time for you to take a rest period, should I alert Tria."

The thought had actually crossed my mind, but I found the intention behind Justice's statement irritating. I chose to ignore him. "What was the total on the credits we recovered?"

I was heading to the down tube and it had been more than a couple of minutes since I made my inquiry. Just when I determined Justice was ignoring me back, he answered.

"In excess of six-hundred and ninety billion."

I guess I really didn't need an exact count — it was a crap load of credits. The Scrun will be feeling the pinch of our latest attacks. A lot of slimy slaver palms were not going to receive their normal greasing. The uncertainty and unrest this would cause the Scrun underlings made me smile and forget all about the spite Justice was sending my way.

"Justice, when you are done being vindictive, I hope you have a briefing for us on the intel recovered from the data cubes."

While he decided to not answer me, I knew he was not likely to display his less than admirable human traits in front of the rest of the crew. I entered the galley and saw that Klutch was already eating. Tria and Coonts sat two tables away quietly talking. They were trying their best to pretend they could not hear the less than palate pleasing noises coming from Klutch. By the look of Klutch's tray, the rations we purchased from Tam Lin were taking a hit. I sat down next to Tria and Coonts cued me in on their discussion.

"Commander, Tria and I believe it would be wise to question Omarro before we meet with the Operative. It might uncover additional information that both Omarro and the Operative might try to conceal. It could also serve as a way to verify what both might divulge to us."

I had to admit it would be a good way to see if Sael was leveling with us on the information she has access to.

"Justice, do you have a briefing for us?"

"Yes, it appears the Scrun and most undoubtedly the Murlak are trying to improve their security. The decryption method they now use is much better than when we first encountered both races. It took additional time to decipher the information. The vast majority is communications with Scrun motherships and other spacecraft assets. After our recent engagement with their forces, seventeen Scrun ships and five Murlak ships that the base was in contact with, no longer respond to communication traffic."

An evil smile crossed my face. E.T. was never going to phone home this time around. The looks on my crew's face said they were thinking the same thing. I refocused on the briefing.

"A call was sent out for reinforcements to investigate, but most all of those requests went unheeded. The three Scrun motherships that the Sig encountered were part of a larger rescue mission to the system they had set as a trap for us. They were delayed several hours by business transactions. When they attempted to rendezvous with the rescue force that had already entered the system, they could not establish contact with them and chose to come directly to the Scrun base instead of reconnoitering what may have happened to their cohorts."

Klutch thumped his large hand down on his table, making us all jump. "HAH! It sounds like the missiles we left behind found some worthy recipients."

His loud exclamation liberated several pieces of partially chewed food from his mouth and some found their way to the floor beside me. I pretended not to notice. The galley bots would have to work a little harder after the briefing was over.

35

After Klutch's outburst, Justice continued with the briefing. "I have several communications that resemble encryption techniques that we encountered on Drayen's outpost. I have yet to find the proper primer, but it is just a matter of time. I speculate that Omarro might have knowledge of a primer key that will assist us. The proper application of stratagem might get him to reveal the access code."

Coonts gave me a startled look. "Commander, my internment on Drayan's outpost revealed that the most sophisticated encryption was used exclusively for communications with Drayen's closest allies. In this case only one comes to mind — Eiger!"

To even hear that son of a bitch's name got the beast in me stirring. Tria reached over and grasped my hand, but I still felt murderous intentions lurking in the back of my mind. We had already uncovered questionable intelligence that had Eiger recuperating on one of the Murlak home worlds. We might be jumping to conclusions, but now I wondered if that was a smoke screen to hide his true location. I would love to get another crack at the sewage sucking Throgg. As far as I was concerned, shutting down the slavers and bringing Eiger to his final reckoning, took precedence over investigating an old pile of garbage, someone left corroding in the armpit of the galaxy. Now that I had the allies to pull it off, we should be able to go toe-to-toe with anything Eiger could bring to the party.

"Klutch, get Omarro out of his cage. We need to have a talk with him."

The Tibor jumped up and started to leave, but at the last second, in a small display of irritation at having his meal interrupted, he grabbed a handful of food and shoved it into his mouth. I was glad that he made no comment as he rushed by.

"Justice, what is our current ETA to the rally point?"

"Seventeen minutes, eleven seconds."

"If we have to kill a little time to get the answers we're after, you have my permission to take as long as you like to intercept the Operative's ship."

"Acknowledged."

Tria, Coonts and I made our way to the hangar. Klutch had put his combat armor on and was walking up the shuttle ramp. The slave crate containing Omarro came bouncing end over end out of the cargo bay landing on its side. Klutch stomped his way down the ramp and righted it. He jerked the door open and yanked the slaver out onto the deck. Without a word from me, the hangar door opened so we could have a view of hyperspace through the atmospheric retention field. When the Scrun turned and noticed this, he attempted to crawl back into the crate, but Klutch blocked his path. He looked over at me with a pleading look on his cyclops face and extended his hands out, splaying his fingers upward. I could feel no pity for the slaver piece of shit because of the pain and suffering he had no problem bringing to others.

"We have many reasons to put an end to your miserable existence, so you should give us a lot of reasons not to. Some of the information on the data cubes is heavily encrypted. I want you to supply my A.I. with the key. If you do that, we will not kill you."

I was gambling the Scrun were smart enough to have different encryption codes for each facility; if not, the next part of our ruse would be exposed. Omarro's less than forthcoming silence told me he was calculating exactly what to say. It was an expected response, but not one he should be using, considering his precarious position.

Turning to Tria and Coonts, I shook my head. "You both were correct, he is of no use. Judrow values his life more than this fool. We will find other ways to verify the information he has given us."

Coonts took his cue and held his hand up to Klutch and made a shooing motion toward the open hangar door. Klutch, grabbed Omarro and started to drag him to the opening, but stopped when the Scrun yelled out a string of code.

Justice confirmed its authenticity. "I have access, Commander."

Klutch let go of the slaver and he scampered across the deck on all four of his gangly arms and legs. He wedged his lower half back into the slave crate. It was ironic that he would think he could find shelter from his fate by trying to hide in a prison of his own making. Anger flashed through me like a torch at the thought that this is what the slaves must have done when they were in the same situation. Tria sensed the change in me and gripped my arm tightly. I tried to calm myself but felt the beast stalking the fringes of my awareness. If I let my anger, and then the beast, control me, I could possibly reveal that we did not have Judrow to question — or, even worse, kill our only source of information.

Justice pinged my implants. "Commander, we will be exiting interdimensional space in one minute. Do you still intend to meet with the Operative upon our arrival?"

I took several slow, cleansing breaths to clear the homicidal thoughts from my mind along with the instigator that was goading me.

"Yes, make the rendezvous. We will give Sael a chance to prove she is not screwing us over to benefit her council."

518

I felt the small discomfort of our transition back to normal spacetime. There was a static-like discharge that was visible through the open hangar door and the sudden appearance of a normal star field. Coonts took my distraction as his cue to continue our interrogation. He approached Omarro and the Scrun attempted to retreat farther into the slave crate. I was surprised by the Grawl's reaction. He stepped forward and grabbed the sides of Omarro's faceplate and hauled back on it till the Scrun stopped his retreat. He then leaned his face down till it almost touched the thick composite.

"Judrow claims that you know where Eiger hides. He has given us certain information to justify his claim. I advise you to think carefully about the next words that come out of your mouth. If they do not match what we have been told or are verifiable by your communications, my fellow crewmember will crush your appendages and reinsert you back into this crate. When my Commander determines you have suffered enough, we will start the questioning process once again."

The Scrun started pleading with Coonts and tried to lean over and touch him. Coonts batted his hands aside and reached inside of his uniform and pulled the Grawl-sized Tibor pistol he now liked to carry concealed on his person. He stepped on one of the Scrun's hands and pushed the pistol against it.

"We do not necessarily have to crush your appendages — we can remove them one at a time."

The Scrun was easily four times larger than Coonts, but he was terrified of the little Grawl's menacing behavior. Apparently, he had never witnessed such aggressiveness from a Grawl before. I had to admit: the look on Coonts' face was sinister and served its purpose well. The Scrun started talking fast.

"Eiger hides with the last of his fleet in a dense dust nebula near outpost 6854. He has several siblings who operate the outpost and he sells our slaves there."

Justice pinged our implants with a startling disclosure. "Commander, that is the location where the Zaens informed us about a large number of Murlak inquiring about battle armor. There is now the possibility that the Zaens may inadvertently supply Eiger with the armor we took from his clan siblings. If he is able to identify the armor, the Zaens could be in great danger. Eiger would most assuredly torture them into revealing where they acquired the battle armor. Their disclosures could prove to be fatal."

SHIT! I had put that piece of information on the back burner to address at a later date. We may have had a way to find Eiger all along if we had prosecuted the data before we went after the Scrun. My lack of urgency was going to bite me in the ass and may have cost the lives of my Zaen friends. I'm sure if that is what has come to pass, it would not sit well with Felix. If it became known that I cannot protect those who are willing to help me, then no one would take the risk of doing so.

Justice pinged me again. "Commander, we have come alongside the Operative's ship, and I expect she will join us shortly."

I was not in the mood to discuss current developments with Sael. I looked out the hangar door and her battleship suddenly filled the opening. I could see a small speck standing in the massive opening on the Chaalt ship. As we drew closer I could make out Sael in her combat gear preparing to jump across. I was miserable at the present situation, and the beast was transforming my despair into anger and revenge. I walked over to the Scrun.

"You are most fortunate that salvation has arrived. The Chaalt that is preparing to board has agreed to take you."

Tria, Coonts, and Klutch all gave me an incredulous look. They could not believe what had just came out of my mouth. For that matter, neither could I. The Scrun wriggled himself free of the slave crate and started hobbling toward the open hangar door. I waved my crew off before they could stop him. They again gave me looks of disbelief. I saw Sael leap from the deck of her hangar and hurtled across to ours. As she landed she unfolded her helmet and her face took on a look of confusion as she saw the Scrun heading directly at her. I did what any slaver-hating species would do in my boots. I yelled a warning.

"SAEL! WATCH OUT!

The Operative did what she has probably done thousands of times. She drew one of her swords and in one smooth motion slashed the Scrun's legs off just below his torso. The slaver's upper body did a single cartwheel off the deck and bounced out into the void. Sael leaned down and wiped her sword off on one of the legs and then kicked both out to join the rest of the carcass. Klutch thought this was a hilarious turn of events and broke out in raucous laughter.

Coonts looked a little miffed. "Commander, I might have been able to extract more useful information from him."

Tria gave me a raised eyebrow but refrained from any comments. Sael walked up to us with a frown and slid her sword back into its scabbard.

"Has the Tibor lost his mind? Why is he laughing, and what was that scat about? You can't let a Scrun run loose on your ship. I hope you had a chance to question him."

I got right to the point. "Sael, why did your council order you to confiscate the shuttles along with one of

Lashmos's siblings? Were they trying to keep information from us concerning Eiger's whereabouts?"

Sael's frown deepened. "Did you not question the Scrun before you were foolish enough to let him escape?"

My thoughts where swirling with conspiracy theories, but the most prominent one was probably correct. The more I examined the situation, the angrier I became. This was another not-so-subtle manipulation on the part of the Chaalt council.

Tria stepped close to me and whispered, "Nathan, calm yourself. Let's not dwell on the past, but instead focus on the future. We now have a means to stop the machinations of my people's ruling caste. As Sael has pointed out, now that the experimental ship is in our hands we have the advantage."

Advantage or not, I was really getting sick at the interference from our supposed ally. I'm sure this was a universal practice, even on the planet of my birth, but I did not have to put up with this backroom bullshit here. Sael stood staring, wondering what I would say next.

"This is about the derelict ship isn't it? Your council is only interested in gaining access to the technology that might be recovered and don't like the delays my other missions might entail."

I could tell she was carefully thinking about what she should say. "Your assessment is most likely correct, but you left out the part about your death-defying behavior. I believe that more than a few council members think you will meet your maker sooner than later. If that should happen, we will be back to searching the galaxy in hopes of recovering small quantities of useful trinkets."

What a load of crap! The Chaalt were looking out for me for my own good, or more aptly, looking out for their future good. Our technological discoveries were turning into a hindrance to goals that would benefit all races. I needed to get a handle on this before it turns into something more undesirable than what I was currently dealing with. But first things first!

"Sael, I am going after Eiger whether the council likes it or not. The Sig would be more than happy to come along without attaching any strings to the adventure. I would readily share tech with an ally that had no interest in interfering with my goals."

Sael cringed at my statement, but I knew it was theatrics. She knew exactly where this was going, and I was sure she somehow steered me in this direction. We were surprised when she turned and headed for the hangar door. I called after her.

"You are a lot of things, but I never thought a quitter would be one of them."

She turned, momentarily looking confused at my words. She then made a noise with her mouth and a dismissive wave with two of her arms.

"You mindless Throgg. I am going to spin this in such a way my superiors will not think I used duplicity to ensure this outcome. When I am done, they will believe it is what they wanted all along."

"We will be jumping to outpost 6854 and see what we can develop on Eiger's location. If we find actionable intel, we will move on it quickly."

Sael stopped short of the hangar door. "Let me know what you find. If you need my help, I will back you, no matter what the council has to say about it."

That was good enough for me, and it managed to knock the edge off my irritation. "Justice, take us to the coordinates the Zaens gave us."

"Affirmative, Commander. DEHD core transition in three minutes."

"Klutch, get that crate off our ship!"

Klutch grabbed the slave crate and threw it out the hangar door. As he walked by to stow his armor he made it a point to stop and talk to me. "Unless you have further need for me, I will be in the galley finishing my meal."

I let him know what might lay ahead. "I suggest you eat while you can and get some rest. If we manage to find Eiger, there will be no time for a nap or a lunch break."

Coonts and Tria were conversing then turned to me. "Commander, we must make an effort to locate the Zaens. Coonts and I agree they would not be foolish enough to interact with the Murlak if it becomes known that several of Eiger's siblings went missing at their former place of business. We should investigate the Zaen market outlet and determine their whereabouts."

I was going to say I agree, but my hearing muted and everything around me turned bright white, then faded away. When my awareness returned, Justice was talking to us.

"Commander, I have engaged our stealth systems and do not believe our transition has been detected. I am doing a passive scan of the outpost and the nearby dust nebula. There is light spacecraft traffic around the outpost and I have detected power plant emanations coming from the dust cloud. I believe closer scrutiny will reveal the true number and identity of the spacecraft loitering in that location."

"Okay Justice, take us into the nebula and let's get a hard lock on the opposition. Once we know for sure what is there, we can formulate a plan of action."

Coonts had another idea, and it involved him exhibiting a trait not common among his people. "Commander, I volunteer to go to the outpost in an attempt to find Broza and Hylet. It would be extremely unusual if the Zaen place of business was no longer operating. If I cannot locate the business, I will try to confirm the Zaens operating it, have been detained."

I could not argue with his reasoning. Tactically, it was the smart thing to do. Tria thought so too and volunteered as well. Unfortunately, I was going to piss her off. I would try to dampen her anger with a factual explanation as to why.

"Tria, all too often, our combat actions were associated with a Grawl accompanied by a Tibor Troop Master, or a Chaalt warrior, or an unknown biped alien. I know you have to realize that a Grawl by himself is not considered a threat to anyone."

Coonts, in a display of his inordinately large nads, helped me out of a tough spot. "Tria, if I go alone, I will draw very little attention. I will wear a standard issue Grawl cloak suit that will hide my identity. Most will overlook me as just another possible customer for goods sold on the outpost. Should I run into unexpected trouble, I will not hesitate to call for your assistance."

Tria stood with her arms crossed but nodded in agreement. Coonts gave us a thumb up. "I will alert Klutch to our new mission considerations before I board the shuttle."

I was sure Klutch would join us shortly to offer going to the outpost in Coonts' place. I shook my head and prepared my response to his request. I gave Tria a small smile in hopes she would return it, but that was not the case. The warrior in her wanted action, and I could not blame her. This might prove to be a chance to even the score with the bastard that had brutalized her. I knew that I would do everything in my power to make sure Eiger did not slip through my fingers once again. Right on cue, I heard thumping footsteps rapidly approaching. As Klutch stopped in front of us, it was apparent he had not finished his meal. His attempt at speaking included a sprinkling of food bits on my feet. He hastily wiped the remainder from his face and apologized for the well-chewed barrage. Coonts and Xul came out of the ready room discussing the mission. Coonts was wearing one of the Grawl cloak suits from our large supply. He was holding a smaller version of a Tibor fighting knife in his hands. His face mask was transparent and you could see the less than attractive smile on his face.

"Look what Justice has presented to me. He has down-sized one of the fighting knives so I am able to conceal it with my sidearm."

He held it out and Klutch grabbed it, twirling it several times in his big meaty hand. "It is a little flimsy but will still do its intended job"

He handed it back to Coonts, who slid it into a scabbard inside of his suit. Any thoughts of a feud going on between Coonts and Justice were now allayed. While we were all gathered, Justice took the opportunity to notify us about some the armor modifications he had been working on.

"Commander, the results of my experiments have yielded new capabilities for your equipment. I have incorporated what I now believe is an effective cloaking system into your current generation battle armor. My initial experiments revealed numerous inadequacies in the backlighting devices that kept the cloaked battle armor from casting tell-tale shadows. I have now overcome those limitations. The newly designed emitter arrays will allow me to closely monitor all encountered backgrounds and compensate for the constantly changing conditions. The one limitation that makes the cloaking of the battle suits less than optimal is the sound emissions from the armored foot gear on rigid surfaces. The sound deadening qualities of the pads I have installed on bottoms of the boots will still require measured careful strides to negate sound propagation."

I knew Justice had been working on the cloak system since he designed the new armor. The ability to cloak the large metallic monsters our suits have become, was an outstanding achievement. Although we would again find ourselves entering combat with untested systems, Justice's record of success spoke for itself. Tria and Klutch wished Coonts good luck and disappeared down the corridor into the ready room. When Coonts turned away from the shuttle, I knew what the topic would be. To my surprise, I was only half right.

"Commander, Xul has volunteered to accompany me to the outpost. Since we do not anticipate combat operations, I thought it was an excellent idea. While not unheard of, my people are not generally known to travel alone. I also believe it would be wise to purchase food supplies and other goods while we are there. It will further our ruse and make reconnaissance much easier if we are seen making purchases in several different locations on the outpost. I would also like to take my battle armor as a precautionary measure in case unexpected circumstances arise. Xul will be bringing his Zaen body armor as well."

I nodded in agreement and waved them on, they both took off to gather the rest of their gear. I called to Justice. "Justice, give Coonts a credit voucher with a denomination on it that will not draw unnecessary attention. Please keep close watch over Xul — I know he means well, but he will be stepping way outside of his normal comfort zone."

"Affirmative Commander, I have carefully selected the loadout for Xul's battle armor and can take control of the Zaen systems at any time, should it require him wearing the suit."

I should have known better. Justice looked after everyone under his care.

36

I suddenly felt a very familiar feeling that was always accompanied by Tria's presence. I turned around and saw nothing. "Tria, I know you are close, I can feel your aura."

My legs turned to jelly and I staggered forward only to be caught by Tria's large armored arms as she appeared in front of me. The cloaking technology was indeed a masterful stroke of engineering. Klutch appeared just behind me with a croaking laugh.

"Commander, Eiger will never know what happened, because you can slit his throat before he knows you are near."

I didn't say it, but I wanted Eiger to know who was coming for him. *I want him to feel the terror he is inflicting on others.*

Justice alerted us that Coonts and Xul were ready to depart. He pushed the shuttle out of the atmospheric retention field then turned the Legacy on a course that took us into the dense dust nebula. We started picking out what we presumed to be Eiger's fleet. There were twenty-two ships identified as three Union gunships, eleven Murlak-heavy cruisers, six Scrun motherships and two that Klutch identified as very dated Tibor shuttle carriers. The carriers were giant disks with four hangar bays around their perimeter. They normally carried sixteen assault shuttles with a dozen troops on each of them. We had no way of knowing if they had complete detachments with them or not. I already knew the Tibor assault shuttle was a formidable weapons platform. If the carriers had a full complement of mercenaries aboard, it could spell trouble if we mounted a rescue operation at the outpost. The one ship I had hoped to see was not present — there were no Warbringer class battleships detected in our scans. Justice continued scanning the entire dust cloud until we were sure we had tagged all the ships hiding there. We were now at the farthest point from the outpost and skirting the outer edge of the nebula. It was time to turn back when Justice alerted us to a new turn of events.

"Commander, I have an active transponder thread."

"I have been wondering if the Guardian transponder quit working — it has been awhile since it has been active."

"I have come to the conclusion that the device is unable to function while making DEHD Core transitions. I believe we have missed opportunities to make additional discoveries, had we made normal interdimensional transitions."

"How long is the thread?"

"More than ninety light years and increasing. I recommend we let it run its course and map the destination before we return to the outpost."

"OK Justice, show us the nebula and the ships you have located while we wait."

We gathered on the bridge and Justice displayed the dust cloud. It was showing the positions of the twenty-two ships, each had a red triangle marking its location. If this was indeed Eiger's fleet, his assets were dwindling along with his power base. Klutch was for taking a call from the Operative's playbook and launching an immediate stealth missile attack. Tria, on the other hand, was the voice of caution.

"We should not take action until we hear from Coonts and Xul. Once we know what is taking place on the outpost, we can make our plan of action as well as any secondary contingencies."

"Commander, Coonts and Xul report they are now moving to the market areas. I will relay their voice communications through the shuttle IST"

"Thanks, Justice. Alert me if anything changes. When you are ready, move us as close to the outpost as you can without putting us in danger of a collision with other spacecraft."

"Affirmative."

Since Coonts and Xul took our only shuttle, we needed to be close enough to bail them out in case scat finds its way into a ventilator.

"Commander, I have comms traffic from Coonts."

Coonts' voice came online. "Commander, there are a large number of heavily armed Murlak and Tibor mercenaries prevalent throughout the market areas. We have been shadowed by two Murlak from the moment we exited our shuttle. We will stop and make purchases to see if they will continue their surveillance."

It sounded like the Overmaster of the outpost was expecting trouble or trying to dissuade anyone from starting any. I did not want to be involved in another outpost shootout. The Oolaran in me would have loved nothing better. I wringed my hands in a display of impatience. Eiger was out there in the void doing I don't know what, and there was nothing I could do about it until he revealed his location.

"Commander, the thread has terminated at a star system one-hundred and forty-one lightyears from our present location. I have mapped the coordinates and we can now move back to the outpost."

"Roger that, Justice, take us back."

Justice relayed Coonts' comms transmission. "Commander, I have purchased supplies at two Grawl outlets, and the Murlaks that were following us have ceased their surveillance. Xul has identified a Zaen supply shop two levels above our current position. We will investigate and report back to you when we have useful information."

So far so good. No hostile actions were a plus and my crewmates could move about freely. I was beginning to feel like we were going to get in and out with no trouble. I hated playing the waiting game but had no choice but to sit back and see what Coonts and Xul could find out. Tria seemed anxious and Klutch looked bored.

"Tria, is something on your mind?"

"Yes. I had fears this was another trap designed to lure us to this location. I now think otherwise — Eiger or the Scrun would not have enough time to set this up. There is no way they could have transferred the data on our last engagement before we arrived. Unless Eiger has obtained DEHD Core technology, they would have no reason to think we will come here."

Tria was right: there was no way the information could have beat us here. "So, you think this is where Eiger has been hiding?"

"I cannot be sure if that is the case because his flagship is not present. It does make sense that he would frequent the area to collect the credits being earned on the outpost. He must keep his underlings paid or they would most assuredly abandon him. I suspect that Eiger spends little time at any single location. Our success at destroying his assets has him fearing for his life."

"Commander, I have comms from Coonts."

"Commander, we made contact with the Zaens operating the outlet, they say that Broza was on his way with an armor shipment and never arrived. He is missing and the merchants say this is a very unlikely scenario. They fear the worst. They are waiting for the right moment and they are going to flee this location"

Shit! This was not turning out as I thought it would. Broza obviously confided in the Zaens on the outpost to some extent or they would not be so forthcoming. I could not blame them for not wanting to hang around. An old Earth dictum came to mind: SNAFU. It described my current dilemma perfectly. Not only was Eiger still at large, but now the Zaens were missing as well. "OK Coonts, you and Xul get back to the shuttle and meet us at the rally point."

"Roger that, Commander. We will load our supplies and leave as soon as possible."

I was relieved that Coonts and Xul had no problems on the outpost. It was a definite departure from the shootouts that seemed to plague our every move.

"Justice, don't we have a way to locate the Zaens?"

"Yes, through their star drive signature and comms. Unfortunately, one or the other has to be operating before

I can attempt to get a fix on their location. They will have to be within our scanner range as well."

Tria and Klutch were exchanging ideas and came up with what the most likely answer could be.

"Commander, Klutch and I believe that with the large number of pirates in this sector, the probability of the Zaens being hijacked is a very likely scenario. It is not a stretch of the imagination to assume the Murlak or others would place an order for armor or materials that they can ill afford, then wait for the supplier to deliver and intercept the cargo."

Although this did not indicate a direct relationship with us, and probably not the reason they might be detained, it did not rule out the possibility of the armor Broza was transporting being identified as captured by us.

"Commander, we have arrived at the shuttle rally point and I have detected the transition of our shuttle. Coonts and Xul's ETA is seven minutes."

"Thanks, Justice, we will meet them in the hangar."

Tria, Klutch and I went down tube to the hangar. Justice had just pulled the shuttle in with the tow beam and was locking it down to the deck. The rear hatch came down and Xul stepped off with a relieved look on his face. Coonts joined him and we congratulated them on a successful intelligence gathering mission — one that did not involve shooting the place up. Coonts walked us to the shuttle's hold and showed us the generous supply of goods he purchased on the outpost. The Grawl back at Alpha base would be very happy to learn that there would be no rationing of Grawl related consumables anytime soon.

I was interrupted by an IST transmission from Sael. "Nathan, what is your status?"

I filled her in on everything that had transpired and the fact we were still no closer to finding Eiger. I told her of our concerns for our allies, and what we thought had happened to them. She was not a lot of help and stated what we already knew.

"If I were you, I would think long and hard about attacking until you can locate the Zaens. If they are being held on one of the ships, you could very well kill them with your preemptive strike. Another thing to consider is that Eiger must know we are actively hunting him. If he does not have the Zaens and you make a big stink trying to rescuing them, what do you think will happen if word gets out who is responsible? You may never get another shot at him."

"We will wait for the time being and concern ourselves with finding the Zaens. We can only hope that Eiger does not have them."

"Keep me appraised of the situation and I will make my way to your location as soon as I am able."

The transmission ended with me wondering what was keeping the Operative from joining us. My crew was having a discussion on how to find the Zaens. They came up with an idea, which, at the moment, was more than I had. It was simple and straightforward. We would make an IST transmission back to Alpha base and contact young Felix. He would know standard communication codes necessary to contact Broza's ship that would not compromise our discrete code system. We would then put a message on a comm buoy and launch it into the system so it arrives close to the outpost. The message on the buoy would say that he was not able to contact the Murlaks on outpost 9765 and was stuck with twenty suits of Murlak armor. We would have him say something to the effect, he would sell the armor at a discount to recoup the investment made to build them. We had hopes that greed would take over if the Zaens comms were being monitored. If an acknowledgement is broadcast to the buoy from their ship, Justice would be able to locate them.

I made the call to Alpha Base and Felix wanted to help anyway he could to find his clan members. He was more than just a little concerned for Broza and Hylet. It took him three tries to get the panic out of his voice while making the message. Justice snuck us out of the local system and prepped and launched the buoy. He programmed it to make four different jumps that would take it on a roundabout course. The buoy's last vector would jump it to the location of the outpost from the far side of the system. We would have plenty of time to pick a strategic location to observe the dust nebula and the outpost if our little trick raised a response from the Zaen's ship.

Justice hid the Legacy in the edge of the dust cloud near the most direct route to the outpost. I sat doing one of my least favorite things: waiting. I was slowly learning how to control the Oolaran soldier that haunted my thoughts, but I could not stifle its constant goading. The yearning for combat was still highly contagious and the anxiety that came with it an unwelcome distraction. I wasn't sure if Tria could sense my restlessness, but she got up from her console and stood by me. When she placed her hand on my shoulder it was if she was siphoning off my pool of bloodthirsty thoughts. I partially relaxed.

"Commander, the buoy has transitioned into the system and is broadcasting now."

I didn't have any idea how long it would take to get a response, but Tria's touch was now having a different effect on me and I wrapped my arm around her waist. She looked down at me and cocked an eyebrow. The damn fool machine put his two cents worth into an already increasingly awkward situation.

"Commander, perhaps it would be wise for all crew members to take a rest period while we wait to see if the Zaens respond."

Klutch and Coonts gave each other a frown then both looked back at Tria and me. They both quickly turned back to their consoles but could not contain the snickers that were easily audible. Tria rolled her eyes and let her hand fall from my shoulder. The spell was broken, and I leaned back in my chair drumming my fingers on the armrest. Tria went back to her station, but not before walking by Klutch and cuffing him on his bullet head. The pair could no longer contain their laughter and both broke out in a loud guffaw. Xul looked on with a very confused expression on his face. *Sweet mother of my maker! My crew is turning into clowns just like Karl and me used to be back in high school.*

I had my fill and got up from my chair. "Tria would you like to join me in the galley?"

"Yes, I believe I would."

As she got up to walk out, she passed by Coonts, giving him a slap to the back of his head as well that shut up the cackle coming from his pie hole. Klutch found Coonts' reaction to being cuffed even funnier than my embarrassed behavior. He was now laughing loud enough I considered it an assault on my ears and wondered if he would commence rolling about the deck. Xul beat me to the drop tube and disappeared down; Tria and I quickly did the same.

We had not been seated for more than a couple of minutes, and I was working on my third bite of food when Justice alerted us. "Commander, a response from the Zaens has been sent and it originated from the location of one of the Tibor shuttle carriers! I will play the transmission and I believe you will find the message very interesting."

There was a short pause and then Broza's voice filled the galley. "Felix! I am so glad to hear from you! Yes, I can sell all of the armor suits. Can you let the shipping department know that the large shipment of Dorta sea snakes that was to be shipped to Haras on outpost 9765 needs to be shipped to 6854 along with the armor? Let Haras know I will give them a discount on the replacement order for the inconvenience. I await your arrival schedule — please transmit it as soon as possible."

Broza was one smooth operator: he just slipped us a warning about the Tibor pirates holding him. They probably thought the Zaen was trying to bribe his way out of the mess he was in by stuffing their faces with their favorite delicacy. If I had my way, they were going to get stuffed all right. I heard some thumping footsteps and Klutch rounded the corner into the galley with Coonts right behind him. The expression on his face was pinched and his large dark eyes had tears in the corners. It was about that time that Klutch's scent caught up with him and I shoved my plate away. Looking at Tria, I saw her take a quick breath and do the same.

"Klutch, calm yourself! I can't think with your warrior's scent choking me. Let's go to the conference room and figure out how to get the Zaens out of trouble."

Tria, Xul, and I quickly headed to the lifts to get a breath of fresh air. Coonts wasted no time bringing up the rear. Klutch had a disturbing look on his face and was pounding his fists together but had the decency to give us time to put distance between us and him.

He yelled after us. "Commander, the pirates that hold the Zaens dishonor all Tibor clans and they must be cleansed from the galaxy!"

I put my arm around Tria and gave him a thumb up with my other as we disappeared upward. As we stepped into the conference room Justice put a holographic depiction of the Tibor shuttle carrier over the middle of the table. We took our seats and then Klutch joined us, but his odor was not quite neutral yet. I gave a slight cringe and shook my head. It would have to be enough for now, and I pointed at his chair until he sat.

"Klutch, if you have additional knowledge on the carrier, please fill us in."

"Commander, the vessel you see was used very little because it had a large number of flaws in its design. It was never accepted into service but led to a much better design. I know of only eight ever built for trials, and of those, only five survived to be sold for scrap. How the pirates came into possession of two is anybody's guess."

"Well, they are here and we will have to deal with them. What are the weapons capabilities and what could we expect if we attempt to board that thing?"

"The initial design had sixteen shuttles, as Justice already pointed out. The number of troops he mentioned was also correct if all the shuttles have complete assault crews. The ship itself had three officers and twenty-one crew members to operate it. I have serious doubts as to the pirates having a complete crew."

Xul held a finger up to me and silenced Klutch for the moment. I gave him a nod. "Is there something you would like to add, Xul?"

"Yes, Commander. While Coonts and I were on the outpost I kept count of all the possible hostiles we encountered when we departed the shuttle. In the docking areas we passed through, there was forty-seven Tibor and sixty-two Murlak including the two that shadowed us. I only counted these numbers because they were openly displaying weapons. All of the market areas we passed through had two hundred and five Tibor, and one hundred and seventy-one Murlak that were armed. If we were to assume the rest of the outpost was as heavily guarded, that would make the chances of the shuttle carrier having a complete crew very unlikely."

The little Grawl took his seat. I looked over at Coonts and could see he was embarrassed by the fact he did not think to do the same thing.

"Thank you, Xul, that is an important piece of intelligence and will make a big difference in our threat assessment."

We gave Xul a nod and Klutch continued. "What we are not seeing is whether or not the ship has its original armament. The ships had large quad energy beam weapons on the top and bottom hidden in armored bays. Next to the batteries were two missile tubes for a total of four. Around the perimeter guarding the hangar bays were eight defensive energy weapons. Again, I can only speculate because if the weapons are present, they are hidden behind armored hatches."

An idea was forming in my head. "Justice can you get us in close for a detailed scan of the ship?"

"Yes, moving now Commander."

"Klutch, what were some of the design flaws you were talking about?"

"For starters, the star drives were much too small and underpowered to give the carriers sufficient speed to keep up with normal fleet combat maneuvers. The powerplants also lacked heavy enough armor to protect them in combat. Some brilliant fool decided that the extra weight would be detrimental to the already slow design and gave it very good shields in an attempt to offset the shortcoming. Initial testing revealed the shields could withstand a good beating, but once they were overwhelmed, it only took a couple of strategically placed shots to completely disable the ship. This may sound like it would be an easy fix with a power plant and armor upgrade, but what really killed the project were the fire suppression systems. The piping supplied by a third-party vendor was substandard and not properly tested. It was internally plumbed throughout the ship and not tested until void trials. The first time the piping was pressurized, it leaked so badly the chemical suppressants flooded internal machine spaces, disabling critical combat and life support systems. More than a few military leaders thought that it was espionage and the project was abandoned to the scrapyards. If the Throggs on those ships don't know that, we should start a fire to show them."

In the back of my mind the beast in me was contemplating a bonfire complete with a war dance. I shook my head, clearing the image from my brain. Justice put a viewscreen on the wall and we got a close-up of the target ship. It was still ready for the scrap yard. I suspected it was more of a base of operations than a space-worthy combat ship.

"Justice, have you picked up any comms coming from the carrier or any of the other ships?

"Negative, only the transmission from the Zaen's ship. My scans detect thirty-nine life forms on the Tibor carrier. I am unable to differentiate between the Tibor and Zaens. All of the target ships are running on minimal systems and their powerplants are working at negligible output. The probability of the vessels being maintained by nominal crews is high and I believe that the remainder of the personnel are on the outpost."

Our view was growing larger by the second and finally stopped when we were looking directly into one of the hangar openings. Sitting just inside hangar number four according to the identifier on the deck, was the Zaens oblong culvert pipe shaped starship. Scanning the rest of the opening, Justice put the images of four Tibor assault shuttles in the back of the hangar. It was obvious from his scans that at least three of them were partially disassembled. A plan was starting to come together in my head. Tria squeezed my hand and then called to Justice.

"Justice, take us to the other carrier, if it is crewed in the same manner we might be able to do a covert recovery mission and depart the area before any are the wiser."

She must have been doing that annoying Chaalt mind-reading trick because I was thinking the same thing.

37

Our scans turned up nineteen crewmembers on the second carrier. It seemed that most everyone was on the outpost, possibly out of necessity. Justice alerted us that the second carrier had no operational atmospheric retention fields. The subzero temperatures in sixty-nine percent of the ship indicated that most of it was in perpetual vacuum. I wondered what sin the remaining crews had committed to be stuck aboard those wrecks. *Sucks to be them and they had no idea just how bad yet!*

"Klutch, are you familiar enough with the deck plan to search for the Zaens if they are not being held on their ship?"

The Tibor looked thoughtful for a long moment. "Familiar would not be the optimal word I would use, but I do recall where the bridge and comms are located. From that location there is a service tunnel that runs through the ship to the machine spaces. If we control those areas, we control the ship."

"Start working on a plan to rescue the Zaens. I want it to be a covert attempt, and if that fails, things will become difficult very quickly."

"Justice, we need to make contact with Felix so we can give Broza a reply message."

"IST transmitter is online and ready, Commander."

I made the call to young Felix and he was only partially relieved that we had located Broza and Hylet. The reputation of Tibor pirates was well known and he feared his relatives would be killed in our attempt to free them. I could not blame him because I was more than worried it might turn out that way as well. He made us a message that stated he would arrive with the inventory in two standard rotations. If the plans we were making panned out, we would broadcast the final message we had Felix make. It was a call we knew would never be answered by Broza if we rescued him and Hylet. It was a request for coordinates to a meeting place to transfer the cargo. When he did not get an acknowledgement, he would broadcast he was leaving the sector. Looking at my crewmates I made eye contact with each of them.

"We need to do this in such away the Zaens won't be a target of the pirate's revenge. Since we haven't got a solid lock on Eiger yet, we need to get in and out without tipping anyone off as to who is behind what is about to happen. Klutch, you said that thing was a fire trap. Well, we are going to make sure that is the case if we get the Zaens out of there. We need to make sure it looks like a tragic accident. If Eiger does show up, we try to take him out with as many of these Throggs as we can. OK. let's hear some ideas."

551

Klutch stood back up. "The accident you speak of will be the easiest part of the operation. The hard part will be making sure no one can use the comms on the carrier or the Zaen's ship to call for help. We must make those targets our first priority. Like I stated earlier, the bridge will be another important target once the comms have been silenced. As far as a fire goes, if we make it to the service tunnel unhampered, we open every service hatch we pass and start a fire in the lower spaces. The fire will spread quickly, so we will want to make a very hasty retreat."

Klutch sat back down and Tria added something I really hadn't thought of. "We should invite our new friends the Sig. They tend to make all races nervous because their motives are always suspect."

Everyone nodded and Coonts added to her comment. "Commander, if they were to make a close pass, the security teams on the outpost would be on their highest alert."

I liked the idea and wondered if it would trigger a call to Eiger to bring his Warbringer into the system, or if it would scare the coward off. No matter the consequences, we needed to get the Zaens out of the dilemma they were currently in.

"Justice, launch a comm buoy to our closest communication relay and contact the Sig."

"Commander, I recommend we move to the outer reaches of the system before we launch a buoy. There is a small possibility it will be detected this close to our target area."

"Roger that. Let me know when you reach them."

I was going to wait until I knew if the Sig could free up some of their assets before we sent Felix's response to the Tibor holding the Zaens. Timing was going to be on the tight side if they were more than a couple of days out. They should have several vessels in the neighborhood around the Scrun base we captured. I knew those ships were within a day's jump to this location.

"Commander, Sushi has responded to our message."

Justice put a viewscreen on the wall of the conference room and Sushi's image appeared. "Nathan Myers, I hope you and your crew are well. How can I be of service to my fellow clan member?"

It warmed my heart knowing we had made friends with another race and it did not involve shedding each other's blood to do it. "I have a favor to ask and it should not include any major risk to your people."

The look I got from Sushi indicated he was disappointed.

"I was hoping you were going to tell me you had some more slavers that needed to be eradicated."

"Not this time my friend. I need you to make a fly-by of outpost 6854."

The Sig looked puzzled. "I know of the trading post and it is rumored that a large number of pirates are firmly entrenched in that sector. If you are attempting to capture the trading post I will have to summon a larger fleet. We have had a few run-ins with the Scrun over our new base of operations. It has been quiet for a while, so we think they may have given up and moved on to other places."

"I have no intention of capturing the outpost. I just need a small distraction so we can pull off a rescue operation without them discovering that it was me and my crew that did it."

"Normally we only purchase our supplies on outpost 9765 at Haras. We like to keep our business within the family. But I think we could make a small exception in this case. I believe I could arrange for ten battleships to make a supply run. If I recall correctly, they used to sell intoxicants of reasonable quality at that location. Perhaps we need to determine if they still do."

"I will reimburse you for all of your expenditures involved in the operation."

"Nonsense! The Scrun base we have inherited more than makes up for such a trivial pursuit. We will use the purchases to celebrate the opening of our new regional headquarters. When would you like us to swing by?"

"As soon as you are able."

Sushi looked to one side and said something is his native language. He nodded and turned back to me. "We will assemble the fleet and jump within the next four hours. You can expect us in one standard rotation."

"Thank you. I am in your debt."

The Sig gave me a dismissive wave with his hand and the screen went blank. I smiled at Tria. It would be a rare occasion if her ideas did not bear the sweetest of fruit. We now had a diversion that should get even the Tibor a little nervous. We needed to get back to planning our rescue. I could tell Coonts had something to say.

"Coonts, you have something on your mind?"

"Yes. The Zaens may not wish to leave with us."

"What do you mean?"

"They will get out with their lives if we are successful but they cannot take their ship with them. If we are going to pull this off with no one knowing the better, it must appear as if the Zaens perished with the shuttle carrier. They must sacrifice their ship. You might not be aware of it, but Zaens consider their ships as they do their siblings. We may have to subdue them in order to get them to come with us willingly."

"You have got to be kidding me! They would rather die with their ship than be rescued?"

"It is not unheard of. I can guarantee they will resist leaving it behind."

I silently cursed. *SHIT! They have to be rescued AND I will have to beg them to leave with us!*

"Alright everyone, we will cross that bridge when we get to it. Let's continue planning how to pull this off."

Coonts and Klutch looked a little puzzled by my statement but let it pass. Klutch took the problem by the horns. I was glad he didn't fall asleep on us like he had been known to do in the past.

"Justice, put the surveillance video of the carrier's hangar on the screen."

"Affirmative, Troop Master."

"Commander, the way I see it we can easily slip into the hangar with our battle suits in stealth mode. When we enter, an alarm in the launch control room will sound, so we need to go in all at the same time. Hopefully when they do not see anything they will assume it was a false sensor reading. We will then eliminate any guards that are present and secure the launch control room so word cannot get out if we are discovered. Once that is done, we have to disable their remaining assault shuttle and secure the Zaen's ship. If all goes well, we leave someone in the hangar to watch our escape route. The rest of us will make our way to the lifts and go up two levels to the bridge and secure those areas without anyone calling for help. We have to go in with maximum surprise and maximum force. If we get bogged down in a shootout, they will call for help and you can expect a conveyer full of scat. The next objective is to climb down the service tunnel, opening all unsecured hatches as we go. There is a brig on sublevel three which is also the engineering spaces. That is where we should find the Zaens. We take out all resistance and I will rig a charge on the coolant pumps and the power terminals. Both will overheat and start a fire. Once that happens we need to get out quickly because the atmospheric systems will suck the fire through the service tunnel. It will rapidly increase in intensity as it rises due to the oxygen being fed to it by the open hatches. We will have about fifteen minutes to clear the AO or risk serious injury when the carrier blows."

No one else had anything to add and it was just a matter of delegating who did what and when. "OK Troop Master, your plan sounds solid and you have covered most all of the issues that face us. Xul, you will be our shuttle pilot. You will drop us close to the hangar door while Justice patrols to ensure we don't get jumped hard if we are discovered. I want you to stay cloaked and close in case we can't handle the pirates. If that happens, you need to pull us out and evac us back to the Legacy."

The little Grawl looked nervous but nodded affirmative. "Once we are in the hangar we will spread out and attempt to silently kill any pirates we come across. When we have secured the hangar, Tria, you will stay behind in launch control and ensure we have a viable escape route."

The briefest of frowns crossed her pretty face but quickly vanished. She gave me a nod and I moved on. "Coonts, you and I will follow Klutch to the bridge and eliminate anyone we find. It will be your duty to secure the comms and disable them while Klutch and I engage any stragglers. You will then secure the lifts so Klutch and I can access the service tunnel and go below. We will find the Zaens and set the charges then join up with you and head to the hangar. When we have collected Tria we will call Xul to come and get us before the carrier goes up in flames. Any questions?"

There were probably a lot of them, but no one said a word. We have done this kind of thing before and knew we would have to wing it once the scat hits the ventilator. We had our objectives and would try to accomplish them in the order we had laid out. Whether it would happen that way or not was anybody's guess. One way or the other, we were going to get the Zaens.

"Justice, relay Felix's message."

"Message sent."

I was hungry because my meal was interrupted. It was time to give it another try. I said, "If you have any more questions or ideas, you can find me in the galley." I stood to leave and Tria joined me. When I stepped into the down tube with her, she leaned in close.

"I would like to be in the forward strike team with you."

"Your skill sets are a magnitude better than Coonts. I knew between the two of you if things go really bad, you would be the one to ensure we could get back out. I am not saying that Coonts could not get the job done — what I am saying is that I know for a fact you can."

Tria digested my words for a moment and then nodded. I leaned in to kiss her but only got a cheek. I let it go and I hoped she would do the same. I had a feeling she was, in some way, wanting to be my protector. The more I thought about the subject, the more I realized it was what all Chaalt women did in her society. The males fulfilled another role and warrior was not one of them. She was stepping outside of normal Chaalt behavior by taking up with a race other than her own. Admittedly, I was doing the same. The alien in me was very much attracted to the alien in her and for some reason it felt perfectly natural. I did not give a crap how many arms she had. I was drawn to her from the minute I met her and I truly felt nothing would change that. She reached down and held my hand. Again, I wondered if the Chaalt could read minds. She squeezed my hand hard enough it hurt. I smiled and squeezed back till I saw her flinch. She smiled and we walked hand in hand into the galley. She would be fine.

Coonts, then Klutch both joined us in the galley. Coonts sat down next to me. "Are we bringing the Zaens back to Alpha base?"

"If we force them to leave their ship, they might want to be dropped off elsewhere. They have indirectly saved our lives more than once by selling us their armor. Now we have young Felix to thank them for as well. I know what it is like to value something like that. Back on my planet I had an old land vehicle that I would never sell, regardless of price. I threw away countless credits restoring it. I wonder what will happen when word spreads that we could have saved the ship and did nothing? I hope this will not cause trouble with the other clan members."

Coonts shook his head. "I hope so too. From what I understand, the ship is owned by the entire clan and all share in the benefits it provides."

"With the amount of credits, I have given the Zaens lately, you would think they could afford to buy a new ship. At the very least it should keep anyone from having hard feeling."

"That would depend on how big the clan is. I suspect the funds they received were split among the entire clan. It would most assuredly raise Broza's and

Hylet's status among all members and make them the senior providers. Losing the family starship could possibly diminish that status."

I rolled my eyes and wondered if it would be less hassle to just leave them to their own means. I let the thought pass and would do what had to be done when the time came. Klutch got up and walked to the galley dispensers. I was momentarily relieved when he got a pitcher of water and cups for us all. He brought them back and placed them in the middle of our table but turned and went back toward the food processor. I tried to keep my face neutral, hoping he would not sit across from me when he returned. Tria was on my left and Coonts on my right; we were intently watching the Troop Master's progress as he heaped a tray with food. When he turned to approach our table, it looked like he would sit on the opposite side facing the three of us. The rest of our meeting was about to become unpleasant.

In a stroke of genius, Tria stood up and made a show of pouring us all a glass of water and she placed Klutch's next to hers on our side of the table. Klutch made a slight detour around the table and sat next to Tria. I hope I hid the relief on my face well enough no one noticed. When Tria sat back down, I leaned over and kissed her. Among other things, I thanked her for pouring me a glass of water. She gave me a heartwarming smile. When I looked at Coonts, I could tell he was thinking the same thing.

Klutch gave us a puzzled look. "There is nothing to worry about. There is only thirty-seven untrained pieces of scat against the four of us. If anything, you should feel sorry for those Throggs." His comment sprinkled the table beside Tria with small bits of food. She quickly picked up her glass and took a drink then placed it next to mine, just out of range of any additional flying particles. Xul wandered into the galley and got a tray of food then turned to our table. We were trying our best to get his attention and have him sit on our side. Coonts even patted the seat next to him, but Xul was oblivious to our intentions. He sat down across from Klutch. It was a choice he was about to regret. I got up and gave the giant viewscreen showing the dust nebula one last look before I excused myself from the table. We still had the better part of a day before the Sig would arrive in the sector.

"Justice, jump us to the location where the transponder thread terminated."

"Affirmative Commander, I have preselected a location to observe and scan the system. DEHD core transition in thirty seconds."

I stepped out of the lift tube on the bridge deck with Tria at my side. Everything went dead still and bright white. *Hot damn, Oolaran tech was crazy freakin' cool!*

When we returned to normal space time, we went to the bridge and Justice showed us the system on the view dome. It was not what I was expecting. There were massive, planet-sized chunks of debris cluttering the system in a huge band around the central star. Justice highlighted a Mars-sized planet out at the edge of the band. It had a heavy brown foggy atmosphere obscuring its surface.

"Commander, there are no signs of life anywhere in the system. After carefully studying the large rocky debris in this system I have determined that they were once planetary bodies. My estimations conclude it is what remains of at least two planets and, depending on size, possibly a third."

That was an eye-opening statement. Something chewed up two or three planets and spit them out around the central star. "Show us the thread, Justice."

A green thread leaped out from the Legacy and made contact with the only remaining planetary body in the system. "Let's get a closer look and then jump back to the outpost."

Justice made an inner system jump and the small planet filled the view dome. "Commander, the radiation levels I am recording on the planet are six-thousand times the fatal dose for all species I have records on. If I was to venture a guess I would say the planet was purposely sterilized. There is the possibility the planet's current condition is permanent."

"Can we safely take the Legacy down to look where the thread terminates?"

"Yes. As a safety precaution, I will enter the atmosphere with our shields at maximum output."

Coonts and Klutch showed up and took their seats. I had to stifle a laugh when Xul walked in with a frown, wiping his face. Justice, took us down through the dusty brown atmosphere of the planet. We were shocked at the devastation. There were craters miles across and impossibly deep. The dusty conditions were the results of one-hundred sixty mile per hour winds blowing the pulverized surface into a sand blaster of a hurricane. We could see in small sections here and there what used to be parts and pieces of a civilization. What used to be roads and building structures were now nothing more than rock covered debris fields. The green thread attached itself to the side a massive crater. Justice took us down below its rim and we got a close up look at what might have been some sort of tunnel or perhaps a complex similar to Alpha Base. It seemed impossible that the radiation could have been any higher, but Justice informed us it was. The planet and all who lived here had been murdered. *HELL! The whole star system was murdered!* I could only think of one foe on record that would do such a thing: the Prule! I now wondered how the planet escaped the fate the others had succumbed to. The only reasonable answer was they put a fight and help arrived much too late. I hoped that, whoever they were, some managed to escape this hell. The Legacy would not fit in the tunnel entrance, but our shuttle could. At some point in time I wanted to return and investigate the tunnel, but we were running out of time.

"Justice, you can jump us back when you are ready."

"Affirmative, I will have sufficient charge to transition in eleven minutes."

I was shaken by what I had seen. *If the races in this galaxy could not pull together for the good of all, then all will perish if the Prule return.* I was relieved when everything went quiet and the bright glow of transition whited out the reality of the devastated world. When my awareness returned, we were just outside of the dust nebula. Justice cloaked the Legacy and dove into the murky light-year wide cloud. Nothing had changed and we took up station where we could surveil the outpost and the pirate ships. My crew seemed like they were just as shocked by what we had seen a I was. We knew what death up close looked like and in most cases were the cause of it, but none of us could easily come to grips with what we had just witnessed.

"Commander, I am detecting large distortion waves emanating from the edge of this star system. I can now confirm ten Sig battleships have transitioned into the sector and have aligned with a course that will take them close by the outpost."

I was glad I had something to take my mind off the devastated star system. "Let's gear up and get aboard the shuttle"

As I exited the down tube with Tria, Justice called to us. "Commander, the Sig fleet has taken up station close to the outpost and has launched ten shuttles. I have intercepted their communications stating they are not a threat and wish to purchase supplies. I have twenty-two spacecrafts of various designs, leaving the outpost on vectors that will take them away from the Sig fleet and out of the system."

I smiled thinking the pirate crews were shitting themselves. I bet a great many of them would be demanding a raise when the Sig departed. Coonts, Klutch and Xul were already geared up and wasted no time boarding the shuttle. Tria and I stripped off our uniforms and put on our suit liners. My dark mood changed for the better when I leaned down to stow my boots. Tria slapped me on the ass none too gently and stepped up into her armor before I could return the favor. The lighthearted stunt did manage to keep the beast at bay and put a small smile on my face. We joined the rest of the crew in the back of the shuttle. We took a jump seat and I gave everyone a thumbs-up. They nodded to me and we closed our helmets.

"Xul, we are ready when you are."

38

I felt the shuttle's gear thump up into the hull and Justice pushed us out the hanger door into the void. Justice put a view of the surrounding area up in our visors. He had the Legacy facing away from the target so the open hangar door would not be detected. Once it closed, there was no indication that the Legacy was even behind us. Xul nosed us over on a course that took us directly to the carrier. I finally got a glimpse of the target as we closed with it. Xul pulled up sharply and made sure the hold was pointed away from the carrier. The ramp opened and we jumped as a group. I looked back at the shuttle, and when the hatch closed, it seemed to disappear. Turning back to the target, Justice put an outline of my cloaked crewmembers in my HUD. We took up our customary positions with Klutch in the lead. As we got closer to the target, Klutch started slowing down. He sent me a clipped message on my Backscatter transmitter. I guess he thought our regular comms might be detected.

"I have movement in the hangar and guards next to the entrances."

I sent back a quick reply. "We will follow your lead, Troop Master."

We dropped below the rim of the carrier deck and Klutch had us hold there until he could assess the situation. After what seemed like an excessive amount of time that in reality was only a couple of minutes, Klutch returned and we huddled.

"There is a single sentry by each entrance and two standing next to the Zaens' ship. There are lights inside the assault shuttle sitting on the flight line. I am not sure if it is occupied or not. There are a number of engineering hatches open, so it may be undergoing maintenance."

Tria asked the question that was bothering me. "Why would sentries be guarding the hangar openings?"

Klutch's visor was clear and we saw the toothy smile on his face. "Because I don't think the security sensors are operable."

That got the beast in me laughing and I could feel adrenaline flowing into my system. "OK, let's get moving. Coonts, I want you to wait until we have the sentries eliminated and then I want you to check out the shuttle and report back what you find. If it is not occupied, I want you in the launch control room as fast as possible — and make sure no one can use the comms."

He nodded and moved off in the direction of the active flight line. "Tria, Klutch, we need those sentries down without setting off any alarms. As soon as we take them out we need to get to the Zaens ship and take down

569

the two standing around the hatch before they notice the missing guards. If the Zaens are being held inside, we will take out any hostiles and secure their ship. We need to make them understand we can't leave until we plant our charges. Let's get moving, I will meet you behind the ramp to the Zaen's ship."

Tria moved off toward her designated target and Klutch moved to the other. I was trying to stifle the anxiety I was feeling. The Oolaran soldier in me was chomping at the bit to bloody the pirate troops. It would get its wish. I eased up to the massive hangar opening and peeked inside. There was a Tibor standing about two feet just inside. He had his helmet face plate up and was chewing on what looked like a stick of some sort. He turned his back to me and was waving the Tibor over from another hangar opening. I was going to slip up behind him but as I prepared to enter he turned back to me and stood looking out into the void. I had pulled away from the entrance and had my back to the hull right beside him. I snuck a peek, and now there were two of them standing right beside the opening on the other side of the atmospheric retention field. I could have easily shaken hands with either of them. The first one pulled the strange stick from his mouth and offered it to the other Tibor. The pirate took a quick look around and popped his helmet open. He took the offered stick and put it in his mouth and began chewing on it. I felt a tug on my leg and looked down to see the outline of Klutch below me. I slowly moved from the edge of the entrance. Once below the deck line Klutch pulled our helmets together.

"Commander, the Throggs are drugging themselves. We should invite them out for a walk to clear their heads."

An evil smile crossed my lips and I nodded. "After you, Troop Master."

We both popped up from below the pirates' feet. We were cloaked and no more than a foot away. They had no idea we were standing right in front of them. We reached out and pulled them through the atmospheric retention field. They both thrashed for a few seconds and went still. We gave them a healthy push and sent them on a one-way tour of the dust nebula. What a couple of dumbasses. That was one high they would never come down from. Coonts gave us a sitrep.

"One hostile in the shuttle: he will no longer be a problem. I have disabled the communication equipment and I am moving to the launch control room."

I had yet to hear from Tria but knew she took care of the guard because a Tibor corpse caught my eye as it sailed out of the hangar into the void. Klutch and I stepped through the retention field and headed for the backside of the Zaen ship. Halfway there I saw Tria's outline crouched behind the ramp that led to the boarding hatch. The two pirates that were loitering outside of the hatch were still oblivious to their fate. We worked our way around the rear

571

of the ship and quietly made our way to Tria's position. There were several crates sitting around the base of the ramp. Apparently, the pirates had taken everything of interest out of Broza's ship. Klutch pointed at the crates next to the ramp and then me and Tria. He made a climbing motion and the two of us complied. We carefully climbed on top of the crates and were now directly behind the pirates. He held up a finger and then cautiously started up the ramp. I guess he was going to introduce himself when he got there.

Coonts called back again. "No contact in the launch control room and the comms are now disabled."

I love it when a plan comes together — right up until it doesn't. The hatch on the Zaen's ship opened and Broza was shoved out. He collided with the cloaked Klutch, who was getting ready to do something unpleasant to the two pirates standing there. The Zaen bounced off the armor like he had hit a brick wall. The pirates stopped cold, staring in disbelief at the Zaen lying crumpled at their feet. We were caught off guard and temporarily frozen with indecision. Klutch did not miss a beat and jumped over Broza crashing head first into the pirate standing in the airlock. The hatch abruptly closed leaving the pirates outside struggling to determine what just happened. Tria came around from left field with a roundhouse punch that connected with the pirate's helmet that was closest to her. That spurred me into action and I did the same but missed when the Tibor Tria had punched collided with my intended target. The Chaalt climbing hook I was going to bury in the pirate's helmet scythed just over his head and clanged loudly off of the hull of the ship. I had put so much force into my swing I lost my balance and tumbled forward on top of the two pirates. The one still moving had his helmet open and was yelling for help. Broza came to his senses and started crawling down the ramp on all fours. I managed to get up on my knees and was going to shove my climbing hook down loud mouth's throat. He put a stop to that by getting a grip on his pistol. I didn't want any part of that and rolled my knee onto his arm, pinning his pistol hand. I jammed my needle gun into his face and gave him a burp of the high velocity shards. Man, did that ever make a mess.

I heard Tria calling to Broza asking him how many Tibor were on his ship. He never answered, but the question got him crawling faster. I got to my feet and saw a portal toward the front of the Zaen ship. There were repeated flashbulb-like flashes emanating from it. I did not have a clue how to open the hatch and pounded on it a couple of times to no avail. Tria had ceased cloaking and was carrying a terrified Broza up the boarding ramp. She set him down in front of the hatch and I uncloaked so he could see it was me.

"Broza, how many pirates are on your ship and how do I get the hatch open?"

He seemed to stare in disbelief but his eyes finally locked on my face. "Mr. Myers! I was hoping Felix would contact you!"

"Broza, open the hatch now!"

He reached for the side of the hatch but it opened before he could touch it. Klutch stepped out and gave me a toothy grin and a blink of both his eyes. "I took care of the pirate scat, but the Throggs shot the ship up pretty bad."

Broza looked like he was going to freak out and pushed his way by Klutch. We heard him start wailing in disbelief and screaming "NO, NO, NO!"

Klutch gave me another wink. "Commander, we need to get to the bridge and secure the comms."

I stepped into the Zaen ship and moved forward to where Broza stood shaking his head. "Broza, where are they holding Hylet?"

The Zaen turned to me and his scaly skin was roiling. "They have destroyed my ships controls. My clan has lost its only means of transporting merchandise!"

He was ignoring my question and could only think of his ship. I gave him a small shake and he finally focused on my face. "I will find you another ship! Where can we find Hylet?"

That seemed to bring him to his senses. "They hold him on subdeck three!"

Coonts came running up to us and we cloaked. "Tria, we are going for the bridge. If things get out of hand, be ready to evac Broza."

She nodded and waved us on. Klutch lead us to the lifts. They were good old-fashioned elevators. We piled in and Klutch hit the bridge level button. It was a high-speed lift because it only took a handful of seconds before the door opened again. There was a pirate standing in the corridor leading to the bridge. The look on his face said he was mystified as to why the empty car opened on this level. We all stood still hoping our cloaking systems kept us invisible until the pirate got close enough for us to overpower him. His stare intensified and his curiosity turned to suspicion. He pulled his fighting knife from his armor. My olfactory sensors were in void mode, and for good reason, Klutch's suit was venting his scent non-stop. I suspected the pirate could easily smell it and was doing some stinking of his own. The pirate stopped in front of the elevator and extended his knife forward. The beast in me was going berserk and I reached out and grabbed the Tibor's arm with both my hands. I jerked his elbow down and shoved his hand violently back, planting his fighting knife in one of his eyes. He started thrashing like a fish out of water as I jerked him into the lift and we quickly stepped out. Klutch hit the down button and we continued down the corridor.

The next room on the right was weapons management systems. A pirate was asleep in a chair with his feet up on a console. Klutch extended his climbing hooks and stepped inside, closing the hatch behind him. I heard a thump come from the room. The door opened and Klutch stepped out into the corridor. I caught sight of a rapidly spreading pool of Tibor blood. Klutch closed the hatch and pointed at another on our left just up the corridor. Coonts happened to be out front and leaned into the open doorway. He stuck his hand back out holding up a single finger and then a fist so we would hold our position. The Oolaran beast felt differently and I stepped to the door just as the Grawl drove a climbing hook into the pirate's throat, almost decapitating him. The pirate thrashed around and crash loudly to the floor. The beast in me surged forward and I was on the verge of letting out an insane war whoop.

The hatch behind us opened and a Tibor stepped out yelling. "Grebber, if you are eating stim sticks again, I will space you!"

He froze when he saw the nearly decapitated corpse. If it was Grebber on the deck, I was pretty sure the pirate would not get an answer to the charges. The pirate had his armor on but no helmet. It was a bad decision on his part. I jerked my arm back leading with the sharp protrusion on the end of my elbow. A gruesome ditch appeared in the Tibor's face from his forehead to his jaw. He fell back into the doorway like he had been poleaxed. There was three more Tibor on the bridge and their eyes were as big as silver dollars. I was shoved from behind by Klutch as he stormed into the command station. Coonts was right behind him and there was no hiding the ruckus we were making. The Tibor were going for their weapons and we had no choice but to hose them down with our needle guns. Coonts was using his wonderfully smart Grawl brain and closed the hatch behind us. The three hostiles and everything behind them were engulfed in thousands of hypersonic hull alloy slivers. They might have survived had they been wearing their helmets, but now their bullet heads looked like deformed sponges. When the fragments quit ricocheting off the equipment and consoles, quiet returned to the room. Coonts checked the bodies and shook his head negative. I heard a gurgling groan coming from behind me that ceased with the stomping thump of Klutch's armored boot. The beast was appeased by the gory mess, and my thoughts became mission-focused once more.

"Klutch, check the corridor and see if anybody else heard the racket we were making."

I saw his outline open the hatch and disappear outside.

"Coonts, find the comms and disable them."

Klutch stepped back onto the bridge. "All clear, Commander."

Coonts came over to us. "Our weapons wrecked the comms console."

Klutch lead us to the corner of the room and showed us the maintenance hatch on the floor. He reached down and turned the latch. The door slid to the side and we could see a dark tunnel leading straight down into the guts of the ship. A solid metal ladder pointed to our destination.

I called Tria on my Backscatter transmitter. "Tria, the bridge is secure and we are moving to the lower decks now."

"Roger that, the hangar is secure and I will have Xul land our shuttle in bay number three. Broza is acting unstable and I want him secured aboard. We will be waiting to extract you."

Coonts wasn't kidding when he said the Zaen's were pretty weird about their ships. Hopefully Broza doesn't go off the deep end while we are doing our thing.

"Coonts, keep the bridge secure until we send Hylet up to you. As soon as you get your hands on him go straight to our shuttle in bay three. Make sure he doesn't do anything crazy when he figures out we are not taking their ship with us."

He gave me a thumbs-up and headed to the corridor to bring the elevator back up so it would be open and waiting for their retreat. Klutch went down the ladder first and I climbed down after him. We hadn't gone far when I felt him grab my boot.

"Commander, look to your left. I want you to grab the pull handle on the side of that hatch and yank it downward. When you see an orange blinking light, push the hatch open. We must do this until we reach sublevel three."

I did as I was instructed. Looking down I saw Klutch doing the same to another hatch just below me. We went down a couple more levels and repeated the process. I felt another tug on my boot and stopped.

"This is subdeck three's maintenance hatch. We get out here and the brig should be at the end of the corridor. We must use caution and be as quiet as possible because we will be passing by the crew quarters."

"Roger that. I will follow your lead Troop Master."

He slid the release down on the hatch and opened it. It was dark down the corridor but the far end had a bright light illuminating the way to the brig. We could hear the rattling snores of several Tibor in a hatch to our left. To our right was a large archway that was the entrance to a latrine. Further down the corridor was another bunking area, then the brig. We made it past the first crew quarters and were halfway to the brig when we heard a noise in the latrine. Klutch slipped into the entrance and stepped around the wall that blocked a direct view into the room. I heard a fairly loud, wet-sounding smack and a grunt, then the distinct whoosh of a toilet flushing. I looked behind me and we got no reaction from the bunk room. Klutch stepped back out into the corridor and waved me on toward the brig. We came even with the second bunking quarters and a pirate walked out of the hatch and right into Klutch. The beast fed on my surprise and I came around with a punch that crushed the pirate's cheek and eye socket. He fell backwards squalling out in agony. I don't know what the Oolaran soldier in me was thinking. As if by magic a grenade appeared in my hand. The next thing I know, it seemed to jump into the bunk room without any effort on my part. Klutch slapped the close button on the hatch and jerked me down the corridor toward the brig. There was an impressively loud metallic clang and the hatch bowed outward.

We made it to the end of the corridor. The brig was on the right and another hallway went left. Klutch pushed me at the brig doorway. "Get Hylet! He should be in there somewhere. This hall leads to the other crew quarters, I will be back after I have mined the passage."

I stood for another second and turned back to the doorway. It was made of a thick transparent material. Standing on the other side of it was a Tibor pirate squinting out at me. He could not see me, but he definitely knew something was wrong. There was a loud blast from the next corridor over and I wondered if Klutch needed my help. I didn't know how to get the pirate to open the door so I headed in Klutch's direction to give him a hand. No sooner than I turned my back, the pirate opened the door and rushed directly at me. He had no idea I was standing there. I spun around with my armored boot and kicked him in the face hard enough to crush his skull. He went down hard and did not move. I tromped over his body and ran into the brig. The forth enclosure down was where I found Hylet. He was down on the floor of the cell in the fetal position. I uncloaked and banged on the clear enclosure. Hylet rolled over and his coal black eyes looked like they could burst from their sockets. I forgot to clear my visor. He was looking at my war face and probably just wrecked the lower half of his uniform. I cleared the visor so he could see my face and was going to tell him I would get him out of there.

It was as far as I got because I was blasted violently into the wall. I didn't know what hit me but whatever it was had my weapons pack and launcher tube showing red and inoperable in my helmet. I rolled over and my minigun feed tube was flopping around. It would only do that if it was no longer connected to the ammo pack. My eyes refocused and I saw a pirate with a big rifle in his hands and he was drawing another bead on me. *OH SHIT! THAT IS GONNA HURT!* There was a tremendous blast that bounced me off the wall once again. The pirate was there one second and the next he was scattered about the room. Hylet was covering his head and curled up in the corner of his cell again. I was crawling on the deck when Klutch ran through the door.

"ARE YOU INJURED, COMMANDER?"

I shook my head and waved him off. "I'm glad you didn't use anti-matter munitions."

My sarcasm was lost on him and he disappeared out the door again. Another series of explosions let me know all was not well. The thought of being trapped in here crossed my mind in a bad way. I got my head together and joined Klutch at the door.

"Did you get a look at the rifle that Throgg shot me with?"

"Yes, it was a Galactic Union heavy rail rifle. I believe they call them sniper rifles on your home world. It launches high explosive penetrators at very high velocities. It is a quality weapon. If they have more than one, we could be in trouble."

That was an understatement. I felt like I got hit across the back with a baseball bat. The Tibor pirates were better armed and trained than any Murlak troops we had come up against, and these guys weren't dicking around. A homing grenade came flying down the corridor and Klutch shoved me back inside. He hit the hatch button and managed to get the door closed before it went off in our faces. I hoped like hell the door could stand up to the abuse. The explosion bowed the door inward but it snapped right back.

Klutch looked at me with a toothy smile. "If I remember correctly, this door was one of the few items that my military liked about this ship."

I rolled my eyes and shook my head. "Get Hylet out of that cell and get him ready to move."

I pulled a couple of grenades out and opened the hatch long enough to toss them up the corridor. Only one exploded right off, the other must have been waiting for targets. I saw a flash and a loud explosion come from the hall Klutch had mined. His booby traps just sent more pirates to their final judgement. Klutch had to drag Hylet to the door. He was having a mental breakdown, judging by the complete nonsense coming out of his mouth. Klutch was no longer smiling. I couldn't blame him — we were trapped like rats. At some point the pirates would figure out there were only two of us. When that happened, things were going to get ugly, and Hylet would be the first casualty. My second grenade finally detonated or was shot down. Opening the hatch, I ventured a peek down the corridor. I jerked my head back as withering fire blasted the corner. There was a lot of movement going on out there.

We had the crew's attention and they were getting more aggressive by the moment. The wall next to the brig was being blasted to shit and the fragments were bouncing around us. I closed the door again and it turned out to be perfect timing. Two more homing grenades came around the corner and exploded right in front of the door. The door must have had a duty rating and it was now exceeded. The clear composite had cracks all over it. The beast in me was ready to test my duty rating, because like it or not, I was going out there to get this over with one way or another.

My beam weapon was still in the green and ready to go. You mess with the bull you get the horns. I popped the hatch and Klutch attempted to push me aside. We both hesitated when we heard nonstop explosive blasts accompanied by a familiar whine. I leaned around the corner and saw a stream of fire coming from the service tunnel. Coonts was mowing down everything in the corridor with his minigun. The pirates never knew what hit them. The remaining survivors were attempting to turn and charge at him. Klutch and I took the opportunity to toss grenades into their flanks and the Tibor offensive was permanently halted. Coonts stepped out of the service tunnel and checked to see if any of the pirates were playing possum. He seemed satisfied with the results of his handy work and waved us on.

Klutch grabbed Hylet and carried him up the corridor, he couldn't seem to get his legs moving properly and we were in a hurry. By the look of the riddled corpses, the pirates had gathered together and were going to charge the brig in mass.

I clapped Coonts on the shoulder. "Thanks for evening the odds."

"I grew tired of Tria asking what was taking so long."

I smiled at his comment. Evidently our comms would not work this deep in the ship or I would have heard the same thing. "Get Hylet out of here while Klutch and I set the scuttling charges."

He nodded and took Hylet by the hand, pulling him into the service tunnel. We followed and watched him take Hylet up the ladder. The Zaen found his second wind and rapidly climbed out of sight. Klutch and I went down one level. He was being cautious as he eased the engineering access hatch open. Anybody hiding down here had to hear what happened on the deck above. My armor had taken enough damage that cloaking was no longer an option. Large portions of my suit were visible, so Klutch let me know in no uncertain terms he was the leader and I would follow. If it meant not getting shot again, I was all for it.

We climbed out of the tunnel into a brightly lit room that was humming with machine sounds. There was no one visible on this side of the largest pipes and monitoring consoles. We moved quietly among the machinery for any signs of an ambush, but it looked like we were alone. Klutch pointed across the room at a pipe that was painted bright orange.

"Plant your charge on the backside of that pipe where it meets the deck. We don't want anyone to find and disable them. I will rig mine on the power conduits."

Justice had fabricated the explosives out of HE rounds for our tube launchers. He had installed simple digital timers on them to give us enough time to escape.

"How much time, Troop Master?"

"Fifteen minutes should be enough time to get clear. It will take the systems another ten to fifteen to overheat and catch fire. We will be long gone by then."

I was skeptical because things were not going as planned already. Who was I to question a Troop Master? I nodded and moved away to set my charge. I tucked it behind the pipe as instructed and ran for the service tunnel. After a couple of minutes Klutch came thumping around the side of the machinery. I ducked into the tunnel and headed for the ladder. Klutch insisted going first to make sure it was clear. I was not going to argue with a clock running. Tibor were surprisingly nimble in one-gravity conditions. He was outdistancing me when I heard a croaking Tibor oath. I looked up in time to see an explosion above us and Klutch's big ass heading straight for my visor. I found myself lying in the bottom of the service tunnel with Klutch on top of me.

"KLUTCH! ARE YOU INJURED?

"No, Commander. Someone threw a grenade into the tunnel. I am not sure where it came from. We need to get out of here now!"

"Can we take another route?"

"Possibly, but this is the only one I am familiar with."

A flash and another explosion from above made us look upward. We were knocked sprawling by a pirate corpse that landed right on top of us. That was the second time I had been hit in the face with a Tibor's ass. As far as I was concerned, it was a lifetime's worth.

Our comms went live with Tria yelling at us. "You can rest when you are dead — you need to get moving because Justice alerted us to a shuttle that launched from the outpost and is headed this way, ETA twenty-nine minutes!"

That was not the only reason. The clock was still ticking on the charges and the timer in my helmet was down to six minutes. Klutch jumped up and rapidly ascended the ladder with me in hot pursuit. We came out of the service tunnel and Tria was at the bridge door with her weapons up and ready. She led the way to the lift and we made the fast trip to the hangar. The shuttle was cloaked and all we could see was the open hold with Coonts waving us in. I could see Broza and Hylet leaning forward in their jump seats, sullenly staring at the deck. We just risked our lives to rescue them and they could only think about losing their ship.

As soon as our feet hit the deck Xul closed the ramp and told us to hang on. He launched hard and I could hear him talking to Justice over the comms. He set up an intercept course and Justice came in from the direction of the outpost and grabbed us with the tow beam. He quickly pulled us into the hangar and gave me a sitrep.

"Commander, the Sig departed the system seven minutes ago. The Tibor shuttle that launched from the outpost will intercept the carrier in twelve minutes and I have detected a large surge in temperature inside the carrier's hangar area. Before we departed the area, I deployed a surveillance drone to monitor the carrier."

Justice put the drone video on our visors so we could see the fruits of our labor. It was not hard to see something was drastically wrong inside the carrier. The pulsating glow emanating from the hangar openings said that Klutch's plan had worked perfectly. Justice put a red triangle around the shuttle that was rapidly closing the distance with the carrier. It made a close-in approach and then veered sharply away.

"Commander, there is a large amount of encrypted comms traffic being broadcast from the Tibor shuttle. It will take time to determine the encryption algorithms, but I surmise the crew is reporting the fire."

A grim smile crossed my lips as all evidence of our incursion was being incinerated as we watched. The Zaens just got a new lease on life but still had nothing to say. A large fiery flash burst from the bottom of the carrier only to be quickly whisked out by the vacuum of space. The glow from the hangar diminished then disappeared as the explosive decompression sucked the oxygen from the fire. The Tibor shuttle turned and made a close pass, then started circling the burnt-out hulk. Just when we thought the show was over, something high-order detonated inside the carrier. A large portion of the lower spaces erupted out into space. It kind of reminded me of a fireworks display.

"What could have caused an explosion like that, Klutch?"

"I am not sure, Commander, but my guess would be a large quantity of munitions. Those Throggs were really well armed for a bunch of scat eating pirates."

I had to agree. They had better weapons than any pirates we had ever come up against. We may have just kicked ass on Eiger's first string. It made me think that what we just went through would have been a lot more difficult if the fools weren't drugging themselves stupid when we made our insertion. If the alarm had gone out early, we would have had serious problems on our hands. I got a surprise from Justice that interrupted my thoughts.

39

"Commander, my subsystem at Alpha base has alerted me via IST that the Operative is now at that location. She has requested our scientists to leave the Chaalt experimental spacecraft and to help make preparations for it to get underway."

"WHAT!?"

"Commander, my subsystems are picking up tell-tale emissions from an A.I. supplemental power source. I believe the Operative is bringing the ship's artificial intelligence with her to install aboard the ship. I speculate she and her superiors fear I will subvert the new intelligence."

"Can you do that?"

"Yes. Much the same way I absorbed the Overseer, only easier."

"So, she is going to manually pilot the ship away from Alpha Base and then install the A.I."

"Yes, but her security measures are futile. I already inhabit systems throughout the ship."

"OH SHIT! When are they going to discover that little nugget of information?"

"Unless I choose to reveal my presence, they will never know. The Chaalt scientists have set up what they believe to be impenetrable detection systems designed specifically to keep me out. They feel confident in their conclusions."

"Why would the fools think that? They should already have an inkling of just how sophisticated you actually are."

"I gave them a sense of false security by letting various items of technology appear to be infected by my systems. It was amusing to see them covertly destroy several pieces of valuable equipment to appease their fears of contamination."

I was startled by the admission Justice had made. It was now leading to other questions that he would have to answer. "Justice, when were you going to tell me about your intrusions?"

"Now."

"They are our allies — is there a good reason why you would do something like this?"

"Yes. They have proven on several occasions to be less than trustworthy confederates. I have effectively removed any possibility of deceit being perpetrated on us through the use of that vessel. We will now have access to their most valuable secrets."

I was a little floored by what was happening. Justice had commed this information to Tria, Coonts and Klutch as well. They sat speechless and I was sure they were just as stunned by this as I was. Well, Tria and Coonts anyway. When I glanced at them, their faces had looks of surprise. Klutch's, however, was blank because he was sleeping. I kind of wished I was — I would write this off as a bad dream. I looked back at Tria. She was staring at me and most probably knew what was on my mind.

"Tria, I want to hear what your honest assessment is and what action should be taken, if any? After all, we are talking about actively spying on your people. There is no other way to describe what Justice is doing."

She took more than a minute to answer me. I really had no idea how she would lean, given the current circumstances.

"I would like to give the subject more thought before I answer. I do know that I am ready to get off this shuttle and out of this armor. I suggest a private meeting in the conference room one hour from now if it is agreeable to you."

She nodded her head at the two sullen Zaens. I had all but forgotten that they were sitting in the jump seats behind me. They had still not said a word and it was starting to get on my nerves. I really needed something else to annoy me right at the moment. My maker must have heard me, because my IST beeped and then the Sael's voice started talking in my head. I cringed and shook my head. *THANKS A LOT!*

"Nathan, I know this is short notice, but I have been ordered to depart your base with our new ship. It is close enough to completion that my tech teams will be able to finish the project. I have to return to my home worlds to have the transporter devices installed. My people and my superiors want to thank you and your scientist for your cooperation and support. The project would have never been completed in such a timely manner without the help of your followers."

Before she could carry on any further I cut her off with what I was now feeling was the real situation. The A.I. was just part of this equation. "You were ordered to take the ship before I could return and demand transporter technology in exchange for a completed project."

"Nathan, as much as I wished for that to be the outcome, you had to know that getting transporter technology from my people was never a certainty."

I had my fill for one day and cut her off again. "Sael, get your ship and your people out of my base."

I ended the transmission. "Justice, shut down the IST and Backscatter equipment. I don't want to hear from the Operative until further notice."

"Equipment disabled, Commander."

I stood up and took one of Tria's hands. She stood up and I turned to the Zaens.

"Broza. You have helped us in more ways than you know. I know losing your starship is causing you great anguish. I will see to it you have another ship."

That got both of the Zaens attention. A glimmer of hope returned to their faces. "The new ship will unfortunately have military grade shields and a full array of offensive and defensive weapons. I hope those items won't be too much of an inconvenience. The cargo hold will be slightly smaller than the one on your old ship but can double as a transport if need be. I am confident it will be much faster than your old ship as well."

Broza and Hylet's faces lit up. "Nathan Myers, those systems will only be a small nuisance. Where can we find this ship?"

"It is my Coram assault shuttle. I am going to let you have use of it until a freighter becomes available. We are going to take you back to outpost 9765 and put you in the protection of the Sig. The owner of Haras is a close personal friend and ally. She can change your I.D. chips and give you a new identity. Once that process is completed, you will be free to move about without worry of the pirates seeking revenge for the loss of their carrier. We will deliver the shuttle to the outpost as soon as we complete the necessary modifications to remove any chances of it being associated with me or my people."

The Zaens were full of smiles now that their future would include a fully armed ship to transport merchandise. Little did they know, one of Justice's subsystems would now be watching over them. He would make sure we knew everything they were up to, and where they were located if we had need of them. I told Justice to alert the scientists back at Alpha base to assign a few engineers to start work on the shuttle immediately.

Coonts left for the ready room, but Klutch still sat sleeping. After what we had just been through I didn't have it in me to screw with him for sleeping. Tria pulled me toward the ramp and we left him there until he woke on his own. We escorted the Zaens to the crew quarters and then went back to the ready room to get out of our armor.

"Justice, will you be able to repair the damage to my armor?"

"Yes. It will require an extended period of time, but I foresee no major issues. I have already started the process."

I was still bothered by the fact we did not find Eiger — that was one son of a bitch I wanted off of my to-do list. "Justice, make a pass around the system and put surveillance drones in strategic locations. I want to know if any Murlak Warbringer ships enter this system. Before we leave the dust nebula, I want you to launch all of our stealth missiles and have them go dormant. Program them to attack any ship with a Warbringer profile and then any remaining ships we have already tagged."

"Affirmative, Commander. I will commence launching now. The Sig are leaving a trail of comm buoys in their wake. I can make use of their systems to substantially decrease the time lag on information being gathered by our surveillance drones."

"Roger that, Justice. When we reach the outpost, I will tell the Sig we are using their buoys."

"Commander, I am ready to make a standard transition to outpost 9765. Our transition time will take more than thirty-one hours. I would like to make a suggestion."

"OK Justice, I am all ears."

"I know it is your intention to not reveal the true capabilities of the Legacy to non-essential personnel. I would like to suggest making a standard transition until such time the Zaens take their sleep period. Once they do, I will drop from interdimensional space and make a DEHD core transition. It appears the Zaens are preparing to bed down now."

"OK Justice, that sounds like an excellent idea. Do me a favor — if Klutch sleeps more than another twenty minutes, please alert him to our meeting."

Tria and I went to my quarters and stripped off our smart cloth and stepped into a very hot shower. I felt the slight discomfort of Justice making the jump to hyperspace but had enough on my mind to dismiss the mild nauseous feelings I usually get. Tria didn't seem very troubled by Justice's actions and I wondered why. We stepped out of the shower and into the warm air stream of the dryer.

"Tria, does it bother you that Justice is covertly spying on your people?"

She put a fresh uniform on then looked at me with those big emerald eyes. "Sael is not a fool. She knows what Justice has done, or at the very least she suspects it. She is putting on a show for the council. If it is ever revealed what Justice has done, she will be exonerated by her actions. She is faithfully following the orders of her superiors. When the transporter tech is installed on her ship, Justice will have access to the systems and transporter capability will finally be ours."

I was more worried about Justice being discovered than I was about the implications of him snooping. I had reasoned he would at some point gain access to the tech but never realized it was his intention all along. I would have to cut Sael some slack if Tria is right about her knowing what Justice was doing. The old witch was playing both sides masterfully. She now had plausible deniability and could claim ignorance if we were ever exposed.

"Justice, is Tria's theory correct?"

"Yes."

"When were you going to get around to telling me about it?"

"I would have made all available information known at the crew briefing."

I shook my head thinking the evil robot didn't want me thinking about what he was up to and wanted me concentrating on my interactions with Tria.

Tria took me by the hand and we went to the conference room across the hall. Coonts and Xul were already seated and Klutch came rushing through the door."

I looked on at him with mild humor. "I trust you slept well, Troop Master?"

He gave me his usual toothy grin and shrugged his wide shoulders. "I should have gone to the galley instead."

I would make sure to skip that adventure and take a meal well after he was finished. I had Justice brief the crew on his mischief. Everyone was excited about the possibility of gaining a transporter. Coonts went as far as telling us he suspected what Justice and the Operative were doing all along. Rolling my eyes to the ceiling, I waved at him to sit down. I was telling the crew about lending the Coram shuttle to the Zaens and was momentarily interrupted by Justice dropping us from hyperspace. I started to continue, but all went quiet and then everything around me glowed a brilliant white.

When we returned to normal space-time I became aware of Tria holding my hand. She must have done it just as we transitioned. The gentle nature of Oolaran transitions always brought a smile to my crew's faces, and I was no exception. It was unfortunate that the next order of business rained scat on my elation.

"We have failed to find Eiger and correct the mistake I made by letting him slip through my fingers. I want your opinions on what we should do next. Once we deliver the Zaens to Tam Lin, we have multiple objectives to consider."

After much discussion, the crew was unanimous in their decision to move on and let Eiger continue running from us. I was the sole dissenter. It was hard for me to determine if it was the alien imprinting driving me to kill the pirate or my failure to protect all of the innocent beings he would terrorize while he continued living. My crew finally convinced me the Throgg would make a mistake one day and we would be there to correct it, permanently! Coonts came up with a plan that could partially appease the beast in me. His suggestion was to investigate the latest transponder thread because it was a short jump from the dust nebula. If Eiger was fool enough to visit that location, we could be there in a matter of minutes. Klutch, on the other hand, wanted to make the trip across the galaxy to see if we could identify the origins of the derelict ship. My interest on that subject was waning because I felt we had more pressing matters. My vote was for Coonts' plan of action.

Justice had some very interesting updates for us, the first being the Operative's new command. "Commander, the Chaalt A.I. is now in full control of the Operative's flagship. The new enhanced intelligence is more refined than previous generation A.I.s. In some cases, they have mirrored Oolaran designs but have hobbled its processing capabilities. The Chaalt have placed an inordinate amount of restrictions on its processors and have limited any chance for it to become truly self-aware. The design has promise, but its current configuration will never reveal its full potential. I believe they fear true sentience and freedom of choice."

Coonts asked the thousand-credit question that was on all our minds. "Is the Chaalt A.I. aware of your presence?"

"Yes."

601

That brought the chatter level up a notch or two. I held my hands up for silence. "Justice, does the Operative know for sure you inhabit her ship?"

"She has a strong suspicion and has called out to me in the privacy of her cabin."

"WHAT!? I hope you didn't answer!"

"No, I did not, because she referred to me as a defective machine."

I slapped my hand to my forehead. *OH SHIT, SHE KNOWS!*

"What did she say when she called out to you?"

"And I quote, 'Alright, you defective machine, tell the Earth primate to turn the IST back on, or I am going to shove it in one of the two orifices that he produces scat from."

The conference room was momentarily quiet as a tomb, then we all burst out in a raucous laughter that almost brought a tear to my eye. There was no hiding the fact that Sael Nalen was the master of manipulation. The old witch knew exactly where, what, when and how things were going to happen because she had somehow set them in motion.

I waved everyone to silence. "We can play at Sael's game. Just because she thinks she knows does not mean that we should admit to it. For now, we will not let her know she is correct in her assumptions. Is everyone in agreement?"

I got nods of approval from everyone. "Justice, turn the IST and BS units back on."

"Power has been restored, Commander."

I had not yet composed myself and the message I was going to send to Sael when my IST gave me a secure beep. "It is about time you got my message, you primate. I was beginning to think the defective machine was not as bright as I gave it credit for."

"Sael, I am not sure what kind of scat you are throwing at me, but if you think you can call and make jokes after backstabbing us again, you can forget about ever seeing the derelict ship. We will keep our discoveries for our own research projects. You and your council can continue using your previous methods to find artifacts."

The silence was deafening and I had to bite my tongue to keep from snickering. Tria gave me an elbow and a stern look. She must have thought I was laying it on a little harder than was necessary.

The Operative's next words confirmed I had thrown a proper size spanner into the works. The doubt in her voice was not well hidden. "Nathan, I was not trying to make light of removing my ship from your base. My superiors were afraid Justice would somehow infect our A.I. and compromise our systems. To be perfectly clear on the subject, I assumed the same conclusion. My orders came directly from the highest offices of power. I was to remove the Fury from your base before the A.I. was installed and brought online. It was the council's intention to prevent any possibility of our security being compromised."

"So, you are telling me this has nothing to do with keeping us from getting transporter technology?"

"I cannot in all honesty say that either. It would be foolish to assume it has not crossed the council's minds you might hold our ship for additional tech."

"I was going to call and update you on our mission to apprehend Eiger. You saved me the trouble. Eiger was not present in the sector but we did manage to safely recover our allies unharmed. We left surveillance drones in the area and stealth missiles set to autonomously attack any Warbringer class star ships that enter the dust nebula. We will now continue our discussion on whether we will include you on our investigation of the derelict ship. I will call you when we have made our decision."

"Nathan, don't you think we have been down this same road enough times? I have been more than generous with supplying you with advanced tech. You have received equipment that many of our closest allies have been denied. Please consider what I have already offered you before you decide to go your own way. I know it may not mean much to you, but my superiors have authorized me to pay you and your followers one hundred billion credits for services rendered."

"I think I already mentioned we have more credits than we could spend in a lifetime. I will call you when we come to a consensus. Oh, and by the way, I love the name you gave your new ship."

I ended the transmission before she could comment further. Tria frowned at the verbal thrashing I gave Sael.

"I realize you wish to keep Justice's capabilities a secret from the military council, but you should not be so hard on Sael for being intelligent enough to know otherwise."

Of course, Tria was right, but I knew if we conceded the information to Sael she would, at some point in the future, beat me over the head with it. At the very least, she would use it as leverage to gain something from us that we did not wish to give away. I needed to change the subject and get back to some of the real reasons we called this meeting.

"Justice, you said you had additional updates for us. Would you please continue?"

"While many of our scientists and engineers worked on the Chaalt project, I enlisted the help of Graf, Jaran and Felix to help me unlock the operating processes of the Dagger spacecraft. Together we have devised a modular cockpit system that will fit each of the crew's physical dimensions and will be interchangeable with the existing configuration. We removed Sentinel race four's seating arrangements and have nearly completed the necessary adaptors to connect our pilot modules. I have already begun simulations and believe we will move to actual flight testing in the very near future."

"If I recall correctly, you were bragging to Sael that the Chaalt scientists were wrong about their operational theories. I would like to hear about your findings."

"I was going to demonstrate the Dagger's capabilities during flight testing, but since you have asked, I will admit that I have made startling discoveries. The small compact star drive on the Dagger is capable of sub-light maneuvering and meant mostly for docking procedures. The ship's true mode of propulsion is the phase jump drive."

Justice, had all of our attention now. Klutch held up a hand, but Coonts was the first to get his questions in.

"Are you insinuating the spacecraft makes continuous jumps in and out of hyperspace while maneuvering!?"

"Yes, Engineer Coonts, your description is an accurate assessment. When the drive is operating at its lowest attenuation, the ship is phasing in and out of normal space-time at more than a hundred times a minute. The vessel is capable of transitional velocities in normal space-time. Only an A.I. is capable of maneuvering the spacecraft while the phase drive is engaged."

Coonts looked shocked. I could only sit and look stupid because I didn't have a clue. I ventured a question anyway. "So, if I understand correctly, you are saying that was its low speed, so what is its highest speeds?"

"By modulating the phase to one or two transitions a minute, or indefinitely, you would effectively be traveling in interdimensional space and traversing light years in seconds. Once flight testing begins, we will be able to benchmark the velocities against the Legacy's recorded transitions."

Klutch looked like he was going to ask a question, but Tria weighed in. "Alright, we have established it is fast, and we already know about the missile launchers and beam turrets. What do you know about the primary weapon?"

"It is a scaled-down version of the Oolaran anomaly weapon. It projects micro-collapsing anomalies that are capable of inflicting massive damage. It will require testing to determine its true potential."

The room had a hint of something unpleasant wafting in the air. Seeing the frown on Klutch's face it wasn't hard to determine where the odor was coming from. "Klutch if you have something to say, please do it now!"

The wide meathead stood up and leaned his knuckles on the table. "How can a ship that small have powerful enough shields to protect it from incoming fire?"

"The Daggers do not have shields, Troop Master."

That statement had all our mouths hanging open. Klutch snapped his shut, then pointed a finger at me. "You are not stuffing me into one of those deathtraps unless it has shields."

"Troop Master, shields are not necessary. The warp bubble surrounding the ship when it is phase jumping, protects it from incoming fire. Any weapon that is accurate enough to actually hit the spacecraft, harmlessly passes into interdimensional space. The ship can effectively fire its weapons into normal space-time but incoming fire transitions. What I find interesting is that the Daggers are capable of phase jumping while stationary."

Holy crap! We have technology so sophisticated it's like magic!

"What are the odds Tria's people have gained access to the Daggers we gave them?"

"Less than two percent unless they have recently recovered a Guardian transponder and an artificial intelligence with Guardian architecture. It takes a combination of both just to gain access to the spacecraft. There are multiple safeguards to prevent access to any A.I. not of Guardian design. It would be advisable to warn the Operative about the anti-intrusion self-destruct devices built around the processing module"

I turned to Tria with a questioning look. She didn't seem alarmed. "My people have studied Dagger fragments for many years. I am sure they have determined that the safeguards may have been involved in the destruction of some of the artifacts."

That was good enough for me. "Justice, alert the Zaens we have arrived at our destination and tell them to be ready to board the shuttle."

"Affirmative, Commander, I have already prepped the shuttle for departure."

I stood up and adjourned the meeting. "I want to continue our discussion on our next mission over dinner at Haras."

That got me smiles from everyone. "Justice, could you please contact Tam Lin and let her know we are in the area?"

40

I was pleasantly surprised to receive an invitation to dinner for my crew and me in Tam Lin's personal dining room. We were directed to land in a private hangar normally reserved for the Sig, and we came to find out it was in honor of us freeing the single largest number of slaves since Tam Lin started smuggling them to freedom. We had bested the Sig by a couple of hundred.

We said our goodbyes to Broza and Hylet and let them know we would be returning soon with their new mode of transportation. They were led away and Pasta escorted us to large, ornately decorated dining hall. A long table that could have seated fifty had a large, throne-like chair at the end. Three smaller chairs were on one side and two on the other. Pasta seated Tria and I and then the rest of the crew.

Tam Lin made her entrance and greeted each of my crewmates and then came around to Tria and I. "It is easy to see why you are attracted to the Chaalt. They are such a beautiful race of people. It is a rarity to find someone so attractive and lethal in the same package. I can only wish for such luck."

I wasn't sure how to comment on her statement so I just smiled and nodded. Tria placed one of her hands on my knee and squeezed. I felt a slight vibration in the room that wasn't present earlier. Tria's hand went a little farther north and she squeezed harder. I jumped and grabbed her hand then felt a little wobbly. Tria smiled at me. I caught Tam Lin giving me a raised eyebrow but her face quickly turned neutral when Tria looked at her. Tria was making sure no one had any doubt who her chosen one was.

Tam Lin finally chuckled and clapped her hands loudly together. A side door opened and carts loaded with food were wheeled out and served to us. It would have been an amazing meal if it were not for Klutch chowing down on Dorta sea snakes. At one point we all sat and stared while the Troop Master laid waste to his heaping plate. My crew and I were growing immune to such displays, but it took Tam Lin more than a few minutes of wide-eyed staring to finally pick at her plate.

The table was cleared and drinks customary to the various races were brought out. Tam Lin addressed us. "You and your crew are becoming quite popular among the Sig. Some of your exploits are becoming so blown out of proportion they are becoming mythical. I must admit: for such a small band of warriors, you have managed to kick some very large asses. When word of your deeds started spreading among the cesspools full of pirate and slaver scum, there was a lot of talk about collecting the crazy big bounties placed on your heads. Now there is only a few that even consider the subject noteworthy conversation, and it is only in whispers."

While it was nice to know we were scaring the hell out of the appropriate people, I really didn't have anything to say about it and tried to change the subject. Tam Lin wasn't ready to.

"The word going around is a certain outpost full of scum has disappeared. You know anything about it?"

I didn't come here to brag about how many I sent to my maker for judgement. I almost let her know it was the Operative but let it slide. "I am sure it happens all the time."

"What about the Scrun hit teams that were sent out to whack you?"

I just shrugged my shoulders. "They are welcome to try."

Tam Lin had a disappointed look on her face that turned into a big smile but she was not looking at me. I followed her gaze and saw that big ox Klutch drawing a finger across the stump that passed for his neck. If I thought my foot would reach that far, I would have kicked him regardless of what the place smelled like afterwards. I instead drummed my fingers on the table and rolled my eyes at the high domed ceiling. I again went for a change in subjects.

"I know it is a very tricky and delicate matter to change permanent personal IDs, and I will pay you well for taking care of my Zaen friends. They are going to be hanging around until I can supply them with a new ship to transport goods. I will supply them with one as soon as possible, but it might take a week or so."

That seemed to do the trick and Tam Lin held up her hand and paused me before I could continue. "We have a large assortment of freighters and other ships for sale. What do you need?"

I hadn't thought of asking that question. "We were going to lend them an assault shuttle until we could find a small armed freighter. I wanted something easy for them to handle and with enough armament to keep them from falling prey to pirates."

She pushed a spot on the table next to her and a small holographic keyboard popped up. She poked at few buttons and a screen appeared on the wall showing several types of spacecraft. She changed ship types several times, finally arriving at what she was after.

"This is a Sig-flagged military transport and the smallest in its class. It is a dated design but has several recent upgrades. It has good quality shields and weapons. This class is moderately fast, and oh by the way, did I mention it was Sig-flagged? No one in their right mind screws with the Sig. I will sell it to you for a little over cost and lease a training crew of five for twenty-five billion credits."

I had no idea if it was a good deal or not. I looked at my crewmates and they all had blank stares on their faces. I guess Tam Lin took my indecision as haggling instead of lack of knowledge.

"Sheesh! I'll throw in a new paint job as well, but you're not getting anything else out of me! I can't just give this scat away for free."

I didn't know what else to do but hold out my hand. We shook on it and she poked at the floating display a little more. "It will be ready in ten work periods and I will make sure your Zaen friends get new permanent ID chips. Is there anything else you need while you are here?"

I pointed across the table at Klutch, Coonts and Xul. "How much to give these three and thirty-seven of my Grawl scientists new IDs?"

"Holy shit Nathan, you are talking some serious credits. To begin with, it is a highly illegal surgical procedure pulling original ID chips from people's brains. It is slightly risky, but we have not had anyone die in several years. We have had a one hundred percent success rate on the slaves that had chips. We have developed a way for the neuro tentacles to reattach to the originals within seconds without any serious side effects. That is the least expensive part of the procedure. It is greasing all of the

615

crooked palms it takes to get the new information into the Galactic database. That costs a fortune!"

I just shrugged because I really didn't care how much it cost. At some point in the future, I would take the Chaalt council's hundred billion and this expenditure would be a wash. Coonts, Klutch and Xul were giving me an affirmative — they were happy about getting a clean slate. I looked at Tria questioningly and she shook her head a definite no.

"How much?"

"A hundred million a head is the going rate — that is why it rarely happens. Very few can afford it and it keeps demand for the procedure low. The price is set so I can afford to do the slaves for free."

"How long does the surgery take?"

"The surgery only takes minutes, getting the information into the database takes a couple of weeks. I have enough chips to do these three, but because of the large number of slaves you recently freed, it will take me a little while to get my hands on enough virgin chips to do your staff."

I had a pocket full of vouchers because I never left home without them. I passed them to her and she made the withdrawal.

"Bring the scientists in a week and we will be ready by then."

Pasta led Coonts, Klutch and Xul to Tam Lin's private elevator. Tria and I waited with Tam Lin and made small talk. "So, Sushi tells me you had a solid lead on Eiger, how did that turn out?"

"Not well. Eiger was not there. We did however recover the two Zaens I brought to you. They were kidnapped by Tibor pirates and held for ransom."

"Hah! Knowing you, I bet that worked out well for them."

"They got what was coming to them."

"Sushi said the little side trip was well worth the time. Whoever was running the outpost was pissing their pants when he showed up with three platoons asking to buy liquor. He scored enough Pluga to last their new outpost a year. The pirates sold it for half of what we normally pay. They must have really wanted Sushi's crew of ass kickers off the outpost pretty bad to sell at those prices."

"Have you heard anything on Eiger's whereabouts?"

"Not really. What I have is dated and still states he is holed up on one of the Murlak home worlds."

The slippery Throgg would continue breathing for now, but one day soon I was going to fix that. I started thinking about what arrangement I needed to make with the Zaens to get some small return on my investment. They were at the very least going to haul any freight and supplies we may need for an indefinite length of time. I might as well get that set up right now.

"We are going to need supplies on a regular basis. I will take enough for our immediate needs, but when the Zaen's freighter is ready, inform them of their new duties. Before we leave, please make sure Justice has all the necessary access codes for our new acquisition."

Tam Lin smiled and gave me a nod. She was making credits off us left and right. At this rate, our supply was finite and we would have to go pick on the Scrun and Murlaks to make sure we didn't run short. Pasta escorted my crewmembers from the elevator. Each had a small patch at the base of their skulls but was looking no worse for wear and tear.

Tam Lin walked over to them. "You are now unknowns. Any previous security clearances you may have held are now null and void. Any reputation you might have enjoyed, good or bad, is forfeit. You are now strangers to your past and can only build on your future. Your names never mattered, but your ID numbers did. I know I don't have to say this, but you are going to hear it anyway. There is no such thing as getting a new personal ID chip, and you damn sure didn't get one here!"

We shot the breeze while I our supplies were being loaded. When Pasta and Klutch had everything secured we said our goodbyes and boarded our shuttle for the return trip to the Legacy. When we were well clear of the outpost, Justice came alongside and pulled us into the hangar bay with the tow beam.

"Justice, take us to Alpha Base so we can restock our missile magazine and unload supplies."

"Affirmative, Commander. I have been deep charging the matrix while you were on the outpost and we can make a DEHD core transition on your order."

"Take us home, Justice."

We were still walking to the lift tube that would take us to the bridge level when everything went dead still and glowed a bright white. When we returned to normal spacetime, Justice reported his subsystems had no unusual activity to report, so we made a straight-in approach for landing. The first thing we noticed after landing was a large new building structure where our replicator was once located. Several of our Grawl engineers were busy using gravity jacks to set building panels in place on an adjoining building that was yet to be completed. Felix came to meet us and was overjoyed that we had rescued his clan members. He pointed at the new buildings and was beaming as he explained what they had accomplished in our absence.

"Nathan Myers, the fabricator building and my personal quarters are now complete. I am currently manufacturing the final forty-one panels that will finish the warehouse structure."

The rest of my scientists and engineers stopped what they were doing and started congregating around us. They held out their hands and I smiled as I walked around and touched each. My crew did the same and I once again stood in front of young Felix. He held his hand out to me and I touched it. A small cheer went out from the Grawl. Every face I made eye contact with looked genuinely happy. I only knew a little about their past lives, and it had nothing to do with being happy. My next announcement should really get them going. I held up my hands and they quieted.

"I have made certain arrangements that can never be divulged to anyone outside of this base. As with everything else here, you are sworn to secrecy. I repeat, you must NEVER speak of what I am about to tell you."

I had everyone's attention. They stood wide eyed and wondering what I was about to tell them. "It is now possible to wipe your past lives from the Galactic records."

This got me several small frowns and looks of uncertainty. Jaran came forward. "Nathan Myers, that is not possible without removing our ID chips. To do such a thing would leave many permanently brain damaged and unable to function normally."

Coonts and Xul stepped forward. Coonts turned Xul around so the crowd could see the small bandage at the base of his skull. "As you can see, Xul and I have suffered no ill effects. We now have new chips and no record of our past. No one will be able to track us through our old identities. We can now travel freely without the threat of someone finding out who we really are."

Man, oh man, that got them stirred up. The excited murmur that went through the crowd was getting louder by the second. I held my hands up again and they quieted. "Any who wish to have a new identity and be able to safely make excursions to outposts on our new freighter, raise your hands!"

I had to bite my tongue to keep from laughing out loud. As one, they raised both of their hands as if they were surrendering to me.

Young Felix turned to me. "We have a freighter?"

"Yes, I now own a Sig-flagged freighter that Broza and Hylet will be permanently in charge of. Their ship was destroyed when we rescued them and it will be the replacement. As long as they give our needs priority, they will be free to use it for their normal commerce. They will be making the journey to a rendezvous point where we

621

will meet them on a regular basis. The Grawl will join them on their first excursion and will get new identities. Once that is done they will be able to travel freely and spend their new wealth as they please."

Turning to the Grawl, I addressed the crowd once more. "I hope that you will all decide to return and help me continue my mission to help others."

The cheer that went out was deafening, then it settled to excited talk and quieted once more. They were looking at me kind of funny.

"Is there a problem?"

The Grawl looked to Graf and he stepped forward. "Nathan Myers, why would we not return to our home?"

That put a smile on my face you couldn't slap off. "I just meant that you now have freedom of choice. You can have a normal life and go wherever the freighter might take you."

"Nathan Myers, this is our home and it is where we wish to live out our lives. We have purpose now because we do not work for the wealth of a corrupt few — we work for the good of all."

There was no arguing with that, and I told them to carry on with what they were doing before I interrupted. I saw that Justice took it upon himself to operate the automated overhead cranes to get the missiles on board the Legacy. Klutch, Coonts and Xul departed to help with the cargo. Tria took my hand and pulled me in the direction of the artifact building. I looked over my shoulder seeing that everyone was busy, then gave her an arched eyebrow. She just smiled rolled her eyes and shook her head. We stopped in front of the big atmospheric hatch and she called to Justice to open up. The doors parted and sitting just inside were the five Daggers. The flush fitting cockpit doors were folded to the side, beckoning us to come look inside. I peeked over the edge and saw everything had been stripped out and a track lock system installed into the opening. Tria waved me over to four large tub-like modules sitting behind each Dagger. They reminded me of the reinforced drivers compartments of rail-style dragsters I used to watch on TV when I was young.

Tria walked around two of them then stepped up on the small scaffold next to the third one in line. She threw her leg over the edge and climbed in. I stepped up on the scaffolding and watched as she sat back into the protective enclosure. It fit her like a glove. She placed her arms on the four rests designed just for her and holographic displays came to life right in front of her. I was going to lean forward for a closer look but folding doors popped up out of the edges of the module and closed like the sections of our Chaalt battle helmets.

"HA HA, Justice, very funny. Now let her out of there."

"The Grawl scientists and engineers were adamant we should have redundant safety measures in place to protect command personnel. This design was adopted to ensure survivability in the event the Dagger's phase shielding were to become inoperable during combat situations. The control module can sustain life for up to fourteen Earth days. There is a supply of water and emergency rations in a compartment under the seat. If need be, the module can be ejected and is able to make limited maneuvers with its gravity thrusters. It can re-enter into atmospheres as well but will be irreparably damaged if that option is exercised."

The closure retracted and I was startled to see Tria holding her Chaalt combat rifle. The god of war was covering all the bases. If we took off in the Daggers and somehow found our asses buried in Throggs, we could always shoot our way out.

"I took the liberty of preparing for all contingencies. There is a Tibor pistol secured in the cockpit as well as two Chaalt homing grenades. The seat pads can expand or contract to fit both of your current armor types."

Tria secured the rifle back in its rack and pulled herself up out of the module. "Justice, when can we test fly them?"

"Tria, November One and Tango Two are the closest to completion and approximately eight work cycles from flight testing. Charlie Three and Kilo Four are still more than twenty work cycles away from the module fitting process and subsystem integration. X-Ray Five is being held for reserve status."

"Justice while we are here and I am thinking about it, I want at least twenty of our nanite missiles in our loadout."

"Affirmative, Commander. I would like to fill the reservoirs on your battle armor with weaponized nanites now that the suits have been combat-tested. I have completed several program sequences that should cover most combat nanite dispersion scenarios. I have taken the liberty of introducing the DNA of you and all personnel in this complex into the stop code algorithms programmed into the nanites. Using Tria's DNA, I have also eliminated any chance of Chaalt personnel being mistakenly attacked."

"Thank you, Justice, I know I am capable of being extremely careless in combat. Keep me posted and give everyone a heads up when we are ready to depart. We will be going to investigate our latest transponder find."

"Roger that, Commander!"

I took Tria by the hand and we exited the artifact building, closing the large access door behind us. One the

Grawl engineers was on an intercept course, so we stopped to see what he was up to.

"Nathan Myers, the second Coram shuttle should be complete in another two work cycles. We have removed all useable equipment and ordinance from the damaged shuttle. We have been ordered by Felix to cut up the remains. We know he is in charge of the replicator but many of us are hesitant to take orders from him. I thought it best to consult with you before we follow...his request."

"Did Felix say why he wanted to cut it up?"

"No, he said to cut it up and transport everything to the replicator facility."

"Thank you for alerting me. Hold off on the demolition until I find out what he is up to."

I moved off with Tria in tow toward the replicator building. I wasn't sure how I felt about young Felix giving orders any more than the Grawl did. As we entered the building, I was surprised to see one of our Chaalt-manufactured stealth missiles disassembled on a large bench. I was even more surprised to see the anti-matter warhead sitting on a cart next to it.

"Felix! What are you doing?"

The young Zaen jumped at my exclamation. "Mr. Myers, it should be obvious I am proofing the replicator settings in preparation of manufacturing our first stealth missile. The Grawl engineers have yet to bring the salvage from the wrecked shuttle. I require it for the casings."

"Where did you get the spec sheets and processing plans?"

The Zaen walked over to a long crate. "While inventorying the shipping crates that were left by the Chaalt, we came across this unmarked crate. When I opened it, I found this missile and a strange cryptic message along with the manufacturing specifications."

"Show me the message."

Felix rooted through the mess on his desk and gave me the message.

If a simple-minded primate were to somehow find these sensitive documents, he should ignore the contents and go back to stacking his scat.

I grimaced and wadded the message up putting it in my pocket. Tria had a huge smile on her face. I rolled my eyes and shook my head in exasperation.

Felix gave me a quizzical look. "Is it a coded message?"

"You could say that. I will have the engineers start cutting up the shuttle. In the future you should consult with Justice before you start issuing orders. And just to be clear on the subject, you are in charge of the replicator —

not the scientists and engineers. If you need help, you can ask for it. If the Grawl have free time, they will give you a hand. In the event it is an urgent matter and I am not present, you are to ask Justice's subsystem and you will receive the help you require. Are we clear?"

A small frown crossed the young Zaen's face, but the look on mine made it quickly vanish. He gave me the proper acknowledgement.

"Once you have the programming for the missiles entered into the replicator, I want those documents fed into it and not another word mentioned about them."

Felix nodded in agreement and went back to work on the missile project.

"Justice, alert the engineers to go ahead and demolish the shuttle."

Tria looked me in the eyes. "Perhaps it is time to quit blaming Sael for the actions of the military council. I think she has proven she can be trusted and she is firmly backing our cause. When our current supply of missiles is expended, we will not have to beg the military council to sell us more at inflated prices. I believe the council was thinking that credits paid to us would be recouped at some future date. Sael knowingly saved us large sums of credits"

"I agree. She practices her brinkmanship at such high levels, I find it difficult at times to decipher who's interest she has at heart: hers, the council's, or ours. It still irks me that it seems she has been dangling transporter technology within our grasp only to pull it away."

"I think she has tried to manipulate the council in such a way that we might possibly end up with it, but they have taken actions to ensure we don't. It must never look as if Sael knowingly assisted us in gaining my people's most closely guarded secrets. She could be stripped of her rank and status and cast out from our home worlds. Now that the Fury is operational, she might have the freedom to be the ally we were expecting her to be."

"I am still not ready to let her know Justice has inhabited her ship, but I will try to drop all pretense that she is not welcome to investigate the origins of the derelict ship. Once the Chaalt install the transporter on the Fury, it will be just a matter of time before Justice figures out how it works and we can put our science teams to work on the project."

"My people will certainly have very robust security measures in place to prevent that from happening. I surmise they will take steps to insure Sael cannot give the technology away either."

"Only time will tell, and I am pretty sure if Justice has set his sights on the transporter, there is little your people will be able to do about it. He has already shown a propensity toward taking and not asking — something, I might add, your people enjoy doing as well."

Tria just nodded and decided the matter would settle itself. We left Felix to his work and were going to board the Legacy. As we stepped outside the building, we encountered the engineer I had spoken to earlier. He was operating a gravity lift loaded down with parts of our wrecked shuttle. I flagged him down.

"When the Coram shuttle is repaired, let it be known that it is now the personal transport of the scientists and engineers."

The little Grawl was shocked speechless.

41

Tria and I had just stepped into the personnel hatch when Justice gave us a sitrep. "Commander, our munitions are at maximum capacity and the crew has boarded in preparation for departure. The engineers have finished the loadout for Eagle One, and as soon as Graf completes his checklist, I will load it into the shuttle bay. I have no anomalous activity to report in our star system, and we can transition once clear of Alpha base. The matrix is charged and DEHD core operations are available on your orders."

"What is the status of my battle armor?"

"Cloaking emitter arrays have been repaired, and I have strengthened the armor sheath over the minigun ammunition feed tube. Nanite reservoirs on all armor suits have been filled and all are ready for combat operations."

"Thank you, Justice, launch when you are ready."

"Acknowledged."

I went to the bridge level and found Coonts, Klutch and Xul already at their stations. Klutch was bragging to Xul how he had managed to get four prisoners on board the Legacy with no assistance from Coonts. He was rubbing in the fact he had won a thousand credits from

Coonts because two of the prisoners were not wearing void suits and neither one had perished as Coonts wagered they would. Coonts turned his back on the two with a less than amused look on his face. I always wondered what that bet was about; now I didn't. Tria sat at her station and just shook her head. Justice rescued us from any more of the mindless chatter.

"Commander, the shuttle is secured and we are ready to depart."

"Roger that Justice, take us out and DEHD core transition us to our last transponder detection."

Justice brought the Legacy up off the deck and rotated one-hundred and eighty degrees and had us in open space in just a few seconds. Klutch was starting in on Coonts again when the silence of transition finally shut him up. When we returned to normal spacetime we were on the edge of the devastated star system. It was such a bleak sight Klutch lost the urge to pick at Coonts and the bridge was quiet once more. Justice weaved us in and out of the massive debris and made a beeline for the only surviving planetary body.

"Justice, will our suits be enough to protect us from the high radiation?"

"Commander, your armor is resistant to most all types of radiation but they still have their limits. I recommend that you stay in the shuttle as much as possible and make your excursions less than an hour at a time. My subsystems will alert you if your exposer reaches dangerous levels. The Chaalt-designed airlock on the shuttle has efficient decontamination systems and they will suffice to clean your armor. However, you should not open the shuttle's cargo bay unless it is absolutely necessary."

"No problem. We are going to look around and only debark if we find something unusual. We will keep any excursions to thirty minutes or less."

We boarded the Shuttle and Klutch took the pilot's seat. Tria sat in the other and I stood behind her. Coonts and Xul joined us and we stared out the view screen as Justice picked the shuttle up and pushed it into the void. Justice's subsystem highlighted the target area and Klutch nosed us over into a dive for the massive crater. The radiation quickly rocketed to crazy high levels as Klutch centered us up for an approach to the tunnel. We noticed that the mouth of the tunnel had large piping and conduits ringing the top and sides of the opening. All were sheared off clean by whatever created the gigantic crater. The tunnel must have been attached to the target of the weapon.

Klutch slowed the shuttle drastically as we entered the opening. He pushed a highlighted button on the control panel and the tunnel was flooded with bright light. There was a lot of dirt, rock and debris in the entrance, but soon it thinned to just dirt and dust. We had gone about a half of mile and the radiation started falling. It would never be a safe level, but if we decided to go for a walk, it would not involve a time limit. I was beginning to think the tunnel went on forever when it opened into a massive cavern. Klutch started skirting the edge, and it quickly became apparent we were looking at a mining operation that had been abandoned during or after the attack on the planet. There was mining equipment that at one time was actively working at different places in the cavern. We could see conveyers that had once moved the materials to the large clear storage containers we were already familiar with. Justice's subsystem was running non-stop scans and alerted us to its conclusions.

"Commander, this excavation was for mining the materials identified by Scholar Burlor as Containium. There is approximately six hundred tons in storage crates and I have detected large veins of the material in the surrounding walls of the excavation. Most of the equipment is old but in good condition. If the tunnel entrance was properly prepared and atmospheric purification systems installed, there is no reason why this operation could not be brought back online."

This was an interesting turn of events and not what I expected to find. Another thought occurred to me: why would the Guardian transponder point out a mining operation? What artifact in this cavern could send a signal that the transponder would respond to?

"Justice, could you show us the exact location where the thread terminates?"

A bright green line appeared on the cockpit viewscreen. It connected to the wall of the cavern. Klutch slowly maneuvered us closer and we could now see an open doorway into the rock wall.

"Klutch, find a spot to put us down and let's go for a walk."

"Roger that, Commander!"

Klutch swung us around and landed the shuttle just inside of the tunnel entrance.

"Justice, are you still negative on life scans?"

"No life forms, Commander. Not even rodent or insect life is being detected."

"Alright, let's go for a walk, and remember — don't touch anything unless you absolutely have to."

That last part was for Xul's sake. The rest of the crew knew better. We jumped down from the airlock to a dust-covered floor. There were no signs that anything had moved about in the thick dust except for the occasional small crater from debris dropping from the overhead. As usual, the Troop Master took the lead and we trudged toward the cavern wall. Klutch was being overly cautious: he led us on a route that would not expose us to a direct line with the open doorway. He led us to one side of the door and held up a fist, then pulled his weapon from its clip. He stepped into the doorway, and a few seconds later, an armored hand waved us in.

We entered the door way and found ourselves in a good-sized atmosphere lock that separated the mining operation from what looked like a large open room just beyond another open door. The no light sensors in our visors gave us a detailed look at what use to be a common area and bunking quarters for the miners. We spread out to get a good look around and Coonts called out.

"Commander, I have the skeletal remains of two aliens."

We went to where Coonts was standing and saw two biped aliens lying in a bunk together. It was obvious that at some point in time there were, in fact, rodents or something along those lines. The faces and skulls of the bodies were chewed open, leaving a grotesque, ragged opening so the critters could eat the insides. The exposed hands were nubs missing all traces of fingers if they actually had them. One of the corpses had a shoulder bag. Coonts extended a climbing hook and carefully cut it free, pulling it from the remains. He handed it to me and I opened it. It looked like several small personal possessions, but what was really interesting was the

Guardian transponder in the bottom of the bag. I pulled the device out and laid the bag back in its place. Our transponder showed us yet another capability. It could point out other transponders. Perhaps, one day, we might find one with a live recipient in possession of it.

We searched the crew quarters for anything else of interest but found nothing. Klutch led us back to the shuttle and we flew back out of the tunnel to the Legacy. Justice pulled us in with the tow beam and locked us down in the hangar. We each stood in the shuttle's airlock and went through a decontamination process. When Justice was satisfied we were clean, he let us stow our gear. I placed the transponder on a table in the science lab and went to my quarters for a hot shower and a nap. Tria and my crewmates were right behind me. When Tria slowed to let them pass, Coonts and Klutch gave us some large eyed looks and big smiles. We could hear them snickering as they made their way down the corridor. It put a frown on Tria's pretty face, and she gave me a quick kiss and made it a point to say I will see you in the galley later. She turned away and walked to her cabin. When Coonts and Klutch saw her coming their way they sped up and disappeared into their quarters. Justice constantly watching my interactions with Tria was annoying; apparently Tria felt the same way about her fellow crewmates.

As I stepped into my cabin, I called to Justice. "Do you have any notable updates from our surveillance drones around outpost 6854?"

"Negative, Commander. A small number of spacecraft have visited the outpost and departed. None have been Murlak, and only one was Scrun. There is a possibility our covert operation may still be linked to us even though there is no evidence supporting that theory. If Eiger is taking every precaution to avoid contact with us, he might decide to stay clear of the outpost and have his underlings transport his profits to a location of his choosing. This scenario has a high probability of being correct."

If it was not for finding the mine and the transponder, I would say my day had turned to shit. I was no closer to finding Eiger and wondered if I should go ahead and strike the remnants of his fleet in case he decides to move them elsewhere.

"Justice, if it looks like Eiger's assets are getting ready to move from the nebula, I want our strike package to take them out. Use everything we got. I want nothing left for Eiger to make use of."

"Acknowledged!"

"Jump us to the Sig's new base of operations, standard transition."

"Affirmative, Commander. Jumping in sixty seconds."

I took a hot shower and laid down to take a nap, wondering what Tria was doing. I woke several hours later with Justice calling to me. "Commander, I have a secure IST link coming from the Operative."

I heard a beep in my head and then the Operative. "Nathan, the Fury is now fully operational and I thought we should take some time to talk. I have been alerted that you are not at Alpha base and seem to be jumping to obscure locations on the fringe of the galaxy."

I didn't know how likely it would be for the Chaalt to find the mine, and I wasn't going to admit I found one either.

"While we were working to uncover information on Eiger, we stumbled across a star system that had been destroyed. Whole planets, moons, everything was decimated. We were close enough to the fringe to speculate it was a victim of the Prule when they first came to this galaxy. All signs of life have been wiped out and the one remaining planetary body is a wasteland of immense craters and incredibly high radiation counts."

"Perhaps we could find the time to meet and discuss your findings. I would also like to convince you my people wish to have no more conflicts of interest with you."

"Sael, I have a keen nose for bullshit. You have been ordered to find me and tag along until I decide to go to the derelict ship. Am I right, yes or no?"

"Why must you act like a primate when I am trying to work with you?"

"Sael, we are jumping to the Sig's new base of operations. If you wish to talk, you can join up with us there."

My IST beeped and the Operative went offline. I had the feeling she was pissed because she didn't like the Sig. She needed to get used to it because they were allies that would stand behind me come hell or high water and they have yet to demand anything in return. I was actually considering taking them along to investigate the derelict ship. If we get lucky and the ship is not a pile of junk, I will offer some of the take to secure the area from any possible interlopers. A Sig fleet operating in the area would keep most races from snooping around.

"Justice, what is our ETA to the Sig base?"

"Forty-one minutes, seventeen seconds, Commander."

There was enough time I could sit down and have a meal before I had to meet with Sael. I got cleaned up and put on a fresh uniform. As the door to my cabin opened, I came face to face with Tria. I could hear Klutch talking to

640

Coonts or Xul somewhere down the corridor. The thought of pulling her into my cabin crossed my mind. The chatter down the way got louder and Tria took me by the hand and cancelled the thought by pulling me down the hall.

"Let's have our meal before Klutch decides to go to the galley."

There was no arguing with her logic, and I picked up the pace enough I was pulling her along. She thought that was funny and we ran to the down tube and dove in head first. We laughed all the way to the galley deck righting ourselves at the last second and then stepping out. I got the equivalent of soup and sandwiches and we sat at our usual places. We had little to say as we hastily ate our food. Our timing could not have been better; Klutch stepped into the galley and nodded to us. We returned the gesture and picked up our trays. This was one sideshow we would be missing. As we exited we almost ran into Coonts and Xul. They were waiting in the corridor for Klutch to pick his seat. We smiled and kept walking.

Justice alerted me of an impending call from the Operative. "Commander, the IST link is active."

I got a secure beep and then the Operative. "Nathan, we are currently holding outside of the system the Sig base is located in. Since the Fury will be an unknown and I do not want to disclose my cloaking capabilities, I suggest you let your defective A.I. track us down."

"No problem, Sael. I will see you when we arrive."

I ended the call with a small chuckle. That was not the answer she was probably expecting. Her new ship may be harder to find than her old one, but with Justice onboard it will be it will be a very short search. I would call her on the IST when the time comes and that will give Justice's subsystem a chance to send us her location piggybacked on the transmission.

"Commander, we will exit interdimensional space in thirty seconds."

"Thank you, Justice. Alert the Sig we will be passing through the neighborhood. I would like you to prep a comm buoy with a message to Sushi. Have it ready to launch in the event we need it. I want the message to say we have made another discovery and will share the wealth if he will supply a couple of fleets for security patrols."

"Message sent, and I am prepping the buoy. I am also detecting return message traffic cued on the local comm buoys."

"Let's hear it."

Tam Lin's voice broadcast from the overhead. "Nathan, the Zaens have launched with your new freighter.

If you need anything, feel free to stop by and talk English to me. Fair skies and calm seas, my friend."

I smiled at the references to my place of birth. The Legacy and Alpha base were my home now, and it would be hard to return to what many might consider a normal lifestyle. Practicing galactic justice back on Earth would land me on everyone's most wanted list. The beast inhabiting my mind would most assuredly get me sent to a prison for the criminally insane.

"Justice, have you got a lock on the Fury?"

"Yes. I am closing the distance now."

"I thought you would need a signal from your subsystem?"

"It will not be necessary now that I can control the Fury's drive emissions. It is a simple matter to introduce minute fluctuations into the drives that are easily detectable."

"Do you think it is wise to go directly to Sael's location? She is already suspicious as it is. I think it is a little early in the game to be tipping our hand."

"I will ensure the Senior Operative still has her doubts about my presence aboard the Fury."

I was starting to get a little nervous because Justice's voice had a familiar edge to it. He usually talked like that just before I was a victim of one of his pranks. The Operative called Justice a defective machine on more than one occasion. I should probably have cautioned her against unnecessarily picking at him. I wasn't sure of her motives other than to see him exhibit emotions rather than programmed responses. I had a bad feeling about this. Justice said we were closing the distance but it looked like we were significantly increasing speed. The stars on the view dome were now long streaks of light: this was not a good thing. Suddenly a bright blue box appeared in the center of the view screen. The Fury uncloaked and a yellow circle appeared around it. In a blink of an eye, we past just to port of it and then it was gone. My IST beeped and Sael came online and she sounded pissed.

"Nathan! What is that defective A.I. doing? You nearly collided with our shields!"

I was kind of lost for words, as was the rest of my crew. I could not think of any reasonable explanation for the crazy close pass other than spite, so I threw her a half ass excuse.

"Sael, we had you tagged further out in the system."

The noise that came over the IST was not a ladylike response.

"The A.I. could have altered your course. Your drive emissions registered as a strike on our shields. This had

644

better not be some kind of foolish game you are trying to play on me."

My response to her statement would be the truth. "Sael, I would not pull a reckless stunt like that. Justice said he was closing the distance to your location."

"Nathan, it is time for you to take charge of the Legacy and take the important decisions away from that arrogant A.I. If the Legacy is truly your starship, then TAKE COMMAND!"

I had to admit it was a foolhardy stunt on Justice's part and his response to Sael's continuous jabs were getting out of hand.

"Sael, we are coming about and will rendezvous with you."

"No, Nathan, let me spare you the indecision. We are coming to you."

Now the old witch was getting on my ass and my nerves. I would let her have her way for the moment.

"Acknowledged!"

Justice must have been eavesdropping on my implants and knew I was getting pissed.

"Commander, I find the Senior Operative's disparaging comments towards my crew and myself distasteful and offensive. It is irritating to my human sensitivities."

"Really, Justice, that's all you got for rationalizing the dangerous stunt you just pulled? What could that old witch possibly say that she has not already said to our faces."

"Commander, while in her cabin she loudly vocalizes insulting comments about you, the crew and myself."

"She is purposely doing it because she knows you display human emotions. She is trying to prove her suspicions are correct that you have stowed away on her ship. I know you don't need me to tell you this, but you should be able to see her true intentions. I'm sure you have heard me call you worse than she can come up with."

"You have never claimed that the A.I. of your toilet is more intelligent than I am."

"She is just trying to anger you."

"She is succeeding."

"Justice, don't get mad. Eventually we will get even. Just ignore her. One day we will reveal she was right all along and it will aggravate her twice as much, especially when we gain transporter technology."

"Her superiors have taken several steps to prevent that from happening. The transporter systems are isolated from the rest of ship operations. The Chaalt have gone to great lengths to make the transporter bay a modular self-sufficient compartment within the Fury. It has its own power and control systems and can only be accessed with the use of three separate encryption keys that are held by command personnel other than the Operative. Someone would have to physically bring a device I inhabit into the transporter room and allow me access to the computer systems."

Tria stated what was already bouncing around in my simple mind. "My people's scientists and engineers are not underestimating Guardian technology. I am confident that every time Justice has displayed small samples of his true potential, Sael has reported what she felt was necessary to remain our handler. It would be foolhardy to believe they do not suspect Justice is present aboard the Fury. Sael is trying her best to prove it before her science team does and then reports it to the council."

Once again, I felt like transporter technology was within my grasp only to be pulled out of my reach. One day in the future, that was going to change.

"Commander, I have allowed the Fury to come alongside. Should I also allow the Operative to board?"

I transmitted an IST signal in the open to the Operative. "Senior Operative, how about a tour of your new command?"

Tria was shaking her head no. She had already informed me the council forbid such actions. I was trying to see if we might be an exception to the rules. Sael's answer confirmed we were not.

"I am sorry, Nathan, I am governed by Chaalt military law. Even though you have proven your loyalty and shed your blood in our defense, it is forbidden for another race to board Chaalt military assets. This law was established well before my time to prevent espionage. All Chaalt command personnel are bound to this rule. I am no exception."

Coonts gave me an 'I told you so!' look, and Klutch just shrugged his wide shoulders. Xul just sat wide eyed at our conversations. He was quickly coming up to speed on our love-hate relationship with Tria's people and the Operative in particular. I ended the transmission. That was sure to piss Sael off.

"Justice, is the matrix charged?"

"Yes, Commander, and I have already taken the liberty of covertly placing a comm buoy out the starboard side of the Legacy."

A smile crossed my lips when my IST came online. "Nathan, I am sure you are already familiar with my military laws. I would like to meet with you to present a gift from my people for your generous support and the hard work of your followers."

The way Sael's statement came out of her mouth it was easy to tell it wasn't intended as a polite request.

"Justice, open the hangar for the Senior Operative and then DEHD core jump to a location where we can reach the derelict ship in a couple of standard transitions."

"Acknowledged."

My crew seemed to be trying to ignore the fact I was going to kidnap the Operative, again. One by one, Coonts, Klutch and Xul headed to someplace where they would not have to listen to Sael blow her top. It was about five minutes before Sael came storming onto the bridge.

"You are an ungrateful primate, you could have at least met me in th—"

The ship and everything around us went dead quiet, then started glowing blinding white. The last thing I saw was the look of anger on the Operative's face as she faded away. I thought I felt Tria grab my hand just before my reality disappeared. My return to normal space-time might have been pleasant if it were not for the very colorful Chaalt epithets being yelled at me. I did, however, take some small comfort in the fact Tria was indeed holding my hand. The small smile I gave her was rudely terminated by the impact of several credit vouchers bouncing off my chest and face.

"Now who is acting like a primate?"

"Take me back to the Fury, NOW!"

"We were going to take you with us to investigate the derelict ship, but if you insist on going back, JUSTICE—"

42

My comment registered the proper response from Sael when her mouth snapped shut, but the look on her face was still anger. Justice's timing for our next jump couldn't have been more perfect as the slight nausea of a standard transition gripped me.

"WAIT! I want to know what kind of scat you are pulling on me now?"

"No scat involved, Sael, we are trying to ensure what we have discovered remains ours."

"Don't be ridiculous Nathan. We have no intentions of seizing your discoveries."

"While it is easy for you to say that, past events have proven otherwise."

Sael had nothing to say to that and instead said what I knew she would. "Take us back. I want to go with you."

Justice again jumped us at the most opportune time, further convincing Sael we had turned around and were now jumping back. She had no idea we were attempting to make it harder for her people to track us down. I knew they would eventually find us, but not before we got a good look around. Justice alerted us we were entering the gaseous nebula. My crew finally wandered back to the bridge from their cabins when they heard me shut the Operative up. They took their stations and Justice brought the view dome online. We could see the gas and dust was thinning out at the edge of the rocky debris field the junkyard for a ship was hidden in. We got a surprise call from Justice.

"Commander, it appears that the dimensions of the ship have been slightly altered."

"Altered? What do you mean?"

"The ship is larger than our previous visit. I will superimpose the current image over our previous recordings and highlight the areas of change."

I didn't know why, but I was getting a bad feeling, and it was contagious because I could feel the Oolaran in me stir.

"Justice, bring the shields up, maximum output."

Everybody turned and gave me questioning looks. The image Justice showed us had two areas that were now obviously larger. One of them appeared to resemble part of a ship's hull. We were still closing with the target but I could tell Justice had slowed us down. Tria's curiosity got the better of her.

"Justice, I am not showing any power sources, but I do have very weak heat signatures scattered all over the wreck. Could you magnify and highlight them as well."

Justice added them to the outline of the derelict and it was like several hundred candles were suddenly lit all over the ship. Coonts asked the next obvious question.

"Justice, were any of the heat sources present on the shuttle scans?"

"Negative. The Legacy's scanners are several magnitudes more powerful than the original systems aboard the Chaalt shuttle. As we close the distance, I am now detecting a very faint power source. I will add my findings to the display."

Goosebumps crawled all over me and it didn't have a thing to do with Tria's Sha'leen. The entire ship had faint lines that resembled blood veins pulsating throughout the hull. The goosebumps were now accompanied by a chill that ran up my spine. Klutch and I had considered boarding that piece of crap.

I jumped when Xul called out rather loudly. "Justice, magnify the largest highlighted area!"

The screen zoomed in closer to the area he was referring to. "Maximum magnification please!"

A large round shaped hump filled the view dome and all of our eyes grew large with the recognition of what we were seeing. It was a huge piece of an Ilor habitat ship's hull and it was somehow melded into the huge junk piles that made up the ship. Justice made a crazy hard turn away from the ship and broadcast for all to hear.

"ENERGY SPIKE, BRACE FOR INCOMING FIRE!"

A blinding flash whited out the view dome and the Legacy was violently thrown aside by a massive impact. The Operative was the only one that chose to stand, and it turned out to be a poor decision. She was thrown into an instrument panel and came to rest against the side of the view dome. She lay in a heap on the deck and was not moving. The crew and I had braced in enough time to not be ripped from our seats. My crew hastily fastened their combat harnesses as Tria and I ran to the Operative's prone body. She was unconscious and bleeding from the mouth but appeared to be breathing normally. Tria was holding the Operative's head off the deck and showed me her hand. It was covered in blood. We rolled her over as gently as possible and found an ugly gash on the back of her head. Out of the corner of my eye I saw a gurney moving in our direction when we were suddenly knocked sprawling by another weapon strike.

"JUSTICE, WHAT THE HELL IS GOING ON?"

"The hostile ship has a powerful main weapon system that appears to recycle enough energy to fire in one minute and fifty-seven second intervals. It is similar in nature to our beam weapons with very impressive range and is extremely accurate. The weapon has a capacitive capability and an effective method of masking the power surge before discharging. The first strike brought our shields down to twenty-nine percent but they recovered to just under ninety percent before the ship could re-engage us. Our return fire has dislodged massive amounts of debris from the ship's hull but has made no detectable difference in the main weapon's discharge capability. We are now cloaked and the hostile ship's last two discharges missed their mark by several thousand yards. I sense it is still able to track us because the misses are almost exactly the same clearances."

Tria had the Operative loaded on the gurney and it disappeared off the bridge. We took our seats and securely fastened our harnesses. I was still shaking my head, thinking Klutch and I should be dead right now. I was pretty sure we were within the weapon's envelope when we first discovered it. Apparently, something as small as a shuttle didn't warrant the release of so much energy. I thought about it a little more and my thoughts went in another direction completely. A ship the size of a shuttle would normally be accepted as a precursor to boarding. Did someone or something on that pile of shit want people to come aboard?

"Commander the ship has ceased fire. I surmise it can no longer track us and we are out of its range. I find it interesting that when I turned off our shields, the ships attack missed by a very large margin of error. I now believe the ship can detect the minute emissions of our shields even while we are cloaked. Fortunately, the hostile's systems cannot process the correlation in a timely enough manner to determine the proper lead necessary to effectively strike us."

"That's just lovely and wonderful, but I am not going to risk the ship and crew by turning off the shields and going back to play chicken with that pile of crap."

"It will no longer be necessary to prove it."

"What do you mean by that?"

"I have made two passes through the hostile ship's weapons envelope and it made no attempt to fire on us."

That got me wide eyed stares and gaping mouths from my crew. I slapped both my hands to my forehead and then proceeded to massage my aching temples.

"Justice, you will NEVER, and I use the word EVER for emphasis, pull a stunt like that again without first asking one of us first! YOU GOT THAT!

"OK."

"What is the Operative's medical status?"

"I have felt better, but I will live."

We spun around to see Sael Nalen walk back onto the bridge. One of her eyes had a ring around it much darker than her normal deep tanned brown complexion. Other than that, and a small gob of nanite gel on the back of her head, she didn't seem injured. At least I had one less thing to worry about. That was until she opened her mouth and let it run some more.

"Now are you going to heed my words and reel in that out of control machine you let run this ship?"

I redoubled my efforts to massage away what might turn into a doozy of a headache. It was a wasted effort, as it blossomed into a real ring-dinger. I stood up and approached Sael. Tria jumped up and grabbed onto my arm. The look on my face made her promptly let go. With great effort and control I calmly told Sael what I thought of her little outburst on my bridge.

"Sael, that machine just saved our lives whether you choose to believe it or not. He also has a name and I know you are familiar with it. While on my ship you will use it or you can get the hell off so you can exercise the right to call him whatever you want. To make myself perfectly clear, AGAIN! You are not a member of this crew and are not in our chain of command. You have no say when it comes to the operation of this ship, so you will kindly keep your mouth shut about command decisions pertaining to how it may or may not be run. I give you a certain amount of leeway when it comes to your behavior that I would never

657

grant to another alien outside of this ship. Do not make me regret that decision. Think about what you might have done had someone pulled the same scat on the bridge of the Fury. You might also take into consideration what might have happened if the Fury was the target of the surprise attack. Would your A.I. have responded the same way Justice did to save our ship?"

The Operative was momentarily lost for words. Then she tried to rationalize her outburst.

"The A.I. recklessly endangered us all by testing its theories—"

I pointed my finger in her face. "Not another word, Sael! He would not have done it without having a high percentage of success."

Justice could not stand the thought of not adding input to our heated discussion. It made me involuntarily grit my teeth and roll my eyes when he did.

"Ninety-six-point eight percent—"

"JUSTICE!"

You could have heard a pin drop. My crew had made it a point to turn their backs and pretend they weren't listening. It was at that point I ran out of steam and my anger was subsiding. Sael was coming to grips with what could have happened to her and the crew of the Fury. She took a seat at an unoccupied console. She belted herself in and sat quietly with all her arms crossed. It was time to get back to what we were going to do about the attack we managed to live through. Evidently a great number of races could not claim the same feat and were lured to their deaths by the monstrosity we were again closing with.

"Justice, have you located the source of the weapons fire?"

"Yes. We were fired upon from three different locations on the ship. It appears the weapons are of a pop-up turret design and all three are ringed by immense piles of spacecraft or other debris. Do you still wish to board?"

I looked at my crew and, with the exception of Xul, got nods of agreement. Turning to the Operative, she gave me a less than enthusiastic answer.

"I guess if I have a choice I would rather die killing the Throggs who attacked us than get reduced to atoms sitting on this ship."

I gave her one last chance to back out.

"Give me the word and we will take you to the Fury and we will finish this ourselves."

"Don't be foolish. The five of you can't go in there by yourselves. You need my help and my troops if you want to capture that thing intact."

"You seem to forget I have other allies who would be willing to help, and I intend on asking for it."

"Commander, the Overseer has warned me you should avoid involving others in your initial investigation. If this ship is a Prule asset, the chances for subjugation of unprotected personnel is high and could lead to a mass Prule infection of non-Guardian designed systems."

Sael could not stand it anymore. "WHO OR WHAT IS THE OVERSEER?"

"Justice do you wish to clarify your statement or the nature of its origin?"

"No."

Sael looked like she was on the verge of a meltdown, but to her credit she just shook her head and held her tongue. I could tell my crew was anxious and ready to go no matter what we were up against. I felt the same way, because there was no chance I would leave that piece of crap floating out there without getting some payback for the countless races that fell prey to it. If the amount of junk on the outside of the ship was an indication of how many victims stopped to investigate, the number was substantial.

The beast inside of me was restless and I could feel its need for mayhem infecting me. Tria noted the change in my demeanor and came over to me. The Operative must have felt it too because she got up and moved away with a frown on her face. I reached out for Tria and she stepped close to me holding onto my arm. My eagerness to bloody whoever was controlling the ship vaguely ebbed. Revenge for the innocent would be the only surefire antidote for the juggernaut infecting my thoughts. Trying to kill us was going to cost someone or something on that pile of shit dearly.

Sael was standing next to the bridge hatch and would come no closer to me. She instead chose a different tack. She must have finally figured out she was not going to get anywhere unless she interacted with Justice in a proper manner.

"Justice, what did you mean when you said unprotected personnel could be subjugated, and what is the nature of the protection that can prevent it?"

We all turned to the Operative, wondering if Justice would answer her. To our shock and surprise, he did the unexpected. Two arms extruded from the overhead and wrapped around Sael. She freaked.

"WHAT SORT OF TREACHERY IS THIS? RELEASE ME NOW!"

We weren't absolutely sure but had a pretty good idea of what was going to happen next. The goofy smiles on our faces did not ease the Operative's trepidation.

"NATHAN MYERS, YOU TELL THIS DEFECTIVE MACHINE TO LET ME GO OR I WILL CUT YOUR HEART OUT!"

"Sael, if you want to go with us you need to calm down! Justice is going to ensure you will not be a threat to us or the rest of the galaxy once you step foot on that ship. You would be doing us all a favor if you quit your whining while Justice takes care of the problem."

Sael's eyes were practically bugging out of her head. If she gritted her teeth any harder they would break off in her mouth. I thought about letting her know it was not a flattering look but decided to keep that little jewel to myself. Just when we thought it couldn't get any better, another arm came down and wrapped around her head. I might have thought it funny if it were not for Sael's body suddenly going rigid."

"Justice, don't you think you are getting a little carried away?"

"Commander, I must introduce Guardian architecture into the Operative's implants. Unfortunately, it is an invasive procedure that is absolutely necessary for her own protection. I had to temporarily paralyze her and block coherent brain function to complete the procedure. Tria underwent the same procedure during the weaponization process. The Operative will suffer no ill effects."

662

That was nice to know, but it was not going to make Sael any less angry when she got her senses back. She wanted to tag along and this was the admission fee. Coonts had a frown on his face.

"Justice, did you perform the procedure on me as well?"

"Yes, it was necessary to ensure your safety."

"I do not recall you asking me if I wanted the procedure. When did you do it?"

"I performed the procedure on both you and Xul during your sleep period. Your safety is my responsibility, and I take that duty seriously. You and Xul are now immune to Prule subjugation and manipulation of your implants. Klutch does not possess implants, so he did not require any alterations."

Xul put his hands to the sides of his bulbous head and walked off the bridge. It left me wondering how many procedures were performed on me without my knowledge. I let the thought pass. I did not want to know.

"Justice, in the future, you need to ask us BEFORE you experiment on us, understood?"

"Acknowledged!"

Justice's extruded arms fell away from the Operative's body and retracted into the overhead. Sael

663

momentarily stood there with a blank look on her face. It was a good start, and I tried to put on a cheery face for her. Her eyes blinked and then locked on me. Thinking a bigger smile would smooth things over, I laid it on her. She reached over her shoulder and drew one of her swords. Not the reaction I was expecting at all. She twirled the four-foot long pulsating blade and headed in my direction. Klutch introduced a bouquet into the air that brought tears to everyone's eyes but Sael's — I was pretty sure there was fire coming out of hers. Tria and Klutch quickly stepped between us and the Operative poked the sword in my direction.

"If you ever let that machine touch me like that again, I will adorn the walls of my quarters with the souvenirs I cut from your body."

After seeing the look in her eyes, I developed an itch in all the wrong places. I was glad that Tria and Klutch did not budge until she finally returned her sword to its scabbard.

"Sael, I did not let Justice do anything to you. You should appreciate the fact that Justice chose to protect you against possible Prule manipulation. If he had not, and you were subjugated, you could have possibly infected your entire race with a machine virus that is capable of destroying entire worlds."

"We have no idea if that scat factory is even of Prule origin."

"Justice was not going to let you gamble with the lives of your people to find out."

That seemed to mollify her anger and give her the proper perspective.

"Now that I have been declared immune, why are we still standing here?"

"Justice, have you got a plan to get us in?"

"We are fortunate another race was kind enough to furnish us with a safe docking area."

"What docking area? All I see is junk and weapons damage."

"Precisely, Commander. The Legacy will fit inside of the crater that was blown through the holds of the ship. The ship will be unable to target us and there should be plenty of access holes to board."

Justice superimposed an outline of the Legacy in the massive crater. It would be a tight fit, but I had no doubt that Justice could do it. It was very unlikely the ship would have internal weapons large enough to penetrate the Legacy's shields. It was a brilliant idea and as safe a place as any.

I took Tria by the hand and stepped into the down tube. The crew and Sael jumped in right behind us. When we got to the ready room I started stripping off my smart cloth uniform and was shocked to see Sael intently watching me. My cheeks warmed and I turned my back to her. Tria noticed what was going on and turned me back around and planted a wet one on me. This was neither the time nor the place for such horseplay, and I grabbed my suit liner and hastily put it on. I didn't think it was possible to get into battle armor as quickly as I did, but I somehow managed. I promised myself if I lived through this I would make it up to Tria for all of the times we were rudely interrupted.

Justice momentarily displayed my armament meter and highlighted anti-matter. He supplied me with twenty rounds. I wasn't sure if he finally relented because I had gained control of the Oolaran soldier in me or he thought I would need them to survive. Either way I hoped it would not come down to using them.

The Legacy was cloaked and our negation systems engaged. We were far enough out from the target it was almost invisible against the background of the dusty rock field. Justice dropped our shields and accelerated to maximum velocity. The speed of our approach made the derelict ship rapidly increase in size as we closed with it. Justice shut down the star drives and all unnecessary systems. We were coasting in at breakneck speed and defenseless against incoming fire. I sucked in a breath as the junkyard filled my visor. We were not fired upon and Justice once again validated his theory. Just when it looked like we would crash into the belly of the beast, Justice spun us around in a crazy one-eighty maneuver that parked us in the huge belly wound nose out. The ships reaction to the disturbance we created within its guts was to randomly fire its main weapons in angles so depressed it was blasting debris from its hull. We were in, and apparently the ship could do nothing about it, or so we thought.

"Commander, I am picking small devices measuring less than a meter across emerging out of the debris and moving rapidly in our direction. I do not recommend you depart the Legacy at this time."

"What are they and how many are coming this way?"

"Unknown and the count is at two hundred and forty-two."

My visor went live with the exterior feed and small red boxes appeared to be leaping out of the trash and junk surrounding the ship and were making a beeline for our location. Our point defense and rail cannons started picking them off as fast as they appeared. I was expecting large explosions but the devices made a bright spark and disappeared under Justice's withering fire. Several made it to our shields and abruptly stopped. They extended some sort of probe that made the part of the shield it was touching fluctuate.

"Justice, what are they doing?"

"They are attempting to drain away power from our shields. It is an interesting phenomenon, but they are only capable of fractionally siphoning power from the areas they make contact with. They would have to blanket our shields in order for them to be an effective power diverter."

Justice had knocked down more than a hundred of the drones and then ceased fire. I guess he was curious whether or not they could pull our shields down. He let the balance collect outside our shields and was content to observe their actions. At first, they were spread out and ineffective, but as we watched they quickly started to congregate and our shield started glowing brighter where they collected. They finally collected into a blob and our shield was flaring brilliant white. I was going to ask Justice why he was dicking around when he turned the whole pile into atomized gas and dust with a shot from our main weapons. We no longer had to worry about the tight squeeze into the ship. The shot opened up a hole large enough we could turn around if need be. The beast in me loved the results and I wanted more.

"Justice, wasn't there a weapons turret somewhere above us?"

The Legacy moved slightly backwards and then up. I could see the red outline of where the turret was located. A flash whited out my visor, and when it reset I could see an awesome glowing tunnel all the way to the starfield peeking back at us. Justice was projecting an image on the bulkhead so the Operative could observe what was happening. She now stared back at me wide eyed.

"You may have just destroyed hundreds of priceless artifacts."

"Easy come, easy go. Justice do you have any movement on your scanners?"

"Negative, Commander. You are clear for departure. I have highlighted several passages for your consideration. I have avoided any that had the power conduits we discovered."

The Operative closed her helmet and moved to the open hangar door. Klutch was standing in his usual forward position and Sael attempted to step in front of him. He would have none of it and pushed in front of her. Tria and I were stepping up behind them with Coonts just to our rear. This was our customary combat formation and Sael was an odd cog in our normally smooth-running combat machine. She once again attempted to elbow Klutch aside for the lead position. I could see the vents in his suit lock in the open position. I thought there was going to be a scuffle but Klutch's response was measured and to the point. He promptly pushed the Operative out the door and she disappeared over the side. Justice did not link our comms to hers and any swearing she may have broadcast was in vain. Xul was standing on the ramp to Eagle One wearing Coonts' old Zaen combat armor. I waved to him and he returned the gesture. If for some unforeseen reason we needed shuttle support, the little Grawl would immediately launch and provide assistance with every weapon available to him.

We took our positions and I rapped Klutch on the shoulder. He hit his gravity drives and jetted upward with us close behind. We formed up to follow and my Backscatter transmitter beeped and then filled my head with lovely Chaalt idioms.

I didn't have time for the Operative's leadership pep talks.

"Sael, the Troop Master drives this train, so either get aboard and shut up or you can go your own way!"

The transmission ended with a disparaging comment about my ancestry.

43

Most of the passageways above us were huge. Klutch guided us to the smaller ones Justice had highlighted. We knew from experience major passageways were direct routes to essential compartments and usually defended. Klutch took us into the closest one. It was still fairly large but nothing like the main corridors. I'm sure he didn't like the idea of being out in the open and an easy target. We set down in a dark service tunnel laced with pipes, wires and tubing of every size. Klutch took the lead and the Operative brought up the rear. There were passages branching off in all directions, many of which were so choked with piping we could not go that way even if we tried. After about a hundred yards our tunnel ended at a large room filled with what looked like more alien junk. We passed through a retention field and the room was registering a thin atmosphere. We had no choice but to go forward or turn around and backtrack until we could find another passage that we would fit into.

Klutch cleared his visor and gave me a questioning look. I waved him on. It was as good a place as any to start looking around. We were maintaining radio silence, and to the Operative's credit, she was too. We jumped down amongst the hoarded booty and picked our way down several narrow paths to the far end of the room. It was as if someone had taken a thousand pieces of equipment apart and stacked it into piles until the room would hold no more. I turned to Coonts and pointed at random piles. He just threw his hands up so I turned back to Klutch and waved him forward.

The no-light setting in my visor revealed the outline of a large hatch on the wall we were approaching. It surprised the crap out of us by opening when we were about five feet away. We yanked our weapons from their clips and dove behind the piles of equipment remnants. Tria was by my side covering my back. Coonts and the Operative went to the left and Klutch to the right. We waited to see what would happen next and got nothing. The door stayed open beckoning us to enter. Klutch got tired of waiting and cautiously moved to the edge and peeked out. He waved us over and slipped out into the huge passageway. Like it or not, we were in one of the main arteries of the ship.

We had gone maybe twenty steps when some sort of electrical current shot out of the walls, surrounding us in a glow bright enough to light the passage. Our comms were overwhelmed with a deluge of languages. Our suits were able to mute the volume of the verbal assault. Justice's subsystem translated the speech and alerted us the rest of the languages made no difference because they all said the same thing.

"BOW TO THE WILL OF YOUR GOD AND MASTER OR BE CONSUMED AND NEVER RISE TO SERVE!"

It would never be a catchy jingle, and we didn't come here to bow to anyone. Klutch took off on a dead run skirting the wall of the corridor, the bizarre bolts of electricity jumping from the wall to his armor as he ran. We closed with him, and the glow surrounding us lit the passage ahead. We had no idea what it was for or what it was doing, but it suddenly stopped. I didn't know where we were going but running seemed like the prudent response to the bullshit that was just laid on us.

"Klutch! Where are we going?"

"To find our new master and kick the scat out of him!"

While it seemed a little rhetorical, it was better than anything I could come up with at the moment. I wondered if Justice had anything to say about our current situation and was going to hail him for a sitrep. He saved me the trouble and embellished my concerns with a bucket of piss.

"Commander, the heat sources Tria detected appear to be multiplying."

"OK Justice, I am going to need a little more than that before I can concern myself with multiplying heat sources. How many more are you talking about?"

"Six-hundred and counting and they are now moving."

673

"Moving where?"

"Toward your current location."

That made us slam on the brakes and take pause. My team took a knee with their weapons pointing down both directions of the corridor.

"Do I even need to ask how many?"

"All of them are converging on the passageway you occupy."

"Are the numbers still increasing?"

"No, they are holding at twelve hundred and six."

The corridor we were in stretched for more than a quarter of a mile. I looked back the way we came and could see a faint light appear. It had to be the weird static electricity and it also meant we were going to have company. The beast in me was surprisingly calm, but no one had shot at us yet either. My visor picked up the outlines of several side passages well ahead of us. There was no light at our end but the other end was getting a little brighter by the minute.

"Klutch, find us some defensible cover. Coonts, go with him and cover his back."

They boosted away and quickly disappeared into the darkness. Sael turned to me and I could see by the look on her face she wanted to start giving orders. She surprised me by asking a question.

"Do you want me to go back and slow them down?"

"No — how many grenades do you have on you?"

"Four, because a primate took me from my ship without my combat loadout."

She had a point — it wasn't one of my brighter moves and not worth commenting on. Tria and I had fourteen a piece.

"Let's go back and mine the passage."

We engaged our gravity drives and flew toward the gathering light making its way up the massive corridor. As the distance between us and the heat sources closed, I upped the magnification on my helmet to maximum. What I saw made my skin crawl. There were beings of every description; some I could identify, some I could not. What was creeping me out to the max was they all had some kind of metal looking protrusions sticking out of their heads or bodies. The crazy electrical current that was coming from the passageway around them was dancing between the protrusions and daisy chaining among the aliens. Tria and the Operative must have taken a look as well and didn't like what they saw any more than I did. They both pulled out grenades and were going to toss them to the overhead.

"No, save them, we may need them later."

The beast in me was crawling out of his cage. The Operative backed away from me and I could see the apprehension on Tria's face.

"No Nathan, you must control the rage!"

The fear in Tria's voice brought back some of my coherent reasoning. I ground out a reply.

"GO! I will catch up with you."

The Operative grabbed Tria by the arms and they boosted down the passageway away from me. I turned back to face the coming onslaught and raised my launcher. Anti-matter appeared in my visor and I dialed it up to full yield. The weapons release code changed from green to orange. The aliens were moving faster now but it would not matter. I fired the round and boosted hard after Tria and the Operative. I could see my crew huddled in the distance. They were at a junction in the corridor. Everything whited out in a blinding flash that was accompanied by an insanely loud metallic clang. The shockwave traveled up the hallway at supersonic velocities, dislodging hundreds of years of dust and debris. I was flipped over by the turbulence and driven into the deck. I rolled several times then got back up and boosted through the filthy dust cloud to my crew. They decided to ride out the shockwave prone on the deck. I landed next to them and they got to their feet. I could see their faces and the looks of concern were obvious. The Operative stood well away from me with two of her hands on her pistols. My crew was probably wondering why Justice would give a proven psychopath anti-matter rounds.

Klutch finally broke the silence. "Commander, we have found an access tunnel to the upper decks!"

That seemed to snap me out of my daze. "Lead the way, Troop Master."

We used our gravity boosters to put some distance between us and the passageway. Klutch led us to a large, capsule-shaped hole in the wall that was at least fifty feet wide. We landed and I peeked into it. It went a long way down and a long way up. If I had to guess I would say it was an inoperable gravity lift tube. The beast in me wanted to send some of my hate up and down tube to see what would shake loose. I stifled the thought with a deep breath and gritted teeth. I wasn't sure if Justice regretted giving me our most destructive ordnance, but he did give me a warning.

"Commander, the already fragile superstructure of the derelict ship has been further compromised by your weapons release. Additional anti-matter discharges may sever the aft section of the ship in the location the Legacy is sheltered in."

OK, I got that part and would heed his warnings, but that didn't mean I planned to save my heavy ordnance for a rainy day either.

"Did I manage to thin the herd?"

"Yes, by more than five hundred, but I have detected six large heat signatures that do not match existing sources. They are on the deck above you."

"Are they moving?"

"Yes, they are advancing on your position."

Coonts was guarding our rear and broadcast a warning.

"Commander, Klutch and I mined the corridor we searched. The munitions are detonating. We cannot remain here much longer."

"Klutch take us up, but don't stop on the deck above us. Go until we have to stop!"

"Roger that. Justice has warned us. Follow me and stay to the sides of the deck openings. We do not want to be exposed to any direct fire."

Klutch and Coonts stepped into the opening and went left and up. The Operative looked back at me and promptly joined them. Tria and I went up the opposite side, keeping pace with them. We cautiously bypassed three more openings leaving a parting gift hovering outside of each as we moved on. We were left with two choices when the tube terminated: go out or go back. I usually never used the second option.

"Justice, do you have any movement on our level?"

"Justice?"

I heard my crew trying to raise the Legacy as well, we were getting nothing, I tried my IST and the Backscatter transmitter and still nothing. I thought for sure those devices would work, but I got no response. Sael hissed the most obvious conclusions over our comms. She didn't sound like her normal unflappable self during combat situations.

"We are encountering advanced shielding or possibly jamming. There is one other scenario I do not care to voice."

I wanted to tell her not to worry, that we had been down this road before, but I couldn't in all honesty say it at the moment. In the past we always had a Legacy to return to, but this wasn't the past and presently I could only speculate why we couldn't make use of our multiple communications capabilities. The thought of being marooned on this wreck was terrifying and was encroaching on the fringes of my mind. I could almost hear the Oolaran soldier in me laughing at my worry — it was immune to such frailties.

I was startled back to reality by the grenades below us detonating, creating a strobe-like effect on our end. We made the judicious decision to unass the tube. We found ourselves standing in the edge of a huge room full of large pieces of unidentified machinery and equipment. Before we moved away from the opening, Tria stuck her arms back in and launched a twenty-round burst of high explosive down at any would be pursuers. Coonts was still on the comms trying to raise Justice, but to no avail. Klutch and the Operative had their weapons out and ready. They were moving from cover to cover trying to establish whether or not we were alone. I took a grenade and tossed it into the top of the tube as a tripwire to alert us to any unexpected company.

Tria, Coonts and I unclipped our weapons and started making our way quietly around the edge of the room. Coonts alerted me to the fact that this room had a constant gravity of almost three as compared to the one G that the other decks registered. The powered exoskeletons of our armor didn't even register it as an inconvenience. He also said there was an atmosphere in here that had very little oxygen and an abnormally large amount of nitrogen and ozone. There was no point in asking what that meant because I did not need a thirty-minute oration on what his thoughts on the subject might be.

The Operative commed me and she sounded excited. "Nathan, you need to look at what we have discovered."

Using the cues in our helmets Tria, Coonts and I quickly made our way over to Sael and Klutch. They were standing near a huge domed piece of equipment that reminded me a lot of the early warning radar domes I had once seen while flying along the coast of Alaska with my friend Karl.

"What have you got, Sael?"

"If this is operational and we manage to get out of here alive, you no longer have to look for the power source for your anomaly weapon!"

"How would you know what an Oolaran weapons power plant looks like?"

"Because a Chaalt transporter power source is reverse-engineered from this design."

"If you already have the designs, why didn't you make the weapon operational?"

"Because we don't have a Justice to control the anomaly. Our initial experiments resulted in a disastrous accident that cost the lives of a great many people."

Coonts was examining the power plant and voiced the question on my mind.

"I wonder how it ended up in here?"

Before we could further contemplate the discovery, the bizarre electrical current we saw coming out of the passageway below us, started snaking around our feet and arcing to our armor. We were assaulted once again by the loud blaring torrent of languages. They translated to more of the same bullshit.

"SUBMIT TO THE WILL OF YOUR MASTER OR BE CONSUMED AND NEVER RISE."

I pretty much had my fill and was going to spout some drivel of my own when the grenade I left in the tube started spitting fragments. We cloaked and ran back toward the opening. We spread out behind the pieces of equipment waiting to see what would come out. The current arcing around us stopped but started going crazy somewhere in the tube below us. The glow was getting brighter by the second. My armor's subsystem alerted me the lift tube was now functioning.

The Oolaran in me was not a patient entity, so I held up a grenade so everybody would notice. I threw it at the opening and it came to a hover just above it. Not to be outdone my crewmates did the same. I got a piercing stare from the Operative because she was fresh out. A mass of aliens boiled up to the edge of the opening. The protrusions sticking out of their bodies were alive with the inexplicable electrical discharge flaring from all around the tube. A large number were carrying a stubby barreled weapon with a spike sticking out of the end. They never got a chance to show us how they worked; our grenades filled the opening with exploding shrapnel.

The beast spun up my minigun and a red circle appeared searching for anything that might make it out of the entrance alive. My crew did the same and gave anything moving in front of us a short burst, blowing them to pieces. Tria was launching single rounds of high explosive into the shaft whenever there was a lull in the outpouring masses. It was a horrific sight to see the eviscerated bodies being forced up and out of the opening like lava flowing from a volcano. The ground up remains were being pushed all the way to our positions, forcing us to retreat back away from the morbid mess. Whoever was in charge was pulling out all the stops trying to overwhelm us.

The aliens had jerky, almost mechanical movements leading us to believe they were being remotely manipulated. They were trying to level their weapons at us as they came out of the tube, but we were gunning them down before they could accurately engage us. Many started firing even before they left the tube, in some cases gunning down the aliens in front of them. I tossed another grenade, only leaving me with five. It would have been wise to hang on to some of them, but the Oolaran soldier in me pulled rank and tossed one after another until they were gone. Coonts became emboldened by the opposition's piss poor accuracy, stepped into the open and gave them hell with his minigun until it ran dry. The firehose stream of exploding slugs only slightly slowed the boiling sea of alien cyborgs. Tria opened fire with all four launcher tubes. The anti-personnel munitions ground down the bodies till they flowed like a mud filled river, inundating our positions until we were forced to retreat once again through the knee-deep carnage. We now had so much gore splattered on us, our cloaking capability was severely degraded. The whole room was glowing brightly from the static discharge until it stopped as suddenly as it started. The aliens literally fell back down the tube, disappearing somewhere below.

The beast half of me felt disappointment, but my rational half felt elated. At this insane attrition rate, the fool that had declared himself our master had to be running low on cannon fodder. That thought lasted maybe two seconds because large metallic hands with six spiked fingers gripped the edges of the tube opening. My eyes grew wide as recognition settled into my brain. A Prule Hunter pulled itself into the room.

We opened fire on the metallic monster but a pale green bubble flared out in front of it and our rounds harmlessly exploded or were deflected away. Evidently our cloaking was no longer effective because the machine came right at us. It moved incredibly fast and was amongst us in a blink of an eye. It whipped one of its lower arms out, smashing Sael in the side, sending her flying. Klutch and Coonts ducked under a swing that crushed the side of the machinery they were sheltering behind. The rope-like appendage sticking out from its upper body started glowing and it lashed out at me. I trying to follow my crew's example but ducked late. The glowing cord wrapped around my upper body. I was jerked off the floor like I weighed nothing and smashed into the ceiling, then the floor. My vision blurred from the impacts. My armor's subsystem called out a warning that the Prule was trying to overwhelm my operating systems. The Guardian firewalls were holding, but none of us had any idea how long they were capable of doing so.

I caught a glimpse of Tria as I was pulled toward the ceiling once more. She was pouring a barrage of armor piercing rounds into the lower portion of the Prule's shield. Just before I was whipsawed around and hurled into Klutch I thought I saw sparks flying from its legs. My vision cleared and I rolled off Klutch to my knees. I saw the Prule raise an appendage with a device on it. What I thought might be a tool flared on the end and lightening like bolt flashed from it striking Tria dead center. She was blown across the room by thunderous explosion. I screamed out her name but got no answer.

The beast in me raged and I threw my arm up and gave the Prule a beam shot from about forty feet. The

685

energy release flattened me and sent a hurricane of body parts flying in all directions. The green bubble in front of the Prule flared a blinding white and disappeared, knocking the creature to the floor. It let out a warbling screech and tried to point its weapon at me. I was surprised to see the weapon explode leaving a ragged stump where it was once mounted. I glanced to my right and saw Sael fire another volley from her pistols collapsing one of the Prule's legs. The creature ducked behind a piece of equipment before I could re-engage it. Coonts and Klutch were still trying to regain their senses from the beam shot. They were crawling through the grotesque collection of ground up body parts. I could not locate Tria and she still would not answer my desperate shouts.

The beast in me must have felt I had rested long enough and forced me to my feet, my burning anger and hate for the loathsome machine egging me on. I stalked after the wounded Prule with the deadliest of intentions. I saw the glow of its power whip before I actually saw it coming. I extended my climbing hooks and shielded my face as it came swinging around for a head strike. There was a flare of bright sparks as the bludgeon cord broke one of my hooks and severed. I staggered backwards from the blow but kept my footing. I was being driven forward by sheer will and a thirst for revenge. I could see the monstrosity scurrying to the back of the room flailing its severed whip and dragging a shattered mechanical leg. We once again heard the blaring loud cacophony of languages, and now they were singing a different tune.

"YOU ARE THE MINIONS OF THE ANCIENT ENEMY! YOU MUST BE STERILIZED!"

A bright beam flashed from somewhere in the back of the room connecting with the Prule. The upper half of its capsule-shaped body burst open in a shower of molten metal. The remains of the machine were brutally smashed into a wall where it collapsed and did not move. I could not think of a more fitting way to shut up that wretched warbling noise the oversized blender was emitting. I was stunned by the shockwave of the beam blast and when I fully regained my senses, I heard Tria shouting my name over our secure comms channel. Her voice was like a cool calming breeze to my heat-driven rage. I saw her stagger around the side of a piece of machinery and all thoughts of the beast were gone. I ran to her and held her in my arms. The front of her armor was crushed inward and burnt down to the inner liner. I could only think of evacuating her out of this hell hole, but she held up a hand.

"Nathan, the air was forced from my lungs by the creature's weapon strike and I was unable to speak. The weapon depleted its energy on my outer armor and did not penetrate my nanite reservoir. As long as the reservoir and my inner armor remain intact, I am still combat effective."

I was going to voice my doubts but was interrupted by a warning from the Operative.

"NATHAN, ANOTHER PRULE IS EXITING THE LIFT TUBE!"

I had forgotten all about the nanites we carried in our heat sink reservoirs and the menu appeared in my visor. One simply said, "attack mode." I selected it and a target designator appeared on my HUD. I threw my arm up and a high-pressure nozzle extended from the top of my hand. The Prule was moving incredibly fast and leaped to the side before Tria could hit it with a beam shot. I was trying to get the nanite weapon to discharge when the word "Hold" flashed in front of my face.

Coonts and Klutch were covering our backs and were used to the fact that our troubles always came in multiples. They were blowing the hell out of everything trying to hit the Prule Hunter with simultaneous double taps from their beam weapons. The machine was making insane leaps back and forth behind pieces of equipment firing its energy weapon at us. We were maneuvering equally as hard to avoid being struck.

A great number of the artifacts closest to the lift tube were now useless piles of slag. Coonts or Klutch made a lucky hit on the Prule's shield. It flared and disappeared, staggering the machine and driving it into the deck, but it quickly righted itself and loosed a barrage that sent all of us scurrying for cover. Tria was pulling me along with her and I finally noticed my HUD was blinking back in attack mode. I lurched away from her toward the machines position. My crew was yelling for me to stop and the beast was ignoring them. I ran around the side of a piece of machinery and ducked under the flailing blow of the machine's bludgeon whip. I fired the nanite weapon and was shocked that it only fired a fist sized gray glob onto the machines armor. The Prule thanked me by savagely smashing me to the floor and trying to drive one of its ice pick appendages through my armor. I was too close for my crew to engage it with their beam weapons. They were yelling out my name and unleashing a firestorm of anti-personnel rounds at the machine, the shrapnel sounded like a hail storm on my armor. The Prule Hunter was forced to retreat.

I shook my head to clear it and got up on all fours and crawled as fast as I could through the carnage around me. I rounded the corner on one of large machine pedestals and came visor to visor with the Operative. She struck me a proper blow to the side of my helmet with one of her fist.

"YOU PRIMATE! IF YOU PULL SOME SCAT LIKE THAT AGAIN, I WILL KILL YOU MYSELF!"

Tria came crashing into us as she leaped behind our cover. She was not happy! I was going to let her know that I was not harmed but she cracked me upside the head.

"NATHAN! DO NOT LET THE DEMON INSIDE OF YOU THROW YOUR LIFE AWAY!

I was going to explain what I was attempting to do, when we heard the Prule screeching out its high-pitched warbling. We could hear it thrashing about wildly and I was afraid that Klutch was brawling with the machine. We got to our feet and peeked around the pedestal. I could see both Coonts and Klutch just across from us and they were doing the same thing. The crashing noises intensified as well as its warbling screech. We could see ground up body parts and debris being thrown in all directions. We started slowly advancing toward the ruckus with our beam weapons up and ready. All of the sudden the Prule Hunter rolled out of cover thrashing about on the deck. It was smashing its whip and appendages into its own body, then dove toward the lift tube leaving us staring wide eyed in disbelief of what we just witnessed. The machine disappeared down the shattered tube and Klutch stormed forward yelling a warning.

"ANTI-MATTER OUT!"

He let one fly and boosted away. The whole room seemed to buck under our feet and we were all sent crashing into the ceiling and then dumped onto the floor or a piece of machinery. I wasn't sure what Klutch saw in the tube but was thinking maybe Justice should take away his toys for being a bad boy. We were attempting to regain our footing in case another Prule tried to make good on the voice's declaration of sterilization. It was a mistake. The whole ship shook, knocking us to the deck. I was sprawled out on top of Tria and she grabbed me in an embrace. It was comforting but left me wondering 'What the hell?' I decided that Klutch was not satisfied with my earlier attempt to blow us all up and must have been trying to one up me.

"Klutch! Cease fire!"

I thought I heard a retort of some kind over the ringing in my ears. Then we were sent flying by back to back bone-jarring impacts. This time I knew it had nothing to do with Klutch because his big ass was sitting on my helmet. I rolled him off none too gently.

"Commander, I only fired one round!"

I wasn't sure what to think about the crazy big secondaries. I was looking around for Coonts but he was nowhere in sight. I saw Tria was a few feet away and she was digging in the debris and body parts. She pulled the Operative upright from the surreal mess we were crawling through.

"COONTS ARE YOU INJURED?"

"Commander! I am up here!"

I looked up in time to see the little Grawl come flopping down off of a large piece of machinery.

"Commander, I must caution you on releasing anti-matter in such close proximity to our positions. The probability of serious injury is high!"

I frowned because I always get the blame whenever shit blows up in our faces. The point wasn't worth arguing because my past record for such destructive behavior spoke for itself. I was going to plead my innocence and tell them about shooting the Prule with the nanite weapon but was interrupted when the voice of the real guilty party came over our group comms.

"Commander! Your telemetry indicates all armor suits have serious battle damage and are less than optimal for combat operations. I also note all strike team members have abrasions, contusions and trauma. I have closed with your position but wreckage is blocking access to your location. I recommend immediate evacuation."

I don't think I have ever welcomed the sound of Justice's voice more than I did right at the moment.

"How did you find us? Our comms went dead when we entered the upper decks."

I detected your anti-matter detonation. It was necessary to disable the ships primary weapons before I could close with your estimated position. My attempts to re-establish communications with you resulted in the alien ship shearing in half."

That explained our rough ride. The only way Justice could do that was with the Legacy's main weapons. He was making surgical strikes dangerously close to our location.

"Justice, we still have unfinished business. We were attacked by Prule Hunters and more may be present near our location."

"The six large heat signatures I detected while you were investigating the ship pursued you when you disappeared from my sensors. They are no longer emanating traceable emissions and I detect no heat signatures near your location. I do however detect a much larger heat source that is also the terminus of the unidentified power current flowing throughout the remains of the ship. The heat is radiating from a bulkhead located nine-hundred and sixty feet aft of your position."

We slowly got to our feet and looked each other over. All of our armor suits were a mess. My needle gun was missing and the three barrels of my minigun were bent. I didn't have a clue what fate befell my shotgun because I lost it right after the battle started. I was surprised to see the Operative was actually in fair shape. She was fortunate she did suffer the same treatment as Tria. It was debatable whether or not the Chaalt armor would have saved her life.

693

44

We were never given the chance to discover what was beyond this room. Now I wondered what the mysterious source of the weird static discharge would turn out to be. But first things first.

"Justice, contact the Sig through our buoy relay and tell them we need this sector isolated from outside interference."

Sael didn't like it and was very vocal in her protest.

"Nathan, you should alert my people to what we have discovered. They will dispatch a containment team to secure this area and the surrounding system. They have the experience when it comes to these matters, the Sig do not!"

"Nice speech, Sael. In the event I put you in charge, you can exercise that option. Since I am not likely to do that, we are going to do it my way."

"Message relayed, Commander!"

I looked Sael square in the eyes. "If you choose to signal your people against my orders it will be the last time your will ever do it in our company."

The look on her face said the thought had crossed her mind. She nodded and turned away. Coonts tapped me on the back and presented me with my gore-covered shotgun. I smiled and banged it on piece of machinery clearing the barrels.

"Justice, do you have a hard lock on our location?"

"Yes, Commander. I am also detecting a moderate quantity of highly contaminated atmosphere leaking from your location. Do to the nature of the combat damage on Tria's battle armor I recommend she be evacuated to the Legacy. I can start immediate repairs to restore the full protective capabilities of her armor."

I turned to Tria but the defiant look on her face said "OH HELL NO!" on so many different levels that I was sure broaching the subject would turn out to be futile. I had to at least try because not inquiring might turn out to be a pitfall as well. Maybe if I asked politely as a favor to me.

"Tria, woul—"

"NO!"

That was good enough for me and it was time to move on. "Klutch, take the lead, let's go!"

I stepped behind Klutch as he took off wading through the carnage. Tria attempted to go next, but I took her by the arm and pulled her behind me. I trudged forward and she followed without comment. Coonts lined up behind her and then the Operative. The mess on the deck finally thinned out and movement became much easier. Coonts called to me.

"Commander, I have a theory on the nature of the machinery in this chamber. While it might be speculation on my part, I believe I will be proven correct."

"I am all ears, Coonts. Let's hear it."

"All of the devices in this chamber are captured power sources the Prule were attempting to take back to their home galaxy for reverse engineering."

That statement gave me pause and we slowed to inspect one of the large pieces of machinery. I didn't have a clue what I was looking, at but I was thinking Coonts might be right. I thought back to the data the Overseer related to us. According to the intel, all outbound resources were being transported out of the galaxy on Prule supercarriers. This ship was immense but nowhere near the reported size of a supercarrier. Until we could thoroughly investigate the ship, it would only lead to more questions than answers. I waved Klutch on and we moved out once more. We came to an area void of machinery and could see a huge ribbed bulkhead with an equally large hatch on it. Klutch stopped in front of the door and rapped his armored fist on it.

"Commander, this door may be several feet thick. I don't know what they are hiding, but they must place great value on it."

If the Prule had something valuable enough to hide it in a giant vault, then I wanted whatever it might be. The infrared setting in my visor showed the wall glowing orange with heat. The exterior of the bulkhead was reading two-hundred degrees. Now I was wondering if this was a generator room of some kind. The only way to find out was to open the door, and we just happened to have skeleton keys that usually opened all locked doors we encountered. Klutch lead us back a safe distance and raised his beam weapon. Sael ducked behind one of the pieces of equipment, but not before commenting.

"You would think that my generosity with my people's military and industrial tech would have rewarded me with a similar weapon."

Coonts, as a rule, was always the quickest on the draw when it came to verbal sparring. He was a silver-tongued devil that got his say whether you liked it or not. This time was no exception and I was actually pleased with his retort.

"You would think shedding our blood in service to your people would have rewarded us with transporter tech!"

That netted him a sour look from the Operative. Klutch decided we had talked enough and hit the giant door low on its left side with a beam shot. Molten metal blasted outward like a fountain, but the door held tight. Klutch looked back at me and nodded toward the door. Tria, Coonts and I lined up with him and raised our arms. The Operative disappeared, seeking shelter and safety.

Klutch yelled, "FIRE"

The blast blew door fragments in all directions. We could now see a hole with bright light shining back at us. It was big enough we could crawl through. As we got closer to the door, we could see that it was more than four feet thick. The edges of the molten hole rapidly quit glowing, but my sensors still detected a torrent of two-hundred and sixty-degree heat jetting from the hole. Klutch leaned down and looked inside and then turned back to us with a frown. He got down on all fours and started crawling through. We quickly lined up behind him and followed. Exiting the hole next to Klutch, I could see why he frowned: in front of us was a shimmering pale green wall spanning the width of the room. On the other side was a gigantic globe sitting on several metal supports. It was twenty-five feet wide and almost a sixty-feet tall. I wanted to laugh because it was glowing brightly and kind of resembled a light bulb. It had a metal dome hanging over it that had large, rope-like cables extending all the way to the ceiling more than two-hundred feet above us.

I was going to step forward to take a closer look when the blaring voices yelled out in hundreds of dialects.

"STOP! IT IS FORBIDDEN FOR BIOLOGICAL VERMIN TO PERVADE THE DOMAIN OF YOUR MASTERS. ALL SPECIES OF THE ANCIENT ENEMY WILL BE SINGLED OUT FOR ERADICATION. THE WORLDS YOU INFEST WILL BE STERILIZED FOR ETERNITY.

I wasn't sure, but I thought the voices were coming from the glowing globe. I wasn't about to take crap from what appeared to be an oversized lightbulb.

"We noticed you already tried that. How is that working out for you?"

My crew and the Operative gave me incredulous looks for mouthing off in the Scrun dialect. I was just covering my ass and the planet of my birth, in case the freakin' lightbulb had the ability to back up the threats. It was almost funny, right up until its supports started lengthening into legs and it stood up. Justice decided it was time to give me a no-shitter.

"Commander, after carefully studying your observations and findings, I now conclude you are speaking to a Prule Hivemind. You should exercise great caution in what you choose to say or reveal to it."

Thanks Justice! It would have been nice if you could have said something ten minutes ago!

We opened fire with our beam weapons, but they only made the green barrier field flare and turn opaque. The barrier was a starship-quality shield system. If our heaviest weapons could not penetrate it, we were in trouble up to our eyeballs. Shields were designed to stop incoming fire, but not outgoing. We decided it might be better to go elsewhere and discuss tactics. Coonts and the Operative turned and headed toward the hole in the door. Tria and I grabbed Klutch by the back of his armor and started dragging him with us as he kept firing away at the shield.

"Klutch! We need to get back to the Legacy. Take the lead NOW!"

He finally turned away and judging by the way his suit was venting, he was pretty pissed off. That is when I started hearing a whining noise that was gaining in intensity. We glanced over our shoulders and saw that not all of the machine's metallic appendages were legs. One of them was, in fact, a large-barreled weapon with a spike sticking out the end, and it was glowing brighter by the second.

"COMMANDER! YOU MUST EVACUATE THE AREA IMMEDIATELY! The current that once flowed throughout the remains of the ship, is now flowing back to its source. I am detecting a massive power spike coming from your location!"

The Operative and Coonts disappeared through the hole. I was trying my best to shove Tria through behind them while Klutch was doing the same to me.

Justice's voice boomed out over our group comms. "TAKE COVER NOW!"

We were assaulted by the earsplitting sound of a jackhammer directly over our heads. The shock and vibration bounced us about the floor. There was a blinding flash behind us that was followed by an explosion that drove Klutch into me with such force I was blown through the hole in the door and into my sprawled crewmates. I was seeing double and shook my head several times to clear my vision. When I could see clearly, I realized I was staring into Sael Nalen's faceplate. I had no idea how I ended up on top of her.

"Are you enjoying yourself primate!? Get off me!"

I rolled over and found Tria pulling Coonts to his feet.

"KLUTCH!"

I heard a groan. "Over here, Commander."

He was spread-eagled half buried in debris on the other side of the Operative. The back side of his armor looked like the front of Tria's. He rolled over and slowly sat up.

"I would be fine if it were not for my helmet colliding with the rear of your armor."

I could now dismiss the thought he had been putting his boot to my ass. I looked back at the hole in the door. Gore, dirt and debris were flying into it. Whatever happened caused explosive decompression on the other side of the door. The remaining atmosphere on our side quickly depleted and all was still once more. We were fortunate to still have gravity or we would be swimming in an ocean of gore.

Klutch crawled back to the opening in the door and peeked through. He gave me a wave of his arm and I crawled in behind him. The once brightly lit room was now a dim, shadowy chamber. The first thing we noticed was the shield was down and the Hivemind was in a heap. The metal dome and cables were collapsed on top of it. I looked to the ceiling high above us and saw three large ragged holes blown downward through the overhead and the Legacy's bright search lights flashing around the exterior of the holes. The huge round junction where the Hivemind's cables terminated was destroyed and glowing a bright orange that was slowly fading. The rest of my team was now through the hole and cautiously approaching the huge Hivemind. They had their beam weapons up and ready. The large weapon and two of the metal monster's legs were shattered, splayed pieces of scrap.

Justice commed a warning to us. "Commander, the Hivemind is still emanating heat and energy. While it may appear to be gravely wounded, I recommend you keep your distance."

Klutch and I decided we would remedy that situation and raised our weapons once more.

The Operative yelled out. "NO NATHAN!

We turned and stared at her in disbelief.

"Please Nathan, let me call my people and take the Hivemind back to our Prule research center. The knowledge we could gain from this creature is priceless!"

Then Justice surprised the crap out of me. "Commander, I concur with the Operative. To destroy the Hivemind would be the loss of valuable information on thousands of subjugated races and possibly locations of other Hivemind lifeboats.

"Lifeboats?"

"Yes, it was the closest human word to describe this vessel. The Hivemind's supercarrier was destroyed by Guardian forces and this vessel escaped the wreckage. It was pursued under intense fire but managed to blind jump to this location. Its damaged power source went critical and had to be ejected before it detonated. It has been trapped here for more than two hundred and seventy years."

"How the hell would you know that?"

"The Hivemind was attempting to subvert my systems from the minute we arrived at this location. When that failed, it tried coercion. It said it would spare your lives if I submitted to it. My rail cannon strikes destroyed its power conduits and its ability to manipulate the ship. It knew I could defeat it and destroy its existence, and it has offered me amnesty if I shelter it from further harm."

To say we were stunned by this revelation would be an understatement.

"Justice, please tell me you did not attempt to absorb that thing."

"No Commander, I was well aware of the machine's deceitful intentions. I did, however, let a measured amount of information download into the data device I designed to contain the Chaalt predatory programs."

"WHAT?!"

"The Overseer was confident the anti-intrusion programs from his former reality are more than capable of containing any Prule infectious attacks. When the Hivemind determined it had been tricked, it attempted to corrupt the information we gained, but it only managed to delete or encrypt a small portion of the data. The Overseer shut down its access and closed off all firewalls. Xul is in the process of building an isolation chamber from our supply of artifacts. Once completed, the data cube will be sequestered in the brig."

Tria, Klutch and I were speechless at what had been taking place while we were getting put through a ringer. Coonts, on the other hand, had a smile on his face, and for the life of me I could not figure out why.

"Commander, Justice and the Operative are correct. The information could lead us to hidden Prule facilities or possibly reveal the coordinates of other worlds that were subjugated."

My small human mind was just now comprehending the possible benefits of what I was hearing. Klutch looked like he just ate a spoiled sea snake. He took matters into his own hands and threw his arm up and blew one of the Hiveminds legs to shrapnel, sending the machine crashing into the wall.

Everyone yelled out at the same time. "KLUTCH!"

The frown on his face turned to a smirk. "Commander, I saw it move!"

"Justice, it that thing still alive?"

"Yes, Commander. It is attempting to bargain for its existence."

"Oh, really? It wants the vermin to stop destroying it. What is it offering us?"

"It is not offering *us* anything. It is offering *me* a share in the rule of this galaxy when they return to end the biological infestation."

The beast in me roared its displeasure and without conscious thought I threw my arm up and blew its only remaining legs to pieces. I yelled out at the machine. "IT MIGHT BE A GOOD IDEA TO BEG THE BIOLOGICALS IN THIS CESSPOOL FOR YOUR WORTHLESS EXISTENCE!"

"Commander, your attack has breached its containment dome and has destroyed a number of its processing entities."

"Is it going to die?"

"No, as long as it still possesses active processing entities, it will survive."

"How many are in there?"

"It has not revealed the actual number, but I surmise more the a million."

We all jumped when Klutch unexpectedly beam shot the Hivemind's base structure, blowing a large piece off and sending it crashing once more into the side wall. We all stared at him with shocked looks on our faces.

The big lug had a huge toothy grin on his face. "HAH! How many are in there now, Justice?"

"KLUTCH! Hold your fire!"

Sael was on the verge of blowing her top. "Nathan, you need to put a leash on that mutinous Tibor before he destroys more irreplaceable data!"

"Sael, do me a favor and SHUT UP! I do not need you adding your input. Do you understand?"

Tria grabbed ahold of my arm and I took a deep breath. I gave Klutch the worst stink eye I could muster and pointed a finger at him. The smile disappeared from his face and he gave the Operative a stern look. The vent covers were blown off the back of his armor and the vents were sending a steamy, non-stop stream of stench into the void. The Operative stormed to the hole in the vault door and stood there with all her arms crossed. I waved my crew over and we put some distance between us and her. We huddled and Coonts let us know what he thought should happen. I had to agree with the little Grawl's assessment.

"Commander, we should let the Chaalt take the Hivemind, but tell them on one condition: they must take a scientist and an engineer from our science team with them. Make it understood our people will share in all information and research. We are to have unfettered access and a dedicated IST to transmit the findings back to Alpha base. If they don't agree to that, tell them we don't need their help."

It was an excellent idea and we had to give the little Grawl his due. He was definitely using his high IQ to our advantage. I clasped him on the shoulders. "Coonts, why don't you inform the Operative what we have decided."

That put a big smile on his face. He turned to where Sael was standing and headed in her direction with a noticeable strut. Tria got us back to business.

"Nathan, we have a tremendous amount of tech in and around this ship. We need to take steps to secure as much of it as possible."

I heard a few choice Chaalt oaths and the Operative stalked in my direction. I shut her down. "Sael, if that doesn't work for you, then option number two is your people can send one scientist and one engineer to Alpha base. They can study the Hivemind under the watchful eyes of my science team."

Justice interrupted our parley. "Commander, Sushi is on station just outside of the nebula with four Sig combat fleets. They are moving to encircle our location."

"Thanks Justice, open a comms channel I can link with him."

"Comms active!"

"Sushi, thank you for your assistance. We have stumbled across a large quantity of artifacts and technology. We need you to secure the area so we can collect as much of it as possible. Can you send a message to Tam Lin that we have need of immediate freighter service?"

"Freighter service into the nebula?"

"Yes, how many do you have available?"

"We have two that are capable of holding a ship the size of the Legacy in their holds and six additional sized down to slightly larger than what you purchased from us. One of our largest is presently offloading supplies and military hardware at our new base of operations. It can be available in one work cycle if that will help you. Will that be sufficient?"

"It will be a start, but we will need all of them."

"Did I correctly hear you say you need all of our available freighters?"

"Yes, the sooner they can arrive the better."

Now my brain was working overtime. The ex-Scrun base that the Sig took over was a single one hour and twenty-minute jump from our present location. It would be an excellent relay point and storage area for the materials we were going to strip off of the ship. I would call Broza and get my new freighter involved as well. It would only cost me crew time to pay him and Hylet.

"OK Sushi, send the freighter when it is available and as many tugs as you can spare. I would like to make a proposal that will pay for all the upkeep on your new base."

"I like the sound of that, Nathan Myers. What do you have in mind?"

"I would like to rent storage space at your facility. I want to store all of the recovered artifacts at your location and keep them under your protection. I will, of course, share some of the artifacts after they have been properly cataloged and sorted. How does that sound to you?"

"That is most agreeable to me and my people. How much space will you need?"

"Based on my previous visit, I would say all of it. Name your price."

"Nathan Myers, if it were not for you, we would not have a base of operations in this sector. I have a suggestion. You pay us for the use of our freighters and pay us standard shipping fees for the distance traveled. Once everything is moved, we will supply secure storage and personnel to watch over it for twenty percent of the artifacts after you catalog the merchandise."

I was speechless because I was going to offer thirty percent and two million credits every forty work cycles.

"Sushi, you have a deal. You and your people will also net additional considerations as they become available."

His booming laugh filled my helmet. "Nathan Myers, we have not spent the profits from our previous dealings. You have made a large number of my people extremely happy. You have made lifelong friends with the Sig! May you grow inordinately old and wealthy!"

"You too, my friend!"

My crew seemed jubilant, and it was catching on until I turned and saw the look Sael was giving me. Tria gave me a nudge in the Operative's direction. I frowned at her and she gave me her golden smile. There was no bitchin' about it after that.

"What's it going to be Sael, your place or mine?"

The look on her face darkened another shade. "Save your fancy play on words for someone who gives a scat. After all we have been through and the wealth of tech I have turned over to you, this was the last thing I expected."

"What may I ask were you expecting?"

"Not to be treated like a Throgg, but as a partner!"

"Now who's full of scat? You have been playing both sides against each other since we've met."

The grimace on her face said loads. Her silence verified the truth of the matter.

"I don't know why you are so down in the dumps. You are about to be the most famous Principal Investigator the Chaalt people has ever known. You are going to bring home a live Prule Hivemind. Nobody that I know of has ever managed a feat like that. You will be able to write your own ticket from now on, and nobody, with the exception of myself, will ever question your orders."

She chewed on my words with gritted teeth and the frown eased from her face. "You might be correct in your assumption that I may finally be given untethered freedom from the council."

"You know the deal. Make the call. As a special gift just for you, I will throw in the whole Prule ship when we have everything we want."

Her voice was laced with sarcasm. "You are so generous!"

"OK, I take it back, I will give it to the Sig instead."

"NO! I didn't say I did not want it!"

I smiled and turned my back on her. "Let me know when your people arrive. I will have Justice let the Sig know so they will let them pass."

Sael made a very unladylike sound, but no further comments.

"Justice, we are going to need an opening in the next chamber over. Use your tow beam to fill the hangar and cargo bay with as much of the salvage in there as possible."

"I have been discussing the matter with engineer Coonts. We have already determined the best course of action. I will remove the remains of the lift tube where Klutch detonated an anti-matter munition. It will require several strikes from the Legacy's rail cannons. I suggest you assemble in the far end of the Hivemind's chamber. I also recommend you make yourself comfortable on the deck to avoid the adverse effects generated by the shockwaves."

"Have you located any more of the cyborgs that were attacking us?"

"Most had gathered behind the larger heat signatures. The Troop Master's anti-matter round exploded right in the middle of the formation. The hostile combatants were either disintegrated or blown out the bottom of the tube into the void. The discharge enabled me to locate your position."

"Roger that. I will let you know when we are ready."

"Acknowledged, Commander. I am maneuvering to that location now."

The crew had listened in to my conversation and was already moving to the back of the chamber. Sael was still talking to the powers that be and was making wild gyrations with her arms. I would have loved to hear the story she was laying on them. I shook my head and walked over and looped my arm in one of hers and led her to the back of the chamber. That netted me a frown and her trying to tug free. I refused to let go until were in a group once more. We sat down and she gave us a funny look and turned her back to continue her report. Tria leaned into me and held on. I smiled at her.

"Ready when you are, Justice."

45

The Operative picked herself up off the deck with a look of disbelief on her face. "IS THAT DEFECTIVE A.I. TRYING TO KILL US ALL!"

I tried to warn her to sit down, but she chose to rage on, only to be toppled again. This time she was smart enough to stay seated. Justice made his third and final strike.

"Commander, the opening is of sufficient size I can begin loading."

"OK, Justice. Starting with the Oolaran power generator, I want everything that hasn't been demolished loaded onto the Legacy. If the Hivemind thought it was important enough to load onto its lifeboat, I want it."

"Affirmative, Commander."

We got to our feet and moved to the hole in the door. Sael was still pissed about being knocked on her ass and was giving me a withering stare.

"Come on Sael, we are going to the Legacy."

"Are you mad!? We must stand guard over the Hivemind!"

"Be my guest. As far as I am concerned, if that shit sack can sprout a new set of legs and crawl out of here without Justice reducing it to atoms, it can carry on."

My crew disappeared through the hole and I turned to look back at Sael. She decided to join us after all. There was no longer gravity on the back side of the door and the crap floating around was being swirled around by Justice pulling the Oolaran power plant from its pedestal and out the huge opening he had made.

"Justice, is the Hivemind capable of repairing its battle damage?"

"Negative, Commander. It would require assistance from other Prule assets and all have been eliminated. I have cautioned the Operative on the need to keep unprotected personnel and A.I. operated machinery away from the area to avoid possible subjugation attempts by the Hivemind."

"What did she say to that?"

"She was insulting and claimed her people were capable of handling the situation."

"Let it go. It's just Sael being Sael."

"She will find when she returns to the Fury that the sanitary facilities in her personal quarters are not as intelligent as she claims."

Oh man! The squabbles Justice has with Coonts were irritating enough, but this thing with Sael was turning into a full-blown feud. I needed to change the subject before I got dragged into it.

"What do you make of the Oolaran powerplant being here?"

"It shows signs of battle damage that was not inflicted upon it during your assault on the Hivemind's lair. I suspect it was taken as salvage from a battle involving Oolaran warships. It was a battle the Prule obviously won. I believe it was the Hivemind's intent to take it back to its home galaxy to reverse engineer the device and incorporate into the Prule arsenal. Many of the pieces of machinery are similar in design but some appear to be parts of weapons. I believe our scientists will be able to properly assess the nature of your discoveries."

The crew and I boarded the legacy and exchanged our combat armor for the lighter Chaalt recon armor. We spent several hours exploring parts of the ship that were not totally wrecked. It was determined that a large quantity of the salvage was collected from the races that stumbled across the Prule ship. The collection was an accumulation from almost three hundred years. Tria, Coonts and the Operative described much of the clutter as junk and we assumed it was being collected for the materials.

Justice informed us a fleet of forty Chaalt warships transitioned into the sector and were in route to our location. Sael's flagship was already working its way through the rock fields and would join up with us shortly. Justice moved the Legacy well away from the Prule ship to rendezvous with the Fury. We were glad to be able to get the Operative off the Legacy; her irritating behavior was getting on everybody's nerves. When the Fury closed with the Legacy, I escorted Sael to the hangar door, waiting for it to come alongside. In a pretentious display of indifference, she extracted herself from her armor and stood naked waiting for a boarding tube to be extended into the Legacy's hangar. She gave me a sneer. "Tell the defective A.I. I no longer have use for his services and he can keep the armor."

Man, was she ever going to have a meltdown when she finds out she was right about Justice inhabiting her ship. She stepped into the tube and it was retracted into the Fury. I laughed out loud because I wondered what she would tell her crew when they opened the boarding tube to find their Captain battered, bruised and naked. I was glad Tria was with Xul and Coonts inspecting the Oolaran powerplant. I was pretty sure she would not have appreciated what just took place.

A huge Chaalt research vessel maneuvered over the Prule ship and engineers cut an opening into the top of the Hivemind's control room. They lowered an isolation chamber big enough to contain the Hivemind down into the hole. A specially prepared containment team with manually operated gravity jacks loaded the Prule into the chamber and hauled it up to the research vessel. The ship rapidly moved away with a thirty-warship escort surrounding it and quickly jumped out of the system. Ten of the Chaalt warships took up station around the nebula to await the Chaalt salvage armada that was on its way to our location.

I once again enlisted Sushi's aid in speeding up our salvage efforts. I offered up another large quantity of credits and he happily volunteered a large number of his fleet's engineers to aid us. By the time the freighters started showing up, we had a good idea what we would take with us and what we would leave to the Chaalt. We spent more than a week methodically picking apart the massive junkyard, only taking enough time to eat and sleep for short periods. We were exhausted but were nearing the end of the project.

During my short rest periods, I was thinking hard about the mining site on the sterilized planet. If we could get some work crews started on the tunnel entrance, we could get the cavern decontaminated and cleaned out. I was thinking a visit with Tam Lin might get the ball rolling. Our current salvage operation was costing upwards of one-hundred billion credits. The value of our salvage should easily pay that figure back with dividends. The mining operation could make huge profits if I was to get it back up and running. There was already a large quantity of valuable material just sitting there for the taking. We would need to decontaminate the containers and find the right person to sell it to. I suspected Tria's people would take great interest in the material, but Tam Lin's outlets would probably bring in higher profits. At some point I would consider buying a larger, more modern freighter.

We were in the tenth day of our salvage operation and I was dead tired. At the end of the work period we would be turning over the remains of the Prule ship to the Chaalt. Their salvage fleet was orbiting the wreck like a flock of buzzards circling a carcass. I couldn't wait to get out of the nebula and had promised my crew we would take a vacation. They had never heard of such a thing and knew nothing of the concept. After explaining it to them, they gave me funny looks. Laying around aimlessly wasting time doing nothing while squandering credits did not seem to appeal to them. I assured them I would pick up the tab but was voted down by the majority. We would be returning to Alpha Base to make modifications and improvements to the Legacy and our battle armor. Flight testing the Daggers was also high on our list of agendas.

The salvage operation was now complete. The Sig returned to their base with the final shipments of artifacts. I paid Broza and Hylet for their time and sent them on their way to take care of clan business. I found it interesting that we had heard nothing from the Operative. When the Chaalt salvage fleet showed up, she disappeared without a word. I guess her new-found fame was enough to keep her occupied and she could find no spare time to annoy me.

The crew and I were sitting in the galley picking at our food, trying not to fall asleep. If it were not for Klutch's unique eating habits, we might have. Justice gave us a sitrep that opened all our eyes.

"Commander, the Overseer has decrypted a small quantity of the information from the Hivemind's memory files. Extraordinary information has come to light. Two-hundred and twenty-seven Earth years ago, the Hivemind sent an incredibly powerful energy burst at a target outside of this galaxy. The target was a location in the Andromeda galaxy. The Overseer was able to accurately decipher the coordinates."

That got our attention and we were wide awake now. "What are you telling us Justice?"

"Commander, we now have the target coordinates necessary to travel to the Andromeda galaxy."

I was speechless — we now had intergalactic capabilities. We had a way of striking at the Prule if they still existed in Andromeda. There was only one way to find that out, and it would require a trip to the target location. A sobering thought crossed my mind. It might turn out to be a suicide mission. DEHD Core jumping into the middle of a Prule installation could prove to be a very unhealthy decision.

"Did the Overseer find anything else of interest?"

"Yes. He has uncovered what appears to be a number of inquiries to encoded locations throughout this galaxy. We are working together to break the encryption and identify the locations. I will alert you to any additional findings."

My crew got up from the table and was headed to the lift tube. They deserved a long uninterrupted sleep period. I took Tria by the hand and we followed them to the bridge level. I had made some promises and decided it was time I kept them. I smiled at Tria and could tell she was tired. I took matters into my own hands and grabbed her up, throwing her over my shoulder. At first, she seemed surprised but after I grunted and beat on my chest a couple of times, she started laughing out loud. I didn't care who was watching and carried her down the corridor toward my quarters. My crew just smiled and shook their heads as they disappeared into their rooms. I didn't have a care in the universe right up until Justice hailed me.

"Commander, the Operative needs to urgently speak with you!"

"Justice, you can tell the Operative to go jump in the void, I am not taking her calls and I want the IST and Backscatter units shut off until further notice. "

"Commander, she said to tell you the Prule research facility has gone dark!"

"WHAT!?"

THE END

If you enjoyed this book please let others know by leaving feedback.

Made in the USA
San Bernardino, CA
04 December 2019